ECHOES OF MAGIC
WHISPER OF WITCHES BOOK 2

NIKITA ROGERS

Copyright © 2022 by Nikita Rogers

Cover Art by Emilie Snaith

All rights reserved.

No part of this book may be reproduced in any form or by any electronic or mechanical means, including information storage and retrieval systems, without written permission from the author, except for the use of brief quotations in a book review.

For Corri
Without whom I would never have made it this far.
Thank you for being the compass of my literary journey.
You deserve the world.
x

TRIGGER WARNINGS

- Fire
- Witch burnings
- Knife cutting for rituals
- Torture
- Starvation
- Death
- Blood
- Murder
- Visual sex scenes
- Very briefly mentioned (but not shown) sexual assault

CHAPTER 1

"Come here, child."

She couldn't stop her feet from moving towards him. Why could she not control her body? Why was she moving straight into his arms and letting him hold her? His hand rested on the base of her back, holding her like they were in some kind of dance, but there was no dancing. Only the hollow feeling inside her chest and the screaming inside of her head that refused to come out of her mouth, and then pain. Pain that shot into her stomach and radiated through her body like a flame, turning her insides into ash and ripping her world apart. She wanted to let go of him, she wanted to fight, to scratch at his eyes instead of lying with the dirt on the ground, bleeding and helpless.

"Now, where would be the fun in that?"

"We are here."

Ana jumped awake as she sat upright in her seat. She blinked away the spots of light that hovered in her eyes, squinting and raising her hand to shield herself from the brightness of the sun as it poured through the windows of the campervan.

After Alexander had taken the purple VW Beetle, Genevieve and Ezra had been left with nothing but a brown moulding van as a means of transport. The sliding door that led to the back seats was rusted, making it hard to open unless pulled from the outside. It smelled stale, like the doors hadn't been opened since the seventies, and when Genevieve had turned the engine on, it ignited with a smell that Ana could only akin to the smell of rotting eggs.

"Ana? Are you okay?"

Ezra was looking back at her from the passenger seat in front of her, his arm draped over the back of the chair loosely. His eyebrows were knitted together in concern, his eyes watching for any sign of pain or discomfort.

Ana cleared her throat and nodded once, wrapping her arms around herself as she looked out of the grimy window. Ezra said that once she had completely recovered, they needed to leave the Sullivan house for somewhere safer, but she hadn't expected to be so far away from the city, and so soon.

The magic that was now flowing freely through her veins had been dangerous in the following days after she had awoken. Every time she felt unhappy or angry, the room would fill with a fog so thick that she couldn't see through it. It would settle around her skin and make the hairs on the back of her neck stand at attention while the room would shake the paintings from the walls and topple over tables. Any time Ezra tried to teach her how to pull her magic's reach back in, she would lose all control and send him flying across the room or set the carpet on fire. The magic was untrained and raw, Genevieve had explained. Dangerous. Like a child with a loaded shotgun. She was so unsafe for everyone around her that Genevieve had to bind her magic by charming a talisman, which would lock away her magic while she wore it.

Ana reached to hold the silver charm that hung from the rope around her neck, feeling the smooth surface under her fingers. If only it would keep her nervousness bound too.

"Where are we, exactly?" she finally croaked, pulling her eyes away from the window and onto Ezra's face.

"Home. At least for a little while until we can figure this out." Ezra gave her a tired smile that didn't quite reach his eyes as he turned back in his seat and opened the van door so that he could slip outside.

Genevieve followed, pulling the keys out of the ignition and closing the door with a slam. Aside from saving her life and binding her magic so that she couldn't hurt anyone, Genevieve hadn't spoken to her at all. She deserved that, she supposed, after everything she had said about her in *The City Herald*.

Sighing, Ana pulled her phone out of her pocket and flicked through her notifications. Where once she would have seen calendar updates from Elianna and happy messages from Bexley, now there were only spam emails for sales at her favourite online shopping stores and 20 per cent off coupons for the city cinema. She gulped back the thickness in her throat and pushed the phone back in her pocket as Ezra pulled open the sliding door of the van, filling the inside with light and birdsong from the surrounding trees. He was smiling at her, and even though she could tell he was still hurting after everything that happened, his smile settled somewhere between her lungs and her heart, and she smiled back.

"Ready?" he asked, reaching behind her to take her backpack and throwing the strap over his shoulder before he offered her his hand.

"Ready." She nodded.

As Ana took his hand and jumped out of the van, she looked up at the tall trees that surrounded them. They were in the middle of another forest, though this one seemed so much brighter than the previous one they had visited together. There was no fog or statues of banshees. Instead, only light streamed through branches, and the air smelled of wild garlic. Lacing their fingers together, Ezra led Ana along the gravel pathway and around the trees. His mother was walking ahead and had stopped at a clearing where the trees and path seemed to simply stop.

A large dilapidated building stood in the middle of the clearing. It was huge. The windows were smashed or had wooden boards nailed to them, and the door was hanging off its hinges, with crumbling brick walls. Ivy crawled up the bricks and spread out across the roof, disappearing into the holes where the wooden beams and slate roof had collapsed, and thick briars and weeds covered the pathway and gardens.

"*This* is where we are staying?" Ana asked, her eyes widening at the collapsing walls and the graffiti sprawled over them.

"You sound ungrateful," Genevieve said as she looked over her shoulder at them from where she stood at the edge of the path, her arms folded against her chest.

"No! I'm not. I'm grateful." Ana gulped. "Totally grateful. It's just . . . I mean, it has character."

Ezra smirked as he looked down at her and shook his head. "She is messing with you, Ana." He let go of her hand and moved towards his mother. "Can we play nice and go inside, please?"

Genevieve sighed and uncrossed her arms with a small nod, the white badger stripe of her hair falling in front of her face. "Fine. I will meet you both inside."

Turning away from them, she walked ahead onto the grass

towards the house. Something was shimmering in the air around her as she walked, and it moved out of her way as she stepped onto a patch of darker grass. She was gone. No longer walking towards the house or trying to climb over the briars. *Gone.*

"Where did she go?" Ana asked with a gasp, stepping to Ezra's side and watching the space in front of her.

"You are a witch now, Ana. What is a witch without a little magic?" Ezra replied as he wriggled his brow at her and stepped forward, following his mother's footsteps. When he stepped onto the same dark patch of grass, the shimmering in the air came flooding back and he was gone, disappearing to somewhere Ana couldn't see.

Something heavy settled in Ana's stomach as she tried to find him with her eyes, but they found nothing but the decaying house and the weeds that surrounded it. She looked behind her to where the path led to the brown van. She could leave. She could get in the van and drive off, but where would she go? What if the talisman broke, or the Council finally found her, or worse, Alexander? And Ezra . . .

Ezra was calling her name from somewhere far away. It was coming from the house, but she couldn't see him. He sounded warm and happy, and as she stood alone, watching the shimmering in the air, she realised how much she wanted to be standing next to him.

Ana took a deep breath and tried to quiet the beating of her heart in her ears as she forced her feet to move towards the patch of dark grass, reaching her hand out in front of herself. The air moved, and the shimmering came back in glittering blues and pinks. The more she watched, the more her hand faded until she couldn't see it. She waved it, wriggling her fingers, but all she could feel was a light tickling breeze on the other side.

"Okay. Here goes nothing." She winced, snapping her eyes

shut and trying to shield herself as she stepped through onto the dark grass.

Tingling spread across her skin, covering every inch of her body in ice-cold pinpricks. Smiling from the sensation, Ana fell forward as she stumbled through the barrier, coming to a sharp stop on top of a beautiful freshly cut green lawn.

The gardens were no longer covered in briars and weeds, the house was not falling down with rotten wood and graffiti, and the windows were no longer broken. Instead, the place in front of her was full of expertly cut hedges, blooming pink rose bushes and a garden patch near the side of the house that was kept especially for wildflowers and herbs. She could smell them, like her senses here were heightened and the colours too bright for her eyes to take in.

The only similar feature of the house was its shape. A long porch ran down each side of the house, and its large windows were now intact. An upper room with a pointed roof that wasn't there before had a spire on top with a wind vane pointing to the north. The walls were now a beautiful cream colour, with little boxes filled with flowers on every windowpane.

It took a long moment for Ana to realise this wasn't an illusion.

It was *magic*.

"You took your time." Ezra chuckled from where he stood on the porch, his hands in his pockets and a smile spread across his face. He was so handsome, standing there with his floppy brown hair and his greener than green eyes. He looked so much *more* here.

Wide-eyed, Ana walked across the luscious grass and towards the porch, a smile tugging at her lips and a look of disbelief on her face.

"What on earth is this place?" she asked, pausing on her

climb up the wooden steps to look around at the garden again. Butterflies fluttered in a breeze she couldn't feel, making her skin almost long to sense it.

Magic. Definitely magic.

"Well, we had to go somewhere the Council couldn't track us. This is our hideout. Only people with magic in their veins can pass the barrier, and on top of that, only the people that my mother has sanctioned. You are number four on that list, after herself, me, and my sister. The Council can't find you here. Neither can my father."

Ana smiled as she took the last step so that she was standing in front of him and reached out to take his hand. She ran her fingers along the back of it, trying to ignore the flinch he gave when their skin touched.

"Thank you. For saving me and helping me figure everything out," she said, looking up at him before she let go of his hand and reached into her pocket to produce her phone. "Should I get rid of this, so they can't track me?"

"What?" Ezra asked with a smirk, looking down at her phone with a small shake of his head and a laugh. "No, not that kind of tracking. You have a lot to learn. Come on, I will show you to your room."

Ezra turned and walked to the open door, stepping through the threshold and into the foyer. It had a large wooden staircase that went up at least two storeys, with a large stained-glass window at the top and two wings on either side of the house. Right in the middle of the foyer was a black grand piano, its top open and the seat tucked neatly under it. It was a little dusty, probably from the house being vacant for a long time. Why it would be empty, however, she didn't know. It was a beautiful place. She could hide away here forever.

"You play piano?" Ana asked as she walked past the instrument and pressed down on a few keys, smiling as the sound filled the room. It was perfectly tuned, and the notes sounded almost dreamlike.

"Sometimes," Ezra said from the staircase, adjusting her backpack on his shoulder as he turned to look at her with a shrug, "I am a man of many talents."

"I know." Ana smirked as she looked up at him from the keys, then reached to close the lid.

He blinked, a grin pulling at his lips as he scratched the back of his head awkwardly. "Your room is this way."

The room he led her to was at the top of the house. It was the same room she had spotted outside that had the spire on top with the wind vane. The room had a small door and a high pointed ceiling, and the little window gave way to a stunning view of the gardens and trees. There was a four-poster bed that sat against one of the cream panelled walls, with white transparent fabric as a canopy that hung loosely over the top.

Ezra ducked under the tiny doorway and approached the bed, setting her backpack down on it heavily and rolling his shoulder out from the numbness that must have settled there from carrying it.

"Home sweet home. At least for a little while," he said as he turned to her.

Ana stepped inside, holding the talisman on her neck between her fingers. Anxiousness settled inside her stomach again as she studied the room. It was beautiful, clean, and perfect, but something about it seemed *wrong*. She realised as she turned to look at him that it felt that way because she didn't deserve it. Not after what she did to them.

"It's a lovely room," she commented, trying to paint a smile on her face.

"But not your own," Ezra relented, sitting down on the edge

of the bed and giving her a patient smile. "I know this is an adjustment. I know you miss your apartment and your friends and your job but–"

"I don't miss my job. I told you I quit after everything that happened between us," Ana said, shifting awkwardly when he wouldn't meet her eyes. He was still hurt; she could see it all over his face. "You know I am so sorry for everything, don't you?"

"I know. You have mentioned that a few times," Ezra said, leaning on his knees with his elbows. "I have forgiven you, Ana, but I can't help but be disappointed. I thought we . . ." He shook his head and stood from the bed again. "My mother, on the other hand, is still angry, so maybe it would be better if you stay out of her way for a little while."

"Yeah, that is probably for the best." Ana gulped dryly. "So, what do we do now?"

Ezra's smile renewed, and he shrugged, opening his arms to indicate the room. "Get your bearings, explore, unpack. I am going to make some lunch and head to the house library. You are going to need books to help you study." He walked past her and rested his hand on the doorknob before starting to close the door.

"Ezra," Ana said, turning to look at him as she stood in the middle of the room by herself. She waited until his eyes met hers, hugging herself for comfort. "I really am sorry. For everything."

Ezra leaned against the doorframe as he watched her, having to duck down under the little doorway to see inside. "I know."

CHAPTER 2

The house was quiet as Ana sat alone atop the bed in her room. She had unpacked the limited amount of clothing she brought with her and found spaces in the drawers for her toiletries and makeup. The room was already filled with perfumes on the vanity, and a dressing gown hung from the back of the door. A pair of fluffy pink slippers sat beside the bed, just like the ones she had at home in the city, like the room itself knew what she liked and where she liked them.

Pulling her phone from her pocket, Ana scrolled through her emails and messages.

They were still empty.

Her mother hadn't messaged her in months, which was normal for her, considering she was always being whisked away on a cruise or vacation of some sort with another suitor. She wouldn't know she was missing for a while yet, and even then, it would be weeks before she would even care enough to call.

Flicking through her contacts, she found Bexley's name and pressed down, the screen opening to the last texts they shared with each other. There was a string of messages from Bex, asking her where she was and if she was okay, all dated from the night Ana took the keys to Bexley's BMW and disappeared into the darkness.

The messages had flooded her phone in the days following when Ana was asleep, asking in hysterical concern why she wasn't picking up her phone.

Then they got angry, telling her she was worried and that she needed her car, and how it "just wasn't like her" to steal her car and bail on her when Bexley needed her the most.

She hadn't meant to bail on her. She hadn't meant to leave her engagement party and not come back. She hadn't meant to go that far and to be left bleeding and unconscious for days. Ana tried to explain it to her, but she knew Bexley would never understand her excuse. To Bexley, Ana had more important things to do than be present for one of the biggest times of her life, times that a best friend should be there for. How could she explain to her she hadn't abandoned her? That she had died, been brought back to life, and was now a *witch*, of all things?

Instead, she told her she needed some time alone, and Bexley had taken it badly. She had taken it so badly, in fact, that she hadn't answered any of her calls.

Or answered any of her messages.

Or replied to any of her emails.

She had lost her best friend, and she felt totally and utterly alone.

Ana sighed as she looked down at her phone, clicking it off and holding it in her palm. There was music coming from somewhere below her. She could hear it building and moving through the halls and up the stairs to her door. It was getting so loud that she could have sworn the notes themselves had knocked against her door, rattling it on its hinges. She stood from the bed and shoved her phone into her pocket before she headed to the door and opened it wide.

It was piano music.

Ezra.

With a renewed smile on her face, Ana stood from her bed and opened the door wide. The music floated around her body as she walked down the stairs of the top floor, her footsteps feeling lighter and her head becoming less foggy. The more she followed the corridors and the staircases, the louder the music seemed to become.

As she got to the staircase that led to the foyer, she could see the grand piano in the middle of the room. Ezra was sitting on the seat, his head tilted downwards so his floppy brown hair fell in front of his face as his fingers moved gracefully over the keys. His eyes were closed, and he looked as though he was gone with the music, like nothing and no one could break him from his rhythm.

"What are you playing?" Ana asked as she made her way to his side and smiled weakly at him.

His eyes snapped open, and he turned his head to look up at her, his fingers continuing to play and a smile creeping over his face. "*Sonata quasi una fantasia*," he said, the words rolling off his tongue.

"Huh?" Her eyebrows raised. Ezra shifted in his seat so that she could sit down beside him, all without the music stopping. It was a haunting song, slow and precise, like whoever composed it had been hurting when they wrote it.

Ezra chuckled at her confusion and looked back down at the keys as he played. "The Moonlight Sonata, in C-sharp minor. Composed by Beethoven in 1801."

"Oh." Ana blinked, watching him as he rolled his shoulders

and swayed with the movements to keep his timing. "It sounds so sad."

"Yeah, it is. At least, it should be. It's a funeral ballad," Ezra mumbled, his fingers coming to a stop on the keys. "I thought you were never going to come out of that room. I figured a little music might get you moving. It is past dinner time, but I can heat some leftovers if you want?"

"No, thank you. I haven't had much of an appetite." She leaned into him and rested her head on his shoulder. "Did you find any books that might help me?"

"I think so. It's hard to tell until we start. Magic isn't something that can be taught. It's an ability we are born with. Like instinct." He placed his chin on her head. "But there is always a way."

Genevieve cleared her throat behind them, her arms folded and a worried look on her face. "Whatever way that may be, you better think of it fast. The Council is going to come for her one way or the other, Ezra. You are already skating on thin ice with them as it is. If they think you are causing them pain again, they will banish you *completely*. Is that what you want?"

Ezra flinched as he turned to look at his mother, frowning. "Have you had word from them?"

"No, not yet, but I am a member of that council, and when they directly ask me to bring her to them, you know I will have to, right? And if she isn't ready, if she cannot control herself–"

Ana cut her off, her finger in the air to silence them both. "Can we all stop talking about me like I'm not *right here*?" She frowned, dropping her hand and turning in her chair fully to look at Genevieve. "What will happen to me if I am taken to them and still can't control it?"

Genevieve dropped her crossed arms. She looked like she

still wanted to be mad at her, but her worry was overpowering the anger, making her face pale.

"Humans should not possess magical abilities. The magic running through your blood is not yours. You don't naturally hold the correct instincts to use it. If they know you cannot control it, that you are dangerous to everyone around you, and more importantly, to the anonymity of our coven, then they will take the magic out of you."

"That would be amazing!" Ana gasped. Ezra's hand was wrapping around hers, cradling it like he always did when he was trying to shield her from something. She frowned at how he wouldn't look at her, and worry pooled in her stomach. "Right? That's good. I don't *want* the magic. We could go now, and they can take it back . . ."

"You wouldn't survive it," Genevieve said as she shook her head, her arms crossing over her chest again. "The magic travels in your blood, Ana. It was a blood magic ritual that Alexander performed. The only way to get it out of you is the process of exsanguination."

"To drain all of your blood," Ezra explained before she had to ask what it meant.

"All of it?" Ana gulped.

"Every drop," he said, squeezing her hand and looking down at her. He gave her a small smile and held the back of her hand against his chest. "But that isn't an option."

"No, it's not. Which is why you both should be in the library studying, not canoodling by the piano. Go. Scoot. Now." Genevieve swatted at them both until they jumped out of the way of the piano so that she could close the lid and push the chair under it again.

Ezra guided Ana down the long corridor that led to the library. Paintings in gold frames and white statues of old literary heroes filled the hallways, but instead of taking in the beauty of them, she couldn't take her eyes away from staring at her feet. A knot of fear had settled inside her stomach, and it weighed heavily, making her feel nauseous and lightheaded. She barely noticed how long they had been walking until she almost bumped into Ezra when he stopped to open the door.

"Are you okay?" he asked, looking back at her.

Ana shook her head, pushing past him to walk into the dimly lit library. It was filled with bookcases that lined the walls, a large marble fireplace and deep red rugs. The middle of the room had been left empty, with nothing but a table and some comfortable-looking chairs to furnish the room.

Ezra sighed as he closed the door and followed her, reaching out his arm to take her hand when she paused in the middle of the room. "Ana. I know you are scared, but I will not let anything happen to you, okay? We will figure this out."

"How?" she asked as she turned to him. Her eyes were filling with tears, and her mouth was turning dry. "I have literally *days* to learn how to control myself, and if I can't, I die."

"And I am going to teach you. You just need to calm down. You can't control your magic if you are letting your emotions get the better of you."

"Teach me *how*, Ezra? How can someone with *no magic* teach me how to use mine?" Ana sniffled, slumping down into the sofa.

"I have magic. I was particularly skilled at it, actually. I am just not allowed to use it anymore. Banned, remember?" he said with a frown, letting her go and walking away to the table where he had left spell books sprawled over its wooden surface.

Heat rose into Ana's cheeks as she watched him walk away from her, filled with a mixture of guilt and embarrassment.

"I'm sorry. I am just frustrated." She groaned, pushed herself up from the sofa and walked to his side, studying his face as he read over the titles. "You never told me why you were banned from doing magic."

"No. I didn't," he mumbled, opening one of the pages and beginning to read the writing inside. "And I am not going to tell you either. We don't have time for gossip, Ana. You need to study. First, you can read the books I studied when I was learning." He pointed at the books on the table.

"I thought you said it was instinct?" Ana frowned as she ran her finger over the spines of the books.

"It is, to a certain extent. I could feel exactly how *much* magic to use and how it came to form itself, but the rest was down to training. Fine-tuning, if you will. Once we get your emotions in check, we can help you wield your magic. You will protect and heal yourself, bring down an opponent with a flick of your wrist. The opportunities are endless, really."

"Sounds promising. When do we start?"

"Tomorrow. For tonight, you need to take this stack of books and read. You must know the terminologies and the basics, so we don't have to waste any time on them tomorrow. You won't be able to feel any of the magic that the books reference until you take off the talisman, but if you familiarise yourself with it now, it will be easier for you to understand tomorrow." He passed her the open book.

Ana took it with a small nod. The book was heavy. It was leather bound and handwritten in delicate cursive, but the letters had a wobble to them as if they were written by someone young. Ezra's name was inscribed on the top of the first page below the date. It read, "Ezra Sullivan, Age 8."

"Wait. This is a *kid's* book?" she asked as she scrutinized him with wide eyes.

"Yeah. I told you, it's the book I first used when I had to learn the basics. Why?" he asked with a shrug.

"I am twenty-five years old, and I have to learn from a kid's book. I am *so* screwed." Ana groaned, closing the book and running her hand through her hair. It was getting tangled and direly needed clean water.

"If you keep moaning about it, then yes, you are screwed," Ezra said as he folded his arms and turned to look at her fully. His brow was furrowed again, and he appeared to be getting irritated. "I am trying to help you, Ana. It's not like you to act so powerlessly. You always find a way to get what you need, right? You don't let things beat you down, so why are you letting this get to you? We work well on a deadline, remember?"

"Yeah, I guess we do," Ana said as she sniffled. Her throat was raw, and her face felt hot as she tried to keep her tears at bay. "I guess I am just scared. Scared that I can't control myself and that I will end up hurting people or being killed by a council of people I haven't even *met* yet. I am scared Bex won't ever forgive me for running out on her when she needed me. I am just . . . *scared*."

Ezra frowned as he reached to take her by the shoulders, holding her at arm's length and trying to make her stand up straighter. "All your emotions are heightened by your magic. When you get scared, you will feel sheer panic instead. When you feel love, it will be uncontainable. When you feel angry, it will burn through you like a fire. That is why you feel so helpless now, the talisman that is binding your magic can't help you with that, but you *can* channel it and you will live with it someday. Magic *is* emotion. Control your emotions, and you can control your magic."

Ana watched his green eyes as they stared back at her, a sense of calm filling her as she tried to listen to the weight of his words. She nodded, trying not to shake under his hands. "Okay. Control my emotions."

"Better," Ezra said, renewing his smile. "I have one more book that might help you, but it's in my room. I will walk you upstairs, and we can get it on the way."

He was already walking away by the time he finished his sentence. Ana secured her hold on the books in her arms, rushing after him out of the library and down the corridor to the staircase. Ezra was climbing the stairs two at a time, reaching the landing quickly and flashing a smile over his shoulder as he waved her to follow him.

Ezra's bedroom was on the first floor at the end of the hallway. He stopped outside the door, resting his hand on the gold doorknob and pausing with an unsure expression clouding his face. Turning to look at her, he dropped his hand again, instead opting to run it through his hair at the back of his neck. "Wait here, I will get the book."

"You aren't going to let me come into your room? You have been in mine. How is that fair?" Ana smirked, noting the red tones that were tinging his cheeks.

"It's not like that." He squirmed, opening and closing his mouth a few times like he wasn't quite sure what to say. "It's embarrassing."

"Embarrassing?" Ana laughed. "Are you a messy person, Mister Sullivan? Or is it the posters of topless women and bookcases filled with raunchy magazines that you don't want me to see, huh?"

"No, nothing like that," Ezra said, standing in front of the door to block her from going inside. "But I haven't been here since I was a teenager, and I haven't redecorated. My mom finds it funny, and she won't change it. It's the magic. Seeing as I'm banned, I can't magic it away."

Ana smiled wider at how uncomfortable he was becoming and how he was avoiding her eyes. "Oh, well, now I have to look!"

"Promise you won't laugh."

"I'm not going to laugh," Ana said, already giggling as she pushed past him. Reaching for the knob, she opened the door, her eyes going wide in surprise when she gazed at his room. Or more, what she could *see* of his room.

Everything was black. The walls were black, the ceiling was black, the four-poster bed was black, and dark stained wooden panels lined the floor. Blinking, she walked in farther, noticing the details of his room. Huge posters displayed band logos she didn't recognise, odd-shaped guitars hung from the walls on stands and sculptures made from metal sat in the corners.

Ana turned in the middle of the room to look at Ezra, a teasing look on her face as she watched him lean against the doorway, with his arms folded, as if waiting for her reaction.

"It was a phase," he defended, flicking his eyes around his room with a furrow of his brow.

"Were you a scene kid, Ezra Sullivan?" she asked, amusement lacing her tone as she tried not to laugh.

"You said you wouldn't laugh," Ezra argued as he walked through the threshold of the door and reached her side, shoving his hands in his pockets and shrugging. "I went through a rebellious stage, you could say."

"No shit," Ana said, fumbling with the books in her arms to free a hand so that she could poke his side with her finger.

Something hanging on the wall caught her eye, and her mouth dropped open. Pictures littered the black wall of his bedroom. Lots of them.

She approached them before Ezra could stop her, standing on her tiptoes so that she could study them. Ezra was in most of them, his hair long with the fringe covering his right eye. He looked about fourteen. Skinny and lanky, tall and not yet grown into himself. He had such a young baby face and a happy smile as he roughhoused with his friends and pulled stupid poses for the camera.

"Oh my God." Ana smirked, looking over her shoulder at him. "This is the cutest thing I've ever seen."

"Stop it," Ezra said, shooting her a glare at first but then laughing. He stood against her back so that he could look over her shoulder. He pointed to a picture of him and another boy with dark skin and black clothing much like Ezra's. "That's Jasper. You met him at the Litha celebration. We were in 'The Black Death Society.'"

Ana smiled warmly at the photo of the boys hanging over each other in one-armed hugs. Ezra looked so different now from what he did in that photo. It was almost hard to tell that the tall, sophisticated, muscled man could have ever been a scrawny scene kid with too much guyliner and a head full of hair gel.

"What's 'The Black Death Society?'" she asked, looking over her shoulder and up at his face as she rested her back against his chest, enjoying his warmth.

"Our band," he mumbled.

Ana's jaw dropped open, gasping through her smile and turning to face him. "You were in a *band*? Tell me there are photos. *Please*."

"No. And even if there were, you are never seeing them, lest my soul leave my body," he said, taking her by the arm and pulling her away from the wall and towards the bookcase.

"Wait, was that a lyric?"

"No!" Ezra laughed. "Stop. You have had your fun. You need to take this book." He reached for a black leather-bound book that sat at the top of the shelf. He brought it down, blowing dust off the cover, and set it on top of the stack in her arm. "And you need to go study. You have a big day tomorrow. Mocking my youth is not going to help us right now."

"But it did make me feel better," Ana said, giving him a thankful smile as she shuffled the books to get a better grip on them. She wasn't sure how she would manage to read these by the morning. There were so many.

"Glad to be of service," he said with a roll of his eyes as he guided her back to the door. "Do you want me to carry the books to your room for you?"

"No, it's all right. I got it," she said, turning to face him in the doorway. "Thank you for the books. And the laugh." She rose on her tiptoes to plant a kiss on his cheek before she started on her way down the hallway.

"You are welcome, Davenport."

Ana turned to catch a glimpse of him as she started on her ascent up the second staircase, but he was gone, followed seconds later by the sound of his door closing.

Maybe if she could get a hold of her emotions and learn to wield the magic she possessed, she would survive.

If she could learn to use her magic, she could help him redecorate that *bedroom*.

Grinning at the thought, Ana stumbled into her bedroom with her books, looking around and setting her face.

She could do this.

She had to.

CHAPTER 3

*L*ight streamed through the windows of her room as Ana sat atop the sheets of the bed. Ezra's leather-bound books were sprawled in a fan all around her, their pages open and skyward. She had been reading while the black moonlit sky outside had turned to purples and pinks and finally to bright blue as the sun rose. She hadn't slept even though Ezra said she should be well rested for training, but the books were thick, and she knew if she didn't finish reading them by daybreak, she had no chance of learning anything from him.

So far, everything inside the books read like gibberish. The books suggested that magic came from the blood through generations of ancestors that shared their wealth of knowledge and power with everyone in their line. It said that it settled in a place behind the stomach, building up and storing itself to be called upon and used whenever a witch had the need. The trick, however, was knowing how much to use and how to control it. For that, there was no chapter.

Other chapters showed the components of spells. It listed

ingredients and incantations for "simple" spells that helped a young witch learn control, but no matter how many times she tried to read them aloud, she felt nothing. Nothing except for the subtle pang of magic that stirred behind her stomach, willing to be let loose.

There were chapters on the religious holidays that Ezra and his coven kept sacred. There were times of the month they kept called "Esbats" that studied the phases of the moon and the corresponding uses and powers of each phase. She could see little drawings of the different shapes of moons, scribbled upon the pages by the hand of an eight-year-old Ezra.

Ana ran her finger fondly over the little drawing of the full moon. It was shaky, and the shading was spiking out of the lines.

A knock sounded on the door, bringing her mind away from the drawings of the moons. She stood from the bed quickly and walked to the door. Ezra was standing on the other side, two steaming cups of coffee in his hands.

"Good morning." He smiled, and as he looked over her face, his expression became confused. "Or not? Did you stay up all night? I told you that you needed rest."

"I know." Ana sighed as she took the coffee cup from him and followed as he walked around her and into the room. "But every time I closed my eyes, all I could think about was how screwed I am. So I thought maybe I should study the books you gave me, but nothing inside them is making any sense." She rubbed her forehead. Her brain felt like it was throbbing and sticking to the sides of her skull.

Ezra rolled his eyes as he moved to sit down on the edge of the bed, looking over the pages that littered the sheets. "That is because you are still thinking like a human."

"You say that like you don't consider yourself human," Ana said as she slumped on the opposite end of the bed, taking a sip of her coffee with a thankful hum. Tiredness pushed against her eyelids in a dull ache for sleep. She tried to blink it away, but it hovered there anyway.

"I don't. Not really," Ezra argued as he reached to flick a few of the pages. He looked up at her when she gave him a raise of her brow in question, and he shrugged with a breathy laugh. "What I mean is, we are human, obviously. It's the same body, the same makeup of genetics I guess, but in energy and capability, we are a completely different subspecies. Every witch is born with the ability to manipulate energy and use it to our will. It's an instinct, like I said, which is why it is so hard to teach someone who hasn't always felt it. You are an anomaly. You shouldn't exist, Ana. You can't just *make* a witch. At least I didn't think it was possible, until you." He furrowed his brow before he stood from the bed again and continued.

"It's like when a baby is born. It knows how to suckle and breathe without being taught, right? A witch is born knowing what that pull of energy feels like, where it lives, how to tame it and bring it to the surface and what kind of energy is needed to do certain things. The rest we learn as we grow. We learn the morality of how to use our magic, how much of it to use to have the desired effect so that we don't drain ourselves into a coma, and chemistry. The spell work in these books only applies when you need to call upon other energies and deities to do your bidding for you, but you don't need to know those things yet. Hopefully, if you are wise, you will never need them at all."

"How is any of this supposed to help me if I don't understand what you are saying? I don't *feel* what you say I should be feeling. I don't feel rushing energies I can bend, and I don't feel magic coursing through my veins," Ana said as she gripped her head in frustration.

Ezra walked around the bed towards her and knelt beside her

legs, trying to give her a comforting smile. "But you did, right? Before my mom had to bind your magic, you felt it."

Ana sniffled back her tears and nodded slowly, her throat feeling tight and her cheeks growing hot. "Yeah. I guess."

"Then when we take this off you," he said, reaching to tap the talisman that hung from her neck with his finger, "you will feel it again, and you will understand. You will stop thinking like a human and start thinking like a witch. Though I would appreciate you not blowing my body apart atom by atom while I try to teach you."

Ana looked down at his warm smile, and his eyes were big and hopeful. She found the nerves in her stomach beginning to quell. She nodded once, then smiled when he reached to wipe a tear from her cheek. "Yeah. Okay. I'll try not to kill you."

"Thanks. That would be great," Ezra said with a laugh. "I will go downstairs and get the library ready for our training session. You should get changed and brush your teeth. You have horrible morning breath." He laughed, waving his hand in front of his face jokingly.

"Hey! Shut up! It's the coffee!" Ana laughed through her tears as she shoved him back onto the floor at her feet, putting a hand over her mouth.

"I'm kidding! Don't hurt me." He chuckled as he scrambled to his feet, trying not to spill his coffee. "I will see you downstairs when you are ready."

Ezra gave her a smile as he turned on his heel and walked out of the door again, closing it tightly when he left, leaving her sitting on the edge of her bed.

After finishing her coffee, Ana set the cup aside on the dresser and slipped out of her pyjamas, moving to the wardrobe. She pulled out a red sweater and a pair of black skinny jeans that she quickly unfolded. After slipping them on, she rushed into the bathroom, fished out her toothbrush and paste and brushed her teeth before she rinsed her mouth and washed her face. The face that stared back at her looked different from the last time she remembered looking in the mirror. That girl had rosy cheeks and a bright smile, eyes full of excitement and hope. The girl that met her eyes now was a shadow of that person. Her face was pale, and her eyes were dull, full of worry.

Gulping down the disappointment that was building in her chest, Ana brushed out her hair and walked back out of the bathroom so that she could slip on her black boots and make her way down the many staircases that led to the library.

When she got there, she noticed Ezra had pulled the table away from the middle of the room, leaving the area clear. He was standing near the marble fireplace at the back of the room, rolling the sleeves of his white shirt up to his elbows neatly when he noticed her walk inside.

"You look a little better. Are you ready?" He smiled as he walked across the room to her.

"I guess I am." Her hands balled into fists at her side as she tried to hold in her nerves.

"Okay, good. We are going to work on containment. You have the magic of almost all the witches of the Marion Coven inside you, just waiting to burst out and create havoc. If you want to survive this, you need to keep it all inside. You need to learn to control it and how to contain the magic inside you without damaging those around you. Understand?" Ezra said as he led her into the centre of the room.

Ana nodded once and took a deep breath as she faced him, looking up into his eyes. "How exactly do I do that?"

"Firstly, do you remember where a witch's magic radiates from?"

"The stomach."

"You did your homework," he said, grinning as he continued, "The solar plexus is the centre of every witch's magic, and it lives right here." He reached forward and placed the palm of his hand on her stomach, pressing her there gently with a warm hand.

Ana blushed deeply as she looked up at him, feeling his hand against her stomach. "Am I supposed to be feeling something there?"

"You will, when we take the binding from you," Ezra said as he took his hand back. "The solar plexus is the area that controls self-discipline, motivation, confidence and, most importantly, willpower. Will is what is going to help you control your magic. If you can use your Will, if you can focus it, you will learn how to tame it and it will listen to you, but you need to pay attention to every word I say. Don't take your eyes off me, okay?"

"Okay," she replied nervously, gulping thickly as he moved a few paces away to stand opposite her.

"Good. Take your pendant from your neck and set it on the table," Ezra instructed, giving her a warm smile. "You can do this."

Ana nodded once and raised a shaky hand to her neck, where she lifted the rope up and over her head. The second she walked to the table at the side of the room and dropped the pendant on the wood, the ground under her feet rumbled. In the middle of her stomach, where Ezra had placed his warm hand, was now turning ice cold, making her body shiver and her eyes wide.

"It's okay! Ignore it, it's just your magic being set free after being dormant. You can do this. Come here." He held his hand out to her to indicate the space in front of him where she had stood before.

Ana inhaled a deep breath and took small steps into the middle of the room, her body tense and her arms rigid at her sides. The floorboards under her feet rattled and groaned at the rumbling that radiated beneath them. The corners of the room were filling with a thick fog that clung to the walls and crept its way around the room as the temperature plummeted.

"E-Ezra," she whimpered, her eyes wide as she watched the walls.

"It's okay! Look at me!" Ezra called out, frowning when she focused on the growing fog. "Ana! Look at me!"

Ana snapped her eyes to look at him, trying to focus as her head began to throb and ringing started to fill her ears so loudly that she could barely hear him.

"You need to concentrate on that area I told you about, okay? Focus." His hand patted his stomach to show her where he meant.

Now that she was aware and searching for it, Ana could feel the sensation he had told her about. It swirled and throbbed, like there was a whirlwind of energy contained inside, ready to burst from its confines behind her ribs. It was uncomfortable and overwhelming, and it must have shown on her face because Ezra was mouthing the word "focus" to her repeatedly. She closed her eyes, taking another deep breath and trying to concentrate on the area, willing the energy to slow from a whirling to a gentle flow.

"Keep going, Ana. Reel it in."

The ringing in her ears had quietened, but when she opened her eyes again slowly, she noticed the fog that was filling the room had only gotten thicker. The floorboards were groaning louder, and the lights attached to the walls were flickering as she looked back at Ezra's face in a panic.

"Ana, your eyes . . ." He took a step towards her, his eyes wide with worry.

She frowned as she turned her head to look at her reflection in the large antique mirror hanging on the wall. Her face appeared normal, although it was paler than usual, but when she glanced over her eyes in the mirror, she could see why Ezra seemed so startled. Her eyes had turned obsidian black, covering her irises and the whites of her eyes. She gasped at the reflection, and as she snapped her head back to look at him, another loud rumble sounded under her feet. The mirror smashed, making them jump from the crash and her eyes grow wider.

"What do I do?" Ana panicked, her hands shaking at her sides as more vases and lights smashed around the room, shards raining on the floorboards and making her flinch.

"You need to calm down! You are letting it slip. Solar plexus, remember? You need to focus!"

The room was full of fog now, and the more she lost control of her magic, the more the blackness of her eyes seeped and stained the skin below them. Raising a hand to her face, she wiped at her nose, feeling a wet, hot stickiness. Blood. Her nose was bleeding.

"Ezra, I can't hold it in anymore," she sobbed.

"It's okay! It's okay, just wait. I will get the talisman. Don't move!" Ezra said as he walked to the table through the fog. He held it out in his hands and moved back to her, reaching it out to her as he took her hand.

The second his skin touched hers, the talisman dropped from his hand, and his body went rigid. Before she could ask if he was okay, Ana watched as he was lifted from the ground and thrown to the other side of the room through the fog. She couldn't see him anymore, but she heard him crash against the wall and fall to the floor with a sickening *thud*.

"Ezra! Ezra, are you okay?!"

He didn't reply.

"Shit!" Ana gasped, reaching to the floor to lift the talisman.

When she slipped it over her head and let it settle onto her chest again, the feeling she had in her stomach faded. The magic got harder and harder to feel, the fog began to clear from the room and the noise under her feet came to a halt.

Ezra was groaning from beside the marble fireplace, holding his head.

"Ezra!" She rushed across the room to him and sank to her knees.

Ana reached for him and frowned when he flinched at her touch. She took his hand away from his head anyway so that she could look at his wound. There was a large gash there, and it was bleeding freely over his ears and down over his neck, staining his white shirt.

"I am so sorry, Ezra. I didn't mean to." She sniffled, frustrated tears filling her eyes.

"I know. It's all right. I'm fine," Ezra said, looking up into her eyes, searching them for the darkness that had clouded them before. "Your eyes are normal again. Are you okay?"

"I think so," she said, wiping her bloody nose on the sleeve of her sweater. "We need to get you to Genevieve. She can heal you, right?"

He nodded once, his eyes studying her quietly for a few long moments before he stood and brushed down his clothes with his hands. He had a worried look on his face, and he wouldn't meet her eyes.

"Maybe we should rethink our strategy. This isn't working. I'm not sure how many more times I can be thrown across a room." He side-stepped around her and reached to lift the toppled chairs. There was a stumble in his walk, like he was feeling woozy.

Guilt pulsed in her chest as she stood and followed him, reaching out to him to take his hand when he rested against the table.

"What if there is no containing it? What if we keep doing this over and over again and I end up killing you? I don't want to hurt you anymore, Ezra." She tried to hold back a sob. "I'm scared."

Ezra finally turned his face to look at her. He squeezed her hand and nodded before he pulled her hand upwards and kissed the back of it.

"I know. I am too. But we can't give up, right? We need to keep going. First, though, we need breakfast. We should both clean up, and I will meet you in the kitchen. We can rethink our strategy there."

Ana's face softened when he held her hand so close to him. She leaned in to hug herself gently to his side, then sniffled again, let go of his hand and headed for the door, her stomach full of guilt and fear. She wasn't sure she could eat even if she tried.

CHAPTER 4

⚜

Ana frowned as she sat at the vanity table in the bedroom at the top of the house. She had changed her red sweater to a blue tank top and opted to slump on the chair to clean her bloody nose with the little cotton balls in a bowl beside the mirror. There was no sign of the darkness behind her eyes anymore. Instead, her eyes held only tiredness. When she closed her eyes, it pushed against her eyelids, making her head feel fuzzy and her body feel weakened.

She opened her eyes again and finished cleaning her lip and chin from the blood, then discarded the cotton balls into the trash can beside the bed and lifted her phone out of her pocket, looking down at the screen. It was blank. No messages. No notifications. No one.

Heat rose into her cheeks and stung her eyes as they threatened tears. She had never felt so truly and utterly alone, and no matter how much Ezra had been trying to help her, she had the nagging feeling he was only doing it because he felt bad for what his father had done to her. She couldn't talk to him like she could to her friends, no matter how close they were.

She needed Bexley.

Ana opened her messages and found Bexley's name, pressing on it and starting to type, then deleted it and typed again. No matter what she said, she knew Bexley would never understand because there was no possible way she could explain everything that had happened. Instead of apologising again, she typed three simple words and pressed send.

I miss you.

She hiccupped a sob as she watched the message send, and after staring for a while, she spotted the little jumping dots at the corner of the screen, indicating Bexley had seen it and was replying. Then the dots disappeared again, like Bexley had thought better of it and stopped.

Hurt pushed against the space between her heart and her lungs, and she set the phone on the vanity, wiping her eyes with the back of her hands to dry the tears that had formed. Her stomach was growling loudly now. Rather than waiting by the phone all day for a reply she knew would not come, she stood from the chair and moved out of the bedroom, heading downstairs towards the kitchen.

Genevieve and Ezra were talking inside. She could hear them arguing from down the hall as she approached, their voices raising and then hushing down low when they thought they were being loud.

"You have nothing to feel guilty about, Ezra. There is nothing more we can do," Genevieve said as she moved around the kitchen.

She was making breakfast even though it was nearly past lunchtime. The smell of eggs and bacon travelled through the door and hit Ana in the face so fully it sent a wave of ravenous nausea over her body.

When she walked inside, they abruptly stopped talking, looking between themselves tensely. Ezra was sitting at the table, leaning on his elbows heavily while Genevieve plated the food.

"Don't stop on my account," Ana mumbled as she moved to sit down at the table, looking between them. Genevieve was avoiding eye contact while Ezra was staring ahead of himself, his jaw tensed. "What were you talking about?"

"Nothing," Ezra said, pushing off his elbows and sitting back in his chair with his arms folded over his chest. When he finally looked up at her and noted her frown, he shrugged. "Nothing you need to worry about."

Genevieve tutted and threw the frying pan into the sink, her hands on her hips as she waited for the kettle to boil. "Ezra told me what happened during your lesson."

Ana turned in her seat so that she could look up into Genevieve's face as she lifted the plates and set them in front of them. "It wasn't much of a lesson. I didn't get very far before everything went to hell."

"It's fine. We will try again," Ezra said as he took his fork in his hand and pushed the bacon around his plate. He had a tired expression on his face, and his brows were furrowed in concern.

"It is not fine!" Genevieve snapped as she set her plate down roughly and grabbed the kettle when it screamed from the stove. "You have too much magic in your blood, Ana. *Far* too much, more than any born witch should have. You can't stay here. We can't help you."

Ana paused as she reached for her fork, looking up again at her face when she returned with the freshly brewed pot of tea and sat down. "I didn't mean to hurt him, Genevieve. I can try to do better . . ."

"It's not about doing better, Ana," Genevieve said with a small sigh as she studied Ana's face. "I know you are trying, but the binding of your magic is only going to work for so long. It is already weakening." She reached forward and placed a finger on the pendant around Ana's neck. A small crack travelled up over the symbol. She tutted at it disapprovingly and sat back again with a shake of her head. "It is not going to hold forever."

Ana frowned as she took the pendant in her hand. "Can't we replace it?"

"It is not that simple. You have the combined magic of the entire Marion Coven. Even an experienced witch would struggle to tame it, never mind *you*. Either it is going to break out and destroy everything around you or it is going to consume you. Either way, your body will not survive it. It is a ticking time bomb, and I don't think we have the time to defuse it." Genevieve roughly cut at her food. Ana wasn't sure if Genevieve was frustrated because she wanted to help her and couldn't or she just wanted her gone.

"So, what do I do?" Ana asked, looking at them hopefully. Her chest felt tight, and blood was thumping in her ears.

"We keep trying," Ezra answered, standing up from the table without eating any of his food. He still looked woozy from his head injury, but his wound was completely healed.

"You can't, Ezra. It is too dangerous. She needs *help*," Genevieve argued as she watched him walk around the table.

"And I am giving it to her!" Ezra snapped, looking over his shoulder at them both. "I didn't ask for your permission, Mother. I am going to lie down. I need to recover. I will meet you in the library tonight, Ana."

He walked out of the room, and even though he hadn't snapped at her, she still felt like she was the one being scolded. She gulped thickly, tears behind her eyes as she looked away from the empty door to Genevieve's worried face. "I'm so sorry."

"I know you are," Genevieve mumbled, her face softening as she reached to pat her hand. "Eat your food. You haven't eaten in days, and you need your strength."

Ana turned to look down at the cooling plate of food. She lifted her fork, and they ate silently for a while. Her head was swimming in panic. If Genevieve genuinely didn't think there was anything more they could do for her, then she was only prolonging the inevitable by staying here. Either the magic was going to burst out of her, killing her and anyone around her in the process, or the High Council would come and take the magic out of her themselves. Either way, she was going to die.

Bile rose into the back of the throat, and she set her fork down on the table, pressing her hands against her chest to will it down. "Genevieve?" she asked, the sound of her name loud in the otherwise completely silent kitchen. Genevieve didn't look up. "Where does a witch go when they die?"

Genevieve frowned at the question, finishing her plate and lifting her teacup to her lips. She let out a breathy sigh and tilted her head, watching Ana with eyes that seemed heavy.

"When witches die, they go to the Summerlands. It is a place of eternal warmth and beauty, where your ancestors and the long-gone members of your coven meet you with open arms to enjoy the fruits of a magical afterlife. It is said that the Summerlands is a place that makes living on Earth pale in comparison. Witches do not fear death because it is not the end of all things. It is not the end of magic." She gave a soft smile from over the rim of her cup. "But I hope you do not go there anytime soon, Ana. That is why we must take you to the High Council. They might be able to help."

"Maybe," Ana muttered. The Summerlands sounded beautiful, but she was not ready to leave this life. She had so much of it still to live, and her stomach and her heart yearned for the chance. "If I do die, if Ezra or the High Council can't help me, will I go to the Summerlands?"

Genevieve set her cup down and rested her hand on Ana's again, squeezing it gently. "Of course you will. You have magic inside you. You would pass through, but I have hope the High Council will have the answers we need to keep you from there for a very long time. Ezra wants to help you, but his judgement is clouded by his feelings for you. He is stubborn. I fear he will continue to try even when his reason tells him you *both* need help."

Genevieve took her hand back from hers and lifted her cup to her lips once more, sipping at it gently.

Ana nodded slowly, sniffling and blinking back the tears in her eyes. "He is very stubborn. I like that about him, how he never gives up."

"You have that same quality, no matter the cost, hm? Ana, why did you write about us in the way that you did?"

Blood rushed into her cheeks at her question, and she shrugged and wrapped her arms around herself as if trying to shield her body. "I don't know. I guess my ambition for my career got a little out of control. Ezra and I had a fight, and I felt like if I had lost him anyway, he would never see it. I was so angry and upset and I just . . . It was cruel of me. It was not the kind of piece I ever wanted to write. That article, that newspaper, it was not the kind of writer I wanted to be. When I started out, I was invested in real journalism. I was helping people. I wrote articles about topics that really mattered. What I wrote about you was untrue, it betrayed your trust in me, and I am so sorry. Can you ever forgive me, Genevieve?"

Genevieve stayed silent for a long moment, clearly pondering whether she could. "I think I can forgive you, but you need to earn our trust again, Ana. I will help you as best as I can with everything you are going through, but trust will take time."

Ana gave a quivering smile, reaching to wipe her cheek with her hand. "That is very fair of you. Thank you, Genevieve. I will make this up to you. I prom–"

A loud rumbling rolled past the house, cutting Ana's words off in the air. It growled and roared, working its way quickly along the side of the house and making a stop somewhere near the front door. It sounded like a loud engine, and it spluttered as it grumbled to a stop.

Genevieve jumped to her feet from where she was sitting, setting her cup down roughly. As alarmed as she was, she had a smile plastered wide across her face. "Abby!" she gasped, walking around the chair and rushing out of the door to the kitchen.

Ana followed, approaching the kitchen door and peeking her head around the frame to see the front door where Genevieve was waiting. She was almost bouncing on the balls of her feet.

The door opened on its own, and standing on the other side was a girl. She looked to be around twenty. She was the same height as Genevieve, with similar dark hair, but where Genevieve had white badger stripes along the front of her face, the girl had bright purple highlights among her long black curls.

Genevieve lunged and threw her arms around her, bringing her into a crushing hug that made the younger woman splutter and wriggle underneath it.

"Mom! Let me go! I can't breathe!" she choked out, though Ana could see her hands hugging Genevieve back.

Genevieve kissed her all over her head and cheeks, letting her go from the hug so that she could take her face in her hands and stare into her eyes. "I have missed you."

"I have missed you too, Mom, but I am here on official business."

"What kind of official business, Abby?" Genevieve asked as she led her daughter inside the house and closed the door behind her.

Abby. Abby was Ezra's sister. It was Abby's room she had stayed in when she slept in Genevieve's house. It was her clothes she had worn when she had none of her own.

Abby strolled around the foyer, studying the high ceilings like she was taking it in after being away for so long, and when she looked towards the kitchen and through the door, her eyes fell upon Ana, who stood tucked against the frame.

"*That* official business." She grinned. She looked almost feline as she focused her eyes on her, like she was waiting for her to dart away so that she could pounce on her.

"Me?" Ana mumbled, stepping around the door frame so that she could stand up straighter.

"You are the girl my father tried to kill, right?" Abby said, taking a step towards her. "That must have sucked."

"Abby?"

Ezra stood at the top of the staircase, looking down at them with his hand on the banister and a tired frown on his face. He walked down the stairs and into the hall, tilting his head at his sister as she turned away from Ana and smiled widely at him.

"Brother. Long time, no see. You have gotten yourself into quite the pickle, haven't you?"

"What are you doing here?" Ezra said. His expression was hard, like he was trying to figure out his sister's intentions by reading her body language, but from what Ana could see, she wasn't giving anything away.

"What? No 'Hey, Abby, I missed you' or 'Where have you been?'"

Ezra's face softened as he reached her. Mere inches separated them, and he reached his arms out so he could pull her into a hug. "Of course I missed you, but I would be a fool if I didn't think you were up to something."

Abby smiled as she pulled back from the hug, peering up at him. "Well, you would be right. I am always up to something. I got a new job."

"You never told me that," Genevieve said as she walked towards her children and reached out to tuck some of Abby's hair behind her ear.

Abby nodded to her mother and pulled the sleeve of her leather jacket up to reveal her forearm. On it was a brand shaped like a four-pointed star with little dots around its points. "I joined the Venator."

"You are a bounty hunter for the High Council? Seriously?" Ezra asked as he stepped back from her and made his way towards the kitchen where Ana was standing.

"It's a good job. I get to use fancy weapons, travel, kill things. It's perfect for me." Abby smirked as she followed him with her eyes.

"And you have been sent to collect Ana," Ezra said. He crossed his arms over his chest and his face hardened as he watched his sister.

"It was either Ana or Dad, and I don't fancy my chances catching him. Ana is the easier mark. I knew wherever you were, she would be. My instincts were spot on, I see." She shrugged. "Don't make this harder than it needs to be, Ezra. No one is going to hurt her. They just want to talk. The High Council needs to know what is going on. Her magic is unstable. Even the Elders can feel it. It's throwing everything off, so she needs to be contained."

"No." Ezra frowned. "I am helping her. We are so close, Abby. I need to do this myself. Please."

"You are not close. Don't lie to me. Do you think the Council would have sent me if things were going *well* here? She needs to come with me, Ezra, for everyone's safety." Abby raised her hand and tensed as her palm began to glow. Electric purple sparks fizzled in her palm as she held her hand out towards them. "Don't make me ask again, Ezra."

"Goddamn it, Abby!" Ezra shouted. He ran his hand through his hair and stalked towards her, taking his sister's wrist in his hand with a grip so tight his knuckles turned white. "One more night. After *everything* I have done for you, you will give me one more night."

Abby held her brother's gaze through her own narrowed, angry eyes. Her nostrils flared as she breathed out a shaky, pent-up breath, before she suddenly smiled again and closed her hand, the purple sparks disappearing. "Fine. One more night. We leave in the morning."

The room fell quiet as Ezra let her wrist go roughly and his eyes darted between Ana and his mother. Genevieve was watching them both with furrowed brows, but she didn't speak.

"Well." Abby sighed, breaking the silence as she rubbed her wrist. "I guess I have time for a hot bath, then. If you try to leave, I will hunt you down, and I won't be so nice about it next time." She turned on her heel and trudged up the stairs.

Ezra breathed deeply as he watched her leave, and when he was sure she had gone into a room and closed the door, he finally examined Ana, who was cowering in the doorway. His face softened, and he reached his hand out for her to take.

One night.

She had *one more* night.

CHAPTER 5

Ana looked down at the book on her lap. It was big and, judging by the cover, very old. It had little jewels melted into it with sigils she didn't recognise etched into the leather. Its pages were browning, and the writing inside was fading, but she could make out the majority. Understanding it, however, was a different matter. She could read the words perfectly, but they made little sense when they translated from the book into the logic of her brain.

You shouldn't exist, Ana. You can't just make a witch.

Ezra's words echoed inside her head as she listened to the slow rhythm of him sleeping beside her. He was lying on top of her duvet, his white-collared shirt rolled up to his elbows and his hand on her thigh as she looped her legs over his middle and sat upright with her back against the wall. He had his head tilted to the side facing her, his floppy dark hair hanging over her face and his lips parted slightly in sleep. She smiled when he jolted. His hands clenched her thigh, and his muscles tensed momentarily before his body relaxed again and he tilted his head the other way.

He must be dreaming.

He was cute when he dreamed.

After he had taken her to her room and away from Abby, Ezra read with her until his eyes were heavy and his face was pale and he finally passed out on the bed beside her. The man was *exhausted*. Not only had he stayed at her bedside every day while she recovered from her injuries, but he had also been pulling late nights reading every book he could get his hands on to help her, oftentimes falling asleep over his breakfast. Throwing him around the room and hurting him every time she used her magic didn't help him much either.

Ana was happy to see him finally sleeping even if she knew it wouldn't last long. Guilt filled her as she watched the back of his head and the sharp cut of his jaw as he slept. He hadn't shaved in a while, and the stubble looked good on him.

Reaching forward, she ran her hand through the hair at the back of his head, teasing it through her fingers. He groaned, turning around to face her again and curling his head into her hand in a way that reminded her of a cat. She laughed quietly, closing the book and setting it aside before she flopped sideways and leaned over him, stroking his head again.

"Ezra," she whispered.

Ezra groaned.

"I'm going for a walk. You need to sleep. Stay here."

"Mmm," he moaned, pouting and wrapping his arms around her middle to keep her there.

Ana chuckled softly to herself as she leaned down to gently kiss his forehead, then wriggled out of his grip and jumped off the bed, looking back at him with a deep blush on her cheeks. His hand searched for her, and when he couldn't find her, he opted to pull the nearest pillow closer to himself and rested his head on it, hunkering down.

Biting her lip with a smile, she backed out of the room and closed the door behind herself quietly before making her way down the staircases to the foyer. She could hear Genevieve and Abby chatting in the kitchen, catching up on their lives after being away from each other for such a long time. Knowing they would be preoccupied, she opened the front door and made her way down the steps of the porch and out into the garden.

The sun was descending, transforming the sky from bright blues to beautiful shades of oranges and pinks that gave the green leaves of the trees a warmer hue. It was the middle of September, and the breeze was still warm and cosy, but she knew the chill of autumn was on its way. Somehow, she could feel the change of the season coming from somewhere inside her veins, like she was hyperaware of the subtle differences she would never have noticed before. She could feel it, the magic softly swirling in that place behind her stomach that she read about, reaching for the trees and the earth around her, willing to be set free.

Ignoring it, she walked around the house and to the back garden near the doors of the kitchen. Sitting in the middle of the luscious green lawn were two sun loungers with blankets draped over them and pillows nested perfectly atop. She slumped down on one, wrapping the blanket over her legs and hugging the pillow across her middle as if trying to smother the feeling of the magic inside.

The garden was quiet, save for the few straggling birds playing and flying loops around each other near a fence at the bottom of the garden. She wanted to smile at them, but their playfulness struck a nerve inside her she didn't know she had, bringing tears to her eyes and forming a knot in her throat.

Ana pulled her phone from her pocket and unlocked the

screen. She swiped through photo after photo of herself and Bexley at various parties, cafés in the city, and their recent spring trip to Rome. She smiled at the picture of them in front of the Trevi fountain, a coin in each of their hands and their eyes closed as they made their wish. After the photo had been taken, they threw the coins over their shoulders and looked back at where they fell among the other wish coins that littered the bottom of the fountain.

She couldn't remember what she had desired when she threw that coin, but she sure as hell knew what she would wish for now.

She would wish for Bexley back.

Ana chewed her lip and set her face, flicking the photo away with her thumb and bringing Bexley's phone number up on the screen.

"Okay, Ana. Throw your coin. Make your wish," she encouraged herself out loud, pressing down on the number and placing the phone against her ear.

The phone rang in three agonisingly long tones before it cut off and Ana frowned. She brought the phone down from her ear to stare at the screen.

Bexley had hung up.

The stinging in her eyes subsided, and instead of sadness filling her body, anger replaced it. She just wanted to talk to her, to explain herself in a way Bexley could understand, but she wouldn't even pick up the phone. The magic in her stomach swirled angrily, and she huffed out a pent-up breath and typed a message.

"Please call me back, Bex. I just need to talk to you. I need to explain."

The message sent, and Ana sat staring at the phone until she saw the three little dots at the bottom of the message, indicating

Bexley was replying. It disappeared almost as soon as it started, meaning Bexley was no longer typing.

"Damn it, Bexley!" she shouted, throwing her phone onto the grass in front of the sun lounger and balling her hands into fists.

"Bad time?"

Ana jumped, looking over her shoulder to see who was speaking. Abby stood by the edge of the other lounger with a glass in each hand. She shook them, rattling the ice inside when Ana didn't answer right away.

"Mojito?"

"Yes, please," Ana said, trying to even out her breathing and paint a smile on her face, but it was strained.

Abby passed her a glass, then sat down and leaned her elbows on her knees, looking between Ana and the phone she had thrown. "You look pissed. What's wrong?"

Ana busied herself by stirring the clear liquid in the glass with her straw. She watched as the mint leaves spun faster and faster, colliding with the ice and clinking against the sides. "Aren't you supposed to hate me?"

Abby laughed, raising her glass and taking a long sip from it. "Why would I hate you?"

"I don't know. You seemed pretty intent on dragging me to your council or whatever."

"I am. You are going whether or not you and my brother like it, but that doesn't mean we can't be friends." Abby shrugged, taking some of the ice into her mouth and chewing on it. "The Council isn't bad, you know. They just want what is right for the coven. The Elders know something is off. Everything is out of whack with this new magic of yours, so we can't have any mistakes. They won't hurt you." She opened her mouth like that wasn't the end of the sentence but closed it anyway.

Ana knew what Abby had stopped herself from saying.

They won't hurt you, *unless they have to.*

"So . . ." Abby grinned, watching as Ana took a sip of her mojito. "Are you sleeping with my brother?"

Ana choked on her mouthful, having to sit up straighter and wipe the corners of her mouth with the back of her hand as she spluttered. "What?"

"Well, I was wondering why the hell Ezra would throw himself into the middle of such a shit storm when he is already skating on thin ice with the Council, and then I came here and saw *you.*" Abby wriggled her eyebrow. "He is very protective of you, that's for sure."

Ana cleared her throat and shook her head, staring down at the glass in her hand to avoid Abby's eyes. "I am not talking to you about your brother's sex life."

"All right, keep your secrets." She sighed, looking away from her to Ana's phone that was still lying in the grass. "Will you at least tell me what made you throw your phone?"

Ana sighed and flickered her gaze back at the girl in front of her. She was persistent and smiling at her in a way that pulled at the corners of her mouth and reminded her of her brother. She could see the family resemblance when she smiled. Abby was pretty in a dangerous kind of way. Her tattoos peeked out from under her leather jacket, and the cat-eyeliner she had drawn around her eyes made her look almost predatory, although her presence was anything but. She reminded her of Genevieve. Warm and happy, but perhaps more playful and teasing than her mother.

"Why are you being so nice to me?" Ana asked, jiggling the ice in her glass again before taking a sip.

"Because my brother cares for you, and my mother is worried about you." Abby shrugged.

Ana laughed. "Your mom asked you to come and play nice, didn't she?"

"Less *asked* and more *threatened*." She smirked. "Come on, I am open ears."

Ana shifted nervously as she sat. Maybe it would be nice to have someone to talk to again even if that person was hellbent on capturing her. It would be nice, even, to get a different perspective.

"My best friend, Bexley." She sighed. "The night I figured out that your father was responsible for everything that happened with the athame was the same night as Bexley's engagement party. She was so excited and wanted me to be the maid of honour. We have always been best friends, and I knew when I asked for the keys to her car that she would understand. A-and she did, I think."

Abby watched as Ana's voice broke, and she started stabbing the ice in the glass with her straw. "Okay, so what's the issue?"

"She didn't understand why I didn't call her or come back to her party on the biggest night of her life or why I didn't return her car. It was so important to her, and I let her down. Apparently, while I was asleep for those three days, Ezra met with Bexley's fiancé to return her car, and he told him that Bexley was mad. She called me *thousands* of times, messaged *hundreds*, but I wasn't awake! I couldn't answer her and now she thinks I was ignoring her and she won't let me explain." Ana sniffled, turning to look at Abby.

"And if she did answer the phone, what would I say? Hey, sorry I missed your party, but I was a little preoccupied trying to fight off a murderer who happens to be a witch with an enchanted dagger, but it all went wrong and now I'm a literal ticking time bomb."

Abby snorted, then tried to stop her smile by downing the

rest of her mojito and ignoring Ana's narrowed eyes. "There isn't much you can do, Ana. She's a human. You are no longer part of that world; you will never be able to have both. If I were you, I would cut my losses and stop trying. You can't pull her into this if you are still dangerous. She can never know."

"I can't do that, Abby. She is my best friend. I just want to see her again."

"Jesus Christ, humans." Abby groaned, pinching the bridge of her nose like her head hurt. She set her glass down on the lounger and leaned forward to look at her with a raised eyebrow. "Do you have anything of hers?"

Wiping her cheek dry, Ana nodded and looked down at the thin gold chain around her wrist. The letters A and B dangled from it and twinkled in the dimming light of the garden. "Of course. Why?"

"Give it to me and chug your drink."

"What? Why?"

"Just hurry, before I change my mind," Abby said, standing and brushing down her leggings.

Ana drained the rest of her cocktail and set it on the ground, then fidgeted with the clasp of her bracelet. When it fell apart and landed in her hand, she held it out towards Abby, watching as she snatched it and turned on her heel, stalking her way towards the house without another word.

"Abby! Where are you going?!" she shouted, but Abby didn't reply, disappearing into the house through the door of the kitchen.

Ana jumped up from the sun lounger and reached to grab her phone from the grass before following her inside the house and through the kitchen. When she walked into the foyer, she saw a flash of black and purple hair heading down the corridor to the right. "Abby, wait!"

"Good god you are slow." Abby sighed, waiting outside a door near the bottom of the dark corridor. When Ana finally reached her side, she linked arms with her and opened the door, pulling her inside.

Abby flicked a switch on the wall, the chandelier above them turning on to illuminate the dark room. It was a big room, deep red in colour, with a large table in the middle covered with a white tablecloth that had patterns threaded into the fabric. A stack of tarot cards and a bowl of incense that had long gone out rested on the tablecloth. The scent of sandalwood and jasmine lingered. Books on shelves lined the walls, and a table near the back wall was filled with jars of herbs, crystals and candles.

"What is this place?" Ana asked, letting her go and walking farther into the room.

"Mom's divining room. She has a knack for divination. I am more of an elixir and tincture kind of gal myself."

Abby strode for the back of the room, where something tall and wide stood covered in a huge red and gold cloth. She tugged on it, letting it drop to reveal a mirror. Instead of seeing her reflection, however, Ana could only see black.

"Why is the mirror painted black?" Ana asked, walking close to it and placing her hand on the glass. It felt icy cold, and it vibrated against her fingertips in a way that made her snap her hand back.

"It's not." She shrugged, folding her arms across her chest and leaning back to examine it. "It is a scrying mirror. It's made from obsidian glass, and you can use it to see anything you want, depending on the magic you use. Today, we are going to use it to see your friend Bexley."

Ana's eyes went wide. She snapped her head in her direction, reaching out to touch her elbow as she gasped. "Really? I can see her through this? How?"

"You can see her through any mirror, it's how mirror magic works, but this is the biggest one we have in the house. She won't be able to see or hear you, but don't touch the glass or you will travel through and give her the shock of her life."

Ana looked back at the black mirror, studying the glass and how it reflected the light. It looked exactly like her eyes the last time she tried to use her magic. "How does it work?"

"Well, you can't do the spell needed, seeing as you can't use your magic yet, so I'm going to do it for you. Just this once. So long as she is somewhere near a mirror, we can see her."

She uncrossed her arms and pushed Ana out of the way so that she could stand in front of the mirror unobstructed and hold her hand out towards it. Ana's gold bracelet dangled from her hand, swaying and catching the light. Abby started mumbling to herself, and as soon as the unformed words poured from her mouth, she could see her eyes flash in a purple hue, growing brighter. It reminded her of how Genevieve's eyes looked when she was healing her. They were bright white, but she figured it had been a hallucination from the pain she experienced, but it wasn't. It was *magic*.

The obsidian glass of the mirror shifted and vibrated. The blackness rippled like water towards the edges of the gold frame, pushing somewhere beyond it and revealing perfectly clear glass. On the other side, the fuzzy image of Bexley's bedroom emerged, sharpening until Abby stopped her chanting and smiled at her handiwork. She stepped out of the way, indicating for Ana to take her place.

Ana gasped in disbelief as she took cautious steps until she was centred before the mirror. She would *never* get used to this.

Bexley's bedroom looked exactly like she remembered it from the last time she was there. The walls were a light grey, and a beautiful fluffy white carpet covered the floor. She had no idea how she kept it so clean. From this angle, she knew they were looking at her room through the vanity mirror that sat against the wall of Bexley's room. She had used that same mirror so many times when they got ready together for a night out in the city.

It all seemed so long ago.

"I don't understand. Where is sh–"

Bexley entered from the door near the back of the room that led to her ensuite bathroom. She wore a long emerald green dress that hugged her beautiful curves, and her hair was pinned up on one side to show off her long neck.

"She certainly is fancy," Abby commented as she watched, her eyebrows raised.

"Y-yeah." Ana sniffled, seeing her friend as she walked to the mirror and sat down on the stool to secure her diamond earrings in her ears. "This is insane. It's amazing to see her, but I feel like I'm betraying her privacy."

"You are, technically, I guess." Abby raised her hand to examine her nails like she was bored.

Ana frowned, grappling with her conscience as she watched her friend beyond the mirror finish her makeup and spray her perfume on the crook of her neck. Standing up straighter, Ana pulled her phone from her pocket and brought up Bexley's name. She hesitated, her finger hovering until she took a steadying breath and pressed it, putting the phone to her ear.

The phone chimed, and Ana flicked her eyes back at the mirror. Bexley was looking down at her vibrating and ringing phone in front of her on the vanity. She shifted uncomfortably and lifted the phone, looking down at her name as if deciding whether she could answer the call. She declined it, then set it down again, going back to her makeup with a saddened look in her eyes.

"Damn it, Bex, answer your phone." Ana sighed, pressing the name again and holding it to her ear.

Bexley groaned beyond the mirror, lifting her phone once more and biting down on her lip hard. Finally, she raised the phone to her ear and looked into the mirror, presumably at her own reflection, but the way she was staring at it almost made Ana think she was looking at *her*.

Neither of them spoke for a long moment. It took Ana more than a few beats to gulp moisture into her mouth. She spluttered, tripping over her words and starting to cry.

"Bex! Please don't hang up! I-I need to explain." She hiccupped. "I miss you. Please don't hang up."

Bexley tilted her head and chewed on her lip, her cheeks becoming red and her eyes filling with tears.

"Explain what, Ana? Explain how you ditched me at my engagement party and stole my car? Explain why you didn't answer any of my calls and drove me insane with worry? Explain why you quit your job and emptied your apartment? I went by to see if you were there and everything was *gone*, including you. Without one word, you just *vanished*." Bexley's voice snapped down the phone. "I'm sorry, Ana, but I have worried for too long over you when you don't seem to care. Goodbye."

"I was in an accident!" Ana blurted before she could hang up. She watched as Bexley paused, the phone a few inches away from her ear. Slowly, she raised it back to her ear, but she didn't say anything.

"I . . ." Ana started. What could she say that she would believe? She had to give her *something*. "The night of your engagement party, I figured out who killed those people, and he was with Ezra. I needed to get to him and warn him, and that's why I took your car. I planned on coming straight back, but . . ."

"But what?"

Bexley was standing now, her thumb in her mouth as she chewed on her nail nervously and paced the room.

"But . . . I was in an accident." It was the closest thing she could say to what really happened that Bex would understand. "I got hurt, *really* badly. Ezra and his mother cared for me afterwards, but I was unconscious for three days. I wasn't ignoring you, Bex. I just wasn't awake. I would never have purposely hurt you; you know that, don't you?"

Bexley sank to her knees in the middle of her room. She was hugging herself and crying, her dress and makeup be damned. "A-are you okay now? Why didn't you tell me?"

"You wouldn't answer me, and I was feeling so guilty, Bex. I am so sorry I missed your big night." Ana hiccupped, wiping tears from her eyes so that she could watch Bexley in the mirror. "I miss you. I miss you *so* much."

"I don't understand, Ana. If you are awake now, why is your apartment still empty? Why haven't you come home?"

"I am still recovering. Ezra's mom specialises in the kind of care I need, so I am staying with them until I am better." It wasn't a complete lie. "But as soon as I am better, I am going to come back to the city, and I want to see you, if you let me. Can you forgive me? Please, Bex."

Bexley spluttered on the end of the phone, covering her mouth with her hand and wiping her eyes, streaking her eyeliner and smudging her mascara. "Y-yes. Of course, I forgive you. I thought you had fallen in love and run away from me. I was so mad." Her voice grew quiet at the end.

Ana gulped thickly, hugging herself and biting her lip hard to stem her crying. "I would never run away from you, Bex. I'm fine now, really, just some aftereffects I need to take care of, but then I am all yours, for wedding planning and then parties and pizza and wine and anything you need, okay?" she said, finally laughing when she saw Bexley smile through the mirror.

"Okay." Bex laughed back, sniffling thickly.

Ana turned her head towards the door when she heard someone clear their throat. Ezra was standing against the door frame, looking tired and his hair standing at all angles like he had just awoken from his nap. He looked anxious, his brow seeming heavier and worry behind his green eyes.

"Bex, I need to go . . ." she said, looking back at the mirror with a genuine smile. "I need to take my medication, apparently." That's kind of what magic training was like with Ezra, right? Medication for her illness.

"Okay." Bexley sniffled, wiping her nose. "I love you, Ana. Don't ever disappear again. And if you plan to, please tell me first, because I can't live missing you like this."

"I love you too, Bex." Ana smiled, hugging the phone close to her ear before she said her goodbyes and ended the call.

She watched the mirror for a few more precious moments before Abby moved her out of the way by shoving the bracelet into her hand. She waved her hand, the image of Bexley fading away, and allowed the blackness of the mirror to return. Finally, the obsidian glass was solid again, and Abby turned to look at them both with boredom behind her eyes.

"Well, that was depressing." She frowned.

"Thank you," Ana said instantly, moving to her and throwing her arms around her in a grateful hug.

Abby gave her an awkward pat on the back as Ezra walked to them. She let Ana go quickly and turned to look at her brother, poking him hard in the ribs. "See? I can be nice."

"Only when you are looking for something," Ezra said, rubbing the place she had poked him. "Are you all right?"

Surprisingly, she did feel all right. Being able to see Bexley and hear her voice had filled her heart and made it beat just a little bit faster. She took a deep steadying breath and wiped her cheeks dry, giving them a spluttering laugh. "Yes. I keep crying, but I'm all right."

Ezra smiled, but it was strained, like he was too tired to hide his worry. He reached out to take her hand in his, leading her towards the doorway. "Good. Because we have training to do."

CHAPTER 6

Ezra took Ana back to her bedroom, where she sat down on the bed and left him to pace the floorboards. His hands were tangled in his hair, and a look of exhaustion spread across his eyes. He clearly had not slept for long when she left him. The sheets of her bed were still tussled, and the pillow was still imprinted with the shape of his arm.

"What's the matter?" Ana asked. He stopped in the middle of the room and turned to look at her, his hands falling to rest on his hips as he tried to stay still.

"I am worried about you. We have so much work to do and only one night to do it in." He frowned. "I'm so sorry, Ana. I wasn't expecting the Council to come for you so soon. They must be really spooked."

"None of this is your fault," Ana said as she gulped thickly and tried to force her next words out of her head and through her mouth. "Are they going to kill me?"

"No. That is not their style, and Abby wouldn't lie to me. If you were being taken there for that, she wouldn't be so playful about it. If she says they only want to talk to you, then she is telling the truth." Ezra moved around the room, pulling candles from one of the drawers and setting them on any bare surface he could find.

"Then why do you look so scared?" she asked. He was closing the curtains and flattening the rug out on the floor with his feet.

"Because if we go there, there is a chance they will no longer let me help you. The High Council does not like me, Ana. If we go, they are going to take you from me, and their methods of training are harsher than I would like them to be. I highly doubt they will let me help you after they take over, and I don't want to lose you to them." Ezra finished what he was doing and turned to look at her. "And I am probably overdue for my punishment for using magic when I was supposed to be banned, so I would prefer not to go at all."

"You don't have to go with me, Ezra. I don't want you to get into trouble over me. Abby can take me, and if the Council can help me, I can come back when I'm feeling better." She stood from the bed and walked to him, taking his hand when he offered his.

"I am not leaving you. I promised. I don't break my promises." Ezra squeezed her hand and gave her a strained smile. "But for now, we have the rest of the night to do what we can to help you focus your magic."

"No. Please, I can't hurt you again," she replied with a frown, taking back her hand and hugging herself. "I could have killed you."

"But you didn't, and I have a plan this time. Sit down."

With a smile, Ezra slumped down on the rug, his legs crossed underneath him as he nodded to the space in front of him. Ana hesitated, shifting on her feet a few times like she was unsure if she should.

"We don't have time for this, Ana. Just sit down," he said with a roll of his eyes.

Ana sighed and sat in front of him, her feet curled under her and her knees meeting his. "Okay. What's the plan?"

"For starters, you need to relax your shoulders. If you are tense, your magic will be too." Ezra reached forward to rest his finger on the talisman that hung from her neck. "And I need to take this off you. When I do, I am going to take your hands and help you channel the magic by letting mine cool yours down. I am going to be punished for using magic when we go to the High Council meeting tomorrow anyway. It's not like one more time will make a difference."

Ana tensed, her eyes narrowing and her face paling. She hated taking the talisman off. Each time she did, everything went wrong.

"It's okay. Trust me." Ezra smiled.

He lifted his hand to take the rope of the necklace and lifted it up over her head, discarding it on the floor beside them. The room instantly filled with a thick fog that flowed under the door and clung to the walls. Ezra frowned as shadows filled the corners of the room behind the fog, making it seem as if something were moving just beyond the spaces they could see. He reached out and grabbed her hands, holding them tightly in his and moving his head to force her to look at him.

"Look in my eyes, Ana. Focus. Feel me . . ."

Ana tore her eyes away from the shadows to look at him, studying all the different shades of green in his eyes and trying to block everything else out. When he smiled back at her, she felt the place behind her stomach rumble with the telltale signs of magic. It flowed faster and faster, and before she could panic, she noticed his eyes shining in colours of green she didn't know existed. Like Abby's and his mother's, his eyes were turning brighter, like his irises had little glowing lights behind them. When she looked down at their hands, she saw light peeking out from between their fingers. The feeling in her stomach was slowing down again without even having to try, and instead of feeling overwhelmed by the power, it was feeling kind of *good*.

"How does it feel?" Ezra asked, a wide smile on his face.

"Amazing, actually," Ana said with a small laugh, biting down on her lip to keep focused in case she lost control without realising.

"Good." He laughed back. "Now, I need you to turn your hands over slowly, so your palms are facing up. I will hold your hands underneath and keep channelling the overflow of your magic, okay? Keep your fingers closed until I tell you to."

Ana nodded and tried to focus, then slowly turned her hands. Her fingers were closed tightly, and Ezra placed his hands on the backs of hers.

"Okay, open your fingers and look up." He stared up at the ceiling.

Ana opened her fingers, and light poured out of the middle of her palms, shooting beams towards the ceiling. They danced, shining their glittering light across the walls like shooting stars. It was beautiful, and her breath caught in her throat, tears pooling in her eyes. The magic inside her stomach finally relaxed as if it were purring happily instead of fighting against her to be let out. This was the first time since she received the magic that she felt *calm*.

"Am I really doing this?" Ana gasped, her mouth hanging open in awe and a smile tugging at her trembling lips as she watched the lights.

"Yeah, you are really doing it! I am going to take my hands

away, and it's going to be all you. You need to focus on creating that light. Keep feeling it flow through your palms. Push it through, but keep it restrained so that you don't blow us away, okay?"

Ana nodded, and Ezra slowly retracted his hands away from hers. He kept his fingers on the back of her hands until the final moment, and then let go completely, setting his hands in his lap as he watched her manipulate the lights on the walls. She was manipulating them at will now, laughing as she made them blink and brighten.

"This is amazing!" She laughed. She was trying to keep the whirling magic in her stomach at bay, but it was building again rapidly now that Ezra's hands were gone. "I think I need to stop now, though. It's getting faster again."

"Okay, all right, you can do it. Pull your fingers into a fist, close your eyes and force the light away from your hands. Will it to stop, and it will." Ezra nodded.

Ana closed her eyes and hands tightly, willing the magic to pull back in again. After a few moments, her hands cooled and stopped vibrating, and she cracked her eyes open. "Are they gone?"

"Yeah. Nothing but the candles. You can open your eyes. Keep the magic in your solar plexus at a nice purr," Ezra said, grinning when she opened her eyes fully and dropped her hands into her lap.

She gulped, focusing on the area behind her stomach. When she was sure it was keeping the magic contained, she reached out and took Ezra's hands again happily. She liked how they felt in hers, and she had missed them when they weren't clasped together.

"Thank you. This was amazing! If I can keep this up tomorrow, maybe we won't have anything to worry about," Ana said, watching him in the dim lights of the room.

It seemed so much darker in here now that the lights from her hands were gone. He looked good in the candlelight, and she found that the magic that was swirling inside her body made her feel warm in her chest and her face. She bit her lip and slipped closer to kneel in front of him, taking his face in her hands and leaning in to kiss him. She forgot how good it felt to kiss him. The magic inside her purred louder, drowning out the sounds of the room as she deepened it.

"Ana . . ." Ezra mumbled around her lips, trying to pull his head back, but she kept kissing him until he kissed her back and pulled her into his lap.

Ana smiled against him when she felt him cling to her, letting him settle her into a straddle on his lap on the floor. She could feel him tense under her kiss and moan against her lips, which only made her kiss him more feverishly. She grinned when she heard him moan again, but he stopped moving, his hands rigid on her hips as he gripped the fabric in tight fists. As she pulled back to look at him, she realized he hadn't been moaning at all.

He was gasping for breath.

The skin under her hands was ashen, and his lips were blackened as if she was sucking the life from him with her kiss. His eyes were cloudy, and his chest was rising and falling in pants, trying to gasp breaths into lungs that had seemed to stop working.

"Ezra? Ezra! What's wrong?!" Ana panicked, letting him go from her grip and scrambling off his lap so she could lay him back on the rug.

Ezra's back arched off the floor, and his eyes rolled into the back of his head as he suffocated.

Ana whimpered and looked down at her hands. She hadn't

noticed it when she was kissing him because of how good it had felt, but the magic in her stomach was rolling out of control and the fog had returned to the corners of the room.

"No, no, no," she whined, her eyes wide as she searched the floor for the talisman.

She spotted it where Ezra had discarded it on the rug, and she scrambled for it, picking it up with fumbling fingers and pulling it over her head so that it rested against her chest. The fog disappeared instantly, and when she was sure the shadows had followed it, she looked back to find Ezra. He was still writhing on the floor, and for a few agonising moments, she thought he might not recover from whatever she had done to him. Finally, Ezra took a gasping breath, his eyes coming back from their greyness and colour returning to his ashen cheeks. Relief washed over her, making her shoulders sag and her forehead sticky with sweat. Her hands were shaking, and her eyes flooded with tears again as guilt settled into the space between her lungs and her heart.

She could have killed him.

"Ezra, are you okay? What happened?" Ana asked as she hiccupped and reached for him, but he rolled onto his side and held his hand up to motion for her to stay where she was. He coughed and spluttered, gulping thick lungfuls of air into his body.

Ana clasped her hands tightly against her chest as she watched him come back around, and when he finally sat up and looked at her, his eyes were wide. "Ezra, I am so sorry. I-I didn't notice it was happening. Are you okay?"

"I'm fine," Ezra sputtered hoarsely, his hand gripping the neck of his shirt.

She took his hand, trying not to frown when he flinched at her touch. "You are *not* fine. Every time you try to help me, I nearly kill you! I just want everything to go back to normal. I want my life back! This is not a life. I nearly killed you with a kiss!"

Ezra coughed, trying to clear his throat from the rawness that had settled there. His face was still pale, and he looked exhausted again, like what little energy his body had left was completely sucked dry. "Ana, I like you. I *really* like you, but I think until we figure out what is wrong with your magic, we should just be friends. Okay?"

"What?" she asked, her hand going limp in his and her lip trembling. Ezra was the only person she had left to be close to. If she didn't have him, she didn't have anyone. "Ezra . . ."

He sighed, watching her with a frown. Clenching her hand, Ezra shook his head and sat straighter. "I want to, with you, again, but your health and mine must be a priority. No matter what happens with us, I am always going to be here for you, but we need to be smart, okay?"

Ana pulled her hand back from his to wipe her cheeks dry. She felt pathetic, and she wasn't too proud to admit that she was a little heartbroken. She nodded, though, painting a smile on her face. Tears were pricking at the backs of her eyes as embarrassment overwhelmed her. She could have killed him with a kiss. No wonder he wanted nothing to do with her anymore.

"Yeah. I understand."

"You should get some rest. We have an early start tomorrow. You did great today," Ezra said as he leaned in to kiss her cheek, but it was short. He stood, fixing his shirt and rubbing at the redness that covered the skin of his throat before he made his way to the door.

Ana sniffled as she sat on the floor of the room by herself, bringing her knees up to her chest and resting her chin on them while she watched his back. "Ezra? Thank you for not turning me away completely."

Ezra opened the door and looked back at her over his shoulder with a strained smile. "I'd never turn you away, Ana."

The second the door of the bedroom closed, Ana burst into tears, placing her hand over her mouth to muffle the sound. Her body shuddered, the weight of what was happening to her finally settling on her shoulders. Her life as she knew it was over. Bexley might have forgiven her, but if she was as dangerous as it seemed she was, she could never see her again. Ezra, too, seemed just out of reach now that she couldn't even touch him without his skin flinching under her fingers.

Ana hiccupped a sob as she pulled herself up and onto her feet, shuffling across the floor and climbing up onto the bed where she flopped onto the sheets and the pillows. They still smelled like Ezra. His sandalwood and patchouli scent still lingered on the cotton from his nap, and she instinctively pulled the pillow into a hug and rested her head in the same place his head had been. It wasn't warm anymore, but somehow it made her feel less alone. Wiping her cheek, she looked down at the vein in her wrist. She could feel the blood pumping through it, laced with something she couldn't quite describe.

The truth was, no matter how much it felt like she might be alone, she never truly was.

With the echoes of magic that flowed through her veins and into her head, she would never be alone again.

CHAPTER 7

The second dawn broke through the window of her room, the sound of bickering siblings on one of the lower levels of the house woke Ana. She dressed quickly and walked out of the room with a bag of clothes she had packed the night before and headed downstairs. Abby and Ezra were in the foyer, arguing as they tugged on a piece of rope, like children playing tug of war.

"Abby, stop it!" Ezra shouted as he pulled. Abby didn't let go.

"It's procedure!" she said through gritted teeth. "Mom! Ezra's being an asshole!"

Ana chuckled as she walked farther down the staircase, raising her brow at them and clearing her throat. Ezra had shaved and was wearing a dark shirt instead of his usual white that she had grown accustomed to. It was fitting, she supposed. Like a funeral.

Ezra dropped the rope the second he realised she was there, folding his arms. "I am suddenly reminded why I am glad I never had any siblings. Do you always bicker so much?" she said with a laugh.

"It has been a regular occurrence since the day they met, yes," Genevieve said as she walked into the foyer from the kitchen, holding out little brown bags to them all. "I made breakfast, but we need to eat it on the way if we want to get there in time. Why are you fighting?"

"She wants to restrain Ana. I have told her it is unnecessary if we are going willingly. She has been through enough without needing to be bound," Ezra said as he took the paper bag from his mother and peeked inside.

"And *I* know it is unnecessary, but this is my first mark and I need to make an impression. To do that, I need to do things by the book," Abby said as she ignored her mother's extended bag and walked towards Ana. "It's procedure."

Ana gave a patient nod, looking over Abby's face as she stopped in front of her. Her face was set in a frustrated scowl, and her brown eyes stared her down, willing her to defy her so she had a reason to make even more of a scene. "Well, it doesn't look like I have much of a choice. Who am I to upset the procedure?" she muttered, setting her bag down on the floor and reaching her arms out.

Abby grabbed her hands and looped the rope around and around until Ana found it difficult to bend her wrists. Abby held the rest of the long rope in her hands and pulled her towards the door, making Ana stumble.

"I will get your bag, I guess." Ezra frowned.

He walked around them and lifted her bag up over his shoulder before taking the rest of the breakfast bags from his mother and following his sister out of the house.

The sun still hung low in the morning sky, cascading pinks and purples over the clouds. The colours calmed her nerves and settled her thoughts, and she was thankful for the distraction when Abby pulled her through the barrier that shielded the house's true form. The shield sent a buzzing through her, like an electric shock mixed with ice-cold pins and needles that pricked all over her skin.

When she pulled her through, the sky looked duller. The colours had faded, and a low-hanging morning mist worked its way through the trees around the brown van sitting in the little layby at the end of the path.

Genevieve unlocked the doors, pulling the sliding door open and nodding for them to get inside.

Abby pushed Ana inside the van and got in behind her, the rope still gripped in her hands as she closed the door in Ezra's face when he moved to get in too. He growled deep in his chest and stomped around the van to get into the passenger side seat, passing Ana's bag and the lunch bags to them over the back of the chair.

Abby grabbed them and shoved one into Ana's bound hands as her mother started the engine with a splutter and pulled out of the lane. Abby didn't take her eyes off her as they drove, and once they moved onto the main road, she lifted her feet to rest them on the seat opposite her, her mud-covered boots inches from Ana's thighs.

"So." Abby grinned, reaching into her brown bag, ripping off part of her croissant and popping it into her mouth. "What happened with you two last night? I heard screaming."

Ana blinked, her mouth pulling into a frown as she looked to the back of Ezra's head for help. He turned in his seat and flashed his sister a warning look.

"Leave her alone, Abby. It's none of your business." He frowned, turning back in his seat and taking a bite of his own pastry.

"Okay, fine. It's complicated, hm?" Abby said, tilting her head and eyeing her for a long awkward moment before Ezra broke the silence again.

"Who is the new high priest since Dad was excommunicated?"

"Thaddeus Alden," she replied, grinning mischievously behind her croissant. "And yes, before you ask, Silas Alden is still the leader of the Venator, meaning he is my boss."

"Shit." Ezra rested his elbow on the window, his head in his hand. "I am so screwed."

Abby laughed loudly, and Ana frowned as she looked between them with a frown. "Who are the Aldens? And why are you screwed?"

"The Aldens are one of the three founding families of our coven. The Sullivans, the O'Neils and the Aldens." Ezra sighed, looking through the window as the trees whizzed past.

"Why is that bad?" Ana asked, looking back at Abby.

"Silas and Ezra never really got along in school." Abby shrugged, biting into her croissant again with a snigger. "It only got worse after Ezra slept with Silas's mom."

Ana's mouth dropped open, whipping her head towards Ezra. His cheeks were a deep crimson, and he wouldn't look back at her. "His *mom*? Seriously? How old were you?"

"It's not as creepy as it sounds. I was eighteen. She's nice," Ezra said, leaning back in his chair and closing his eyes, trying to block out the sounds in the car.

"I am sure she was." Abby laughed, finishing her croissant and rolling the paper bag into a ball, throwing it at him over the chair. "But Thaddeus has been waiting a long time to get his hands on you for sleeping with his wife, so I suggest when you walk into this meeting, you do so with your tail between your legs."

"Abby?" Ezra mumbled, not opening his eyes. "Shut up."

∼

THE JOURNEY TOOK around two hours. Thankfully, the car had fallen silent for most of the way there, and she got a few extra moments of sleep before the van lurched and stopped with a squeak of its brakes. Looking out of the window, Ana could see that they had parked inside the grounds of an estate. It looked similar to the Harrow mansion, though instead of beautiful cherry trees littering the lawns, there were tall weeping willows and long stalks of grass.

"Are we here?" Ana asked as she sat up in her seat, trying to roll the strain out of her wrists from the ropes.

"That's usually what it means when a car stops," Abby said, shuffling her way to the door and grabbing the handle. She had to yank it a few times because it was so rusted, but she finally pulled it open with a loud squeak. She jumped out, smoothing down her leather jacket and smiling at the large gothic mansion.

Abby pulled at the rope when Ana wasn't fast enough getting out of the van, making her slip onto the gravel. Ezra rushed around the van after closing his door, reaching out to take her arm and steady her.

"Are you ready?" he asked, looking down at her seriously.

"Do I have a choice?" Ana asked, looking over his shoulder at the building with a frown. The building looked ominous, and the mist that hugged its walls sent an unsettling feeling into the air.

Ezra reached into the van to lift her bag and threw it over his shoulder as Genevieve made their way to them after locking the doors.

"I am a member of the Council, so I need to take my seat.

Wait in the hallway until you are called. I will see you all inside." Genevieve rested her hands on their shoulders and gave them a comforting nod before she walked up the path and into the building on her own.

"What is the Venator?" Ana asked suddenly, thinking back to their conversation in the van as she watched Genevieve walk away. She was disappearing into the mist around the house, and she had to squint her eyes to see her as she walked through the doors.

"The bounty hunters. We capture the people in our coven who need to be tried, perform executions and punishments, that kind of thing," Abby explained as she walked, tugging on the rope again and making Ana lurch forward.

"And Silas Alden. He is your boss? What is he like?"

Ezra's face set in a frown as Abby turned to look at her. "I've seen him pull a man's teeth out with a pair of rusty pliers just for talking too much, if that answers your question." She flashed a proud grin.

Bile and nerves crawled their way up into Ana's throat as they trekked up the path and reached the doors of the gothic mansion. Abby opened the tall wooden doors with a creek and walked inside as Ana's feet stopped dead at the door, her face going pale and her hands shaking.

"Okay," she reassured herself. "Don't talk too much. Got it."

"You've got this, Ana," Ezra said from beside her ear, placing his hand on her lower back to guide her through the doorway. She could feel the warmth of his chest against her back, and she tried to focus on his touch instead of the nerves thrashing through her body.

The hallway inside was dark. The red velvet curtains that hung over the tall archway windows were half-drawn, and most of the light that illuminated the room came from candles that hung on the grey brick walls. Huge oil paintings in gilded gold frames littered the walls, illustrating men and women in old-style garments. The skin on her arms was goosebumped, and her hairs were standing on end.

"This isn't creepy at all," Ana mumbled as she walked inside.

A doorway was at the bottom of the middle hall near the staircase, and she could hear multiple voices on the other side, hushed and buzzing. The sound made the nerves in her stomach lurch up into her throat again. Her head grew light, and she searched behind herself for Ezra, trying to reach for him with her hands until she realised she couldn't because of the ropes.

"It's okay. Don't panic. Everything is going to be fine," Ezra said as he placed his hands firmly on her shoulders, steadying her while his thumbs massaged the knots from her back. "There are a few things you need to remember before you walk inside. Don't speak until you are spoken to, keep your answers short, and try not to look so scared. People in there will feed off your fear, so don't give them the satisfaction. And remember, you have done nothing wrong."

Ana gulped dryly at his instructions, and she was about to reply when the door opened and a young man looked out at them, nodding to Abby.

Abby grinned, practically jumping when she took off in a quick walk and pulled hard on the rope. Ana wobbled forward again and walked behind Abby through the door and down the aisle of the large gothic ballroom. It was grand, with high grey stone ceilings, tall arched stained-glass windows and gold chandeliers. Like a courtroom, the room had rows upon rows of chairs filing out in two wings to the left and right of the aisle, and at the very back sat a long table, with an empty chair in the middle. On both sides of it were six chairs, twelve in total, with Genevieve sitting in the very last seat on the left.

Ana's breath hitched in her throat when she surveyed the room. Everyone's eyes were fixed on her as she walked, and the voices seemed to hush when she passed them. Ezra walked behind her, his hand on the small of her back so that she knew he was right behind her, but his touch did little to quell the bile in her throat.

"Okay, stay here. Thaddeus will be here any moment," Abby said to Ana as she stopped her at the end of the aisle and stood beside her. Ezra stood on her other side and steadied her with his touch.

Peering at the table at the front of the room, Ana looked for Genevieve, who gave them a nervous half-smile and clenched her hands neatly in front of herself. She could tell she was trying to look confident, but it didn't show in her eyes. Sitting beside her was another woman who seemed to be around thirty years old. She had bronzed skin, with long, straight black hair and big brown eyes that almost looked feline. She was wearing a wine-coloured dress with a neckline that reached her sternum and was staring intently between herself and Ezra, like she was watching prey. She was, quite possibly, the most beautiful creature Ana had ever seen.

"Abby. You actually did something you were told. That's rare."

Ana jolted from her gazing and turned to find the voice. The man was tall, with tanned skin and black hair that reached his broad shoulders. He had a well-kept beard that clung to his chiselled jawline and eyes so dark she couldn't see his pupils. He stalked around them until he was standing in front of them, his hands in the pockets of his leather jacket and his eyes narrowed. Heat rose into Ana's cheeks at how intimidating he was. She felt like a rabbit being stared down by a wolf.

He watched her for a few long moments more before he tilted

his head and sidestepped until he was almost standing chest to chest with Ezra.

"Sullivan," he said, his eyes narrowing further.

"Silas," Ezra mumbled, looking bored.

Silas grinned and removed his hands from his pockets, folding them over his chest, his T-shirt stretching to accommodate his biceps. "I can't say I was surprised when I heard your father was a murdering bastard. Like father, like son, hm?"

"That's what they say," Ezra said as he finally looked him in the eye, his face turning from boredom to anger. "How's your mom?"

Silas's smirk slipped from his face, and as he stared Ezra down, Ana could see his eyes flash red. Ezra instantly growled in pain and sank to his knees, holding his head like someone was trying to boil his brain. His eyes shut tightly, and his hands shook as they gripped at his hair, his nose starting to drip with blood.

"Stop it! Stop it, please!" Ana gasped, reaching out to shove the man with her bound hands. He didn't, so instead, she reached to pull Ezra to his feet, but Silas's eyes flashed again, and Ezra screamed.

"That is enough!"

The voice of the man now sitting in the high priest's chair boomed throughout the room, and Ezra's screams stopped instantly when Silas let him go from whatever he was doing to him. He tried not to shake as Ana helped him to his feet as best as she could with her restricted hands.

Silas laughed and leaned into Ezra when he finally stood again. "Nice to see you again, Sullivan." He turned and walked to one seat near the window closest to the council table.

Ana studied Ezra as he tried to compose himself and wipe the blood that had dripped down his face. She rubbed his arms, trying to bring his head back into the room as the high priest spoke.

"Council members, coven members, welcome to House Alden. We are here to discuss the effects of the actions of former-High Priest Alexander Sullivan. Abby, you have returned with the girl, yes?" He looked at them over the rim of his glasses. He had a bald head and a long black beard that came to a point in the middle of his chest and wore a deep red robe that covered his shoulders and reached all the way to the floor.

"I have," Abby said. "Ana Davenport. Human woman, aged twenty-five, stabbed by Alexander Sullivan with the Marion coven athame and thus now has the magic of the blade. Delivered as promised." Abby proudly smiled.

Thaddeus nodded to her and turned his head to stare at Ana as she clung to Ezra. He raised his brow, and she separated herself from him so that she could stand up straighter and clear her throat.

"Ana Davenport. Our Elders have informed us of the magic that is now running through your veins. It is more magic than every witch in this room combined. I am surprised you are still standing. How *are* you still alive, exactly?"

"Uh . . ." Ana started, then cleared her throat when it cracked, "I am not exactly sure. Genevieve saved me when I was bleeding, and I woke up with all this power. It's more than I can handle, if I am being transparent, but Genevieve kindly helped me bind my magic with this." She pointed to the talisman around her neck. "It stops the magic from coming out when I'm not expecting it, so I don't hurt people."

"I understand how a binding works," Thaddeus said tensely, leaning forward on his elbows. "Your magic, what do you mean that it hurts people? How unhinged is it?"

"I can't control it. Ezra is helping me, and I'm making some progress but . . ." She turned to look at Ezra as he tensed. She couldn't lie. She had to tell the truth if she was going to survive any of this. "Every time I try to pull it back, I end up hurting him."

Thaddeus hummed, then sat back in his chair again. "You are human, Ana. You shouldn't be standing, never mind able to control the magic you have."

"If I may interject," Ezra finally said, his eyes sweeping over the members of the Council, "she is learning. I know it may not work, but we cannot just give up on her. I know you all very well, and some of you will want to take the magic out of her, but if you do that, she dies and the magic is gone. It's not like we can take it for ourselves if we take it out of her. The best thing for the coven is to continue training her and keep her as an ally and a member of our coven. If there is one thing I know about this coven, it's that you all thrive on power, and if you want to be the most powerful coven in existence, you need her, and you need her alive."

Thaddeus frowned. He watched Ezra as the members of the coven whispered among themselves and raised his hand to silence them. Then he turned to the left to look at the end of the table. "Elders. How long does she have before the magic consumes her?"

The two old women at the end of the table gazed in his direction. They were ancient, with wrinkled skin, blinding white eyes and long white hair. They spoke in unison. "It is hard to say. The vision is not clear. Could be days, could be never. Something is wrong with the magic."

"I do not like uncertainty." Thaddeus turned toward Ana while pushing his glasses back up onto his face. His shoulders were tense, and his hands were folded in front of him. The room remained silent as he took a moment to think and breathe. His greying brows furrowed, and his lips pulled into a thin line until he finally flicked his eyes back up to look at them.

"She has until the next full moon to prove she can contain the magic. That is three weeks from now. If she cannot contain it and manipulate it by then, it will be taken from her, and she will die. I believe I have been fair."

Ana's face blanched. Three weeks seemed like such a short amount of time to control her magic. It would never work. She was going to die. Tears filled her eyes as they darted to Ezra helplessly.

"If I may, I would like to continue training her," Ezra said as he took a step forward. "Ana and I know each other very well. She trusts me. If anyone can get her through this, it is me."

"Absolutely not," Thaddeus countered. "Silas will take over her training. She will stay here in House Alden until we either know she can control it, or she is executed."

"Me? Why me?" Silas interjected with a frown from his seat.

"Because I asked you to," Thaddeus snapped, his eyes narrow until Silas sunk back down in his seat.

"Moving on to our last issue, Mister Sullivan. You have been banned from practising magic, yet you have used your magic four times in the last month. There is a punishment for this, as you were warned on the day of your banning."

"I am aware," Ezra mumbled, tensing his jaw.

Thaddeus snapped his fingers towards some men who were standing near the wall in front of a large stake that she hadn't noticed when she entered. They moved instantly, grabbing it and helping each other lift the chunk of wood before they lugged it to the middle of the room in front of the Council table and set it upright. It was about seven feet tall and thick and stood by brackets that the men were screwing into the spaces on the wooden floor.

"Lashings. Three for each time you used your magic," Thaddeus said, looking up at Ezra.

Ezra's face dropped, and his confident demeanour fell. "What? You can't be serious."

The woman she had noticed before, who was sitting beside Genevieve, tensed and turned to look at the high priest, a look of shock in her eyes. "Thaddeus, come now . . ."

"I did not ask for your council, Anora!" Thaddeus retorted without meeting her eyes as he continued to stare at Ezra. "Take off your shirt."

Ana gasped as she turned to look at him, her hands trembling in their binds as she shook her head. "Don't."

Ezra shook his head in a silent plea for her to stay silent. He cleared his throat, started to unbutton his black collared shirt and slipped it off, throwing it to the floor. He stared at Thaddeus as he reached to unbuckle his belt from his jeans, doubling it in his hands before he walked across the room and to the stake.

"I volunteer!" Silas smirked, quickly standing and unclipping the whip that was attached to his belt.

"No. We want him punished, not dead," Thaddeus said, scanning the room, and his eyes fell on Abby. "You. You may be his sister, but I hope that won't get in the way of proving your duty to your coven. Take the whip."

Abby flinched, her eyes flicking to her brother. Their eyes met, and he gave her a subtle nod. Ezra turned, putting his belt in his mouth so that he could bite down without breaking his teeth, and hugged the stake.

Abby gulped thickly as Silas walked to her and swapped the rope for his whip, tugging Ana aside roughly and making her stumble. Abby nodded, though it looked more like she was trying to convince herself to move instead of telling herself it was okay.

She trudged across the floor of the room, her footsteps the

only sound that echoed off the walls. Shakily, she stood behind her brother and uncoiled the whip, letting it fall at her side with its sharpened leather tip resting on the floor.

"Any time today would be great." Thaddeus sighed.

Abby set her face into a scowl and lifted her arm. She swung, the whip hurtling through the air and slashing Ezra's back with a sickening *crack*. He jerked forward and cried out into his belt, shutting his eyes tightly as his back opened up in a long red welt. She swung again, and it connected harder, sending the sound around the silent room in an echo that made Ana cry.

Ezra jolted into the wood when Abby struck again, burying his face into the stake and closing his eyes tightly as he tried to take the pain without crying out. By the fifth crack, he was screaming out into the air of the room. His back was bloody, and his legs were weak as he tried to cling to the wood without falling.

Abby struck again, and Ana couldn't watch anymore. She closed her eyes and turned her back to them, trying to block out the noise of the whip connecting and Ezra screaming until she counted the twelfth and last welt. She opened her eyes, wiping her cheeks dry and trying to hide her tremors. She turned again, just in time to see Abby drop the whip and rush forward to catch her brother, who swayed and collapsed. He was bleeding badly, and his back was in shreds that looked inflamed and excruciatingly painful.

"He needs Genevieve. She can heal him! Please," Ana shouted with a splutter as she looked up at Silas. He clenched the rope in his hands, and a wide smile spread across his face.

"She couldn't even if she wanted to. That whip is enchanted. You can't heal any wound it makes. He is going to have to heal normally. And slowly." Silas grinned, watching as Ezra fell out of Abby's arms and knelt on the floor on his hands and knees, panting and trying to even out his gasps.

Thaddeus stood from his chair as the voices of the crowd in the room grew louder. "And thus concludes our meeting. Blessings to you all. Silas, take Ana to her room."

"What? Now? No, I need to make sure he is okay!" Ana yelled, pushing past Silas and rushing forward. His mother was beside him now, rubbing his brow and trying to get him to stand, but he couldn't keep steady on his legs. "Ezra!"

Silas frowned and tugged hard on the rope attached to her wrists, dragging her back and grabbing her by the back of the neck. "He's not worth it. Move." He shoved her toward a door at the side of the room.

She could hear Ezra shouting for her in confused and pained pants from somewhere in the crowd, but she couldn't see him now that Silas had blocked her view of the room. He pushed her again, making her stumble and trip into a heavy wooden door that most likely led to the "room" Thaddeus mentioned.

"No! I need to say goodbye! Please! Ezra!" Ana cried, thrusting at Silas's chest to squeeze past him, but he was much bigger than she was, and much stronger, so he manoeuvred her down the hall with little effort. "Ezra!"

CHAPTER 8

*A*na made her way down the stone staircase that led to the lower levels of House Alden. She could still hear loud voices thundering in the room above, echoing around the walls and coming down through the ceiling. Ezra's voice, though, was long gone.

The corridor at the bottom of the stairs was dark, with a few small candles dotted around the walls so that they could see where they were walking. It smelled damp, like growing moss and decaying wood. The scent worked its way up her nose and welded itself there, making her screw her face and bring her hands up to shield herself from it.

Flanking each side of the corridor were rusted iron-barred cells, each identical in shape and size, with their doors open wide. They were all empty and bare. Only a single grimy mattress rested along the left-hand side of each wall.

"This is a dungeon," Ana commented as she shuffled along the floor.

"You are perceptive," Silas said lowly, walking behind her with the rope in his hands tightly.

"I wasn't told I would be imprisoned. That wasn't the deal. I am supposed to stay here to be trained." Ana stopped in the middle of the corridor and turned to look over her shoulder at him.

"Keep walking," he sneered, reaching to shove her forward.

Ana lurched and walked again, a deep frown creasing her brows and her lips pulled into a thin line. She could hear the blood pumping in her ears. Silas nodded to the second to last cell door, and she approached its entrance, scanning the inside and her frown growing deeper. Just like the rest of the cells, a single mattress lay on the floor near the wall, covered in stains she didn't want to know the origins of. She spotted a small table with a candelabra sitting on top of it, a moulding pillow and a thin grey blanket. At the back wall to the right, one of the stone walls gave way to another little room that had a rusted sink and a cracked toilet, the pipe dripping water onto the dusty ground.

"You can't be serious. I am not staying here. I want to go with Ezra," Ana said, recoiling from the room and backing away from the cell door.

Silas sighed as he came up behind her, leaning back to press his foot to the small of her back and kick her inside. "Ezra is indisposed."

Ana tumbled inside the cell and fell onto the hard stone floor, unable to stop herself with her bound hands. Pain shot up the bones of her arms as she rolled onto her side with a groan, shuffling to sit upright as Silas stalked inside and knelt in front of her. He watched her in silence for a long moment, his dark eyes flicking across her face and studying her until he grinned and reached for his belt. Something flashed in the candlelight, drawing her attention away from his staring eyes and to the decorative dagger he had in his hand.

Ana flinched, throwing her bound hands up to cover her face and turning her head away from him with her eyes shut tightly. Even though she couldn't see him, she could still sense his eyes watching her and feel his breath on her skin. He shifted, and she felt him place the cold steel of the knife against her cheek and flick a strand of her hair out of her face before he grabbed her by the wrists.

Ana snapped her eyes open when the tension from the rope bounding her wrists released. He wasn't looking at her anymore and instead was staring down at the rope as it came apart in his hands.

"Are you going to hurt me?" she asked, watching him in what little candlelight there was in the room. Her cheeks felt wet, and she raised her free hands to wipe them dry.

"That is entirely up to you," Silas mumbled, stuffing the knife back into its sheath on his belt and standing, his hands clenched into fists at his sides.

Ana gulped, helping herself to her feet and stumbling back from him to create some space between them. As dark as it was, she could still make out his facial features and his body. He was tall and muscular, with large shoulders and hands that looked like the bones had been broken and reset badly more than once.

"Why am I down here? I am not an animal you can cage, Silas. I am a person. Please just let me go," she begged, trying not to let the quiver in her voice shine through, but it wobbled her resolve anyway.

Silas said nothing for a long moment. His eyes narrowed and his head tilted before he stepped to her and loomed over her, making her shrink back from him. "How much have you actually *learned* about your magic?" he asked, eyes searching hers.

Ana frowned, feeling cornered and suffocated by his sudden closeness. "A little, I guess. Ezra has tried to teach me what he can." She reached out to shove him, but he didn't budge. "Can you give me some space? Why do you keep looking at me like that?"

"I am looking for your magic," Silas said simply. "You can see magic in a witch's eyes, but I can't see yours. It is probably the binding, but even then, you should at least *see* it."

His eyes flicked down to the talisman she wore around her neck, and he reached for it, turning it over in his hand roughly and then dropping it against her chest. "It comes off tomorrow. Sullivan magic won't help you here."

Ana's face paled, her body feeling limp as she tried to keep herself steady on her feet. "You can't take it off me. My magic is too wild without it. I will hurt you if you take it."

Silas's set frown turned into an amused smile as he laughed softly, then turned from her and headed towards the cell door. "That would be a first, though I would like to see you try."

"W-wait!" Ana stammered, shuffling forward. "Genevieve said you would help me. Please don't leave me down here in the dark. I won't be able to sleep down here alone."

"Genevieve is a fool," Silas snapped, walking out of the cell and moving to grab the door. "And I don't care about your feelings. I am only doing what my father asked me to do. I don't care about you either way."

Anger and panic flushed up into Ana's cheeks. Her hands turned to fists at her sides, and her shoulders squared as she stood up straighter, her teeth clenched and her eyes hard. "Do you do everything your *daddy* tells you to do?"

Silas's body tensed. He rammed the door open and stalked across the stone floor, grabbing her by the hair on the back of her head in a fist and slamming her against the wall. His knife pressed against the skin of her throat as he leaned in close to her face.

Ana whimpered, her head tipped back from his grip and her back pressed against the damp stone wall of the cell. "I'm sorry! I'm sorry! Please . . ."

"Let me make something crystal clear for you, Miss Davenport. I am not a Sullivan, and I'm not your fucking friend. I will not hold your hand and braid your hair and tell you everything will be okay. My training methods will not be gentle, with pretty little flowers and rainbows, and I will sure as hell not stroke your fragile emotions to make you *feel better*. The Sullivans have been soft on you. I will not be. I don't much care if you succeed or if you die in this cell when your magic takes you apart atom by atom. You either listen to me and live, or you refuse and die. Am I in any way unclear?"

Ana gasped, tears dripping down her cheeks as she tried not to flinch at his words and his growl. The sharpness of the knife at her throat was nothing compared to the sting of his words, and she could do nothing but splutter and shake her head in reply.

"Good girl," Silas said, whipping his hand free from her hair and taking the knife away from her skin. He tucked it back into its place at his hip as he exited the cell. He closed the barred door and began to lock it, flicking his eyes up to look at her again, a smirk back on his face. "I am going to have a hell of a lot of fun breaking you down and building you back up again, Miss Davenport."

"Wait! Wait, I need my bag, a-and my phone," Ana stuttered as she rushed to the bars and grasped them, watching as he pulled the keys out of the lock. "And you will bring me food, right?"

"If I remember. I will see you for training."

He turned and walked back down the hallway until Ana couldn't see him anymore. She heard his heavy footsteps echo up the stone steps and the wooden door slamming shut behind him, leaving her alone in the darkness.

Ana hiccupped a sob as she pulled her shaking hands from the bars of the door and to her throat, where Silas had pressed his knife. Sticky wetness dampened her fingers, and when she pulled them away again to look down at them, blood dripped from her fingertips.

"Shit," she cried, spinning on the spot to look around the cell.

There was a mirror on the wall, its glass cracked and its edges chipped, but it was solid. With the candlelight, she could see her reflection well enough to inspect her wound. She approached it, ignoring how pale her face was and how wet her cheeks were, and instead tipped her chin upwards to look at her neck. It wasn't deep, but it was smeared red and bleeding, reminding her of the cuts Ezra had suffered from the whip. He was going to be in agony, and if Silas had told the truth about his whip, he wouldn't be healed for weeks. Her heart tugged as she thought about him, guilt bubbling into her body and making her eyes fill with tears again. He was whipped for using magic, which had been for *her*.

"God, Ana, get it together." She whimpered, wiping her cheeks dry and trying to set her face to make herself look less pathetic, but she couldn't.

She turned away from her reflection, unable to look at herself anymore. Her eyes fell upon the moulded mattress, and she walked to it, wrinkling her nose and slumping to sit down on it. Hugging her knees to her chest, Ana rested her back against the wall and tried not to think about how alone she was inside the dark cell. A cell that would only get darker once the candles in the candelabra died away. She never liked being in the dark. Ever since she had seen the shadow messenger back in Ezra's bedroom, she hadn't been able to sleep in the dark. Something could be waiting to reach out from the darkness and grab her. So many bad things happened in the dark. Then again, so many bad things had happened in the light too.

What could possibly happen to her in the darkness that hadn't already happened to her in the light?

~

"Ana."

There was a whisper from somewhere near the bars.

Ana snapped awake and rubbed her wrist underneath her eyes. She must have fallen asleep because the candles were burning low and she was curled up on her side on the mattress with the thin blanket wrapped around her shoulders. She wasn't sure what time it was, but it had to be around dinner, for her stomach ached in the need for food and her body shivered from the coldness of the cell.

"Psst! Ana!"

Abby was crouched on the floor on the other side of the cell door. She had bundles of something at her feet, and she was waving to her with a smile on her face that didn't reflect in her eyes.

"Abby? What are you doing here?" Ana croaked, sitting up and shuffling across the floor so that she could sit beside the door, her hand instinctively reaching through the bars to hold Abby's.

"Silas is gone. He said he will be back in the morning to start your training. Are you okay?" Abby asked, squeezing her hands and tilting her head at her, pity tainting her expression.

"No," she replied honestly, biting back a sob. "I don't like it down here. It's cold, and Silas is"–she paused to think of the best term to describe the man–"mean."

"That's one word for him, I guess. I figured he hadn't sent any food or thicker blankets to you, so I brought you some supplies." Abby retracted her hands and pushed some fabric through the small space in the bars. It took her a few shoves, but they finally broke through, and Ana took them thankfully.

"Abby, how is Ezra? Is he okay?" Ana asked as she examined Abby's face in the dim light.

Abby winced, looking away from her and at the brown bags in her lap. "He is in a lot of pain." She sighed and pushed one of the lunch bags through the bars for her.

"But he will be all right, won't he? Silas said the wounds can't be healed." Ana tried to catch Abby's eye, but she wouldn't look at her.

"He is right; they can't. The whip is enchanted, so any wound it makes cannot be healed by magic. I tried to be gentle, but if Thaddeus or Silas saw me holding back, they would have made it so much worse for him." Abby took a bite of her food with a furrow of her brow. She swallowed, clearing her throat with a bottle of water and then passing it through the bars to her. "He was asking for you. He was furious that they took you away so fast without being able to say goodbye, but Mom needed to take him home to bandage him up. We had to sedate him. He will be asleep for a while."

Ana's stomach churned as she looked down at the sandwich in the bag she had given her. As hungry as she was, the thought of taking it out and eating it made her want to be sick. "Silas is an asshole."

"He's not an asshole, he is just . . . he has his issues, I guess," Abby said, looking up from her sandwich to scan the inside of

Ana's cell. "You aren't supposed to be here. Your room is upstairs. Nice big bed, a fireplace, a huge bath, but Silas said you needed to earn your way there. He doesn't want your magic blowing up and then have to clean your blood from the carpet, so he said you need to stay here. No one has the courage to argue with him. The last person to argue with him ended up with his mouth sewn shut for a week. I'm sorry, I like you, but I'm not putting myself on his bad side when I have only *just* gotten on his good side."

Ana grimaced and brought the bottle of water to her mouth, chugging the liquid until it was drained. "It's okay. I don't want you to get into trouble over me. He is an animal, though."

"He's not a gentleman, but he is *fine*, am I right? God, I would climb that man like a tree." Abby laughed, leaning against the bars. "I'm sorry you are here. I will come visit when I can. Ezra made me promise to keep an eye on you."

Ana gave a weak smile and sniffled, trying to conceal how weak she was feeling. If Abby was going to go back to see Ezra, she wanted her to tell him she was okay, even if she was feeling light years away from it.

"Hey, Abby? What did Silas mean when he told Ezra he was just like his dad? He said he was a murderer."

Abby's smile slipped from her face, and in its place came a frown that Ana almost thought looked like fear, but it was fleeting and left her face as quickly as it came.

"Uh . . . yeah," Abby said, scratching her head, "that is why Ezra is banned from using his magic. He killed someone five years ago while using it. He was human. It didn't go down well with the High Council, obviously. There was a big cover-up, and Dad had to ban him from ever using magic again. It was the most lenient sentence there was. He was lucky he didn't get executed."

That didn't sound like Ezra, not by a long shot. "I don't believe it."

"I know, right?" Abby said, a fake smile plastered back on her face as she tried to laugh it off. "Anyway, I need to go. I brought more water and your bag, but Silas wouldn't let me give you your phone. I put it in your room upstairs. You should try to sleep some more. You will need the rest for tomorrow."

"Thank you, Abby, for everything," Ana said as Abby pushed her bag through the bars and set the water beside it.

"You don't need to thank me, but don't fuck with Silas, okay? Don't make him mad. He is not known for his patience, and any hostility will only force him to make you suffer." Abby took her hand through the bars. "And I will be here for you when I can be. Don't lose hope, Ana."

Abby stood with the rest of her sandwich and waved to her as she shuffled quietly down the hall. She was light on her feet, and she couldn't hear her leave the hallway. The slamming of the door upstairs was the only indication she had left.

Ana sat by the bars for a long while, finally forcing herself to eat her sandwich before she dragged her bag, pillow and blankets back to the mattress. She made the bed as well as she could, trying to give herself a little source of comfort in knowing she would at least be able to sleep without shivering, then sat down on it and pulled her bag open.

Digging inside, her hand hit something hard, and when she grabbed it, she pulled out a thin red book. Black scrawled text was on the front that read, *A History of Witchcraft*.

Inside, on the first page, was a note in Ezra's handwriting. It was scrawled quickly and chaotically, and a little blood had been smudged on the page, most likely by his hand. He must have tried to write it after his lashings.

Ana,

I will come for you. Don't give up.
–Ezra

Ana smiled weakly at the writing and snuggled down into the musty pillows and blankets, flicking through the pages and reading until the candles completely melted down and burned out.

CHAPTER 9

The sound of rattling against cell bars awoke Ana. She groaned and rolled onto her back, wiping the sleep from her eyes and sitting up. Her back ached from lying all night atop the lumpy mattress on the hard stone floor. She felt grimy, like she needed a shower to rid herself of the sweat that had settled on her skin. Her throat felt dry from a night of crying, and her nose was stuffy from the dust that was hovering in the stale air.

"Get up."

Silas stood on the other side of the bars. He opened the lock on the cell door and walked inside, kicking her bag aside to clear the floor in the middle of the small room.

"Good morning to you too," Ana said as she tried to stop her shivering. The cold had settled into her skin so deeply she was trembling. "What time is it?"

"Does it matter? I said get up," Silas snapped, reaching into the little drawer on the table and lifting out more candles. He replaced the used ones and raised his hand, the candles sparking and lighting with fire. The room illuminated, casting Silas's large shadow against the bricked wall in a way that made him seem even bigger.

Ana licked the dryness away from her lips and stood. She walked to the centre of the room and played with her hands in front of her, waiting for him to stop staring at her, but he didn't. He stared her down as if waiting for her to speak or cry again or try to rush past him out of the room. She refused to give him the satisfaction, and instead, she stared right back.

Silas finally closed the distance between them, making her fight her instinctive flinch when he reached to take the talisman from her chest in his hand. He looked down at it through narrowed eyes, his fingers toying with the carved metal and running over its surface.

"It's cracking. Genevieve is very good at what she does. Even if I find her irritating, I will at least give her that. If your magic is breaking the binding she made, it must be serious." He gripped it in his fist. "Let's find out."

Silas tugged, and the rope snapped behind her neck, bringing the talisman into his hand. She moved to protest, about to tell him to give it back, but it was already on the floor and under his heel. The sound of the talisman cracking and breaking filled the room, and when he pulled his foot back, she could see the fragments of it shining up at her.

"Why did you do that? I told you, I can't be without it!" Ana snapped, sinking to her knees, lifting the fragments into her hands and trying to fuse them back together again, but it was no use.

The little grey bricked cell filled with thick fog. It loomed in the corners and spread around the room, snaking between them and making it harder for her to keep her eyes on Silas. She stood again quickly as shadows crawled their way around the room. A loud rumbling rattled the tiles under her feet so strongly that it vibrated the bars of the cell. The magic in her solar plexus erupted violently, making her scream out in pain and drop the fragments so that she could cling to her red cardigan at her stomach. It rolled faster and faster, like it knew the talisman that had bound it was gone forever and it was free.

"What did you do?!" Ana shouted, stumbling as she tried to stay on her feet. The aching in her stomach burst in a blast of pain again that sent her screaming as if the magic might just burst from there and rip her apart. "W-what's happening to me?"

Silas said nothing. Instead, he ignored her screaming and watched as the shadows crept along the walls and the fog thickened and engulfed the room. His face was set in a frown, and his eyebrows were pinned together in confusion as he watched the effect her magic had on the room. Finally, he snapped his eyes back to Ana and moved towards her, but she flinched and took a stumbling step back.

"Don't! Don't touch me. I will hurt you!" Ana warned. She tried to remember everything Ezra had told her. She tried to keep the magic inside her in a cat's purr, but she couldn't. It wasn't a purr. It was *never* going to be a purr. It was a raging fire, and it was consuming her, making her head spin and her nose bleed freely down her face.

"What are you doing?" Silas asked, tilting his head at her and taking a determined step towards her again.

"E-Ezra said I needed to control it, that I needed to keep it in. He said if I don't control my emotions, it will burst out and hurt everyone. I'm trying, I-I promise I'm trying, but it h-hurts." Ana hiccupped. Her head was throbbing, and her body was trembling, making her teeth chatter.

A smile spread across Silas's face as he laughed lowly, watching the blood from her nose drip down over her lips and chin and onto her cardigan. "If you keep holding it in, it is going to melt your brain. Magic is controlled by emotion, yes, but Ezra has always been good at controlling his emotions. Your magic is not the same. You need to *feel*, and you need to let your magic *go*."

"I can't!" Ana yelled, wincing as the pain in her head worsened and her ears rang. "If I do that, it will blow me apart, and it will hurt you if you get too close!"

"Do you want to die?!" Silas shouted, his amused smile gone.

"No!" she screamed back. A loud boom echoed in the room, and the mirror smashed. Silas didn't flinch.

"Then you need to let go! Your emotions will help you control it. What do you feel?" he asked.

"I have a headache, m-my ears are ringing, it hurts–"

Silas groaned and cut her off. "No! Not physically. Emotionally."

"I don't know. I'm tired. Confused?" she asked, reaching to hold her head while her fingers snaked into her hair and gripped it in fistfuls. It felt like her skull was splitting down the middle, cracking her forehead apart to make way for something.

"That's not good enough!" Silas hollered, making her flinch. "You have had *everything* taken from you. Your friends are *gone*, your job is *gone*, your whole life is in ruins, and you are *tired*? You were nearly murdered by a man who instead turned you into *this*, and you have been taken to a world where you are no longer in control of your life! You are going to die, Ana!" He shoved her, and she stumbled back, and when she didn't retaliate, he pushed her again. "You are going to die! How does that make you feel?!"

"Angry!" Ana screamed, pulling her hands away from her head furiously.

The force of her scream pushed out from all around her body, throwing the table and the candles against the wall, blowing the blankets through the cell door and forcing Silas a few steps back. He stayed on his feet, though, and stepped up to her again with a scowl on his face.

Ana could see blackness taking over her eyes, until they were fully black, like they had been when she was with Ezra. Where the fear in her heart used to be, there was now anger and acceptance, and she found the pain in her head was easing and the panic was filtering away.

"Better," Silas said, dusting off his black shirt from the debris in the room. "You cannot control your magic without accepting its presence first. You cannot control your emotions if you first do not acknowledge they are there. If you allow yourself to truly feel them, then your magic will listen to you. It is yours. Start acting like you own it. Don't let it own you."

"Why am I not hurting you?" Ana asked, wiping the blood from her face with the back of her hand, but it smeared over her cheek instead. "I hurt Ezra. Why am I not hurting you?"

"I have magic too. I can shield myself well enough. Ezra is banned. If he shielded himself using magic, he would have received a lot more lashes than he did," Silas said, looking her over.

Her nose had stopped dripping, but her eyes stayed dark and the fog still lay thick in the room. The magic in her solar plexus was flowing nicely now, and it felt good to be angry and allow the magic to do the work for her.

"When you calm down, you need to start trusting your abilities, or they will take over again. When you are angry, let it out. When you are sad, let your magic do what it needs to, or it is going to burst out of your body and do it itself." Silas moved to right the table and set the candles on top once more so that he could wave his hand and light them.

"Now that it's not hurting me when I have the talisman off, can I go home to Ezra? Thaddeus said once I learn to control it, I can leave," Ana suggested hopefully. Her breathing was still coming in pants, and her mouth tasted like copper pennies, making her wince in disgust.

"No. You think *this* is controlling it? You have tamed it *slightly*. It's going to build up again and again, and you will get out of control once more. You need to know how to keep it as it is now. You have more magic than any witch should have, so what comes easy for me is going to be almost *impossible* for you. Your magic makes your emotions run high. If you blow like that in the human world, the High Council will have you killed. Once you figure that out, we need to work on manipulation so that you can actually *use* your magic. If you use it like how the rest of us do, it will stay content. Right now, because your magic is bored, it is acting out." Silas sighed, turning to walk out of the door and kick the blankets back inside.

"Wait, where are you going?" Ana asked as she rushed forward in the fog to the cell door, holding the bars when he closed and locked it.

"It's breakfast. I'm hungry," he said simply. He turned on his heel to walk away from her but paused a few feet away and gritted his teeth. Sighing, he looked back over his shoulder at her as she clung to the bars and rested her head against them to see him better.

"I will have food sent to you. For now, work on settling the thoughts in your head, and the fog should recede." Silas walked away before Ana could answer him, moving out of sight and down the corridor quickly, leaving her alone in her cell again.

Ana turned, trudging to the centre of the cell. She fixed the mattress and folded the blankets, setting them down on top of it and slumping to sit on them. She took a deep breath, scanning the fog and how it moved with the air, filling every space and flowing out of the cell door.

Settle the thoughts in your head.

That was easier said than done. Thoughts were always rolling through her mind, making her stomach churn and her mood plummet. Silas was right. She had lost everything. She lost her friends, her freedom, her sanity. It was hard to clear her mind of thoughts when they were so heavy.

She sighed and closed her eyes, breathing deeply in through her nose and out through her mouth to calm her beating heart. She tried to clear her mind, focusing on the feeling in her stomach and how it ebbed and flowed in a gentle dance. It felt good for it to finally stop fighting with her, and as she concentrated on it and admired the feeling, a smile finally crept over her face. She opened her eyes to see the fog begin to slowly dissipate and her eyes return to normal. She could see the blackness recede from her vision, making the cell brighter, if that were even possible in the low light.

It took a while for the fog to completely dissipate, but when it did, she let out a deep sigh and smiled, bringing her knees to her chest and resting her chin there.

Silas didn't come back with breakfast.

In fact, it was nearly suppertime before anyone came near the cells again. Her stomach growled loudly in protest when she saw Abby hovering at the cell door. Ana jumped and rushed to it, smiling at her and slumping to sit on the ground.

"You came." Ana gripped the bars.

"Yeah. Silas got word on my father, so he had to leave. I had to get my work done before I was allowed to come and see you," Abby said, a dark frown on her face. She slumped to the ground beside her. "I brought more sandwiches and fruit."

"Thank you," Ana said, her smile faltering and a frown

replacing it. "What do you mean Silas got word on your father? Have they caught him?"

Abby pushed the brown bags through the bars with a shake of her head. She leaned against the bars and lifted her own, holding them in her hands like she had lost her appetite. "No, but they got a hit on the blood tracking spell, so they know his location. If he doesn't move quickly enough, Silas will catch him."

"You sound like you want Alexander to get away." Ana frowned. She could feel anger bubble up inside her, and it made her magic rumble in her stomach and up into her chest, pressing against her heart.

"I don't! I mean, I don't think I do," Abby defended. She had a confused look on her face, like she was battling with herself. "I know what he did was technically wrong, but–"

"*Technically* wrong?" Ana snipped, her eyes beginning to darken around the edges. "He killed two people. He tried to murder *me*. He knocked out his son and was going to wipe his memories. How can you say that to me?"

"I-I know! I know and he should be punished for that, but he's my *dad*, Ana," Abby explained with a sad frown. "He wanted the magic in the athame to help us witches be out in the open so that we didn't have to be hidden all the time. I understand that part. The murder, not so much. It's just . . . I know when they catch him, he is going to be tried, and the only outcome of that trial is execution."

"Good!" Ana snapped, setting the sandwich aside. "He *killed* people, Abby!"

"He is still my father!" Abby shouted, tears spilling out of her eyes. "I know he did bad things, but he is the man who helped me learn how to ride a bike. H-he's the man who showed me how to cast my first spell and who chased all the monsters away from under the bed!"

"Abby, your dad *is* the monster!" Ana argued as she watched her, her anger making the magic swirl harder and faster in her chest. The floor under her was vibrating and the bars were shaking, but it didn't seem to bother Abby.

"This was a mistake. I should go," Abby said as she wiped her cheeks and shoved her sandwich back into her bag. "I will come back soon with more food."

"No! Please don't go. I'm sorry I shouted at you. I'm just so mad!" Ana said, reaching through the bars to grab Abby's arm.

The second she touched her skin, Abby's eyes rolled into the back of her head, and her body went rigid. She collapsed beside the cell door on her back, her body twitching and her back bowing off the ground. Ana retracted her hand, looking down at it before returning her sight to Abby.

"No. No, no, no!" She gasped, grasping the bars and sitting up on her knees, her face turning pale and her brow beading in cold sweat. "Abby! Abby, can you hear me?"

Abby was jerking, her eyes shut tightly and her hands in fists. Her skin was turning ashen, like Ezra's had been when she kissed him.

"Help! Someone help!" Ana shouted. This must have been what Silas meant about not having tamed her magic. She couldn't let it take over, or else bad things happened and people got hurt. Innocent people, like Abby.

"Help!" she screamed down the hall.

No one came. Abby's fit slowly subsided, and she lay beside the bars on the cold stone floor, her body completely still and her eyes softly closed as if she were sleeping. Ana slumped back to sit on the floor and tried to calm her breathing. She realised the room was filled with fog again and the bricks were rattling. She closed her eyes, focusing on the whirling inside her solar plexus.

"Come on, please . . . please stop," Ana begged.

She waited until she could feel the furious whirling calm again as her anger subsided, and when she was sure it had returned to its gentleness, she opened her eyes and reached for Abby's arm through the bars, checking her pulse. Her skin was cold and her pulse was weak, but she was alive. She must just be knocked out.

Ana held Abby's hand through the bars, waiting for what seemed like hours until the heavy door upstairs opened and Silas's footsteps stalked towards them. She had learned what they sounded like. They were always heavy and loud. And angry.

"What the fuck happened?" Silas growled when he reached them. He knelt beside Abby and checked her over before glaring up at Ana. "I can't leave you alone for two seconds?"

"I'm sorry! I got mad and I grabbed her, and she just collapsed! Is she okay?" Ana sniffled, taking her hand back from Abby's and standing quickly, holding the bars in a grip so tight her fingers were turning white.

Silas lifted Abby in a bridal carry, holding her like she weighed nothing. Abby's head lolled back, her body completely limp and her face almost serene. Silas looked down at her face, his scowl deepening, before he started his walk down the hallway and flashed Ana an angry gaze over his shoulder.

"For your sake, Ana, you better fucking hope so."

CHAPTER 10

Silas didn't come back for days.
No one did.

The sandwiches and fruit Abby had left were gone quicker than she would have liked, leaving her stomach starving and cramping. The bottles of water hadn't lasted long either, forcing her to drink what she could from the rusting sink in the little stone bathroom. It tasted stale and it was a funny colour, but after days of nothing to eat or drink, she didn't have a choice. Her magic was hungry too. It filled her head with a thundering so loud it made her eyes fuzzy, her nose bled more often, and it was getting harder and harder to quiet it down when she was so exhausted from lack of sustenance.

She could barely raise her head from where she was lying on the mattress. The extra candles in the drawers had long since run out, but she was finding the darkness in the cell somewhat comforting now. If she couldn't see anything, maybe she couldn't hurt anything.

Rolling onto her side, she curled up with her pillow and wrapped her arms around her starving stomach, gazing through the barred door. The candles on the walls in the corridor never seemed to run out. Magic, she supposed, but it also made her wonder why she was never given any magic candles to illuminate her own room. Perhaps she didn't deserve them.

As the candlelight from the hallway flickered over the stone floor, Ana noticed something near the bars shuffle and move. It was small, with a little nose and beaded eyes, and it huddled against the bars like it was searching for something. Squinting in the low light and raising herself up on her elbow, she looked closer. It was a grey mouse, or perhaps it was brown. She couldn't tell.

"Hey . . ." she whispered softly, shuffling across the stone floor to the bars and trying to see him, but the mouse snapped his eyes on her and darted away. "No, it's okay! Come back, I won't hurt you. I think."

The little mouse stayed close to the wall, watching her for any sudden movement. She stayed still, resting against the bars and waiting as he slowly scurried back towards her. Twitching his small nose, he scampered inside the cell and looked around.

"You won't find any food here, if that's what you are searching for." She tilted her head and placed her hand down on the floor with her palm facing skyward.

The mouse sniffed at her fingers, obviously trying to find any remnants of crumbs that may have lingered there. He nibbled at them, then sat up on his hind legs to look up at her pleadingly.

"I know how you feel, but I don't have anything. As soon as someone brings me food, I will share it, though. What is your name, huh? Do you have one?"

The mouse just blinked back at her and watched her as she

lay down, her head resting in her hand and the other petting his little head.

"God, now I'm talking to a mouse." She sighed, rolling her eyes. "What about Mister Cheese? No. Mister Whiskers?"

The mouse curled his head and ears into her hand and nibbled at her fingers.

"No. Mister Nibbles. That's your name." She laughed.

"I find it amusing how the source of all this chaos is sitting on the ground talking to a mouse."

Ana jumped in shock at the voice, sitting up so quickly she felt something in her side pull and sting. She snapped her eyes to look up at the cell door, seeing a shadow in the corridor. It was a female voice she heard, with her shadow cast upon the wall. The little mouse hurried towards the bathroom, and Ana scrambled to her feet and dusted down her dirty clothes.

"Who's there?" she asked, her eyes searching the hallway.

The shadow moved forwards, and then the woman it cast from came into view in front of the cell door. She flashed Ana a red-lipped smile and leaned against the bars, leering at her. Ana recognised her as the woman who had sat beside Genevieve at the Council table, but for the life of her, she couldn't remember the name Thaddeus had called out. She was wearing the same wine-red dress with a neckline that dipped low between her cleavage to her sternum. Her long black hair bounced around her shoulders and down her back in large curls, and her eyeliner was flicked at the ends. The woman said nothing to her for a long while, instead reaching out her hands and wrapping her fingers around the bars so that she could rest her head against them and grin at her.

"I've seen you before, upstairs at the Council table," Ana said, her mouth dry as she watched her. She smelled amazing, like expensive perfume and musky winter nights, and her big brown eyes held something alluring inside them that Ana couldn't place. "You are a member of the Council, right?"

"Perceptive," the woman replied with a light chuckle. She flicked her eyes over Ana as if taking in every inch of her. "Such a fuss, for such a little lady, wouldn't you say? I just *had* to come down here to see you with my own eyes even if your surroundings are less than impressive."

Ana frowned, crossing her arms against her chest to hug herself. "Can you tell me if Abby is all right? Is she alive?"

"Ah, yes, Silas's new recruit. I wouldn't know. I do not meddle with the Venator. Such a nasty business they deal in." She let the bars go to inspect her perfectly manicured black nails. She flicked her eyes up again, looking at Ana under her long eyelashes and flashing her a grin that made Ana feel small. "They say you still cannot control your magic, that it still runs thick and wild through those veins of yours."

"I . . ." Ana started, but she didn't know what to say. She closed her mouth tightly, narrowing her eyes at her and shifting on her feet. "I'm sorry, but who are you?"

"They call me Anora." She shrugged and flicked a long curl of black hair over her shoulder. "Why are you sitting in the dark?"

"Silas hasn't come back. He has left me here for *days* with no food or water or candles. I need you to get someone, please," Ana begged, tears pricking at her eyes from how hungry and lonely she was. Her stomach growled in protest, and she hugged herself tighter. "Please."

Anora blinked at her, then laughed. It was a pitiful kind of laugh that made Ana's heart sink in her chest. "You ran out of candles, so you are just sitting in the dark? You have magic. Have the Gods forbid you to use it?"

Before Ana could ask her what she meant, Anora raised her

hand above her head. Light flashed in the room so brightly that Ana had to fling her hands up to her face to shield her eyes. Her eyes were sensitive from being stuck in the dark for so long, and the bright light stung like visual acid. She blinked a few times, trying to will away the spots in her eyes as Anora lowered her hand. She grinned up at the shining orb that was hovering in the middle of the ceiling, illuminating every inch of the cell.

"How did you do that?" Ana gasped, pulling her hands away from her face and trying to look up at the sun-like silver orb, but it was too bright.

"Simple illumination magic. It is the magic of children. If you cannot do simple light magic, there really is not much hope for you." Anora sighed as she looked Ana over with her cat-like eyes, now that she could see her better. "Now . . . the magic of children is not what I am interested in. My forte, as they say, is blood magic."

"Blood magic?" she asked, rubbing her arms. Every time Anora looked at her, she felt like a mouse being stared down by a snake, like at any moment, Anora was going to lash out and feed on her.

"And mediumship, yes, but mostly blood magic. The Elders tell me you have an awful lot of magic running through those veins. I would like to taste it."

Ana tilted her head to the side and narrowed her eyes as if she didn't quite hear her correctly. "I'm sorry, what?"

"I don't need much, just a prick of your finger and I will be on my way. I will even have food sent to you, and water, and whatever else you need." She reached her arm through the bars, her tanned skin perfect and smooth. Opening her hand towards Ana, she wriggled her fingers invitingly. "Come now."

Ana flinched and took a step back, attempting to hide the

disgust on her face, but her grimace shone through anyway. "No, I am not letting you *taste* my blood. That's disgusting."

The grin on Anora's face fell, and she retracted her outstretched hand back through the bars, clenching it into a fist. "Disappointing, Ana." She pushed off the door and paced the hallway as if trying to calm herself down. She swivelled her head towards Ana, and her eyes narrowed. "Very disappointing."

"I'm sorry, Anora, but–"

"Your father would be so disappointed in you if he could see you now. Stuck down here in a dungeon, lying on the floor covered in filth and talking to vermin. Not exactly the daughter he thought you would grow up to be, are you?" She stopped her pacing and folded her hands in front of her politely, but the wicked grin on her face betrayed that graciousness.

Breath was pulled from Ana's lungs, and tears instantly fogged her eyes. Something sharp pricked the back of her throat as her face and body heated, yet cold enveloped her as she stared back at her.

"He is dead. He doesn't think about anything anymore," Ana replied in a shaky voice that she tried to keep steady.

"Ah, only a former mortal would think such a thing." Anora laughed, tipping her chin up proudly and looking over the outside of the cell. "But your dear father and I have had quite the chat these last few days."

"You lie." Her tears betrayed her false resolve by falling down her cheeks. She could feel her magic bubbling dangerously in her stomach. This time, she almost *wanted* to lose control. She wanted to stop Anora from talking. "Stop it."

"I do not lie." The woman laughed. "Oscar Davenport, died at thirty-eight. Dirty blonde hair, tall, glasses. He had a moustache that would tickle you when he kissed you and made you giggle–"

"Stop it."

"He loved coffee early in the morning while reading the Sunday papers and a crumpet before the rest of the house woke up. He worked as a freelance writer and was composing a second novel when he died. Murder mysteries, I think he said his preferred genre was. Fancied himself a bit of a detective, didn't he?"

He had. Her father had spent hours at his typewriter, setting her on his knee when she was young and letting her play with the keys and write silly notes when he should have been working. He loved creating masterpieces on that typewriter. That was why she wanted to grow up and be just like him. She always thought that someday she would finish his novel for him, but she had gotten sidetracked with working at *The City Herald* and hadn't opened the manuscript since. Her father was a great writer, much better than she ever hoped she could be.

Pain hit Ana in her chest like a train as she thought of him and how he used to cradle her over that typewriter. She started to cry heavier, reaching her hands to cover her ears as she gasped breath into her lungs. "Stop it."

"Then he died, of course. You were ten, right?" Anora asked, leaning forward with a grin and stepping back to the bars now that she saw Ana was in hysterics. "Hit and run, the car rolled over him like he was a bird and just left him there for you to pick up the pieces."

Ana took a steadying breath and dropped her hands, setting her face in a scowl and gritting her teeth. "You could have learned all of that anywhere. You are a fraud. Why would you want to hurt me like this, huh? What have I done to you?"

"Nothing, except deny me." Anora shrugged. "And I am no fraud. You think he died on the way to the hospital, don't you?

He didn't. He was just too weak to speak to you. He survived right up until they got him into surgery. What was it he used to call you? His little sunflower, right?" she asked, flashing her a wicked grin.

"I said stop!" Ana screamed.

Instinctively, Ana threw her hands out towards Anora and clenched her fists, watching as the woman was shoved back from the bars and thrown to the other side of the corridor. Her back slammed against the opposite cell, and she stumbled to right herself on her feet. Anora laughed, dusting herself down and grinning up at Ana from under her long eyelashes.

"If that is all you have, I think the Elders must have had the wrong visions." She stepped closer to the bars, just out of arm's reach. "Mister Davenport told me to tell you he misses you and that he would like the opportunity to speak with you again, one last time. If you give me a taste of your blood, I can make that wish come true, Ana."

Anger raged inside Ana that she had never felt before. She could feel the blood in her veins literally bubbling every time Anora opened her mouth, and her mind cast a shadow over all her reason. If she could get Anora to come close enough to the bars, she could reach out and grab her, and with any luck, if she held on long enough, Anora's heart would stop beating.

"Speak one more word of my father, and I will kill you." Ana panted in anger. She could see the edges of her vision begin to blacken, and she knew the darkness was consuming all the white and blues in her eyes until they were solid. The fog that came with her magic filled the cell behind her, and the shadows that were crawling over the walls reached their way up towards the bright silver sun, trying to snuff it out. It fizzed and crackled in response, but Ana didn't flinch. She was too angry to move.

"Ah, there it is. *There* is your magic." Anora grinned, taking a small tentative step towards the cell door.

She searched Ana's black eyes, and from the way she was looking over her face, she could tell she was studying how her black eyes leaked inky veins into her cheeks and under her eyes. The last Ana saw them in the mirror, they had scared her, but Anora wasn't scared.

Anora was *thrilled*.

"All I need is a prick of your finger, and I will give you your father, Ana."

Anora stepped forward again, and Ana took her chance, lashing through the bars with her hands and grabbing onto Anora's wrist in a crushing grip. Anora's eyes instantly went wide, and her body shook under her grip. A smile came over Ana's face when she saw the woman's knees weaken, sliding down the bars as she tried to hold on to her consciousness. Just a few more moments . . .

A few more *seconds*, and Anora would be–

Anora set her face and gripped the bars with her free hand, sending a bright electric shock through them that radiated from the centre of her palm, making Ana recoil from the metal and let her go. The woman flew away from the cell door, rubbing her reddened wrist with a look of shock and awe on her face that transformed into a wicked smile.

Ana released deep, angry breaths as she tried to calm the magic that was furiously whirling in her solar plexus. "If you are not going to help me, you need to leave."

Anora smirked and straightened her back again proudly, then flicked her hair back into place over her shoulder. With a raised eyebrow, she walked down the long stone corridor, her shadow blocking the flickering light of the candles on the bricks. The silver orb above Ana's head in the middle of the ceiling shimmered and vibrated, then imploded, sending sparks of twinkling light into the cell around her and making her scream. She covered her head, rushing to the cell door and pressing her head against them to find Anora, but she was gone from sight.

"I will taste your blood, Ana. One way or another," Anora whispered from the dark.

CHAPTER 11

No one came down to the cells for another full day. She could now notice the shift in time, depending on how loud or quiet the noises from the ballroom upstairs were. Right now, light shuffles were rolling through House Alden, signalling breakfast. Her stomach ached, and she had no more tears left to cry. Her body felt drained of all life, and her head throbbed from dehydration. The rusted sink water was making her feel sick, so she had given up and opted to lie on the mattress, staring at the dark ceiling.

Since Anora left her alone, Ana had tried to focus her anger and pain into trying to create light. She couldn't do it in the same ways Anora had. Instead of trying to create the bright silver sun, she tried to remember what Ezra had taught her. He had been so gentle, and understanding, and patient when he taught her how to create the sparkling lights from the centre of her palm. She found it somewhat easy to do it now that she had the time to focus on it. Her magic was working with her better now, and even though it hurt to use and she lost her mind when the magic tried to take over, a small sense of harmony lingered on the horizon. Perhaps, maybe, they could coexist.

Opening and closing her hand weakly, she watched as pinpricks of light beamed up from her palm to the ceiling like stars. She should be smiling at how easy it was and how much she had learned, but she wasn't. It almost felt like she would never smile again.

Mister Nibbles scurried back into the room when she was playing with the lights, looking up at them and then back to her face. He had come back to see her every few hours since Anora left. Even though she didn't have any food to give him, he kept coming back anyway, just in case. He squeaked in protest somewhere around her head and sniffled at her hair.

"Sorry, buddy. Nothing today either." Her stomach growled loudly, making her pull her hands into fists and hug herself around the middle with a groan, the lights in the room disappearing.

After a few moments of hugging herself in the darkness, she heard the heavy door upstairs open, making her snap up where she was sitting and gape at the bars. The door slammed closed again, and heavy boots thundered down the stone hallway.

She could tell it was Silas from how tall his silhouette was and how big his shoulders were, as they blocked what little light was coming from the hallway outside.

"Silas?" Ana croaked, giving a whimper. She was furious at him, but for some stupid reason, she almost felt excited to see him. Right now, she would be excited to see *anyone*.

Mister Nibbles dashed into the bathroom when Silas's tall shadow loomed on the other side of the door. He was menacing in the dark and was standing in angry silence.

The lock on the door clicked, and Silas pulled the door open with a squeak, walking into the room. He moved to the table and placed new candles into the candelabra, the wick sparking into a flame instantly. He turned in the candlelight and frowned at where she sat on the mattress.

"You left me here for *days*," Ana said through gritted teeth, tears stinging her eyes.

"You almost killed my acolyte. Consider it your punishment," Silas said simply, throwing a bottle of water and something wrapped in paper onto her lap.

Ana unrolled it quickly. The smell of warm bread and cooked bacon filled her nose. Her mouth watered instantly, and she pulled the sandwich up to her mouth, then paused and glanced up at him. "Is Abby okay?"

"She woke up today. Our healers couldn't figure out what you did to her. It took many hours and many potions to bring her back from her coma. Genevieve is here with her." He leaned against the wall and folded his arms as he waited. "Eat."

"Genevieve is here? Is Ezra here? Can I see them?" Ana asked, her eyes wide.

"No. We have work to do and not much time to complete it. Eat, or I will take it back."

"Why are you so cruel?" Ana demanded. She wanted to stay strong in her anger at him, but her stomach cramped again and instead she took a bite and moaned at how good it tasted. "Would it kill you to ask me how I am? Make some conversation, maybe?"

"I don't care how you are. That is not my job. I want this over with as much as you do. If you continue to act like a child, your time is going to run out." Boredom was plastered all over his face. "Have you been working with the flow of your magic?"

"Yes. I think it's talking to me better now, but the weaker I became, the harder it got to keep it from taking over," Ana said, taking another ravenous bite. "Food helps."

Silas nodded once, observing the contents of the dirty cell. "Maybe next time, don't try to kill the person who brings you food."

When she finished her sandwich, she rolled the paper into a ball and licked her lips, looking up at him. "I have had a lot of time to think the last few days, and I know what I want to learn next."

"That isn't up to y–"

"I know. I know it's not up to me, but I was hoping you could teach me how to do that thing Alexander did to me in the chamber. He somehow influenced me. All he had to do was ask me to come to him, and no matter how hard I tried not to, my body obeyed. I couldn't get away. I want to know how to do that."

"Influence is a little above your paygrade. You can't even light a flame yet." He rolled his eyes. "And if you're only interested in learning that so that you can influence me to free you, you are just as stupid as you are childish."

"I–" Ana started, frowning and standing shakily. "I wasn't even thinking that. I just . . . I can't get it out of my head. I just want to know how he did it."

A smile came over Silas's face, but it was darker than a normal smile. He took one of his blades from his belt and gripped it by the hilt. The blade was curved like a long black talon, and he turned it over in his hand as he pushed off the wall and stood in front of her.

"Take off your shirt," he commanded, tilting his head.

Heat rose into Ana's cheeks, and she frowned, pulling her sleeves at her wrists down further to cover her hands. "What? No."

Silas's eyes flashed red, like they did when he was using his magic on Ezra, and Ana found herself unable to move, her breathing steady. "I said, Take off your shirt."

Ana's hands moved on their own. They reached the hem of her shirt at her waist and held onto it, pulling it up over her body smoothly and over her head. Pulling her arms out of it, she let it drop to the floor by her feet, her arms at her sides as she stood in the middle of the dark cell in her black bra. Her breaths moved unevenly as she began to panic, and he took a step forward until he was standing right in front of her. Her face only met his chest, and she found she couldn't even move her head upwards to look him in the eyes.

Silas leaned down, his face close to her ear. "You don't get to tell me what I can and cannot teach you. We are not friends. Give me your arm."

Tears swelled in Ana's eyes, and she hiccupped a sob, her throat growing tight as she tried to force her body not to comply. Her arm raised on its own anyway, and he grabbed her wrist in his free hand and moved his face so that it was inches from hers and she could look into his eyes.

"You do not need to learn influence. Not yet. What happened to Abby made me realise you need to learn how to protect yourself and how to heal. You need to focus on the pain and will your body to heal itself, and quickly. Do you understand?"

Ana sniffled, trying to force her arm away from him, but her body didn't respond. She couldn't even shake her head.

Silas didn't wait for an answer. He raised the curved blade, pressed it against the skin on the inside of her forearm and sliced, leaving a long, deep wound. A scream rumbled in her throat, but she couldn't open her mouth to let it out. Instead, she hummed in panic as she watched the blood drip from her arm.

"You have fifteen minutes. If you are not healed, I am going to do it again, and again, until you figure it out. Good luck," Silas said, giving her a playful grin as he dropped her wrist and walked to the cell door, closing it over and locking it before disappearing down the hall.

When she heard the door shut upstairs, her body was released back to her, and Ana let out her scream, raising her arm to get a better look at the cut. It was bleeding freely all over the floor. Her face blanched, and she knelt to grab her white long-sleeved shirt that she had taken off, wrapping it around her arm and shuffling into the light. She couldn't stop shaking.

"S-shit. Shit!" Ana cried, pulling the bloody t-shirt away and looking down at the wound. It was gushing with so much blood that she couldn't see where she was supposed to knit it together. He had gone too deep.

"Bastard," she swore, leaning closer towards the table where the candlelight flickered to see it better. Nausea pushed up against her throat as her head felt light.

Focus. She needed to *focus*.

Taking deep, shaky breaths into her lungs, Ana tucked her hair behind her ears with her good hand. She closed her eyes, clearing her mind and talking to the magic that was ready and waiting in her solar plexus. It rolled and pushed against her stomach and through her chest, calming the nerves in her body and cooling her blood. She could do this. She *had* to do this.

Opening her eyes, she looked down at the wound again, focusing on the sharp edge where the slice started. The corners of her vision darkened as the magic took over. She could see the blood flow slow down enough that she could see where the flaps of skin were. She gagged, losing concentration for a second and having to look away until she managed to pull her focus back. The edge of her skin where it was at its most narrow glowed in a deep gold, shimmering and glittering as it knitted the skin together. She gasped, her hands shaking as she watched it with wide eyes.

It was working.

It started, and stopped, and started again. It was hard to stay focused when the pain became too much, but after some minutes passed by, she healed half of it. The skin of the healed side had a gold shimmer to it, contrasting against the still bleeding and inflamed half. Biting her lip, Ana took a deep breath through her nose and narrowed her eyes on the unhealed half, trying to force the wound to heal faster.

The door upstairs opened again, and she could hear footsteps coming back down the corridor. She was exhausted, and the time had slipped by so fast as she was trying to heal herself. Silas opened the door roughly and walked inside, eyeing her still bleeding wound.

"No! No please! I'm almost there!" Ana pleaded as she cradled her arm and scrambled away from him towards the wall.

Silas reached out and grabbed her, holding her arm above her head so that he could inspect the wound. "Halfway is not almost. Again." He reached his curved blade up and sliced her arm again just under the first wound, then let her go.

Ana dropped to the floor with a cry, holding her bloody arm against her chest. Blood spilled down her bra and over her stomach as Silas turned to leave again, slamming and locking the cell door.

"Ten minutes. Heal them, or the next time, I carve your face." He warned as he walked down the hall and away from her with a shake of his head.

Ana cried from where she was curled up on the floor against the damp stone wall. Her body felt weak, and her mind was clouded with anger. She tried to wipe her face from her tears, smearing blood on her face in the process. She could taste the copper on her lips.

Ana lay on the floor of the cell for a moment longer, refocusing her mind while taking deep breaths. Silas was malicious and cruel, and she knew if she didn't do as he asked, he would pull through on his promise to carve her face. He would enjoy it, too, but she refused to give him the satisfaction of hurting her anymore that he already had.

When her racing heart had calmed, she sat up again and crawled back to the candlelight. She wiped at the blood, waiting until she could see the flaps of skin. Anger filled her veins, her eyes growing fully black again as she focused, and it was like someone else had taken over inside her, like the magic was taking the will to heal her itself. The wounds glowed brighter and knitted together faster.

The second half of the first one healed quickly and was a lot neater than the first time she tried. Then the second weaved together, glowing gold and soothing the pain as it finished healing in a matter of seconds. She gasped, lifting her bloody shirt and rubbing the smeared bloodstains away so that she could see the two golden scars left there.

She studied them until she heard Silas return. The sound of his footsteps pulled at something furious that had built up inside her chest, fuelling her with a hatred that burned and begged to be reckoned with. Her eyes were still black, and her magic was prepared this time when he opened the iron bars and stalked inside.

Ana scrambled to her feet and stood in the centre of the room as he reached for her. Something inside her told her to reach out her hand, and when she did, his curved blade whipped out of his hand and into hers. She gripped it in white fists and twisted his hand to keep it away from her. She pressed the metal up to his throat.

"Touch me again, Silas. I dare you." Ana panted furiously,

her eyebrows furrowing and her teeth bared. "I fucking *hate* you."

A look of surprise washed over Silas's face, an expression she hadn't seen before. Usually, he was grinning or glaring, but seeing him looking anxious made her magic swell and her pride sharpen. He didn't move, but his eyes flicked down to her arm.

"Good. You should hate me. But it worked, didn't it? And it seems you learned to compel objects to you in the process."

He tried to move, but Ana pushed the blade against his throat harder. It bit into his skin. She was so angry and so full of hate that she wanted to rip his throat out. The magic inside her screamed for her to do it, to end his world with one flick of his knife, but her resolve weakened as her heartbeat calmed and her hand shook.

"If you are going to kill me, you better do it before I get that blade back from you," Silas advised, his eyes narrowing.

Ana inhaled shaky breaths into her lungs as she looked up into his eyes. He was menacing, but somehow, he was grinning at her again like he was playing with her, which only made her blood boil more. She gritted her teeth and in one swift movement, she lowered the blade from his throat and pressed the point of it against his skin near his shoulder. She sliced open the skin at his chest in one long swipe, ripping his shirt as well.

"Heal that, you bastard," Ana snapped, dropping the blade at his feet.

Silas didn't flinch. He simply looked down at the wound as it bled into his shirt and laughed, shaking his head. He scooped to grab the blade from the floor and placed it back into his belt, looming over her as she stood firm in the middle of the room. Blood covered her chest, bra, stomach and face.

"This is a much better look on you," he commented, strolling to the cell door and closing it. "I will see you in the morning. This was fun." He laughed.

Silas disappeared down the corridor, leaving her alone once more. Holding her fists at her sides, she let her anger rush through her until she had calmed down enough to walk into the little bathroom and wash away the dried blood under the dirty water. She direly needed a hot bath, but she dried herself off and changed her shirt to a clean one from her bag. Then she lay down on the mattress and stared at the ceiling. She was hurting, starved and bored, but he was right. This was the most she had felt in control of herself in weeks.

A grin tugged at the corners of Ana's mouth, and she ran her hand over the scar on her stomach from where the athame had stabbed her.

For the first time in weeks, she felt *good*.

CHAPTER 12

It had been a week since Silas sliced Ana's arm open and forced her to heal herself. In that time, he had mostly left her alone with spell books and her own thoughts. Surprisingly, he had even left her with a candle that never seemed to die out. She hadn't needed candles since she could now produce her own light, but the gesture hadn't gone unnoticed. The stronger she became and the more she knew how to defend herself, the less likely it was that Silas would blow up and hurt her. Every now and then, he would have a bad day and would barge into the cells in a particularly bad mood, throwing all kinds of magical attacks on her without warning that she had to block. Most of them connected, and she had to spend her time alone in a heap on the floor healing broken ribs and split lips. Silas said if he could attack her so easily, then anyone who wanted her magic could too. She needed to be prepared, but no matter how many times she tried to expect his assaults, he always took her by surprise.

Instead of crying and feeling empty about it, she found

herself frustrated when she failed and possessed a passion to do better so that she could finally leave the cells. Silas never mentioned when that would be, but he was warming to her now. She could tell from how his face betrayed him when he saw her fighting back, making his lips curl into a smile before he could stop himself.

The air seemed different today, like it held an electricity to it. The temperature had changed, and the air seemed somehow fresher, even in the dank smell of the dungeon. Sitting up on the mattress, Ana rubbed her eyes and yawned, looking at the pile of books Silas had left her. As she reached for one, her eyes fell on the cell door. Air was moving there, and a sparkling purple mist filled the space in the bars near the floor. A light flashed, and the purple fog drifted away. In its place sat a small silver plate with a slice of steaming pie.

Ana blinked a few times and rubbed her eyes, but the pie didn't budge.

"Great, now I am hallucinating," Ana mumbled as she moved on her hands and knees towards the door. Scents of apple, berries, cinnamon and sweet sugar worked their way into her nose and made her mouth water.

Sitting in front of it, Ana reached her hand out and awkwardly poked the pie with her finger to confirm it was solid. It was, and when she lifted the plate, a note lay on the floor under it. The paper was hastily torn and the writing was scrawled quickly, but she recognised it. She would recognise Ezra's handwriting anywhere.

Blessed Mabon, Ana.
I'm coming for you.
−E

Tears filled her eyes as she studied his handwriting. He wouldn't have risked doing the magic himself to get it here, so she knew he must have convinced Genevieve or Abby to do it for him. Knowing he was still thinking of her sent her heart thudding in her chest and her cheeks feeling hot.

She missed him.

She missed him *so much.*

Squeaking to her left near the bathroom brought her mind back into the room, and she smiled at the little mouse as it edged closer and closer.

"Party for two, huh?" she asked him with a smile, wiping her eyes and sniffling thickly.

Mister Nibbles crawled up her legs and her arms, making it to her shoulder and settling himself there while Ana broke off bits of the crust and fed them to him. Taking her own bite, Ana's eyes rolled into the back of her head happily. It had been so long since she tasted sugar, and it was *incredible*. Flavours burst into her mouth and made her moan. She covered her mouth with her hand with a small laugh.

"Blessed Mabon indeed, whatever that means." She smiled, her eyes searching for the books beside the mattress.

Lifting the plate, she walked back to the bed and settled down, pulling the book of Sabbats and Esbats onto her lap and flicking the pages open until she found the page for Mabon. She took another bite of the pie, then cleared her throat and read aloud.

"Mabon falls between the twentieth and twenty-second of September, depending on the calendar. It is the second harvest of the season and is the time in which a witch must celebrate the bounty of what the earth has given them during this time. It is a time for being thankful for the world around you, and you must bask in the blessings that have been bestowed upon you."

Ana scoffed, closing the book and lifting the pie in her hand so that she could give Mister Nibbles another piece of crust.

"The blessings around me, huh?" she asked, looking around her cold, dark cell, and rolled her eyes. "Some blessings."

Before she could finish the pie, Ana heard Silas opening the heavy door at the end of the corridor. She jumped to her feet, rushing with the plate in her hands into the bathroom, and finished it as quickly as she could. She didn't want Ezra getting in any more trouble if Silas were to find it.

"Where are you?" he demanded when he got to the cell door, his voice unamused and gruff.

Ana gulped and wiped the crumbs from her face, brushed down her clothes and then rushed out of the bathroom as he opened the lock and walked inside. "Can't a girl pee in peace?"

Silas looked unimpressed as he pushed the cell door open wider. "Since you had a bit of a breakthrough recently, I am moving your training up a level."

"Wait! Wait, before we do," Ana said, stepping to him and looking up into his face with a smile, "it's Mabon."

"Obviously," Silas said with a raised eyebrow. He stood still, waiting for her to continue her sentence, and when she didn't, he sighed in irritation and folded his arms. "So?"

"So, in order for me to properly give thanks for the blessings of harvest," she said, trying not to sound like she had no idea what she was talking about, "I would like to get out of the dungeons."

Silas rolled his eyes and dropped his hands, backing out of the cell. "You don't celebrate our holidays. Why should I care if you give thanks or not? What God are you giving thanks to? Do you even know what we practise here?"

"Ugh! Silas, please!" Ana begged, reaching out and grabbing his arm when he turned away from her. She tugged on the sleeve of his leather jacket to get his attention, but when he scowled at her, she dropped her hand and stepped away from him.

"Okay, so I don't really care about Mabon, but I *need* to get out of this cell. Please. Just for a moment! I want to walk outside and feel the sun on my face, and watch the sky and the trees, and feel the air. Just for a moment. *Please*."

"It's raining." Silas grunted, like that would explain why he was still not letting her through the door.

"Even better!" she answered. "I know you don't like me. I don't like you either, we are not friends, but it is your job to get my magic working, right? How can my magic work correctly if I'm not happy? It might work so much better if I can just get out of this depressing cell for two minutes. Please, Silas." She rested her hand on his crossed arms and looked up at him.

Silas narrowed his eyes, seeming to mull it over. Puffing out a deep sigh, he leaned forward and down so that his face was inches from hers. "If you run–"

"I won't. I promise," Ana replied with a wide smile.

"If you do," he continued, "I will chase you down and rip your spine out through your mouth."

"Okay. I believe you," Ana said, grinning.

Silas let out a breath against her face and stood back again. He shrugged her hands off his arms and turned to walk out of the cell, waving for her to follow him.

"Stay behind me," he ordered, then walked down the corridor towards the steps.

Ana's hands shook gently when she took her first few steps through the threshold. It almost felt wrong for her to be on the other side of the bars, like she was stepping into the real world for the first time. She hesitated at the doorway, staring at her feet as her heart skipped beats.

"If you take all day, I will throw you back inside."

Ana jumped into action before he could change his mind, taking off in a jog to chase him along the corridor and up the stone steps.

When Silas opened the heavy door, light burst into the corridor, making Ana gasp in pain as her eyes stung. The light washed over her eyes like acid, as if they were being seared from her skull if she kept them open too long. She shut them tightly, almost wishing for the darkness back, and reached her hand out to find something to hold on to. Surprisingly, instead of letting her bump into the chairs of the ballroom, Silas grabbed her hand and guided her. His hands were rougher than Ezra's, and they held her in a grip that she knew she would have no chance of ever getting loose from. He walked her through what she assumed were the main doors of House Alden, the cold air hitting her in the face and making her body shiver as Silas slowed to a stop.

Ana opened her eyes. It took them a long moment to adapt to the sting of sunlight after being in the dark cells for so long, but eventually, she stopped squinting long enough to look over the grounds. It was pouring with rain, and the air had a freshness to it. Gasping a thankful breath, she turned to look at Silas with a happy smile and stepped onto the grass.

The gardens of House Alden were simple, yet looking at them after staring at nothing except grey bricks sent tears into her eyes and made her throat tighten. The tall trees that ran along the edge of the cut lawns were now in shades of vibrant reds, oranges and yellows, and their leaves had blown off to litter the grass below. The mist in the air hung low, making the garden look somewhat eerie as it weaved its way around the trees and statues.

She laughed through a sob and trekked over the grass, turning with her arms out and spinning in the rain. She loved how the cool drops splashed on her face. They were cold and refreshing and felt like *life*. Opening her mouth and sticking out her tongue, she tried to catch the droplets with a laugh and then turned to look at Silas.

"Sit with me in the rain." Ana smiled, pointing to the little bench beside one of the trees.

"I am not sitting with you in the rain," Silas replied, his arms crossed tightly over his chest as he leaned against the wall.

"Silas. It is Mabon, and I want to sit with you in the rain. I am even willing to overlook the fact I hate you, because right now, I have no one else in the whole world to share it with. You *will* sit with me in the rain," Ana said, reaching to grab his arm and tug it. He didn't budge, no matter how many times she pulled on his arms. It was like he was made of stone.

"If I sit with you in the rain, will you come inside and get back to work?" he asked, looking down at her. "Without me having to break your bones?"

"Yes." Ana grinned.

She pulled him once more, and he finally sighed, kicking off the wall and sulking with her to the bench. The rain was coming down in a torrent, but it didn't seem to bother him as he slumped down to sit on the bench, one of his feet resting up on his knee as he slouched back.

"You have five minutes," he said.

"That's all I need." Ana tilted her head back and opened her mouth again to catch droplets in her mouth. She didn't normally act so silly, but the magic inside her yearned for play and made the blood in her veins pump faster and happier until she felt a giddy power in her chest. "Silas?"

He grunted in response, his arms folded. He was scanning his surroundings, like he was on edge.

"Can you tell me why Ezra was banned from using magic? Abby said he killed a human."

"He did. I was impressed, actually." Silas shrugged. "It was five years ago. Abby was sixteen; Ezra was twenty-two. He came home to find his sister with her boyfriend at the time. Abby was young and blind drunk, and her boyfriend was hurting her. Ezra lost control. I guess seeing a man hurting your sister would do that to you."

"That's horrible. No wonder Abby tried to change the subject when I asked her." Ana frowned as she looked up at him again. "What did he do to him?"

"I am not sure. All I know is his body was found in the Sullivan living room, with his skin missing. Every inch." Silas smirked. "Ezra and I don't get along *at all*, but that amused me. It didn't amuse the High Council, though. He was lucky his dad was the high priest, or he would have been executed."

Ana gulped thickly as she thought about Ezra and his temper when it came to those he loved. She had been on the receiving end of his temper once or twice and it was fierce, but she never thought he could do something like *that*.

"I don't believe it. Ezra would never kill anyone," she said, looking out along the garden towards the mansion.

"Ezra isn't as innocent as he likes people to believe. He is educated and somewhat talented when he could use his magic, but mark my words, Ana; he has his father in him."

Ana narrowed her eyes. "His father is an arrogant piece of shit."

"Exactly my point. Your five minutes are up," Silas said as he stood. "Are you coming willingly, or do I need to make this difficult for you?"

Silas led her back into House Alden and down into the dungeons again. She felt refreshed, and her magic was flowing happily in her veins. It felt tingly and cold and wonderful. He dried them both off from the rain with a wave of his hand as they reached the cell door, and Ana smiled up at him.

"Thank you. I needed that."

"Don't thank me just yet," Silas said as he took her by the arm and walked her past her cell.

He shoved her towards the next cell, making her stumble and look up at him in confusion. When he stopped her, Ana looked inside the new cell. It was completely bare aside from a mirror, and it smelled like fumes and chemicals.

"What is going on?" Ana asked.

"Your next lesson. If you do this correctly, I will let you sleep in your real room instead of that cell," Silas replied, reaching to his waist to unbuckle his belt. He opened it and dropped his weapons, then started to unbutton his trousers. "Take off your clothes."

"Excuse me?" she asked with a blink, looking him over with a shake of her head and a laugh. "Absolutely not."

"If I were you, I would seriously take off your clothes," Silas continued, pulling his shirt up over his head, and kicked off his heavy boots before dropping his boxers.

Ana's jaw dropped, and she had to clear her throat and look away from him quickly so that her eyes wouldn't wander over his body. She had, however, seen the muscles that rolled under his tanned skin. It was probably from all the training he did, or the killing.

"I will keep my clothes on, thank you," she announced, trying to keep her voice steady and hoping her face didn't get too red.

"Suit yourself." Silas shrugged and pushed her shoulder, making her stumble into the funny-smelling room.

He closed the cell door and turned to look at her as he stood completely naked and entirely comfortable in front of her, rolling his shoulders out as he readied himself. She looked up at him finally, a deep blush filling her cheeks and her heart beating faster when she saw the long silver scar over his chest from when she sliced him open. She was staring so long she almost didn't hear him when he started talking.

"Since you have already learned how to heal yourself, today you are going to learn how to do it faster," he said.

"What does that mean? What's that smell?" Ana insisted, sniffing the room.

"It's petrol. I am going to set the room on fire, and you are going to control it. You can heal yourself faster than it can hurt you. If you can, you will live long enough to get out of this cell and into the room upstairs. If you don't, you burn to death," he explained simply, opening his hands.

"N-no! Wait! Silas!"

Silas ignored her and clenched his fists, the muscles in his forearms tensing with the rest of his body. The floor erupted in flames, and she watched in horror as it crawled over the floor, the walls and ceiling as it ignited the fuel he had laced the room with. It was instantly searing hot, and Ana froze in panic as she watched him through the fire. Flames licked at her clothes, setting them alight as she tried to turn her body away from them, but they were *everywhere*. There was nowhere to go. Silas stood strong between herself and the door, and she knew she could not slip past him. He would never let her just *walk out*; he would sooner watch her burn to death.

"Silas! Please let me out! I can't do this!" Ana gasped, her eyes wild and her hands covering her hair and her head. A flame lashed around her trouser leg, burning her skin and making her scream. "It burns! Please, Silas!"

"Concentrate, Ana! Let your magic take over!" Silas shouted. He was completely calm, and the flames didn't seem to hurt him. They rolled over him like they were his friend, caressing his tanned skin and licking around his thighs and stomach.

Ana tried to calm her heart, and she closed her eyes, ignoring the heat on her face and the roaring of the flames. She had seconds to figure this out, or she was going to burn.

She reached down into her solar plexus with her mind, asking her magic for help, for it to take over and that it had her permission. It responded with a burst of ecstasy that filled her whole body. She opened her eyes, knowing they were black again, and looked down at her hands. Her skin was glowing, and her clothes were burning away, falling off her body and leaving her naked in front of him.

She looked up at Silas, and he was smiling at her. The flames that had now engulfed the whole room were licking at her calves and up her thighs, rolling over her skin like gentle tickling feathers. They hugged her body and curved up over her breasts and her arms, like they were trying to hug her.

Silas walked through the flames, and they made way for him until he was toe to toe with her, staring down at her. "Good. You learn quickly when you have to."

Ana gasped at how good the flames felt against her skin. It was intoxicating, filling her body with a need that burned her insides and made her reach out and rest her hands on his toned chest. She ran her fingers along the silver scar on his chest that she had caused, and a smile started to tug at her lips at the power she felt inside her.

"I have a good teacher. Mean, but good," Ana mumbled.

Silas took her chin in his hands and stared into her black

eyes, studying their darkness. "I have never seen magic do this to someone's eyes before."

He let her go and took her by the wrist, turning her around roughly and wrapping his arm around her middle. She gulped, feeling him press his chest up against her back as he took his free hand and held her jaw steady, forcing her to look at herself in the cracking mirror.

Ana pushed back against him and rested against his chest, her hands gripping his forearms around her middle as she watched their reflection in the mirror, their bodies engulfed in flames. She wasn't sure what was happening to her or why the flames intoxicated her. She didn't feel like herself, but instead, like some other more ethereal version of Ana had pushed through and taken over. She squirmed in his grip at how good her skin felt and examined his reflection in the mirror. He wore a wicked smile on his face.

"How do you feel?" he asked into her ear, his breath on her neck making her shiver.

Ana gulped thickly as her body trembled. Something about the flames did funny things to her magic, made her body shake and respond to him in a way she wasn't used to. It made her feel . . .

"Powerful." She grinned.

Silas smiled back at her and let her go, and she found when his skin wasn't pressed against hers, she missed the feel of his body. "Have fun in the flames. I will see you upstairs when you are finished." He backed out of the cell as Ana turned to look at him over the fire.

"Silas?" Ana panted, walking to him before he left, and took his hand, leaning up to kiss his cheek. "Thank you."

"You are welcome, Miss Davenport," he said, then walked out of the cell, leaving her to enjoy her nakedness in the tickling flames.

CHAPTER 13

*A*na spent a while playing in the flames, learning to sit within them and manipulate the fire by putting it out and starting it up again. Once she gave in to her magic and let it truly speak for her, the instincts Ezra had always raved about made sense, and she bent her magic to her will with a simple thought.

When she finished dancing, she let the flames die away completely and walked back into her own cell, changing into a new set of clothes from her bag and then throwing the strap over her shoulder. She grinned at the open cell door, a sense of pride filling her body as she walked down the corridor and left the dungeons.

Ana pushed open the heavy door, walking out into the ballroom and closing it behind her with a heavy thud. The room was mostly empty, and the chairs were all moved again so that they no longer looked like a courtroom. Instead, a long table rested along the back wall where the council table once stood. It had an altar cloth hanging over it that shimmered in reds and oranges, with tall pillar candles along the back that flickered and danced in the gentle breeze of the room. Right in the middle sat a stag skull, its antlers festooned with fallen autumn leaves, pinecones and acorns. Flanking each side of the skull were large crystal obelisks she couldn't recognise. One was yellow and white, and another was red and black with little flecks of gold inside it. She did recognise the tiger's eye column, which was huge and reflected the light in shimmers of browns and yellows. Instinctively, she reached out and ran her fingers along the smooth surface, a tingling shooting up her arm at the touch. Smiling, she turned to the end of the table, where the offerings lay on top of white cloths. Plates of apple and cherry pie, cinnamon cookies, honey bread and nuts stared back at her, making her stomach rumble. She knew they weren't for her, and that if they were sitting atop the offering table, then no one should touch them. That didn't mean she couldn't *smell* them.

Pulling her grimy hair back in her hands, she leaned over the table and breathed in the smell of the sugar and sticky fruits with a moan. Her mouth watered, and she had to take a few stumbling steps backwards to stop herself from eating them.

Ana walked to the space she had been when Abby first dragged her here, standing in the same spot where she had the ropes tied around her wrists. The last time she was here, she was a scared, dying little girl. Now, she felt like she was reborn after walking out of the flames below. Her body felt alive for the first time in years, and her head was swimming with possibilities. She grinned, scanning the room before she closed her eyes and clenched her fists at her sides, mentally saying goodbye to that scared little girl, then turned on her heel and walked through the door to the foyer.

Now that she was paying attention, Ana noticed how big the foyer of the gothic mansion was. It had black walls and high ceilings with massive dark wood staircases and deep red carpet that spanned every hallway. Large gilded gold frames littered the walls with pictures of battle scenes and portraits of people she didn't recognise in period clothing. Her footsteps echoed back to her as she walked to the bottom of the staircase and looked up, her eyes falling upon Silas, who was leaning on the banister with his elbows and looking at her as she marvelled at the paintings.

"You look different," Silas commented as he watched her walk up the stairs.

"It's funny what a little freedom can do to a woman," Ana replied as she made her way up the carpeted staircase and to his side. He was fully clothed again, donning his usual black shirt, dark jeans and leather jacket.

"Let's hope you are smart enough to stay free." He stood up straighter from where he was leaning. "This is a reward. If you slip back into being uncontrollable, I will put you straight back into those cells. Do you understand?"

"I understand, Silas," Ana said with a small sigh. "Though, I could use a bath and rest in a real bed, if you don't mind?"

Silas waved his hand for her to follow him. He led her down a few long corridors and to another large wooden door with a gold handle. Pushing the door open, he welcomed her inside and stepped back against the wall.

The room was *huge*. It had high ceilings, with black painted walls and a massive four-poster bed. Three archway windows gave way to a view of the front of the house and its gardens. Walking into the room and dropping her bag on the floor, she observed the crystal chandelier and gothic stone fireplace already lit and crackling.

"Are you kidding me?" Ana gasped, her eyes wide as she spun in the middle of the room to absorb every inch. There was a bathroom to the side of the room, and through the door, Ana could see a standing gold bath, his and hers sinks and a huge, gilded mirror.

"I have been stuck in that dirty cell for almost two weeks, and this was *right here*?!" she gawked, glaring at him and gritting her teeth.

Silas shrugged, appearing bored as she inspected the vanity table filled with perfumes, lotions and fancy creams. He tilted his head at her, then cleared his throat and uncrossed his arms.

"I need to go. I have my real job to attend to," Silas said as he moved to the door. "If you need anything, Abby will be getting out of the infirmary today. She will help you. In the meantime, keep practising your magic safely, and for gods' sake, take a bath." He flashed a teasing smile.

"Rude." Ana laughed, turning to look at him as he walked out of the door and closed it behind himself.

Sighing happily, Ana looked around her room one last time, then focused on the bed, where she slumped down on top of the sheets and moaned at how good they felt against her skin. They were soft and crisp, and she felt the aches and pains in her arms and legs begin to lift now that she wasn't on her feet or crouched on a stone floor. It was like she had forgotten what comfort truly felt like.

She rolled off the bed and walked into the bathroom. It was larger than any bathroom she had ever seen, which made her feel somewhat exposed as she undressed and turned the knob of the faucet on the golden tub. It filled quickly, the water steaming hot, and with the new magic in her body, she could get in without burning herself. It was like she could will her body to get used to it quicker.

Ana soaked for what seemed like hours, simply enjoying how the water purified her senses and fixed the aches in her bones. She scrubbed the ashes from her skin, paying particular attention to the two new silvery scars on her arm. Dried blood stuck to her flesh, and when she cleaned it from her skin, she sat up and peered down at the scars, smiling softly. She thought she would have hated having the reminders of magic on her forever, but looking at them filled her with a sense of pride she couldn't explain. Shaking herself awake from her daze, she finished washing her skin and hair, brushing out the knots before jumping out of the tub and reaching for the nearest towel to wrap around herself.

Walking back out into the bedroom, she moved to the wardrobe and opened it wide. Clothes for every occasion filled the inside. Jeans, T-shirts, gloves, a leather jacket, some skirts and a couple of dinner dresses hung from wooden hangers. Chunky boots and strappy heels lay on the bottom of the wardrobe beside a drawer specifically for underwear. She grabbed a bra and some pants and headed back to the bed, sitting down on the edge of it and pulling them on under the towel.

That was when she saw her phone sitting on the bedside table, fully charged and waiting for her. She gasped, scrambling over the sheets to pick it up in her hands as the screen illuminated. There were messages from Ezra, asking where she was and if she was okay, then there was a few days' break in the messages before he sent more, telling her he had just woken up from his sedation and was coming for her. Then the messages stopped. He must have realised she was imprisoned and couldn't reply.

She tapped on his name and pressed the phone to her ear in excitement as she waited for the phone to ring, but it cut off and she frowned, pulling it back down and looking at the screen. No reception.

"Damn it," Ana mumbled, setting the phone aside again. She needed to get a signal so that she could confirm he was okay.

She dressed quickly in a black skirt and a red sweater, pulling on the heavy black boots from the wardrobe and brushing through her wet hair before she grabbed her phone and ran out of the room. Holding the phone in the air, she walked around the top level of the house, eyeing the bars. None popped up, and she growled, stalking down the hall and to the balcony that looked over the entrance to the house.

"Ana?"

Abby was standing in the foyer, looking up at her with wide eyes. She had a blanket around her shoulders and slippers on her feet.

"Abby." Ana gasped, shutting off her phone and shoving it in her skirt pocket as she ran down the stairs to get to her. "Are you okay?"

Abby stepped back from her, holding her hands out in front. "That's close enough," she warned, pulling her hands back to grip the blanket draped around her.

"Abby . . ." she cooed with a frown, dropping her arms by her side and biting her lip as she reached the bottom of the stairs and stared at her feet uncomfortably. "I'm sorry I hurt you. You know I didn't mean to, don't you?"

"I ended up in a coma for days, Ana. I am still *freezing*," Abby replied, her teeth bared. Dark circles were ringing Abby's eyes, and her face was pale.

"Abby, I am so sorry." She tucked her damp hair behind her ears. "I didn't do it on purpose. I couldn't control it, but I can now. See?" she said, holding her hands up to show her nothing weird was happening around her.

Abby shifted on her feet. Finally, she let out a deep sigh and walked down the corridor to the left, away from the ballroom and the stairs. "I am going to the kitchens. I haven't eaten in days.

You don't look like you have eaten in *weeks*, so if you want food, you better come with me."

A smile spread across Ana's face as she watched Abby walk down the corridor. At the mention of food, her stomach rumbled, and she quickly followed after her. The corridor was long, with dark wooden floors and arched windows covered with deep red curtains, plunging the corridor into darkness that was only illuminated by the candles on the walls.

"Someone certainly doesn't like sunlight," Ana commented as she caught up to Abby. "It's like a crypt in this place."

"The Aldens like it that way. Something about darkness and mystery," Abby said with a roll of her eyes.

Abby led Ana through a door to a large clean kitchen, which had ovens and tables set out for visitors. In the middle of the room, a large wooden table held silver platters filled with food of all kinds. There was roast chicken, potatoes, fries, a mountain of roasted vegetables, a massive chocolate cake and wine in crystal bottles. Ana's mouth dropped open at the scene, and she felt her blood boil with anger.

"That bastard had all this food up here, and he left me starving for *days*?" Ana asked, her hands in fists as she approached the table. "I am going to kill him."

"I tried. He said you needed a clear head. I'm not sure how not feeding you helped, but it must have if you are up here and not in those cells," Abby explained as she walked around the table and lifted two silver plates, handing her one.

Ana shook her head as she walked around the table, scooping fries and chicken legs onto her plate, then taking a slice of cake. All the food was still warm, which made her tilt her head in confusion. The kitchen didn't have a chef, nor were any of the ovens on. "Has this just been made?"

"No," Abby replied, struggling to fill her plate while weakly holding on to her blanket. "It is made in the morning; the house's magic keeps it fresh and warm for the Venator. We come here to train and for meetings and assignments, so there can be quite a few hungry mouths needing to be fed at one time in House Alden."

Ana finished plating her food before she lifted a tray and placed her plate on it, then took Abby's.

"Why don't I carry all this upstairs for us, and you can eat with me in my room in front of the fire?" Ana suggested, lifting a couple bottles of crystal wine with a wiggle of her eyebrow. "And maybe get a little drunk?"

Abby chewed on her lip. "Are you sure your magic is controlled?"

"I promise." Ana smiled, putting the bottles on the tray beside the plate. "Come on, Abby. I need some girl time, and by the look of you, you need someone to take care of you. There isn't much of that going on around here. Let me make it up to you. Please?"

Abby sighed and nodded, hugging the blanket tighter. "All right, I guess you do owe me."

Ana led Abby out of the kitchens and all the way up the steps of the house. When she guided her to her room, she set the tray on a table beside the fire, pulled all the blankets from the bed onto the floor and tucked them in neatly. After helping Abby to the floor, Ana propped pillows behind her so that she was sitting upright against the chair to ensure her comfort, then handed her a plate before taking her own and slumping down in front of the fire beside her.

"Thank you," Abby said, giving her a small smile as she glanced sideways at her and ate her bowl of fries.

"You are welcome," Ana replied, sighing happily as she lifted one of the wine bottles. She pulled the crystal topper and set it aside, then took a large gulp of wine from the bottle with a happy hum.

"Straight from the bottle?" Abby blinked.

Ana held up her finger and continued her long gulp. She finally pulled it away, covered her mouth with her hand and laughed, offering Abby the bottle. "I have been through literal hell, so yes. Straight from the bottle."

Abby took the bottle and tipped her head back, taking a much smaller swig than Ana had before she passed it back and studied her face with an expression Ana couldn't place. "What happened to you after I passed out?"

Ana shrugged uncomfortably and took another mouthful of the wine to collect her thoughts. "Silas was angry that I hurt you. He didn't come back for days. I thought he had left me to die, if I am honest, but he came back eventually." She pulled the sleeve of her sweater up to reveal the silver scars on her arm. "You were right. He is a cruel man. He kept slicing me open with that stupid knife of his until I learned how to heal."

Abby blinked, the chicken leg in her hand hovering near her mouth. "Seriously?"

"Uh-huh," Ana said, pulling her sleeve down and setting the bottle aside so that she could eat some of the chocolate cake from her plate. "And today, he threw me in a room full of fire, which was terrifying but actually kind of fun." She smiled. "I am just glad I am out of my cell. He is a psychopath, but I guess he knows what he is doing. I feel fine now."

"Yeah." Abby took a bite of her chicken and wiped her mouth with a napkin, tucking the purple bits of her hair behind her ears. "Ezra came to see me when I woke up. Silas wouldn't let him go down to see you, and Ezra went *nuclear*. The Venator had to restrain him. I have never seen him so angry before."

"He did?" Ana asked. Her smile turned sad, and she set her

cake aside to pick at the bottle's label. "I've missed him *so much*, Abby. He is the only thing that kept me from wanting to give up in that cell. But now I am out of it, that makes me nervous."

"Why?" Abby shoved a fistful of fries into her mouth. "The man is obsessed with you."

Ana shook her head. "No. He is just a really good friend. He is protective, that's all."

"Protective?" Abby snatched the wine bottle from her and took a gulp of it. "He is in *love* with you. How can you not see that?"

"Because he told me as much back at the house. He said he wanted to just be friends. I think almost killing him one too many times was too much for him." Ana cleared her throat and blinked away the tears in her eyes. "I think I scare him."

She wouldn't admit it to Abby, but Ezra rejecting her had made her doubt everything she felt for him. She knew he did it because it was the smart thing to do, but when he pushed her away, her heart had folded in on itself and collapsed.

"I don't want to talk about men, or magic. I just want to get blind drunk and pass out in front of the fire. Can you do that with me? Please?" Ana asked, wiggling her brow and handing the bottle back.

Abby sighed, a smile creeping across her face as she reached for the second bottle and opened it. "Fine, but for the record, no one takes lashings for a woman they don't love."

Ana tried not to think about Ezra and the lashings he received for helping her. Instead, she tipped her head back and downed the rest of the bottle of wine until her thoughts ceased, her head was swimming and her body felt blissfully numb.

CHAPTER 14

"What the hell is going on?"

Ana blinked awake from her spot in front of the embers left smouldering in the fireplace. Shouting voices filled the hallways outside the room. They sounded rushed and angry, and they made Abby jump up and steady herself.

Ana and Abby had been drinking and laughing for hours until their sides were sore and their heads were swimming. They must have passed out, because when Ana wet her dry lips with a wince, she grabbed her phone to check the time.

3:04 a.m.

"Damn it." She yawned, grabbing Abby's hand to help pull herself to her feet. She wobbled, still somewhat tipsy. "I feel woozy."

"Yeah, you drank a lot," Abby mumbled, watching the door. "Something's happening. I need to go."

Ana blinked when Abby bolted for the bedroom door, throwing it open and disappearing over the threshold. "Abby! Wait!"

She didn't come back, and Ana tripped over her unsteady feet as she followed after her. She rushed down the hallways and to the balcony, looking down to the foyer, where all hell was breaking loose. Men in leather jackets were holding the heavy doors of House Alden open, appearing angry and shouting words she couldn't make out. Silas emerged, walking into the foyer with an expression of rage across his face and a rope in his hands. On the other end of the rope, with his wrists bound together and his nose and head bleeding badly, was Alexander Sullivan.

Alexander stumbled inside the house when Silas yanked on the rope. He sank to his knees and panted in pain, his face pale and bruised. He had been beaten badly, and his chest heaved up and down unevenly.

"Dad?" Abby gasped. She was shaking, her face blanching.

Ana wrapped an arm around Abby's shoulders as she watched Silas hand the rope off to one of his men. They pulled Alexander to his feet, and he stared straight at Abby on the balcony, his eyebrows slacking. He didn't even look at Ana, or more likely, he didn't recognise her.

"Abby?" He struggled against his binds. "Abby, baby, it's okay."

The men pulled on the rope hard, dragging him through the foyer into the ballroom.

Ana turned to look at Abby, holding her closer to her side and trying to keep her from trembling. The scar on her stomach itched in remembrance of the last time she had seen Alexander, but she tried to push the idea of him out of her head to focus on her friend. "Are you okay?"

"I need to see him," Abby said, starting to cry while her shoulders trembled in Ana's hands. "I need to talk to him."

"Are you sure that is a good idea?" Ana asked.

"He is my father, Ana. I know he did bad things, but he's still my *dad*." She gritted her teeth, shrugging Ana off her shoulders when she saw Silas ascending the staircase.

Silas's face was pulled in a grimace of anger that made his features dark, and his eyes held a hatred in them that surprised her. He was cradling his arm under his leather jacket, but otherwise, he seemed fine.

"I need to see my dad," Abby said as she pulled away from Ana completely and confronted him. "Please. I just want to talk to him."

"He's a criminal. You are no longer his daughter, Abby. You are a member of my team, so I need you to act like it. Go back to bed."

"I can do both! Please, let me see him."

Silas narrowed his eyes, looking between them both and seeming to consider it for a moment until he saw Ana wobble. His scowl deepened. "Are you drunk?"

"Blind drunk," Ana confessed as she moved to them and tried to hold Abby back, but she stiffened and set her face, snapping her eyes back to Silas.

"I am fine. I am sober enough, and I can keep my composure. I promise. Let me see my dad," Abby ordered.

Silas sighed, his shoulders sagging as he pinched the bridge of his nose. "You can talk to him through the bars. His trial is tomorrow. If he goes missing, Abby–"

"I am not stupid, Silas!" Abby shouted, pushing past him and rushing down the stairs in a flurry of black and purple hair.

Silas sighed, shaking his head and cradling his arm again as he limped down the corridor and opened one of the doors to disappear inside.

Ana looked torn. She wanted to follow Abby, but she knew her magic was unstable *at best*, and she wasn't sure how it would react if she saw Alexander face-to-face. Instead, she followed Silas to his room and opened the door, poking her head inside.

Silas was standing beside his fireplace, peeling his leather jacket off with a wince and throwing it on the floor roughly. His arm was wounded with a coiled burn that looked like a snake that worked from his wrist to his elbow. It was sizzling, like it was eroding the skin. She watched quietly as he raised his other hand to heal it, but it sparked and burned deeper, making him growl.

"What happened?" Ana asked softly.

Silas grunted as he turned away from her and walked towards the alcohol cabinet near the back wall. He grabbed a crystal decanter from the shelf and filled a glass with whiskey, bringing it to his mouth and downing it with a hiss. He filled it again before looking over his shoulder at her with a scowl. "Get out."

Ana rolled her eyes and stepped into the room anyway, closing the door behind her and folding her arms. "You are hurt."

"Yet again, you are perceptive," Silas said, downing his second glass and refilling it. "But apparently you are deaf too. I said, Get out."

"I am not going anywhere, so you might as well sit down and let me look at your arm. It needs to be cleaned," Ana said as she walked toward him with a stumble in her step.

Silas flashed her a look that made her stop. He approached his large leather lounge chair and sat down, watching her from behind his dark eyes. "You are drunk, and this is a magical wound. It cannot be healed." When she shot him a look of confusion, he let out a deep sigh. "Alexander got a hold of my whip and used it to defend himself. My arm caught it."

Ana's shoulders dropped as she walked to him, sinking to her knees beside him and reaching to lay her fingers on his arm. He flinched and growled deep in his chest, narrowing his eyes at her, but he didn't speak.

"Don't be such a baby," she scolded.

She reached to touch his wound again, and he grabbed her wrist, twisting it hard and forcing her hand to release him. "I did not ask for your help, Ana."

"That's the thing about decent people, Silas. You help without needing to be asked. Now, you are going to let go, and I am going to heal your wound with the fancy new magic you helped me unlock, okay?"

"It won't work," Silas said, letting her hand go roughly.

"Shut up and let me try."

Ana watched him as he took another sip of his whiskey, looking away from her to focus on the wall. She frowned, studying the wound on his arm with narrowed eyes. The skin was charred and red, and it was bleeding where the cracks in the burned skin were coming apart. She wrinkled her nose and focused, closing her eyes and digging deep down into her magic. The wine had dulled her senses, though, and she found it hard to hear. After a few moments, she cracked one of her eyes open, peering down at the burn. Nothing had happened.

Silas chuckled from somewhere deep inside his chest and sipped at his whiskey again. "I told you. It is impossible."

"I am trying! You told me to practice, right? Sit still," Ana snapped.

Ana gulped and focused again, wriggling her fingers as she held them above his arm once more, concentrating as hard as she could on the whirling in her solar plexus. It sparked awake, and she smiled, the corners of her eyes going black until it filled her vision completely and her palm glowed. Silas's arm tensed as he noticed the glow, and he turned to look at her as she worked, confusion washing over his face as his arm began to heal. The skin near his elbow knitted together, working all the way around in a glittering silver balm, down over his large forearm and to his wrist. When the glowing stopped and she retracted her hand, he lifted his arm up to his face to inspect it. A thick, silvery scar remained all the way up his arm, but it was completely healed.

"How?" Silas grunted, dropping his arm to eye her suspiciously.

Ana shrugged and stood, watching him through her black eyes. "Practice."

"It is impossible. You cannot heal a magical wound," Silas argued as he took another sip of his drink and shot up from the chair.

"I'm special, remember?" She snatched his glass, downing the rest of his whiskey with a wince. "But I know how you can repay me."

He folded his arms across his chest, and she could see he was trying not to look down at his new scar as he waited for her to state her demands.

Ana grinned. "I want you to teach me influence."

He sighed impatiently and grabbed his empty glass out of her hand so that he could walk around her to refill it from the alcohol cabinet. His jaw was tight, like he was unnerved by his new scar, or more likely, what it meant that she could heal it. "I already told you that it is a little above your paygrade."

"I just healed a wound that was impossible to heal! Let me try!" Ana reasoned, following him.

"It's not exactly the most moral kind of magic, Ana. You are forcing your will into someone else's body to make them do what you want. It is not something to be trifled with."

Ana sniggered, her nose wrinkling with her smile. "You aren't the most moral person yourself, Silas."

He filled the glass to the brim. "Why is this so important to you?"

Ana pouted and tilted her head at him, her hands clenching

and unclenching at her sides. She wasn't sure why, but tears were springing to her eyes, and her face was growing hot. A hangover was looming somewhere around her forehead, like it might just drop upon her any second.

"I guess when Alexander did it to me, it felt like an invasion of my body that I've never felt before. It was like he had taken all of my freewill, I was completely vulnerable. He could have made me do *anything*, Silas. He tried to kill me using that magic." She sniffled, squirming on her feet. Silas raised the glass to his lips but let it hover. "It feels like when he did that to me, my actions haven't been my own since. I want to know how he did it so that I can gain control of my life again."

He took a sip of his whiskey, set the glass down on the mantle and turned back to her. A deep frown settled on his face, but his eyes held a compassionate look. "Fine."

Silas moved back to her again and took her by the shoulders, guiding her into the centre of the room. He let her go and took a step back to put his hands on his hips.

"You need to completely empty your mind and force your magic to connect to the person's brain. It is harder than it looks, and you need to do it with your eyes. Search theirs for their response, reach into their reason and completely break it. Once you have latched on to their reason and they are open to your influence, you can ask for what you want. But if you are going to do it, you need to be fast before they can refuse you. Usually, you can tell when it is working because your magic will flash in your eyes, but yours are different. I can't tell when yours is working because your eyes are–"

"Like this," Ana said, pointing to her eyes, the whites still completely black from when she healed him. Her magic was still rolling in her stomach, and she knew her eyes wouldn't return to normal until it settled again.

"Like that." Silas nodded. "Look in my eyes. Reach into my head. Break my reason. I won't refuse it. I will let you, this time," Silas said, completely relaxing his shoulders.

Ana smiled, then tried to force it away so that she could focus. She let her magic build up until it was rumbling inside her, and she willed it to push out and into him. She wasn't sure what *reason* was supposed to look like or feel like, but she figured her magic would sense it and take over, like it had been doing this whole time.

Her body flinched as she focused on his dark eyes and into his head, and then she felt it, his reason right there, like a bubble waiting to be penetrated. It was as if it was hard to miss now that she was looking for it. She grabbed onto it with her mind and severed it, grinning when his eyes drooped. He didn't flinch, speak, or blink. He stood there, suspended in a way that took her by surprise.

Silas was *vulnerable*.

Ana opened and closed her mouth a few times, like she wasn't quite sure what to ask him to do. In this state, she could make him do anything. She could make him jump out the window or kill someone with a simple request.

The gravity of the situation pushed down on her shoulders. He was right. This wasn't moral or as much of a power trip as she expected it to be. She felt cruel, having him here in the palm of her hand when he could do nothing about it.

Just like Alexander had done to her.

She tilted her head, watching how calm and even his breathing was before a smile draped over her lips. If she morally couldn't do anything else to him, then at the very least she could get her revenge.

"Take off your shirt," she commanded, remembering the same request he had given her in the cells.

Silas crossed his arms at the hem of his black shirt and pulled it up over his body, throwing it to the side and onto the floor. She blushed, her heart beating faster as she allowed herself to look over him. His chest was toned, and the scar she had given him that ran along his skin there stared back at her. Heat pulsed in her body, the telltale signs that her magic needed sedating. Maybe it was the wine talking, or how good that raging magic felt, but he looked good. He looked *really good*.

"Come here."

Silas closed the space between them and looked down at her, his hair falling in front of his face. His brows were knitted together like he was trying to break from her influence, but she had him trapped. A rush of adrenaline ran through her as she raised her hand and placed her fingertips on his scar, running them down the length of it.

"Kiss me," Ana mumbled, looking up at him. Silas hesitated, and she smiled. "Now."

Silas pulled her against him roughly and leaned down into her, kissing her hotly and holding her against his hard chest. His beard tickled her face, and she smiled, but somewhere along the way in kissing him, she felt cold.

He was rugged, and while she should enjoy kissing him, his arms didn't fit in the right places and something inside her stomach felt wrong.

"I don't like you," Ana said as she kissed him again. "I think you are cruel and rude." She bit down on his lip, and somewhere along the way, her influence on him slipped and he wrapped his arms around her tighter.

"I don't like you either. You are childish and irritating," he responded now that he was free, but he still kissed her.

His kiss was hard and firm, and he held her in a way that made her unable to sink into his arms. They weren't soft and cradling like Ezra's. His kiss wasn't passionate and intoxicating. His hands didn't cup her face and snake their way into her hair the way Ezra's had.

Ana's heart pulled so hard in her chest it made her knees weaken and her head lighter. Tears sprung to her eyes behind their lids, and she fluttered them open, pulling back from Silas and placing her finger against his lips when he leaned in again. She sniffled and tilted her head, giving him an apologetic half-smile.

She forced her magic to calm into a gentle rumble, its influence on her eyes and vision fading away so that her normal blues returned to the surface. Her magic reacted when she was around Silas. It wanted him *badly*, but her heart didn't.

Her heart wanted Ezra.

"Silas," she started.

He sighed deeply, his arms relaxing from around her to let her go. "Ezra?"

Ana nodded as she cleared her throat. He rolled his eyes and tried to turn away from her, but she reached out for his hand. Then she smiled softly at him, raised up on her tiptoes and pulled him down to kiss his cheek.

"Thank you, for everything you have taught me." She nuzzled his cheek and let him go.

Silas didn't answer her. Instead, he squeezed her hand and then let her go, returning to where he left his whiskey glass on the mantle. He grabbed it and tipped his head back, draining it as he stood shirtless in front of the fire while Ana backed out of the room quietly.

Making her way back to her room, she closed her door and locked it. Her hangover was back now that the magic inside her had fallen asleep again, and the closer she got to her bed, the weaker her knees became. She grabbed her phone, then undressed and slipped under the crisp cotton sheets. Laying her head down on the pillow and curling up on her side, she unlocked her phone. If Alexander's sentencing was tomorrow, then Ezra would be here to witness it. Her heart tugged, and a smile spread across her face in excitement as she sent him a message.

"*I miss you.*"

To her surprise, it sent, and she watched as the little bubbles at the side of the screen started moving, indicating Ezra had seen it and he was replying.

"*I miss you too.*
Tomorrow, Davenport. Xx"

CHAPTER 15

Knocking on the door awoke Ana with a start from her sleep. She had slept like she was lying on a cloud. Sleeping on the stone floor of the cells had hurt her body in places she did not know existed, yet resting for a mere night on soft cotton sheets repaired the aches that had settled in her bones.

Snapping up in the bed, she looked around the room and took a moment to rub the sleep from her eyes. Light was shining through the gap in the curtains, but she wasn't sure what time it was. Ana yawned, unable to wipe the radiant smile off her face.

Knocking pounded on the door again as she slipped out of the bed, her bare feet slapping against the wooden floor.

"What took you so long?" Abby asked when the door opened. "The coven is arriving, people are filling the courtyard, and Ezra will be looking for you. If you want to see him before the trial starts, you need to move your butt."

Ana smiled as she jumped in excitement. Abby shooed her back into the room, then disappeared down the hallway. Closing the door, she changed into new clothes as quickly as she could, brushing her teeth and spraying herself with some of the fancy perfume sitting on the vanity. After applying makeup for the first time in what felt like forever, she pulled on her black boots and ran out of the room.

Chattering people filled the foyer. The air seemed anxious and electric, and some of their faces even held expressions of fear that pulled the colour from their cheeks and knitted their brows together. She wasn't sure where the courtyard was but figured it was in the direction that the crowd was walking. She rushed down the staircase and joined the end of the line, following them down the corridor to two large stained-glass doors that were propped open. The courtyard was on the other side, with rows of chairs that were filling with muttering people. The Council table was positioned near the front, facing the crowd, and a raised stage stood beside it, with a wooden pole standing in the middle.

When the crowd found their seats, Ana's eyes searched the Council table. Genevieve sat to the left, looking somewhat regal in her beautiful purple robe. Beside her sat Anora, who was wearing a black off-the-shoulder dress that seemed wholly inappropriate for a trail. She was inspecting the ruby rings on her fingers with a bored expression. Walking down the aisle, Ana caught Genevieve's eye, and Genevieve waved, her face looking concerned even though she was trying to smile through it.

Ana waved back before seeing Abby sitting in the front row near the middle. A tall man with broad shoulders sat beside her, his head forward and his floppy dark hair falling over his face.

Ezra.

Ana's heart stopped beating in her chest. Her feet froze to the stones of the courtyard, tears springing to her eyes when she saw

Abby turn to look at her. She jutted Ezra in the side, then pointed over his shoulder towards her.

Ezra looked over his shoulder, and their eyes connected. For a long agonising moment, Ana almost thought he didn't recognise her. He stuck to his seat, his face awash with an emotion she couldn't place. Finally, he stood from his chair, toppling it over as he did, then squeezed his sister's hand to excuse himself and rushed to the aisle.

"Ezra . . ." Ana hiccupped, pushing past the last few stragglers to run to him.

She leapt onto him in a hug, his arms enveloping her and lifting her off the ground as he tucked his face into the crook of her neck.

"Ana." He sighed, his tone had a wateriness to it, like he was struggling with something, but with what, she didn't know. "Are you okay?"

Ezra set her down, but he didn't let her go. He held her cheek close to his chest and rested his chin atop her head, his arms tightening around her as she burst into tears and clung to his black collar shirt with tight fists.

"Y-yeah." She sniffled against his chest, breathing deeply and enjoying how good he felt in her arms. He smelled like a home she never knew she yearned for, and it was because she felt safe when she was with him. The sound of his voice and the flash of his smile made the rest of the world melt away. "I am now."

Ezra pulled back from the hug to gaze into her face. His eyes seemed watery, but he did a good job of hiding it behind the flash of his handsome smile. He reached to poke her nose gently, then tucked her hair behind her ears. "I'm sorry I couldn't come for you. I tried, but every time I came, they kicked me o–"

"Whatever the hell this is, can it wait until later? The trial is starting," Silas snapped from behind them. He pushed past them both and walked down the aisle, then disappeared somewhere near the wall at the back.

He was right. They were the only ones left standing in the middle of the aisle. She tried not to blush when she noticed how many eyes had glued onto them. Ezra didn't seem to notice or care. He was staring after Silas with a deep frown, but he regained his composure, taking Ana's hand and leading her back down the aisle and to their seats beside Abby. He kept a hold of her hand on his lap, then reached to his other side and took his sisters. Abby seemed scared, and she held onto her brother with tight fists and eyes that threatened tears.

The voices in the courtyard quietened to a murmur as Thaddeus glided through the stained-glass doors. He walked down the aisle and across the stoned pathway towards his seat in the middle of the Council table. He stood in front of his chair for a moment until the crowd finally fell silent, then folded his hands in front of him.

"Council members, coven members, thank you for coming to today's trial. Last night, the Venator finally caught up with former high priest Alexander Sullivan. He was apprehended and returned here to face justice for the crimes he has committed. We will be speaking to the accused directly. Please refrain from raising your voices until we are finished." He extended his arm toward the door. "Silas!"

The door on the stone wall to the right near the house opened, and Silas walked out, a rope in his hand. He pulled on it, and Alexander stumbled out into the sun, the rope wrapped around his middle. He held his good arm in against his body, his ashen arm still hanging dead at his side. His eyes were closed, like the light hurt them, and his face was badly bruised. Dried blood nestled around his mouth and in his beard, and his frame was thin, like he hadn't eaten while on the run. Ezra's hand flinched in hers when he saw his father, but otherwise, he didn't move as Silas pulled Alexander towards the raised stage. He tugged him faster up the steps and then grabbed him by the shoulder, shoving him to his knees. He stood beside him, the rope in his hands, and kept an eye on him as if he was waiting for a reason to rip his head from his shoulders.

Alexander kept his head down, only looking up when Thaddeus spoke again.

"You have been accused of two counts of murder and one count of attempted murder. You did so to take the magic from the Marion coven athame for yourself and attempted to commit the highest crime of all: exposing our world to the humans. How do you plead?"

Alexander sighed. "Guilty, and I regret nothing."

He looked over the mumbling crowd to lock eyes with his children, and he tried to give them a smile but it was shaky. Ezra squeezed Ana's hand harder when his eyes connected with his father's, and she gripped it back to steady him. Her heart was beating hard in her chest when she tried to look at Alexander, but every time she did, the scar on her stomach stung and tears pooled in her eyes.

"If you have anything to say before we sentence you, now would be the time," Thaddeus replied, finally sitting down in his chair.

Alexander gulped thickly and tried to clear his throat, but it sounded dry and hoarse. He moved to stand from his knees, but Silas placed his foot to his back and kicked him down again. He gritted his teeth and sighed, glaring back at Silas with a scowl, then turned to look at the audience.

"I was the high priest of this coven. I have spent my entire life trying to convince you all that *now* is the time to come out of the shadows and into the light. There is no reason we need to be second-class citizens in a world we know better than humans. We deserve more than that. With the magic held inside that athame, I was going to take it into myself and free our coven from our confines. The deaths that occurred on the way to that conclusion were a means to an end. I didn't enjoy them; it just needed to be done. And Ana . . ."

Alexander looked at her finally, his eyes boring into her. Her heart quickened as she watched him take a few steadying breaths, his jaw tightening while he shook his head and continued.

"I needed blood, but I was too hasty with the translation. I didn't realise the blade needed the blood of the person who intended to take the magic. That was a mistake and I lost my arm for it, but if my plan had gone correctly, then I would have contained that magic and we would be unstoppable. We cannot stay in the dark anymore. We must take our rightful place."

"Your hubris is your weakness, Alexander, and it is your downfall," Thaddeus responded simply.

"The only thing I am sorry for is for my children. Abby, Ezra, I love you both, more than *anything*. I know you are ashamed of me, but if you could find it in yourselves to forgive me and come to see me in my cell, I will explain further. There are things you need to know that have not been explained."

"There will be no cell for you, Alexander," Thaddeus announced. "You have pleaded guilty, and the Council has decided that your crimes warrant execution. Silas, the stake."

Hushed voices filled the air as Silas pulled the rope, bringing Alexander to his feet and towards the pole in the middle of the stage, binding him as he struggled. Ezra stood from his seat quickly, dropping Ana's hand and gaping at his father. The voices in the courtyard became loud and erratic, echoing off the bricks in a chorus of confusion.

"Thaddeus, please. You can't do this!" Ezra said, looking

between the high priest and his father with wide eyes. "I have absolutely no love left for my father, but this is barbaric! The punishment for his crimes is imprisonment for life. *This* makes us just as bad as he is. Can't you see that?"

"Your father has been deemed too dangerous to live, Ezra. He could potentially break out of any magical binding we perform on him. He is *barely* contained inside the one we have on him now. He was one of the strongest members of this coven; you know this. We cannot risk letting him go. I am sorry."

"Wait! Wait, please! You don't understand. I need to speak!" Alexander shouted, struggling against his bindings with a growl. Silas pulled the ropes tighter. "It is about the magic! It is dangerous! It wasn't what I thought it was. You need to listen to me!"

"Silas is dealing with it, and he assures me it is being handled," Thaddeus responded as he stood from his chair.

Alexander laughed, giving up on struggling. He rested his head tiredly against the stake and grinned, flicking his eyes between Ana and Thaddeus.

"It is handled because she thinks she has control over it? You have no idea what you are dealing with. The control she has on it will not hold for very long. I went to what is left of the Marion coven. I needed to see if there was any way I could transfer her magic to me. They had very interesting things to tell me about the magic they stored in that stone." He laughed. "If any of you hope to survive it, you need me alive."

"Elaborate," Thaddeus ordered through gritted teeth. The coven was now on their feet, some throwing their hands in the air and others shouting their agreements.

"Sentence me to life in prison, and I will tell you." Alexander panted.

"Dad!" Ezra shouted. Alexander looked at his son, who took a few extra steps towards the stage, his hands out toward him in a pleading gesture. "If this is about Ana, you need to tell me. If you want my forgiveness, you need to tell me *now*. Please, Dad."

Ana stood from her chair, watching the events unfold with wide eyes. Her magic was thundering loudly in her stomach, like it wanted to break free, but she kept it at bay, letting it heat her hands against her thighs instead of bursting.

Alexander gritted his teeth. He squeezed his eyes shut, like he was battling between wanting his son's forgiveness and keeping his secret close to his chest. Finally, he buckled, puffing out a sigh.

"I am sorry, Son. The magic inside the stone was *dark* magic. I didn't know when I attempted to take it for myself. If I had known, I would never have tried. It was also never supposed to be contained inside one person; it was meant for a multitude of people. Sooner or later, it is going to get too much for her, and the darkness of the magic will consume her. Either she will die from the pressure, or her body will not be her own. She will go dark, Ezra. She will be taken over by the magic inside her and no longer *be* Ana. She will be a body for the darkness, and nothing will stop the havoc it causes. Then the world will know we exist, in the worst way."

Ezra snapped his head over his shoulder to look at Ana. His eyes were wide, and he gulped before turning his head back to his father. "No. That can't happen. If we take her to them, will they help us?"

"I can take you to them. I had a deal with them. If I take you to them now, they should help you, but we don't have much time. Please, let me go."

Thaddeus cleared his throat and ran his hand through his long beard, his eyebrows furrowed and mouth pulled into a concerned frown. "You have already been given your sentence, Alexander. Thank you for your candour. Silas, the kindling."

Silas grabbed sticks and kindling from the side of the raised stage, positioning them around Alexander's feet. Abby was crying hysterically from her seat as she watched Silas build the pyre around the stake. She stood, leaving Ana alone as she ran for her brother, taking his hand and trying to hug him when he shouted and protested.

"Thaddeus! You are a better man than this. Don't be like him!" Ezra pleaded. "He gave us the information we needed, and he is willing to take a lifetime in the cells as punishment. *Please.*"

Thaddeus ignored him while Silas finished building the pyre and jumped off the stage, walking towards Ana with his hand extended.

"Time to prove you have mastered your fire magic," Silas said.

Ana blinked in shock as she looked down at his hand. Her heart quickened in her chest as she looked between Silas and Ezra, then flicked her eyes to Alexander. The magic in her stomach growled with a fierce fury when she realised what Silas was asking her to do. "You want me to burn Alexander? I-I can't. I won't."

"Do you want to stay out of that cell? Do you want to live long enough to find the magic that can cure you if he is right?" he asked, then extended his fingers when she nodded. "Then you need to do this. You need to prove to Thaddeus whose side you are on if you want any kind of future here, and you need to make Alexander pay for putting you here in the first place."

Ana's magic was thundering in her ears, beating hard against her skull as it willed her to let it out. She knew if she didn't, then she was going to lose control in front of the whole coven. The idea of her magic reaping her revenge sent her head spinning, and before she knew what she was doing, she was taking his hand.

"Ana . . ." Ezra muttered, horror written all over his face as he turned to her, his eyes watery. "Ana, don't. You can't! He needs to pay, I agree, but not like this. *Please*"

"I have to," Ana whispered, releasing Silas's hand so that she could approach Ezra and take his instead. "I haven't got a choice."

"Ana, there is always a choice! Please!" Ezra grasped her hands tightly. "This isn't you; this is the magic talking. Don't let them turn you into a murderer."

"Like you, you mean?" Silas scoffed, folding his arms and waiting.

Ana shot him a warning look, then turned back to Ezra. "If something is wrong with my magic, then I am going to need their help. I need to prove to them I can handle it. You don't need to watch this, Ezra. You should go."

Ezra's eyes softened as his grip weakened. He let her go, then turned to pull his sister into his side and hugged her. He pulled her towards the aisle, but she refused, sinking her heels into the gravel and watching her father.

Ana turned, walking to the front of the stage and laying her eyes on Alexander. He was staring at her, his face void of all emotion until she raised her hands.

"If you burn me, eventually you will burn too," Alexander said. He looked exhausted, like he knew there was no point in fighting it anymore.

"I doubt it," she returned.

Ana closed her raised hands into fists. Her eyes turned black as her magic broke free, leaking inky veins down her cheeks. The kindling smoked then crackled, until a moment later, when it burst into flames around his feet. When the fire increased in height, sweat beaded on Alexander's forehead as he turned his head away from the growing flames. Billowing smoke filled the quiet courtyard and filled her nose, the heat of the roaring flames making her face turn sideways for a second. Alexander's expression twisted, and he pressed his lips together, perhaps to suppress a yell, but he couldn't hold it back anymore. The second he yelled, a rush of power overcame Ana that she had never felt before, and she smiled.

She wanted to watch him burn.

She wanted to see him in pain.

Ana clenched her fists harder, and the flames erupted, roaring high and covering Alexander's body as he screamed into the air. His face was turning black, the skin melting and peeling from every exposed surface, while his body jerked against the rope that didn't seem to burn away.

Ana snapped back from her drunkenness when she heard Abby crying beside Ezra. Genevieve had moved from her chair at the Council table to hold her daughter as she now screamed at the sight of her father being burned. Ezra was frozen solid, his eyes wide in horror. He met her eyes with a painful stare, then shook his head and turned on his heel, walking down the aisle and away from the courtyard as fast as he could. She watched him leave, and while she wanted to go after him to comfort him, she desired more to watch Alexander burn.

His screams fuelled her magic, and they stirred something inside her that felt strong and thrilling. All she could think about was how incredible it felt to watch him die and how powerful it made her feel. Alexander's screams gave her that power in a magnitude that she wasn't prepared for.

She was almost disappointed when the screams stopped.

CHAPTER 16

Once the flames died away and the magic was purring in a blissful sleep inside her stomach, Ana left Silas to deal with Alexander's remains, and made her way through the crowd to find Ezra. He had left in such a hurry and in such anger, and she was too focused on how good the magic felt that she didn't notice what direction he had gone. She walked through the corridors of House Alden and out through the front door when she found him. He was walking towards his mother's brown van with his hands gripping the hair on his head.

"Ezra! Ezra, please wait!" Ana called, taking off in a jog so that she could catch up with him. When she did, she rested her hand on his shoulder, trying to ignore his flinch.

Ezra stumbled and dropped his hands from his head, then whipped around. His eyes were filled with tears, and his voice was shaky. "How could you do something like that, Ana?"

Ana frowned, taking her hands back and shoving them in her pockets as she studied his expression. He looked utterly heartbroken, which sent a wave of guilt through her body. She couldn't tell him she did it because the magic was screaming for her to do it, nor could she say it sent an intoxicating euphoria through her. Instead, she shook her head and stepped closer to him.

"I know you are upset and I know he was your dad, but he was a *murderer*, Ezra. His sentence had already passed. It was going to happen no matter what I did." He clenched his hands at his sides in response. "What did you expect me to do? I have been here for *weeks*. I was lost and tortured and starved, and I must prove myself to a coven I am now part of. You expect me to throw that back in their faces? I can't do that, Ezra. I still need help. If I hadn't done it, someone else was going to, and the outcome would have been the same. I am *so* sorry, Ezra."

Ezra flashed her a look of pain. "You enjoyed it, Ana. I saw your face when you started that fire. I saw your body shake, and it wasn't because you were scared. You loved every second of burning a man to *death*. Do you know how fucked up that is? The Ana I know would never have done something like that."

"That Ana is gone. I am adapting, I am learning. Isn't that what you wanted?"

"Not like this." His shoulders finally sagged, and his face softened when he looked into her eyes. "What did Silas do to you in those cells to make you so cold? You are not in control of yourself anymore. Do you realise that?"

"I am in control, Ezra! I have never *been* in so much control of myself before!" She smiled at him, but he didn't return the gesture.

He frowned, sighing deeply when she rested her hand on his chest, and he reached to hold it. "The fact you believe that scares me."

"I feel fine," Ana promised, reaching to smooth down the collar of his shirt. "And I'm so sorry about your dad. You're right, I shouldn't have done it, but somewhere inside you, you know I had no choice, right?"

"It's not like it matters anymore, he's still d–" Ezra started, then stopped when he looked down at her arm. He searched the skin where her red cardigan was rolled up, her silvery scars poking out from under it. He reached his other hand to push the fabric up to her elbow, running his fingers over them. "What is this?"

Ana looked down at her scars, tilting her head and showing a small smile. "That's how I learned to heal myself. Silas's methods are brutal, but they worked, I guess. Don't worry, I cut him back. He has one just as big."

"He *cut* you?" His expression transformed from confusion to anger, and he dropped the sleeve of her cardigan to grasp her hand. "Come with me."

Ana blinked as Ezra led her back towards House Alden and through the front door again. He pulled her towards the ballroom where the rest of the coven was filing in from the courtyard. He stopped, looking around and panting, then pulled her back through the stained-glass doors and out into the sun. The Council table was empty, and Genevieve and Abby were nowhere to be seen. The only person still watching the dying fire was Silas.

Ezra let go of Ana's hand when he saw him. His body was tense as he stalked down the aisle between the chairs towards him. "Hey, Silas."

The second Silas turned his head, Ezra's fist connected with his jaw. To her surprise, Silas was knocked off his feet and stumbled backwards into the stack of chairs. Silas was unmovable anytime she had hit him, but Ezra was upon him easily, tackling him to the ground and hitting him repeatedly in the face.

"Ezra!" she yelped, rushing forward to try to separate them, but Silas was already shoving him away and throwing his fists into Ezra's ribs. "Please stop!"

They didn't. Ezra recovered quickly, punching Silas square in the face and slamming his head against the ground. "You cut her?"

"Really? Of all the things that have happened today, *this* is what you want to fight over?" Silas snapped.

A look came over Ezra's face that Ana had never seen before. He was panting angrily and flexing his hands and arms like he wasn't sure what fist to throw next. Then he elbowed Silas's face.

"Ezra, let him go!" Ana shouted, grabbing his arm before he could throw another elbow.

Reason returned to Ezra's expression, and his muscles relaxed. He steadied his breath, still using one hand to pin down Silas, who struggled against his grasp. He shook his arm out of Ana's grip and leaned in close to Silas's ear.

"Touch her again, and the next funeral the coven will be hosting is yours. Am I clear?"

Silas laughed through his mouthful of blood, grinning up at him with crimson teeth. He had an amused look on his face, like he almost enjoyed getting his ass kicked. "Whatever you say."

Ana grabbed Ezra's arm again, and this time when she pulled, he finally allowed her to guide him away. He turned to look at her and took her hand again. His hand and his shirt were smeared with blood, but he didn't seem to notice. Somewhere inside, she knew this wasn't about *her*. Ezra was spiralling and hurting, and punching Silas half to death seemed to be the only remedy for his pain.

"What the hell are you doing, Ezra? You are scaring me," she said, trying to get him to look at her, but his eyes were trained on Silas as he stumbled to his feet.

"As truly touching as all of this is," Silas commented, brushing the dust off his shirt and reaching to hold his jaw. His wounds instantly glowed and healed, leaving only smeared blood behind. "Thaddeus is waiting for us in his office. He wants to talk to you about what Alexander said before he turned into a pile of ash."

Ezra flashed him a warning glance, his body tensing as he took a step forward that Ana had to pull him back from. "You are loving this, aren't you?"

"Your pain is highly amusing to me, yes." Silas shrugged, directing his gaze at Ana. "You know where his quarters are. I will meet you both inside. Or not. I really don't care either way." He then left them to head towards the house.

Ana looked back at Ezra, her eyes wide and her eyebrows raised. "What the hell was that?"

"Blowing off some steam, I guess." He rolled his shoulders to get the strain out of them. "He doesn't get to cut you, Ana."

"Oh, but you get to beat the shit out of him?" She grabbed his shirt in her fist to get him to stay stagnant. His body was still full of adrenaline, and he was practically vibrating. "You could have killed him over a few simple cuts, Ezra. That wasn't even the worst part of his training!"

"Don't tell me." He pinched her chin with his fingers and thumb. "If you tell me, then I really will kill him."

Ezra let her chin go and turned on his heel, walking into the building. She followed him inside into the foyer and down the right-hand corridor that she hadn't seen before. It led towards a room, its door open wide with marble statues flanking either side of the archway. Ezra paused before he got to the door, like he was remembering something unpleasant, then he shook it off and pulled her by the hand through the threshold.

The room was decently sized, with high ceilings like the rest of the house and familiar red curtains hanging from the windows. In the middle of the room sat a wide antique desk, carvings etched into the wood along its legs. Rows of books lined the walls behind glass cabinets, and little trinkets filled the spaces where the books and the edges of the wood were. Thaddeus was sitting behind the desk in his chair, with his chin resting in his hand, his face wearing a frown.

"Ezra." Thaddeus stood from his chair, remained where he stood for a few moments, then offered him his hand to shake, which Ezra ignored. Thaddeus retracted his hand and sighed. "I am sorry for your loss. I know you and your father did not have the best relationship, but the Council voted and we couldn't risk the chance he could get loose. He was a good man, in his day, before his madness. You deserved better."

Ezra's jaw tightened. "Thank you. Though if you could tell me why I am standing here so I can go home, that would be great."

Ana squeezed his hand, looking around the room over his shoulder. Silas was lounging in a chair near the window, peering through the glass to the gardens with his head in his hand and his expression seeming bored.

Thaddeus took his seat again with a nod, leaning on his elbow and stroking his long, pointed beard. "We need to talk about what Alexander said before he died. If her magic is truly unstable and can consume her, we need to act. Silas, you said her training was going well."

"It was. It took some encouragement, but she is manipulating it freely now. I haven't seen anything special about it, though, at least not until last night. She healed a magical wound. If her magic can do that, there may be much more inside. She does not seem out of control yet, though I cannot study her eyes to assess the force at which her magic is growing."

"I feel like I am in control. I can handle it," Ana said as she leaned into Ezra, looking between them all. "It is a little overwhelming sometimes, but it's listening now."

"Alexander was clearly trying to stay his execution. What he said should not be taken seriously. It was a dying man's last hope." Silas grunted.

"I know–I *knew* my father very well. He would not have lied about something as serious as that unless he had proof, especially if he only found out because he was trying to get the magic for himself. He has only ever cared about power. On that subject, he would not lie."

Thaddeus raised his brows. "Then how do we proceed? No one knows where the Marion coven is hiding. We don't even know how many of them there are left, never mind how powerful they are. How do we correct this?"

The room fell silent until Ezra looked up from where he was staring at his feet. "I need to go to where the Venator captured my father. I assume he was still doing research on the coven and spells. I should read his work and see where he was going with it. There could be maps or incantations. Where did you find him?"

Silas turned from where he was looking out the window. "He was in a log cabin in–"

"In the Lakelands?" Ezra finished. "He used to take us there when we were kids. If he was there, he was doing research. Whatever information he had, it will be there. I can take Ana and go there tomorrow. We work well together, and once I locate what I need to, we can find a solution on our own."

"Fine, but in order for that to occur, two things need to happen," Thaddeus explained. "One: Silas goes with you." Ezra began to protest, to which Thaddeus held his hand up. "Ana cannot control her magic, and you are not allowed to use yours. If she does go dark, you need him there. I will not argue with you on this, Ezra. Two: In order for Ana to have the support of the coven, she must first become a *member* of the coven. Tonight. Otherwise, we will offer no more protection for her from the Marions or anyone else who might be looking for that magic. Our resources are for our own. If she is not our own, she is not protected. That is the way of the coven."

Ezra flinched, looking at Ana quickly. "Ana, you don't have to do that. We can do this ourselves. This is not the kind of place you want to be part of."

"*You* are part of this coven. Do not forget," Thaddeus asserted.

"Barely, and only because I was born into it. If I had the choice she does, I wouldn't be caught dead in this building," Ezra returned, narrowing his eyes as he switched his gaze to Ana. "You don't have to do this."

Ana frowned as she studied each of the men in the room. Silas appeared unbothered, Thaddeus showed anger, and Ezra looked worried. His expression made her stomach clench.

"I trust you, Ezra, more than I trust anyone." His face relaxed, and she smiled. "But ever since I woke up with all this magic, I haven't been myself. Being here, being trained, being around more magic that I can learn from, feels like some weird kind of familiar. For the first time in a long time, I feel like I belong somewhere."

"You don't need to be here to feel you belong. That is the magic talking. I know it feels addictive. Trust me, I get it, but you don't have to stay here. Come home with me."

"She can go home with you, of course," Thaddeus interjected, "but only after her initiation and after the investigation into Alexander's claims. Until then, she needs to be supervised. The initiation will take place when the sun goes down, followed by the Mabon ball."

"A party? You are going to have a party mere hours after burning my father to death? Don't you understand how distasteful that is?" Ezra flashed a look of anger at Thaddeus, which prompted him to stand from his chair.

Thaddeus sighed and walked around the table to them, resting a gentle hand on Ezra's shoulder. "I am not doing this to hurt you, Ezra. I am just doing what I was elected to do. Your father needed the sentence he got, and for that, you cannot blame me. Plus, you know all members of the coven are expected to attend the Mabon ball. You might as well try to enjoy yourself before you start your investigation. The coven has taken quite a beating with this whole Alexander thing. Spirits are down. We all need to move on together. I would like you to be part of that. No matter our personal history, you are still a member of our fold."

Ezra's jaw clenched, and he had to look away from Thaddeus. He cleared his throat and nodded once, then shrugged Thaddeus's hand from his shoulder. "Fine, but while she is staying here, I am staying too. Just because I am part of you doesn't mean I trust you."

"Wise," Silas murmured from the corner.

"I need to see how my sister is." Ezra turned to look at Ana, his hand fused to hers in a way she thought he might never let it go, which made her smile again. "You should go to your room. My mom will probably help you prepare for your initiation."

Ana nodded, standing up on her tiptoes so she could hold his head in her hands and kiss his cheek. "Thank you, Ezra."

He nodded once, squeezing her hand one last time before he let it go and let her walk towards the door. "Ana? If you change your mind . . ."

Ana paused as she held the knob of the door and looked back over her shoulder at him. "You'll be there. I know."

CHAPTER 17

It was nearing sundown by the time Genevieve knocked on Ana's door and poked her head inside. Ana was sitting atop her bed and staring at the phone in her hand. She had been trying to call Bexley, but the signal was still weak and her messages refused to send. Genevieve entered the room with a tray holding a jug of milk, little ornate glass bottles and some bowls filled with salts and petals. She set them down on the table near the fireplace and folded her hands across her torso while turning to Ana.

"How are you doing? You look well, considering."

"I am great, actually," Ana replied, getting off the bed and approaching her. "I am so sorry for what I had to do to Alexander. I had no choice. You know that, right?"

"It's all right. It is not your fault. I am on the High Council; I knew the sentence. Silas's move for you to carry it out was callous, but it was a good strategy. The Council is satisfied with your progress. If they were not, you would not be initiated."

"Thanks, I think." Ana walked to the tray she had brought

and looked down at the items. "How is Abby? Does she hate me?"

"No. She understands. She is traumatised, but she understands. The outcome was always going to be the same. Alexander dealt his own cards, so his fate was not a surprise to him. You shouldn't blame yourself." She lifted the tray when Ana started playing with the objects.

Ana blinked as she looked up at Genevieve. She didn't feel responsible or that she should blame herself. Deep down, she was still riding her high from burning him, but she couldn't admit that. Instead, she gave a sheepish nod and followed Genevieve into the bathroom.

Genevieve reached toward the faucet of the bath and turned it on. "The cleansing ritual part of your initiation starts now. We must give you a ceremonial milk bath to cleanse your body so that it may take the oath."

Ana watched as she poured the jug of milk into the hot running water.

"Milk, for the mother and the moon," Genevieve explained. She lifted the little bowls of salt, petals and herbs and dropped them into the bath in handfuls.

"Salt to purify, sage to cleanse, rose for balance, protea for transformation, sunflower for courage, orchid for strength and chrysanthemum for fertility." She smiled.

"That sounds like a lot," Ana commented with a smile, watching as the petals and herbs swirled around.

"Not finished yet." Genevieve winked. "Crushed crystals are next. Quartz for focus, moonstone for intuition, serpentine for instinct and hematite for grounding." She took the last bowl of crushed crystals and flicked them into the bathtub. Once the tub was filled, she turned the faucet off and tilted her head. "You need to undress and get in."

"Now?" Ana asked with a blink.

"Yes, now. I need to stay with you and bathe you so I can anoint your skin with the oils. It is common practice; you do not need to be nervous."

Ana nodded and removed her leggings and cardigan. Genevieve turned around to help save her modesty, working on setting the little jars of oils beside the bath so that Ana had time to take off her underwear and step into the hot water. She sank into it, reclining and waving her hands among the floating petals and herbs. They smelled amazing in the hot water, filling her nose with their muskiness and heightening her senses.

Genevieve lit incense and candles while Ana relaxed in the tub. Lifting some bottles of oils and sitting on a stool beside the bath, Genevieve gently took Ana's arm from the water and dried it off before adding oils to her skin and massaging them in.

"Sandalwood to remove anxiety," she elaborated when Ana looked at her curiously. "What are you thinking?"

Ana sighed as she sunk into the water and closed her eyes. "Ezra. He seems to think this initiation is a bad idea."

Genevieve smiled softly with a nod, kneading the oils into Ana's fingers and over the backs of her palms. "He does, but he only has his own experiences to draw from. He doesn't like the idea of losing you. Like Abby told you, Ezra has bad blood with the Aldens. With the rivalry in school with Silas and everything that happened with Thaddeus's wife, he doesn't have the best reputation with them, but he is a valued member of the coven, regardless."

Ana cracked an eye open. "Has he always hated magic?"

"No. He was in love with it, actually." Genevieve sighed. "He was a magical prodigy. When he was young, he could do things no other person with magic could at that age. Alexander and I were so proud of him, and he thrived. That didn't go down well with the other kids. They felt he was showing them up, I guess. He was in line to be the next leader of the coven, if he played his cards right, but then he got banned from practising."

"Because he killed a human, right?" Ana opened her other eye to watch her.

Genevieve's eyes became sad, and she let her hand go, moving her chair to the opposite side of the bath to begin working in the oils to her other arm.

"Yes. I don't know what happened exactly. I came home with his father, Abby was catatonic, curled up in the corner of the living room, and Ezra was kneeling beside the body of the boy on the living room floor. He was covered in blood, and he was so angry. No one ever found his skin. He admitted to the murder, said he peeled off his skin with a spell, but he has not spoken about it since. He refused to talk about it at his trial. Since then, he has been very anti-practice. He doesn't like magic, I think, because he has lost the love of his life. It hurts him to be here and be the only one who cannot feel the power of *using* his magic. It just sits inside him, dormant and pulsing to get out."

That must be torture. Ana knew how keeping the magic inside took its toll and was almost painful. She couldn't imagine how he had done it for so long.

"Is there any way he could get permission to use it again?"

"Not unless he talks about what happened, which he refuses to do. He got off lightly, and I guess he doesn't want to rock the execution boat. I would rather him be alive than run the risk of him being executed." Genevieve sighed. "Do not be upset with him if he finds tonight hard. He has promised to be there, and I warned that he cannot ruin this night for you. He just wants what is best for you, but I think he is scared that when you magically surpass him, you are going to drop him like a hot stone for this place."

"I would never, Genevieve. I . . ." Ana blushed. She loved him, but she couldn't tell her that, not when Ezra's words still rang in her ears. *Friends*. "I really like your son. He is a good man; I would never just drop him."

"Good," Genevieve said, giving her a knowing smile and letting her arm go. "Your oils are done. I will be waiting in the bedroom with your dress for the ball and your cloak. I need to paint some symbols on your skin for the initiation, but take your time. Breathe in the scents, relax your body. Come out when you are ready."

Genevieve stood, drying her hands on a towel and walking out of the bathroom. She closed the door after herself, leaving Ana alone in the dark bathroom with the soft glow of the candles.

Ana stared at the flames as they flickered against the walls. The smells of the oils and flowers calmed her heart and her magic, leaving her feeling cosy and tingly all over. When she was finished, she stood out of the water and stepped out onto the bathroom floor, pulling a towel around her body and running her fingers through her hair. She looked around the bathroom one final time, then opened the door and walked into her bedroom.

Genevieve was standing in the middle of the room. The dress she had seen in the wardrobe was now resting on the bed beside a black cloak. She lifted the dress, holding it on the hanger and smiling when she turned it in the light. It was midnight blue, tight-fitted with an open back and two thin straps that held the front to the hanger. It was long and glittered in the light, the skirt fanning out from the hips with a slit up one of the sides.

"That is stunning." Ana gasped, rushing to it and feeling it with her fingers.

"It is. Everyone deserves to look good on initiation day. Come, let's put it on."

Ana moved to her drawers, slipping on some underwear

before she dropped her towel and let Genevieve pull the dress over her head. Genevieve zipped it up at the back and guided her to sit at the vanity. Once Genevieve dried her hair, she braided the top half of her blonde hair like a crown on her head, the rest of it falling over her shoulders.

After slipping on her heels and applying her makeup, Genevieve lifted a small pot of shimmering gold paint and a paintbrush, painting sigils that Ana didn't recognise on her arms, chest and back. She explained that they were the sigils of the coven: of acceptance, transformation and bravery, power and passion. When she was finished, she lifted the cloak and placed it over Ana's shoulders, pinning it with a gold decorative brooch. She finished the look by pulling the hood up over her head.

"You look beautiful," Genevieve said and smiled widely, taking Ana's hands and squeezing them. "I am going to take you down to the ballroom. You will walk inside and straight to Thaddeus, and he will guide you from there. It is nothing huge, just some oaths and a ritual, and then you can dance the night away. Have fun, Ana."

"It has been a while since I had any fun."

Genevieve leaned in and kissed her cheek, then let her hands go and guided her out of the room and down the stairs. Ana heard happy chattering and laughs from the door of the ballroom, along with soft violin music playing and the clinking of glasses. Ana paused and took a deep, nervous breath. Genevieve flashed her another smile, then reached for the golden knob, opening the door wide.

Hundreds of candles filled the ballroom. They hung from the ceiling, dripped all over the tables and walls and lined the aisle, guiding her to the altar at the front. They looked like a million stars, and she found herself caught so off-guard by their beauty that Genevieve had to place a hand on her back and push her forward. She gulped, walking inside and giving a sheepish smile when everyone quietened down and the music lowered to a gentle hum. The people in the crowd smiled back, their cloaks over their shoulders and their hoods up to cover their heads, but their faces still beamed back at her.

She walked towards the altar, trying to find Ezra or Abby or Silas. Ezra stood near the front, his cloak hugged tight to his body and his hood down as low as he could get it. She beamed at him, reaching for his hand when she passed to squeeze it. He squeezed back, but he didn't look at her, keeping his eyes focused on the altar in front of him.

Ana let him go and moved to stand in front of Thaddeus at the foot of the altar. He was wearing a cloak too, but it was a deep crimson with black swirling embroidery covering the front.

"Ana. Welcome. How are you feeling?" Thaddeus asked kindly.

"Good, I think," Ana replied, peeking over her shoulder nervously to eye the crowd.

"Don't worry, this is very informal." Thaddeus laughed. "I will try to be quick."

He moved to the ceremonial table and lifted an athame and a gold chalice. "This ceremony is usually for the born witches of our coven when they come of age to accept their roles. There has never been a made-witch, so this is new for me too. It will be quite quick, then the party can begin. First, in this chalice, I have the blood of our coven. Every living member of our coven has contributed to the blood in this chalice. I need you to stay still as I continue the incantation, then I will anoint you with the blood of the coven before yours will join theirs."

Thaddeus held the chalice out with an extended arm, the athame in his other hand before he chanted.

"Cum hoc sanguinis ego invite vos ut lorem sacra circulus. Servabit te, volumus honorare te, nos mori pro te."

Ana didn't know what any of that meant, but he was smiling when he finished, dipping the tip of the athame into the chalice. When he removed it, the tip was dripping with blood, and he advanced towards her, nodding for her to remove her hood. She did, and he drew on her forehead with the bloody tip of the blade.

"Ut nostra sacra symbolum in aeternum sequi."

Thaddeus took the athame away from her forehead when he finished drawing the symbol, then held it out to her. "Now you must add your blood to the chalice. Cut your hand and hold it above. Let it drop inside."

Ana gulped dryly and took the athame from him. Now that she could see it up close, she realised it looked similar to the Marion coven athame. Little blue and green gemstones lined the hilt. She placed the blade against her palm and bit her lip nervously, pressing down against her skin and slicing her hand open. She gasped, not having expected it to hurt so much, but when she was done, she clenched her fist and held her hand out over the chalice. Her blood dripped freely, and after collecting enough of it, he pulled it away, took the athame from her and swirled the blood with the tip.

"You can heal yourself."

Ana looked down at her bleeding hand and opened her fingers so that her palm was facing skyward. She focused, letting her magic that was thudding in her stomach bubble over and move to her hand. The wound glowed gold, shimmering and tingling as it began to knit her skin together until it was completely healed, a familiar silver scar left in its wake.

"Cum nos consumet sanguine nova familia, nos erit ligatum in aeternum, in aeternum, tutus, in perpetuum simul."

Thaddeus extended the chalice to her when she was finished

healing, and she took it, looking up at him with a confused raised of her brow. "Drink."

"What?" Ana asked, a grimace coming over her face as she looked down into the cup of blood. "Seriously?"

"Seriously." Thaddeus smirked. "I know, it is a little archaic, but it is part of the ritual. It is not complete until you drink of your brothers and sisters. You only have to take a bit."

Ana blinked and gazed down at it again, then brought the gold chalice to her lips, tipping her head back and taking a gulp. It was thick and cold, and made her choke. It tasted like she had a mouthful of copper pennies, and when she pushed it back to him, she gagged. "Sorry."

"It is okay. It is not to my taste either." Thaddeus then gulped some down and passed it on to the next person. "The rest of the coven will take their sips, and with that, we have our new member!" He grinned, opening his hands to her. "Let me see your gold sigils. Take off your cloak."

Ana wiped at the blood that had dripped down her chin and unpinned the brooch. Thaddeus helped remove the cloak from her shoulders, passing it to Genevieve, then focused on the golden sigils that were painted on her arms, chest and back. Reaching forward to take her hand, he used his free one to wave over her, and the sigils disappeared like they had melted somewhere under her skin.

"They will be with you forever, just as we shall be. You are part of us now, Ana. You have our protection, our love, and our aid whenever you need it, and when we need you, we will call upon your services. Welcome to the coven. Enjoy your party." Thaddeus winked, letting go of her hand and gesturing towards the coven. "Let the Mabon festivities begin!"

Ana smiled widely, then turned to look at the crowd of people as they drank from the chalice being passed around. The music started up again, the sounds of happy laughing and talking filling the air once more. When she turned to find Ezra, she saw he hadn't moved. He still had his cloak on, even as others were taking theirs off to join the party.

"Hey . . ." Ana cooed, walking towards him with a wide smile. "Are you okay?"

Ezra took a deep breath and nodded, looking her over. His face softened, and he gave her a weak smile. "You look beautiful, Ana." He smirked as he fixated on her bloody forehead with the symbol on it. "You have something on your face, though."

"Oh, haha." Ana blushed deeply and leaned into him.

She reached to take his brooch in her hand, unclipping it and peeling his cloak from his shoulders, sliding it off them and letting it fall on the chair behind him. He was wearing a black shirt with black suit trousers, maroon braces and shining black shoes.

"You look very handsome." She took his hand and pulled on him softly. "Dance with me. Please? You can't let me get all dressed up like this and not take me for a little spin. Hm?"

"Actually . . ." a voice interrupted from behind her.

Ana turned, her eyes falling upon Anora as she stood with a wine glass in her hand. She was wearing a sparkling deep purple strapless dress, with a low heart-shaped bustline and a grin on her perfect face that Ana wanted to slap.

"A-Anora," Ezra stammered, standing up straighter and clearing his throat. Redness travelled up his neck and into his cheeks, and he stuffed his hands into his pockets to save himself from fidgeting.

"Ezra," Anora purred and shoved her glass in Ana's direction, forcing her to take it from her as she moved to him and ran a flat hand down one of his braces. "I would like to speak with you, if you don't mind. It has been a while."

Ezra cleared his throat again, then flashed her a smile. "It has."

"Dance with me, then I shall hand you back to the new little witch."

"*Little?*" Ana frowned, looking between them as she clutched Anora's wine glass, which had deep purple lipstick smeared over the rim.

Anora ignored her and tugged his maroon brace, giving him a grin when he nodded and offered her his hand, which she took delicately. "Don't worry, I will take good care of him."

Ana watched as Ezra guided Anora to the dance floor, looking over his shoulder and mouthing, "Sorry." She gaped at him, blinking a few times and looking around the room with an angry blush on her cheeks. She spotted Silas leaning against the wall near a table filled with crystal glasses and bottles of wine. He was still wearing his robe, but his hood was down and he was drinking heavily from the glass in his hand. She puffed out an irritated sigh, then stalked towards him and shoved Anora's glass at him.

"Take it from me before I throw it."

Silas pushed off from the wall, taking it and setting it aside on the table as he watched Ana furiously grab a glass of her own and fill it with deep red wine. "What is your problem?"

"*She* is my problem," Ana mumbled with narrowed eyes, tipping her head back and draining the glass before she filled it again and stood beside him, her arms folded, and her eyes trained on Ezra and Anora.

"Who?" Silas asked, following her eyes to the dance floor.

Silas's body tensed when he saw Ezra dancing slowly with Anora. She was laughing and fiddling with his collar with her perfectly manicured nails and leaning into him closely as he rested his hand on her waist. They were talking in hushed voices, but over the music, she couldn't hear what they were saying.

"Anora." Silas sighed, rolling his eyes and downing the rest of his glass.

"You know her?" she asked, stifling a groan when he nodded. "Who does she think she is? Did you know she came to my cell and asked to *drink my blood?*"

Silas coughed a laugh, a sound that was strange to hear coming from a man such as himself. She wasn't sure she had ever heard him truly *laugh* before. "That is what she does. She is a blood witch. She likes the taste of magic, and the best way to do that is to obtain a witch's blood. That, and she has a knack for youth potions."

"Sounds like you know her well." Ana frowned. Anora had her arms draped around Ezra's neck and she was whispering something into his ear with a sultry look on her face that made the magic in Ana's stomach growl loudly.

"I should," Silas replied, grabbing the jug of wine and refilling his glass. "She is my mother."

Ana almost dropped her glass. The wine inside it swirled and dripped over the rim, splashing on the floor at her feet. "What? But she is barely in her late thirties!"

"No, she *looks* like she is in her late thirties." Silas shrugged, setting the jug back down. "Like I said, youth potions."

Ana gaped at him, then looked back at Anora. Everything seemed to suddenly make sense. Silas and Anora looked so alike now that she was studying her. They shared the same dark hair, the identical brown eyes that almost looked black, the same tanned skin and expressions of boredom when they thought no one was looking.

"And they have history," Ana breathed, remembering Abby's teasing about Ezra having slept with Silas's mother.

Silas was silent again as they observed the couple with equally tense bodies and scowls on their faces. Ezra spun Anora, and she was laughing, leaning into him and kissing his cheek while holding his head in her other hand.

Ana's heart leapt into her throat, and she jerked into action, downing her drink and passing Silas her glass with a shake of her head. "Okay, that's enough."

She lifted her dress in her hands and dashed across the ballroom, snaking between the dancing couples to Ezra and Anora. Ezra cleared his throat with a sheepish smile, reaching to take Anora's hand from his head and pushing it back to her gently before he took a step back to create space between them.

"Finished?" Ana asked, forcing a fake smile when Ezra offered her his hand. She took it, then glared at Anora.

"I guess I am," Anora said, placing her hands on her hips and smiling when she caught Ezra looking at her. Then he stared forward with eyes wide, unsure where to look. "Thank you for the dance, Mister Sullivan." She turned to look at Ana. "Welcome to the coven, little sunflower."

Ana growled deep in her chest as Anora sauntered away, flicking her hair behind her shoulder. She jolted to rush after her, but Ezra looped his arm around her waist to hold her back.

"Woah, okay . . ." Ezra laughed, taking her hand again and spinning her around so that he could make her focus on his eyes. "Why are you so pissed? And why did she call you 'little sunflower'?"

"Because she is a bitch," Ana said flatly and a little too loudly. Some of the dancing couples were watching her now, and she gave them an embarrassed half-smile before she turned to him again. "She knows that is what my father used to call me when he was alive, and she is taunting me with it. She came to my cell and told me she had contacted him, that if I gave her my blood, she would let me speak to him."

"Well, she probably could, but it is never a good idea." Ezra shrugged, pulling her in close by the waist and starting to dance with her. "It just hurts too much to be reminded of those you have lost. You should stay clear of her if you can."

Ana looked up at his face. He was smiling at her again, looking more relaxed and playful. Heat pooled in her cheeks when she focused on the shades of green in his eyes. "Oh, you mean like you do?" Her eyebrows raised. "How many times did she taste *your* blood?"

Ezra laughed, shrugging and turning her in a spin before he pulled her back to his chest. "More than a few times."

Ana grimaced, shaking her head like she didn't want to know any more information. The music in the room changed and slowed, sounding more wistful and longing. She looked up at his face, and the smear of Anora's lipstick on his cheek caught her eye. She licked her thumb, then reached to clean it off. "You have something nasty on your cheek."

"Jealous?" An amused grin played on his face, his eyebrow lifting as he tilted his head.

"No," Ana defended, dropping her hand once the mark disappeared and resting it on his chest. She sighed, rolling her eyes as he placed his hand over hers. She could feel his heart beating under his shirt, and it made her blush. "Okay, yes. I know I have no authority to be, but–"

"You do." He moved his head to catch her eyes, but she continued to stare at her feet, pouting. She wondered if she could keep her heart from bursting out of her chest. Thoughts rushed from her head and out of her mouth before she knew her lips were moving.

"If I do, then why did you push me away?" She finally

looked him in the eye. He looked confused, so she elaborated, "When you told me you just wanted to be friends and–"

Ezra sighed and shook his head, stopping the dance to look at her fully. "I didn't mean forever. If I had kissed you and gone with it when you were in the throes of a magical high, what kind of man would that make me? You were so confused and hurt and angry, I couldn't take advantage of you like that. I–" He cleared his throat. "I like you too much to do that to you, Ana. You deserve better than that. And in my defence, you almost killed me with that kiss."

Tears brimmed in Ana's eyes when he laughed and began swaying with her again to the music. She reached to place a hand on his cheek. "And now?"

Ezra watched her for a long moment, studying her eyes and letting a small smile tug at the corners of his lips. He placed his hand against hers on his cheek, then leaned down and kissed her softly, his arm tightening around her waist and holding her to his chest.

Ana's heart leapt in her chest. She leaned into him fully, his brace gripped in her hand and her cheeks burning. He broke it with a smile, and she looked up at him under hooded eyes.

"I missed that," she said, grinning when he took her hand and spun her fast. She yelped happily, falling backwards to rest her back against his chest as they swayed. "And if this new investigation of ours sends us down another rabbit hole, will you still follow me?"

Ezra wrapped his arm around her to keep her close to him, using his other hand to lace his fingers with hers while he leaned his face down close to her ear. "Ana, I would follow you to the edge of the world."

CHAPTER 18

*L*ooking out the window of her bedroom, Ana watched the sun as it rose. She hadn't had much sleep, considering she and the coven had spent all night dancing and drinking wine. She had only been convinced to go to bed at 1 a.m. when Ezra told her she needed rest if she was going to get up early. He had taken her to her room and kissed her goodnight, but he hadn't stayed. He told her he needed to make sure his sister was okay and left her to get some sleep. But the magic in her stomach was cramping and thudding against the insides of her ears, itching to be let out and keeping her up.

She stretched in bed, slowly sitting up and yawning. Surprisingly, no hangover clouded her mind. Getting out of bed, she walked to the wardrobe and sifted through the clothes inside. She chose a black T-shirt, black leggings and a pair of chunky black boots, then grabbed a wine-coloured leather jacket. Once ready, she settled at the vanity and began her makeup. She opted for a nude lip, brown eyeshadow and flicked eyeliner, trying to make herself look a little more confident than she truly felt.

Finishing her makeup, she lifted one of the fancy bottles of perfume, spraying herself and then looking down at her fingers on the bottle. She frowned, noticing the tips of her nails were black. Flicking her eyes from her eyeshadow palette to her fingers, she tilted her head and tried to rub the blackness away. It didn't budge, and it didn't feel like eyeshadow fallout. Spreading her fingers wide, she looked at all her fingers, which shared the identical shading. Black tipped nails stared back at her, shining and hard.

"What the–"

"Are you ready?"

Ana jumped, pulling her hands back. Ezra was poking his head around her door, a gentle, tired smile spread across his face. "Just about," she said.

She smiled at him, then moved towards the drawer near the wardrobe and pulled out a pair of black leather gloves. She had spotted them when she was searching for underwear, making a mental note to take them later. After pulling them on over her fingers and tightening the buckles, she walked to him and hooked her arm around his. "Let's go."

They left the room and made their way down the staircase and into the foyer where Genevieve was waiting for him, the keys to the van in her hands.

"Please be careful," she said, holding them out to Ezra when they reached the last step. "And call me. Take care of each other."

"Of course, Mom," Ezra said with a smile, taking the keys from her and leaning in to kiss her cheek with a loud *mwah*.

"Silas is waiting for you beside the van. He doesn't look happy, so you should go." Genevieve pushed them both out the front door and waved them off. "Be sensible!"

Ana waved goodbye, following Ezra away from House Alden

and to the crumbling brown van. Silas had the hood open and was working on the engine, a tool bag at his feet.

"What are you doing to our van?" Ezra demanded when he got close. He opened the side door, the squeaking sound of the rusted door echoing around them, then took Ana's bag and set it in the back.

"You seriously expect me to get into this piece of shit? We will be lucky if we make it out of the gates." Silas grunted from under the hood. He finished what he was doing and stood back, slamming the hood and wiping his greasy hands on a towel that was sitting on his tool bag.

"It is all we have. You are more than welcome to walk," Ezra said, strolling around the van to get into the driver's seat. "Or even better, stay here." He slammed his door closed so hard the van rocked.

Silas rolled his eyes, lifting his tool bag and throwing it in the back with Ana's bag. "This will be interesting."

Ana sighed as she watched Silas take the front passenger seat, leaving her to get into the back by herself. She closed the sliding door and sat close to the front to keep an eye on them. Ezra started the engine, which ignited with an angry splutter, and sent the van down the driveway and away from the house. Uncomfortable silence filled the air inside the van, and Ana felt pressure swelling in her chest. It pounded against her ears and tickled her brain.

"So . . ." Ana said, clearing her throat and wincing as she tried to think of something to breathe into the stillness. "Genevieve told me you both went to school together."

Ezra's hands tightened on the steering wheel. Silas grinned widely.

"We did. Ezra was just as insufferable then as he is now." He shrugged and lounged back in his musty seat. "Constantly reading spell books and witchcraft history, outdoing everyone with his magical skills, thinking he was better than everyone else. Not much has changed."

Ezra gave a deep irritated sigh, looking sideways at Silas through narrowed eyes. "I will not apologise for being *good* at something, Silas. Maybe if you read more instead of envying people for trying, you would be more than a glorified hitman."

"And maybe if you weren't so much of a pompous know-it-all, I wouldn't want to rip out your spleen every time I see your face." Silas retorted, folding his arms.

Ezra shook his head as he watched the road. "Why are you always so bloodthirsty, Silas? Everything about you is blood and violence."

"Coming from the man who punched me not even a day ago." Silas chuckled. "And I am not the one who skinned a boy and left his body for his parents to clean up. I liked that, by the way, but you do not get to cast stones at me. I do it for a job, for the coven. You did it because you lost control. You did it because you are more like your father than you care to admit."

Ezra's knuckles turned white, and he clenched his jaw. He glared at Silas before taking a steadying breath. "One more word, Silas, and I will show you what real violence is, and I won't need magic to do it."

The rest of the journey was met with silence, the tension in the air like a static that wouldn't fizzle away. It took two hours of melting in the quiet to get to the Lakelands. The smooth tarmacked road they travelled on turned into country roads over the tops of hills, then onto dirt tracks. The further they drove, the more Ana could see why Alexander had chosen this place for his hideout. Not only because it was somewhere he had shared with his children but also because it was secluded. They hadn't passed another car for miles.

Ezra pulled the car onto another dirt road, which led to a rusted red iron gate. He stopped the van outside, looking sideways at Silas until he got the hint and opened the door. He jumped out, closing it after himself and made his way towards the gate, where he fiddled with the iron latch. Unlocking it, he pushed it wide open, sidestepping to allow Ezra to drive on.

The second there was enough space for him to get through, Ezra started the van again and drove off without him, leaving him waving in the rearview mirror angrily.

"Ezra, you can't just leave him behind." Ana sighed as she leaned over the back of the seat.

"Fuck him. It's not far. He can walk."

Ezra placed the car in park when they got to the little log cabin in the middle of the woods. It looked rundown, like no one had been here to tend its weeds or repair the damages. The windows were intact, but the porch roof was sagging and the front door hung from its hinges, probably broken from the night they caught Alexander.

"You used to vacation here?" Ana asked, her brows furrowed as she looked out of the window. It was so neglected that she couldn't imagine a family living comfortably here.

Ezra's hands were in his lap, and he slumped back against the seat of the van as he looked at the cabin. Sadness clouded his expression, and his eyebrows were knitted together as if the memories stirring in him were physically painful. He looked away from the building and pulled the keys out of the van, clearing his throat. "Yeah. We did. It didn't always look like this. It was actually quite idyllic."

He didn't say anything else, instead getting out of the van and shoving the keys into his pocket just as Silas approached them. He jabbed a finger at Ezra.

"You do that again, and I will–"

Ana jumped out of the van, reaching for Silas's arm and pulling it down. "Be gentle. He is hurting, Silas. *Please*"

Silas growled deep into his chest, and to her surprise, he didn't resist her. "Keep pissing me off, and he will be hurting in more places than he knows exist." He turned back to the van. "Just hurry and do what we came here for. I am going to work on this pile of crap. I am not staying here all day so that he can sift through some emotional family trauma."

Ana frowned as he grabbed his toolbox from the van. She sighed and turned back to look at Ezra. He was standing in front of the porch, his shoulders sagging and his hands in fists at his side. She placed a delicate hand on his elbow, but he didn't acknowledge it.

"Are you okay? You don't have to go in if you don't want to. I can find what we are looking for by myself."

"No. I'm fine."

He wasn't fine, and she could tell just how much by the way he dragged his feet up the steps of the cabin and rested a shaky hand on the door.

Ana followed him inside the cabin, entering the dark living room. It was small inside. Cramped, even. The little house had an old stone fireplace and a little stove and basin that must have been used for cooking, and in the back, a door was cracked open, revealing a small dilapidated bedroom.

Ezra stopped when he reached the centre of the room, trying to draw old memories from the walls. Ana gave him time to adjust, and when he was ready, he confronted the broken picture frames with his family displayed inside. Some of them had been shattered and fallen to the floor, probably from the fight that occurred on the night of Alexander's capture. Ezra sunk down on his haunches to lift a frame, blowing the dust from it and looking over the picture.

"Is that you?" Ana asked, kneeling beside him.

The photo was of Alexander and a boy of around six sitting on his knee at the edge of a lake, a huge fish on the end of a fishing rod. They both looked so happy. Alexander looked young, wearing a proud expression on his face, and the boy was smiling so widely she could see where he had lost some of his baby teeth, pure unfiltered joy in his eyes.

Ezra sniffled and wiped his cheek as he nodded, trying to clear his throat and keep his tears from spilling over. "Yeah. We used to come here on fishing trips. Boys club, he called it. No girls allowed, just me and Dad. We spent two summers trying to catch something with no luck, and then we brought Mom and Abby, who was just a baby, and we finally caught one. My first catch. Dad said it was because Abby was a lucky charm, so I made sure she came with us every year after that."

Ana smiled softly, resting her head on Ezra's shoulder as he stared down at the picture. His hand was shaking, and she reached forward to steady him.

"Ezra, it is okay to be upset."

Ezra took a shaky breath and gulped. "He wasn't always a monster, you know. I know what he did was wrong. What he did to you, to Nina . . . it is unforgivable, but that's not the man I knew. That is not the man who brought me here and taught me how to build a fire with my hands, taught me how to fish, taught me how to be a man. We didn't always get along when I got older and he became high priest, but when I was a kid . . . God, Ana, he was my *hero*."

He was crying now, and Ana removed the picture from his grasp so that she could take his face in her hands. "I know. I am so sorry, Ezra." She pulled him into a hug, letting him lean on her and hold her tightly until he took a few deep breaths. Guilt pulsed in her stomach at what she had done to Alexander, but no matter how hard she tried to shake it, every time she thought about him, a thrill built up inside, like her magic was still excited from watching him die.

Ezra sighed into her shoulder, staying there for a long moment before he let her go and squeezed her hands. "I'm fine. This isn't about me. We need to find his notebooks."

He stood, studying the room. His eyes found a toppled-over wooden table near the back wall, the floor littered with loose papers, old books, scrolls and a journal. He walked straight to it and knelt, sifting through them as Ana flanked his side. Lifting the journal, he sat down on the dusty floor cross-legged and leafed through the pages.

"What does it say?" Ana asked, trying to look over his arms to see what was written inside.

He stayed silent for a long time, reading and collecting his thoughts as he read his father's handwriting.

"His notes are ravings about your magic. He worked out why his ritual went wrong, cursing himself for making the mistake and having you take the magic instead of him." Ezra sifted through to the last entries. The more he read, the more his facial expression grew grim, and his brows furrowed.

"What is it?" Ana asked, pulling the journal down to look at it.

Ezra pointed to the symbol at the top of the page. "This is the Marion coven sigil. He went there, just like he told us, and he spoke to them about the Marion magic inside the stone."

"And?"

Ezra moved his hand down to the next symbol. It was nestled among scribbled notes in cursive handwriting, and it was messy, like he had written it in a rush. "This symbol means dark magic." He paused, wearing a worried frown. "You have dark magic, Ana."

Ana gulped as she looked down at the page, and then up into his concerned face. She didn't know what *dark magic* meant, but whatever it was, it didn't sound good.

"It is magic that has been tainted by dark intentions. It thrives on violence, blood, pain and horror. A witch's magic will go dark when they have connected themselves to a dark entity or a dark god that produces their magic. Once you switch to dark magic, there is no going back. That is why the magic was contained in that stone, so it couldn't escape and cause harm."

Ana's face paled, and her body felt hot at the information about the magic she was hosting. The dark thoughts she had been having were all making sense. The attraction her magic had to Silas when he was being mean to her, the way burning Alexander made her feel, how her anger bubbled up so quickly–it was all *dark*.

"Do you think that is why I feel so different? Is it why the magic makes me act unusual? I am impulsive now. I thrive on the *worst* things. I am easily angered."

"It makes perfect sense," Ezra said as he sighed, closing his eyes for a moment before he opened them. "If you have dark magic inside you, Ana, we need to know exactly how much so we can prepare. If it is a little, then we can handle it. We will just need to train you to make the right choices. But if it is like my father said, if *all* your magic is dark . . ."

"What happens if it is?"

Ezra shook his head. "Then my father was right. You will go dark, and you won't be Ana anymore. It will be your body and your face, but it won't be you. You will be a nightmare."

Ana's face dropped all expression as she closed the pages of the journal. Her body felt tingly, and her magic thudded loudly in her stomach. It spewed out of her the more her heart sank, and her panic was increasing. The corners of the room filled with fog, and the cabin floor rumbled under them, shaking loose the wooden logs that made up the walls.

"No, it's okay! Just breathe. This is why we came here, right? We can fix this, Ana. My father said the Marion coven has a spell that can help you, so all we have to do is find them in time." Ezra reached out to touch her arm.

Ana's eyes had blackened, leaking darkness down into her cheeks, but this time, her touch didn't seem to hurt him when he held her arm. She nodded, trying to breathe deeply and focus on his handsome face and his green eyes, anything that would keep her heart from leaping out of her chest. "Please don't let me disappear, Ezra." She sniffled.

"Never," he said, taking the journal from her and setting it aside to hold her gloved hands. "But we need to work quickly. Do you trust me?"

Ana nodded once, clenching his hands. "Always."

Ezra flashed her a crooked smile and leaned in to kiss her softly, then let her go and lifted all his father's loose papers, books and maps from their place on the floor. He helped her to her feet with his free hand and gazed around the cabin one last time before he led her outside and into the afternoon sun.

"Finished?" Silas grunted. He was kneeling by the back wheels of the van with a wrench in his hand and a bored expression clouding his face. "What happened in there? The house was shaking."

"We will explain later. For now, we need to find somewhere to stay. I need a table and a stiff drink if I am going to make any sense of these texts." Ezra pushed past Silas and got into the van.

Silas grinned as he packed up his toolbox and watched Ana step into the van, studying the blackness in her eyes. "I know just the place."

CHAPTER 19

The town of Mistport was thirty minutes from the Lakelands cabin. It was a fishing town, with docks that lined the shore for miles and little beach cabins for holiday-makers during the summer months. Silas directed Ezra in vague gestures towards the harbour, nodding for him to stop in a carpark beside a wooden fisherman's tavern that sat on the edge of the rocks on stilts. Seagulls screamed outside, and as she opened the van door, she could smell the salt in the air and feel the freshness of the waves as they sprayed over the wind.

"Where the hell are we?" Ezra asked, looking sideways at Silas.

"The Crow's Nest." Silas looked out the window towards the tavern. "It is owned by a friend of mine. She inherited it from her grandfather not too long ago. She lets me stay when I need time away. In fact . . ." He turned in his seat to smirk at Ana. "I was here most of the time you were in those cells."

Ana glared at him, the image of him drinking and feasting and lying with women while she had been abandoned to starve and drink rusting water from a broken sink flashing in her mind. "You are an asshole."

Silas shrugged before opening the door and getting out. He didn't wait for them to follow as he took off towards the building.

The Crow's Nest was a three-storey white wooden building. Torches lined the fence, and a balcony overlooked the docks where the sailboats bobbed up and down in the waters. She would have thought it a pretty place, had it not been for the fear hugging her insides, pulsing against her magic as it bubbled.

"Let's go. We have work to do," Ezra said, giving her a soft smile.

They walked inside the tavern together, her bag over her shoulder and the loose papers and journal in Ezra's arms. The bar spanned most of the middle of the building. Booths hugged the walls, with singular tables littering the floor beside them, and a thin staircase near the back led to rooms for rent, if the signs were correct. The windows were circular, like the windows of a ship, and fishing nets and ropes covered the walls, along with lobster pots with little lights in them that illuminated the room.

The only thing that didn't make sense in the fisherman's building was Silas. The tall broad and muscled bounty hunter was leaning against the bar on his elbows and talking to the barmaid. She had curly bright red hair that flowed to the bottom of her back, a tight white blouse that barely contained her chest and denim shorts that showcased her curves, and she was looking at him like she might just eat him alive.

"Okay, now this makes more sense." Ana smirked as she followed Ezra to a booth in the corner. It had a little window right beside them that looked out over the ocean, and she could tell that when the sunset came, it would be a beautiful place to watch the sun's descent from.

Ezra fanned the pages out in front of him, then set the scrolls beside them and opened the journal to the last entry.

Ana watched him as he fussed with the papers, waiting on him to look up, but he didn't until the waitress left Silas at the bar and walked to their booth, forcing him to clear his throat and smile up at her.

"I hope Silas isn't bothering you too much."

"Quite the opposite." The barmaid winked, giving a giggle that jiggled her whole body. She set menus down on top of the pages and nodded to the tray in her hand that held two glasses filled with a mysterious black liquid. "In fact, he just bought you both drinks."

"Silas?" Ezra asked with a blink, his eyebrow raised and his back straightening. "Are they poisoned?"

"Maybe." She shrugged and set the glasses down on the table with a pretty grin. "Figure out what you want to eat, and I will be right back."

She left, and Ezra gave Ana a confused look before looking back down at his papers.

Ana bit her lip, feeling useless as she watched him read. She leaned forward on the table with her elbows and pulled her drink towards herself with a gloved hand. Now that it was up close and she could swirl the liquid with her straw, she could see that it was actually dark purple. She placed the straw between her lips and took a sip, her nose wrinkling at the taste. It wasn't exactly mouthwatering. It tasted like aniseed, blackcurrant and an alcohol she couldn't place. Looking up from her drink, she studied Ezra. His brow was furrowed, and he looked exhausted. A fire burned behind his eyes, though, like anger was fuelling his blood, and she wondered how he kept it under the surface.

"Ezra, can I ask you a question?"

"So long as I can keep reading while I answer, yes," Ezra mumbled, pulling another page closer and cross-referencing it.

Ana squirmed in her seat as she thought of the best way to frame her question, "What they say you did to that boy–"

"That I murdered him." Ezra elaborated, half listening as he flicked the page and kept writing.

"Yes." She tilted her head. "Is it true?"

He didn't answer straight away. The barmaid had returned with her notebook, standing beside the table and grinning at Ezra with leering eyes that made Ana uncomfortable. He ordered crab claws, fries and beer, and she asked for the BBQ pulled pork nachos. The second she left, her eyes darted back to Ezra, and she folded her gloved hands under her chin. When he didn't reply and returned to reading, she sighed and rolled her eyes.

"Well? Is it true?"

Ezra sighed and paused in his writing so that he could lift his glass and take a large gulp of it, looking at her from over the rim. He didn't wince like she had, instead gulping down more than half of it before he set it down again. "Do *you* think it's true?"

"I don't know. I look at you, and the Ezra I know could never have done such a thing. But I know your temper when you are pushed, and I know how protective you are of your sister. That, and you admitted it."

"Then it must be true." Ezra shrugged, looking down at the papers again.

"Why are you dodging my question?" Her eyes narrowed as she searched his eyes for the truth. They revealed nothing, simply staying focused on his work.

"Because it doesn't matter, Ana. It was a long time ago. I admitted to it, didn't I?" Ezra sighed. "I don't talk about it, I'm sorry. I didn't talk about it when it happened, I didn't talk about it at my trial, and I am not going to talk about it now. Stop pushing. Please?"

Ana frowned deeply, then nodded once and reached for her drink, bringing it to her lips. Ezra was looking back down at his work once more, completely engrossed by the symbols, maps and witches' alphabet before him. When she finished her gulp and set the glass down again, she eyed her gloved hand with a soft frown. Pulling her hands into her lap and under the table, she peeled away the gloves from her skin.

The tips of her fingers still seemed dirty. She grabbed a napkin while Ezra was distracted so she could try and wipe them clean, but when she pulled the napkin away, it was completely white, the blackness of her fingers only seeming darker. She realised now that the colour of her fingers was no accident. The darkness of her magic was starting to make itself known.

Ana fervently rubbed at her fingertips until Ezra noticed her fidgeting.

"What's wrong?" He set the journal down and took another gulp of his drink.

Ana jerked, dropping her napkin and pulling her gloves back on quickly. "Nothing important." She smiled. Ezra watched her suspiciously for a moment, then tilted his head down again.

It was hours before Ezra looked up again. He had only stopped once or twice to take bites of his food and order more beer while Ana watched him in silence.

"Okay, I think I have something," Ezra said, clearing his throat. He was already into his sixth beer, and his eyes looked heavy from tipsiness. "Everything he wrote in this journal is about his journey to retrieve the magic from you, just like he said. He met with the Marion coven, and they told him that the magic was not meant for one person and that it was dark magic.

One witch's dark magic is easily handled, but the amount you have is lethal."

Ana frowned, leaning back against her seat in the booth. "So, I am screwed."

"No, not entirely." Ezra smiled at her drunkenly. "The Marion coven offered him a trade. A long time ago, around 1570, give or take, the Marion coven gave us a bright blue gemstone as a gesture of goodwill. Our covens had been feuding for an age, it was going nowhere, and everyone wanted peace. The stone is called The Blue Draíocht. The truce didn't last long, and only a couple of years later, the Marion coven and our own were back at each other's throats over the future of the craft we practise. We just couldn't agree, and we returned to being rivals. The Blue Draíocht is still in the possession of our coven. The Marions had a deal with my father, which I am sure would still stand if we ask for the same deal for you, that if we return the stone to them, they will hand over the spell that will draw the magic out of you, saving your life."

"Seriously?" Ana asked. She wanted the dark magic gone from her system, but somehow, she wasn't sure how she felt about having none *at all*. She was getting used to having the abilities of magic, and she liked to feel in control of the magical world at her feet. She just wanted it to be *safe* magic. "All of it?"

"Does it matter? This saves your life, Ana." Ezra took his pitcher of beer in his hand with a triumphant grin.

"Yeah, of course." She looked at the sprawled pages of symbols and words she didn't recognise. She puffed out a sigh, her shoulders relaxing. "Now we just need to find the Marions so we can ask them if the deal still stands."

"That's easy. Dad left a map." Ezra finished his beer before setting it down, unrolling a scroll and tapping on it with a pointed finger. "It took him a few tries to find it, coming from the roads he had marked and scribbled out, but he found it eventually. Right here." He pointed to the red circle in the middle of the mountains. "We can leave in the morning."

Ana blinked, leaning over to look at the map with a soft smile. Maybe losing her magic wouldn't be so bad. She could have her life back. She could get a new job, be Bexley's bridesmaid and find some sort of normality to her life that wasn't blowing things up and hurting the people she loved.

"For now, though, I think it is time for sleep." Ezra smiled, packing away all the papers and scrolls, putting them under his arm and jumping out of the booth with a stumble.

"Okay, hold on! I will steady you!" Ana laughed, getting out of the booth after him.

He wrapped his arm around her shoulder and walked with her to the bar where Silas was still leaning against it. He had a glass of whiskey in his hand as he talked with the barmaid in a hushed, flirtatious voice.

"We need keys to a room." Ana smiled tiredly, coming up beside him.

Silas turned to look at them, smirking at how tipsy Ezra was. "Well, Tina here tells me there are two rooms left," he said, holding out the keys, one in each hand as he gave a mischievous grin. "So, I guess you have to choose who you are going to bunk with: Ezra or me?"

Ezra frowned and took his arm from Ana's shoulder, snatching one of the keys from Silas. "You lay your greasy Alden finger on her and I–"

"Ezra, he is just trying to get a reaction from you. Let's go before *someone*"–she narrowed her eyes playfully at Silas–"starts a bar fight and gets us all kicked out, hm? Come on, Prince Charming, keep walking."

Ana helped him around the bar and up the staircase. The key

said "Room 4," and she found it surprisingly quickly, considering how slowly Ezra was walking. She let him rest against the door as she fiddled with the keys, and she could feel his eyes on her as he watched her try to open the stiff door.

"Do you remember the last time you were opening a door for me while I stared at you drunk?" Ezra asked, leaning against her with a coy smile on his face.

"I do," Ana said, cracking the door open and taking his hand to guide him inside. "Litha. You were wearing your Holly King crown while looking *very* handsome." She chuckled, closing the door and turning on the lights.

It was a simple room, with white walls, corny paintings, a double bed and a sofa, a little television and a bathroom. She guided him to the bed and let him sit down, taking the papers from him and setting them on the cabinet as he reached for her clumsily and brought her down to sit on his lap.

"And you were wearing that little white dress, looking like a country fairy." Ezra laughed, looking up at her when she smiled down at him. "I saw you walk across that field, and I *knew* I was screwed."

"Screwed, huh?" Ana hooked her hands behind his neck so he wouldn't focus on the gloves she was wearing.

"Royally." He nodded, leaning in to kiss her gently.

Ana closed her eyes, enjoying his soft kisses that made her eyes flutter. She broke it, though, looking into his hooded eyes. "You are drunk, and you need to sleep."

In reality, her heart was beating in her chest with a happy thud, and she was beginning to blush. She wanted to tell him she was just as screwed as he was, but it didn't feel like the right time and she could see that he was spiralling. It was written all over his face. His worry for her, his need to protect her, the loss of his father–it was all going to spill out of him sooner or later, and she just hoped that she could be here for him when it did.

She kissed him once more, then pushed him to lie back on the bed and tucked a pillow under his head. His eyes were hooded, and his body heavy as he lolled his head to look at her.

"I can take the sofa if you want," he mumbled, but he was already closing his eyes.

"It's okay, I think we are past that." Ana pulled off his shoes and then her own before she lay down beside him and curled up into his side.

"Ana?" Ezra asked, rolling over and pulling her into him with strong arms. "Don't leave me again."

Ana pouted. She reached her gloved hand to his hair, stroking a curl of it away from his face and watching as he slept. "Never."

CHAPTER 20

"*E*zra?"

Ana sat upright in the bed and listened to the sound of running water coming from the bathroom. The door was cracked open, and steam was wandering through the gap and into the room. Rubbing her eyes with the heel of her hand, she shuffled out of the bed and stretched. She must have gotten too warm when they collapsed into bed because she was wearing only her underwear and black T-shirt, the rest of her clothes discarded on the floor.

She spotted her gloves among her leggings, a cold chill running up her spine. Throwing her hands upwards to look at her fingers, she saw that the blackness that tainted her skin at the fingertips was spreading. It now covered her fingers down to her palm on each side, and her nails were longer and growing into points. She pushed one of her dark nails into her finger, surprised at how normal the skin felt. The nails, however, felt thicker, like they were turning into some kind of obsidian. Her brows knitted together as her hands trembled.

"Ezra?" she called again, sniffling and walking towards the bathroom door.

Pushing the door open a little further, she poked her head around the frame, her eyes falling upon Ezra as he tilted his head back in the shower, letting the hot water hit him over his chest. She paused, biting down on her lip to stop her from speaking. He looked relaxed for the first time in what seemed like forever as he grabbed the washcloth and lathered it over the skin of his chest and shoulders. That was when she saw them, the long-welted scars that decorated his back. They were still inflamed and looked like they hadn't yet completely healed.

A sharp breath hitched in Ana's throat as she studied how they moved with his skin when he rolled his shoulders and stretched his arm up over his head to wash his body. She didn't even notice he had turned his head to look at her until she heard his voice over the running water.

"You know, you could just save the water and jump in with me." He smirked and wiggled an eyebrow, turning his body fully towards her. "Save the planet, and all that."

Ana tried not to let her eyes wander over his body, but she couldn't help it. Her face burned, and she wanted to throw off the rest of her clothes and jump into that shower with him. *God, she wanted to*. He was perfect, and when he smiled that cheeky grin at her and his chest tightened as he extended his arm through the glass door of the shower, she almost did. Instead, she shoved her hands behind her back to conceal her blackening fingers and tilted her head at him, flashing him a smile.

"I think I prefer my view from here." She leaned against the door frame and watched as he finished rinsing himself from the suds on his arms. "I'll see you inside."

Ana walked back into the bedroom, closing the door after herself and rushing to pick up the leather pair of gloves. She pulled them on over her fingers and secured the buckled straps, then grabbed her leggings and pulled them on just as Ezra emerged from the bathroom with a towel wrapped around his waist and his wet floppy hair sticking to the sides of his forehead. He must have seen the nervousness in the smile she gave him, because he walked to her and wrapped an arm around her waist, lifting her easily and setting her down on the bed before he sat beside her and brought her into a one-armed hug.

"What's wrong?"

Ana gulped and turned her head to look at him as she fidgeted with her gloved hands in her lap and shrugged her shoulders. She couldn't tell him about what was happening to her skin, not when he looked so relaxed and the day seemed so hopeful.

"Nothing. Just nervous about meeting the Marions, I guess."

Ezra exhaled and leaned forward on his knees with his elbows. "Yeah, me too. But I promise, we are going to figure this thing out. Together. Okay?"

She nodded once, then flicked her eyes to his back, where his scars stared back at her. He caught her looking at them, and she could have sworn she saw a sad look descend over his face, but it was fleeting. She pouted, then shuffled on the bed until she was sitting behind him. Wrapping her arms around his middle and placing her legs on either side of his, she rested her head on his back and hugged him tightly.

"I'm sorry they did that to you. You should never have had to take something like that for me."

"I'd do anything for you. I think we have established that," he said, his chuckle making her head bob on his back as he held onto her arms.

"Do they still hurt?" She leaned back from the hug to study them.

Twelve lashings, three for each of the four times he used magic. Some of them were deeper than others, and they crossed each other like the trails planes leave in the sky, except they were redder and angrier.

"No, not really. The skin heals first, so that was the hard part. I had to sleep on my front, which was awkward. The inside, where it ripped the meat of my back and damaged the muscle underneath, that takes longer. It is still uncomfortable, but it's nothing I can't handle."

Ana bit her lip, reaching her hand to one of the scars and running a leather fingertip down it, making him shiver. "What were these three for?"

A smile appeared on Ezra's face as he looked back at her. "Catching you when you fell in the tower."

She smiled, her eyes creasing as she leaned forward to kiss his shoulder where the tip of the scar started, then pointed to the next one. "And this one?"

He laughed. "Opening the lock of the Harrow Museum."

"And the third?"

"A cloaking spell, so the security guard couldn't see us."

"I figured that one out." Ana chuckled.

She moved her hand lower on his back to the other scars, running her fingers over them until Ezra reached behind himself and took her arms, pulling her forward so that she would hug him again instead. "And the last one?

"Teaching you how to create the lights." Ezra stared off into the corner of the room for a long moment, then looked down at her hands that wrapped around his middle. "Do they bother you?"

"No," she said instantly, crawling away from his back and onto his lap, looping her arms around his neck and shoulders to fit comfortably there. "I don't like that you got them because of me, but they don't bother me."

If anything, they reminded her of why she loved him so much. He was kind, and he cared for her in a way that ran deeper than she realised.

"I actually find them kind of sexy, if I'm being completely honest."

Ezra laughed softly and reached for her hands, looking at the gloves and pinching the fabric. "Yeah? Well, I could say the same about these things. What's with these, anyway? They aren't exactly your usual style. Silas is rubbing off on you, huh?"

Ana's playful demeanour fell, and anxiety replaced the space inside her chest. She shrugged, taking her hands back and looking down at them, red-faced. "Yeah, something like that, I guess."

He watched her for a long moment, waiting for her to elaborate. When she didn't, he pulled her around to his side and kissed her forehead. "I know you are stalling because you are scared, but we really need to get moving if we are going to have time to find the Marions."

Ana let him go and watched him stand from the bed so that he could fish his clothes off the floor. She sighed, tucking her hands under her legs. She didn't have the heart to tell him it might already be too late.

~

"Not to be the one to fuck up this plan of yours, but even if we find this lost coven that no one has seen since the 1600s, what makes you think Thaddeus is going to just *give* you The Blue Draíocht?" Silas's voice strained from the passenger seat of the van.

Ana pulled her eyes away from looking out the window to study Silas. He had his head tilted back against the headrest of his seat, dark sunglasses hiding his eyes and his arms crossed tightly over his chest. He was incredibly hungover.

They had been driving all day, heading northwest from Mistport and deep into climbing mountains that seemed never-ending. The sun was lowering in the sky, cascading oranges and pinks into the clouds, making it look like the heavens were set on fire.

"Because he has no choice. *We* have no choice. If he wants the witch world to stay hidden as it has always been, then Ana cannot go dark. If she goes dark, the world will find out about every single one of us. He doesn't want that," Ezra said to him as he drove.

"I don't like this. We don't know if Alexander was onto something or if he was a raving lunatic, and worse, we could be walking into a trap. You understand that, don't you? We should go back to House Alden and bring reinforcements." Silas snapped, "We need back up."

"If we go in there with a hostile attitude, Silas, they will not cooperate with us. We need them to trust us if we have any chance of keeping Ana alive. I will not have you jeopardise this. Drop it or walk home. The entrance of the cave system on Dad's map is up ahead, so we don't have time for this now."

The magic in Ana's stomach was thundering louder the closer they got to their destination. It screamed in her ears, willing to be let out as if it yearned to go home. It was so loud she could barely hear Silas and Ezra as they argued.

The trees thinned out to reveal a much rockier landscape, filled with different shades of grey volcanic rock. It angled out in weird shapes, hexagonal, then spikes, then boulders, like angry magic itself had carved the stones.

Ezra parked the van as close as he could to the ominous-looking mountain that separated the rest of the land and the sky. The stone it was made from seemed darker than any other small hills that surrounded it. Looking at it made her head swim, chilled her skin and caused nausea to flood up from her stomach into her throat. She wasn't sure what was happening to her, but the vibrations from the magic that radiated from the mountain felt toxic and polluted.

Ezra pulled the keys out of the ignition and looked at Ana in the back seat, noting her ill expression. "Ana? Are you okay?"

"I don't feel too good."

He turned and reached over his seat, resting his palm on her forehead with a frown. "You are ice cold. We need to see them now."

Getting out of the car quickly, Ezra walked around the van and opened the sliding door, offering her his hand to help her get out. She took it, stumbling out of the van and letting him steady her. He looked concerned, and he took a nervous breath as he tucked the collar of her maroon-coloured leather jacket around her face to save her from the wind.

"Let me grab the map, and I will help you walk."

"I can walk fine," she said, trying to paint a smile on her face, but something in her stomach swirled, making her groan instead. She walked a few steps towards one of the worn pathways and squinted at the mountain. "Where is the entrance?"

Ezra watched her with worry, then cleared his throat and moved around the van to collect his father's journal and his map from the back seat. "Just up ahead. Not far, according to the map."

Ana narrowed her eyes, trying to focus on the feeling her magic was trying to make her understand, but it was foreign to her. Instead, she waited for them and looked down at her hands, tightening the buckles.

"You look as shit as I feel," Silas said, suddenly beside her.

She jumped, shoving her hands into her pockets and looking up at him. His eyes behind his sunglasses flicked from her face to her concealed hands.

"I am going to walk ahead and see if I can find the entrance. Take your time," Ezra said, kissing her head on the way past and taking off in a jog up the little foot-worn path.

Silas walked slowly beside her as they followed Ezra. He kept an eye on the horizon as if searching for danger, his eyes trained and focused. "What are you hiding?"

"What makes you think I am hiding something?" Ana asked as she walked and hugged herself tightly.

"Because I am not fucking blind." Silas growled at her. "I do not like being in the dark when walking into somewhere I have never cased out. I am already walking in here unprepared, so I do not need any surprises from you too."

Ana felt woozy and stared at her feet. "My hands. My hands are changing."

Silas stopped walking, placing a hard hand on her shoulder. "Show me."

She tried to keep walking, but Silas grabbed her wrist and pulled her back to him roughly. "I told you I don't like asking twice."

When she didn't comply, he pulled her arm, grabbed onto the buckle of her glove and pulled it. The buckle broke, and the leather came away easily when he tugged, revealing her blackened fingers and long obsidian nails. His face settled into a deep frown as he turned her hand over to see how far it went. For now, it was only creeping over the top of her palms.

"Ana, Jesus Christ . . ." Silas let her hands go roughly. "You need to tell Ezra. He is going to be even more insufferable if you keep it from him."

"I don't want to hurt him," Ana said as she kept walking, her hands now tucked into her pockets. "He is so excited about finding a cure for me he won't admit that it might be too late. If I show him, he is going to lose hope, and his hope is all that is keeping me going, Silas."

Silas groaned, like he was uncomfortable with the conversation. "It is never too late."

"Why are you being nice to me? You don't even care about me."

"Of course I care," Silas said, looking down at her. When she gazed up at him with an unamused expression, he shrugged. "You are a member of the coven. I care. Just keep walking."

They caught up with Ezra at the base of the mountain. He was standing in front of a darker patch of rock and running his hands along it, feeling the stone and furrowing his brows. The patch of dark rock was an archway in shape, like a doorway should exist there, yet it was missing.

"What's wrong?" Silas asked when they stopped beside him, looking up at it with his usual frown.

Ezra consulted his father's journal. "My father's journal indicates this is a doorway, but I can't find any cracks or openings. It must be a cloaking spell. Silas, you need to open it."

"Why me, exactly?"

"Because I can't use my magic, and it needs a magical opening. That's what you are fucking here for, right?" Ezra shoved the journal into his hands. "Just read the incantation and open the damn door."

Silas growled in his chest, his large arms tensing like he wanted to punch him. He didn't, though, instead studying the words before him.

"You can read, can't you?" Ezra demanded.

"Of course I can fucking read, Ezra. Incantations were never my strong point, and your father's handwriting is ridiculous." Silas held his hand out, resting his palm against the rock doorway and reading out loud.

Ana didn't understand the words he was saying, but a glow from his palm radiated and energy shifted around her body. It filled her nose and echoed in her head, making her sway a little and feel faint.

The door rumbled, like an earthquake came from somewhere deep in the mountain. Sigils etched into the stone, carving deep gouges into the face of the wall, until a thud sounded from the other side of the rock. Small rocks shook loose from the vibrating doorway and landed on the ground at their feet before the doorway cracked open, a freezing breeze bursting through the opening and into their faces.

"Told you I could fucking read," Silas said, throwing the journal back at Ezra. "I will go first. Stay behind me and shut up."

Silas walked ahead, stepping over the rocks and into the caves, Ana and Ezra following behind. The caves inside the mountain looked like they had been polished smooth into tall, dark pillars, and the farther inside they got, the grander the caves became until they were no longer caves. In their stead was a perfectly carved black rock palace. The first room they arrived in was a huge foyer, with sweeping staircases made of polished obsidian glass. Chandeliers made from bone–of what species she didn't want to know–hung from the swooping ceilings. Between the staircases stood a tall obsidian throne that seemed to almost glitter.

"This is ominous." Ana frowned, looking around the shining crystal walls. There was an alluring kind of beauty here even if it was dark and gruesome. Her magic scratched at the inside of her stomach and clawed its way through her resolve. She groaned, leaning into Ezra's side as she felt a wave of nausea roll inside her. "Is anyone even here?" she whispered.

"We are always here."

The voice came from nowhere and everywhere all at once. It rang in her ears and echoed off the walls, making her feel dizzy and queasy.

"Show yourself!" Silas's voice boomed in front of them, his eyes trained on the staircase and darting around to find the voice.

"We are here to speak to your high priest. We do not bring any trouble," Ezra said as he stepped forward in front of Silas, standing in the open of the grand foyer.

"I know why you are here, Ezra Sullivan, Silas Alden, and . . ."

A woman appeared in the centre of the grand staircase. She was so pale she was almost glowing, with long silvery hair that reached to the small of her back. She was very thin, with large completely white eyes, and wearing a glittering silver gown that flowed behind her in a wind that didn't seem to come from anywhere.

"And our magic thief." She began her descent down the staircase silently.

Ana watched as she walked to the black rock floor of the room, her hands laced politely in front of her. Ana almost couldn't speak, her eyes wide and her hands shaking at her sides when she finally moved to stand in front of her.

"I did not steal your magic. I never wanted your magic, I swear," Ana said, her voice sounding dry. The woman was beautiful, stunning actually, and she couldn't take her eyes off of her. "Alexander, he–"

"I know what he did. Alexander and I have spoken in great detail. That does not change the fact that you have what is rightfully ours." Her baby pink lips curled at the edges as she focused her eyes on Ana. She walked across the shining floor until she was standing before of her, her head tilted and eyes narrowed.

The woman lifted her pale hand to eerily stroke the back of her long fingers against Ana's cheek. Her skin was freezing, and it left her cheek feeling numb from the contact, her body relaxing from whatever magical vibration she was sending through her.

Ezra walked quickly to their side, but the second he touched the woman's wrist, she flicked her eyes to him and grinned. With a simple wave of her hand, she sent Ezra flying across the room and into one of the stone walls.

"Child." She sneered as he fell, the expression looking bizarre on such a perfect face. "I will not be touched by a Sullivan."

Ana jumped in shock, her body flinching in the want to run after him, but her legs didn't move. The witch calmed herself and turned back to look at her. Now that Ana could study her eyes, she noticed that they were not completely white. Her irises and pupils were like iridescent moonstones that shone with a beauty she couldn't describe.

"You are fading away," the woman commented, circling her like she was eyeing up prey. "The darkness of the magic is beginning to consume you. I can smell it. It wants to come home. Let me see your hands."

Ana's heart was beating fast in her chest, and she could feel her eyes become black, leaking down into her cheeks the more her words sunk into her head. She didn't want to provoke her, so she raised her hand and peeled her glove off, then offered it to her. The witch took it in her white one, turning it over and caressing the back of her hand.

"Beautiful." She grinned. "It starts with the eyes, then the hands, then it infects the arms, your neck and cheeks, then your brain. Once it has consumed your whole body, you will disappear, and in the wake of you will be something rather terrifying." She giggled as she let go of her hand and backed away from her.

With wide eyes, Ezra watched the encounter, holding his ribs from his fall. He got up and steadied his shaking, then walked closer to them again with a caution in his step.

"That is what we are here to stop. We need to speak with your high priest about the deal you had with my father."

"High *priestess*, thank you," the witch said as she walked to the glittering obsidian glass throne. She moved the train of her silver dress aside and sat down, crossing her slender legs and resting her hands on her knees. "My name is Mallory Marion. High priestess of what is left of our Marion coven. You may call me Mal."

Ezra limped back to Ana, looking down at how infected by darkness her hands had become. The blackness travelled up to her wrists, and long black veins were spreading up her arm. Regardless, he took her hand and held it softly, then looked towards Mallory.

"High Priestess," he started, taking some steps toward her, then stopped when she raised her hand. "Mal, we only come for the same deal you gave to my father. In his journal, he wrote that you offered him a spell that could remove the magic from Ana, in return for The Blue Draíocht. Does this offer still stand?"

Mal studied him for a long moment, then gave him a feline grin, leaning forward. "I will give you the same deal, yes. You bring me my diamond, and I will give you the spell that will free the girl from the dark magic. We want our magic back, and she, I assume, wants her life. You are on borrowed time, however. She does not have much of it left."

"What will you do with the magic once you get it back?" Silas's voice boomed. He was moving along the walls, studying the higher levels and balconies.

"That is none of your concern," she replied, flashing him an unimpressed look.

Silas shrugged. "And how many of the Marion coven are left?" He finally looked at her. Surprisingly, his muscles were relaxed.

"Always the hunters, you Aldens, aren't you?" Mal said with a deep sigh. "You do not need to worry; there are only thirteen of us left. You will not need an army. After your combined ancestors wiped out ours and the magic of our Gods was taken from us, we did not have enough magic to go around. You know a witch's line can only continue if there is enough magic to go around. We have stretched our reserves enough already. So far, in fact, that we cannot even leave the safety of our mountain."

Mallory smiled softly, turning her head towards the staircase. Her coven appeared from nowhere on the stairs, all matching with their silver suits and gowns and their glowing skin and white hair.

They glowed so brightly they were hard to look at. Ana's magic was practically ripping at her insides to be let out. She looked down at her hands, watching as the blackness spread higher up her arm, and vomit climbed up her throat. The combined nausea of the magic that was swelling in her veins and the vibrations radiating from the Marions and their mountain were making her knees weak and her eyes heavy. Her legs buckled, and she had to cling onto Ezra's arm.

"Ezra, I need to go. I don't feel good in here." Ana gasped, looking at him with her black eyes.

Ezra backed away from Mallory with his arm looped around Ana's waist so he could lift her weight and help her walk. "We will be back, and you will keep to your end of the bargain."

"Do not come back empty-handed," Mal warned, raising her hand and wriggling her fingers in a goodbye as she chuckled.

Silas ushered Ezra and Ana down the hallway and back towards the entrance. "Let's get the hell out of here. I don't like this place, I don't like this deal and I do not trust them."

When Ana reached the van, clean air rushed into her lungs, and her body shook with adrenaline. Her eyes returned to normal, and the spreading of the blackness at her wrists receded. Ezra helped her into the back of the van, leaning her back against the chair, and checked her over by laying a hand on her ice-cold forehead.

"We need to get to House Alden. Now."

CHAPTER 21

The brown van pulled up outside House Alden. It was late, and the sky was black and pinned with stars that somehow made the gothic mansion seem calm. Ana was staring down at her hands when the engine shut off. They had stopped leaking black just above the wrists, but her nails had grown longer, the black obsidian nails shining back at her like claws. Worry settled in her stomach as she stared at them, and a dark depression descended upon her shoulders, clouding her mind and scrambling her thoughts.

"We need to find Thaddeus," Ezra said, his voice shaky. He jumped out of the van quickly, walking around the side and opening the sliding door. "Come on, I will help you inside."

Ana sniffled and looked at his extended hand before giving him a small smile. "You go ahead. I will meet you inside. I need to talk to Silas."

Silas blinked as he got out of the van and leaned against his door. Ezra glanced at Silas, then back at Ana, taking his hand back with a frown on his face.

Silas rolled his eyes. "I am not going to bite her, Ezra. Find Thaddeus, and we will be right behind you."

"Okay, fine. Please don't be too long. I don't want this to get any worse." Ezra reached to hold her hand, then turned on his heel and jogged towards the house.

Silas sighed and pushed off from the van door, watching Ezra as he took off across the grass. When he was far enough away, he turned to look at Ana. She was sitting still, staring down at her hands. "I didn't train you to be so pathetic, Ana. If you weren't a fighter, you wouldn't be here. Get out of the van."

Ana wiped her cheek and nodded, stepping out of the van and letting Silas close the door. "Silas, I need you to do something for me."

"That depends on what you are going to ask of me," Silas said as he walked across the grass, shoving his hands in the pockets of his leather jacket.

Ana licked moisture into her dry lips as she followed, glancing up at him. "When I go dark–"

Silas sighed. "You are not going to go dark. Ezra isn't going to let that happen."

"*If* I go dark." Ana stopped and laid a black hand on his arm. She waited for him to turn to look at her, and when he did, she looked up at him with pleading eyes and squeezed him. "I need you to put me down."

"What?" His eyebrows raised, and he shook his head. "I am not killing you."

"Please." Ana whimpered, squirming uncomfortably from the pain in her stomach as the magic clawed at her insides. She had tried not to show her agony while Ezra was around. Now that he was gone, she was crumbling, and she had to lean on Silas to stop herself from fainting.

"If I go dark, I will be dangerous. I could *hurt* people, and I can't bear the thought of my body walking around doing all these horrible things while I have absolutely no control over it." She took a steadying breath. "If I go dark, I want you to kill me. Ezra is too close to me to do it, he will always choose me over doing what needs to be done, but you are not like that. You will do what is best, right? For the coven? For me. *Please.*"

Silas gritted his teeth as he looked away from her to the horizon, where the autumn trees swayed in the light wind. "You realise that if you go dark, you will obliterate me before I can get anywhere *near* you, right?"

"You need to try." Ana tugged his arm, withdrawing his hand from his pocket. She held it tightly, forcing him to look at her. "Promise me you will do what needs to be done."

Silas growled. "Fine. I promise."

"Thank you." She breathed out a deep sigh.

Ana pulled on his arm to bring him down close to her and kissed his cheek. She let him go again with a weak smile, then continued to walk over the grass and through the front doors of House Alden. Ezra was standing in the foyer talking to Abby, his hand on his head and a frown on his face. Guilt pulsed in her chest as she moved to him.

"Thaddeus isn't here," Ezra said, looking up at Ana and Silas.

"He had business to do with the Council elsewhere, but he will be back in the morning. What is going on?" Abby asked, shifting her gaze between her brother and Ana.

"We need something from him, and we don't have much time!" Ezra said, his frustration boiling over.

"Hey, calm down . . ." Ana said, approaching his side and reaching to take his hand down from his head. "The blackness is slowing down. We have time."

Abby's wide eyes examined Ana's black hand. Her mouth

dropped open, and she spluttered a little. "What the hell is happening to you?"

"I have dark magic, and it's spreading. Once it reaches my brain, I am gone, so we don't have much time to correct it." Ana sighed as she looked at Abby. She hadn't seen her since her father was burned. Her face flushed at the memory of Abby screaming into the grass in the courtyard. She looked well, considering.

"Shit, that is not good," Abby mumbled as she placed her hands on her hips. "Thaddeus will be back. Don't worry, he will do what he can to help you. In the meantime, I can take Ana to the greenhouse. Tonics are my specialty. Maybe I can whip something up that will help slow the dark magic down."

"That's a great idea, actually. Thank you, Abby," Ezra said, moving to his sister and bringing her into a tight hug. "I love you." He kissed her head. "I am going to grab the journal and papers from the van and take them to the library in case I missed something. I will see you both later, okay? Don't go far."

He let his sister go, then reached to squeeze Ana's shoulder before he walked out of the foyer again. Silas had already walked inside and up the stairs without saying a word to anyone, which left Abby and Ana standing alone together.

Abby broke the silence, bearing a small, thin-lipped smile. "Okay, let's go."

She led Ana through the back of the house towards the courtyard and flinched when she saw the charred raised stage still laid out near the back of the garden, illuminated by lights that lined the old mansion walls.

"Are you okay? I haven't seen you since what happened with your dad," Ana said, walking behind her with a frown and staring at her feet. She felt *awful*. "I am so sorry. You know I didn't have a choice, don't you? If I could take it back, I would."

"I don't blame you," Abby said quickly, looking back over her shoulder at her. "I haven't exactly recovered, but I don't blame you. You did what you had to do."

Ana nodded slowly and followed her towards the apple trees at the back of the courtyard. Nestled among them was a large greenhouse. It was white, with huge windows and a glass door. Little paving stones led the way to the door, and Abby walked over them and opened the door, edging inside.

The greenhouse was warm and bright, filled with flowers and herbs of every kind. Beautiful vibrant flowers climbed the walls and hung from the ceiling, and right in the middle of the room was a wooden table, a stove and a–

"Is that a *cauldron*?"

"It's a *pot*," Abby asserted, giving her a smirk and side-eyeing her. "How else are you supposed to infuse herbs and flowers into a tonic? You need hot water and oils, and you boil them in the pot." She slumped onto a stool, pulling a pestle and mortar closer to her.

"It's a *cauldron*." Ana laughed, sitting opposite her and watching as she flicked through the bottles of dried herbs and seeds on the table.

"So, your magic is going dark, huh? That can't be fun." Abby lifted one of the bottles and opened it to measure out how much of the herb she needed. She dumped it into the pot and then grabbed for another. "Does it hurt?"

"It is excruciating. It feels like there is some kind of demon inside me trying to rip me apart. My head feels like it's caving in, and I'm cold all the time." Ana hugged herself, trying to hold back tears.

"Hey . . ." Abby flicked her eyes up to look at her. "You are going to be okay. This tincture I am making you is going to alleviate the symptoms of the magic. It's not going to slow it down much, but at the very least, you won't feel sick anymore."

"And if we can't get the magic out of me, then what? I die? I don't want to die, Abby."

"Dying is not an option either. Once we are done here, I will take a sample of your blood to the alchemy lab. There, I will do some further research and see if I can come up with a plan B, okay?" she said, stopping at what she was doing so that she could throw a leaf at Ana when she didn't reply. "Look at me. You are going to be okay. Ezra would never let anything happen to you."

Ana sniffled and nodded at her words, finally looking up at her and wiping her cheeks dry. "Yeah, I know. Ezra is stressed over all of this. I feel like all I do is bring trouble to his door, yet he is always there, helping me with open arms. I don't deserve him." Ana pouted, folding her black hands on the table.

"Ezra would do anything for you. It's just the way he is," Abby mumbled as she concentrated on measuring out the herbs.

"Yeah. He has a habit of being selfless like that." Ana tilted her head and studied her for a long moment.

"Why are you looking at me like that?"

"Because I think he has done the same for you." Ana leaned on her elbows. "The things people say he did, I don't think he has it in him. He didn't kill that boy five years ago, did he? The one who hurt you."

Abby's face turned red, and she moved away from the table, lifting her scissors and reaching to snip some flowers from a nearby plant. "I don't know what you are talking about."

"I'm not going to tell anyone, Abby! Ezra wouldn't talk about it, but I *know* him. He couldn't do what they say he did." Abby's hands shook as she dropped the flowers into the pot. "He is covering for you. What happened?"

Abby looked up at her with a deep frown, like a child who

just got caught stealing. She shook her head and grabbed another pot of herbs, opening it with a tremor in her hand. "I don't know what you are talking about."

"Abby." Ana rolled her eyes. "I am probably going to die soon, anyway. Who am I going to tell? Are you really going to let me die thinking Ezra is a murderer?"

Abby sighed and slumped on her stool again, picking at the label on the jar. She was chewing her lip so hard that she left imprints of her teeth in her purple lipstick.

"No, he didn't kill him," Abby admitted, looking over her shoulder at the door. "My boyfriend brought me home, and the house was empty. Mom and Dad were on a date, Ezra was studying at the library and I was *so* drunk. He brought me into my house and he was all over me. I asked him to stop, but he didn't and . . . I don't know what happened. I kept blacking out, I guess. When I came around, I was naked and he was on top me, and I panicked. Something bad happened. I lost control, and my magic went into overdrive. I remember him backing away from me, his skin melting from his body like he was covered in acid or something. He fell to the floor, and I crawled into a corner and closed my eyes for what seemed like forever until I heard the door opening."

Abby was crying now. Her eyes were focused on the label she was now frantically picking at, shame clouding her face and regret knitting her eyebrows together.

"Ezra held me and dressed me and combed out my hair and told me he was going to fix everything. Ezra was a natural with his magic, everything came so easy for him but he never really cared much about using it when he started his studies. He preferred the study of magic, rather than the practice, but he knew it was *everything* to me. He knew it was my dream to be good enough to join the Venator, but if the High Council convicted me of murder, they would ban me from ever doing magic again. They might have even killed me if they didn't believe it was self-defence."

"So, Ezra took the blame," Ana finished, her heart swelling in her chest.

Abby nodded and wiped her cheeks. "Yeah. He said he didn't care about doing magic and that I was too young to lose everything. He rearranged the body, covered his shirt in his blood and told everyone he killed him while trying to defend me. It wouldn't have been so bad if it had been another witch, but the guy was *human*. There was a big cover-up, and Ezra got banned from practising ever again. He was imprisoned for weeks before his trial, and he never once gave me up. He never flinched when they threatened to execute him or hurt him if he didn't talk. I owe him everything."

"Which is why you are helping me so freely, right? That's why you kept bringing me food in the cells. That's why you forgave me when I hurt you?"

"I know what it's like to lose control and not understand why. And I trust my brother. If he likes you, then I like you too." She opened the jar again. "Pass me the eye of newt." She smirked, clearly trying to change the topic.

"The what?"

"The mustard seeds." Abby laughed, pointing to the jar near Ana's black hands.

Ana rolled her eyes and grabbed it, throwing it at her.

She caught it and pried open the lid, dropping some of the tiny mustard seeds into the pot before she stirred it. "Are you scared? To die?"

"Yes. I guess I am holding out hope our plan will work, but it is a long shot and there are no guarantees. The waiting is worse." Ana sighed, wriggling her fingers. "I think I am going to spend the night in the cells, just in case the darkness speeds up. I don't want to risk hurting anyone."

"Probably for the best."

Abby finished letting it boil, wrinkling her nose at the smell as she strained it out with cheesecloth into a tall crystal glass, then handed it over to Ana with a grimace. It was thick and a sludgy moss green colour, smelling like fish eggs and mint. The smell worked its way up her nose and tickled her brain.

"Bon appétit." Abby laughed, waving her hand in front of her face mockingly before she cleaned the mess from the tabletop.

"You expect me to *drink* this?" Ana blinked, taking the glass in her hand and screwing her nose when Abby nodded and grinned. "Here goes nothing."

Ana put the glass to her lips and tipped her head back, drinking the mysterious liquid and trying not to choke it back up again. It was grainy and slimy, and it left her with a fishy aftertaste that didn't seem to go away, no matter how many times she smacked her lips.

"That is the most disgusting thing I have ever tasted." She coughed, pushing the glass back at her and wiping her tongue with her sleeve.

Abby tipped her head back as she tried to stop giggling at her. "I can't believe you drank that. I mean, it will help, but damn, you must really want to live."

"I really do."

"Good. Now we need to take your blood so I can take it to the lab. We might be able to come up with a serum that you can inject into your muscle. With the right combinations, it could work." Abby walked to a drawer and pulled it open.

She lifted out a tourniquet, a needle and some tubes, then walked to Ana and sat down beside her, pushing her jacket up her arm. Ana looked away the second she started wrapping the tourniquet around her upper arm. She always hated getting her blood taken. It used to make her faint and queasy, but she guessed anything was better than how she was feeling right now.

"I never pegged you as a scientific kind of gal," Ana commented, trying to take her mind off what Abby was doing. "I thought this place was all magic and spells."

"Science *is* magic." Abby smiled. Ana flinched when she felt the sharp prick of pain in the crook of her arm. "The trick is knowing when the right time is to use your *own* magic, and when to use the magic of science. They are not always one and the same. You can always find magic in the real world first, in plants and herbs, vibrations and, most importantly, the sciences."

Abby pulled the needle out of her arm and let the tourniquet fall away, setting the needle beside her on the table as she studied the blood in the tube. It was darker than what Ana remembered it to look like, and thicker. "Hmm."

"Is that a good hmm, or a bad hmm?"

"I won't know till we test it, but I will have some answers for you tomorrow. Hopefully, if this plan of yours falls through, this will be our backup. You should get some sleep, though. Resting will slow your heart rate down, making the blood less likely to race through you and hasten the spread of the darkness."

"Thank you, Abby, for everything you have done for me." She took Abby's hand and squeezed it with a smile, then stood from her seat and made her way to the door of the greenhouse.

After saying goodbye, Ana walked out into the chilled night air. The moon was almost full, and it illuminated the garden, benches and trees that lined the walls. The grass was covered in crisp autumn leaves that crunched under her heel as she walked along the pathway towards the gothic mansion. It was a beautiful night, and she found her feet slowing to a stop as she looked up at the stars and moon. They were sparkling here in a way they didn't in the city. She could barely see them there from the air pollution that hovered in the sky and blocked them out. Bexley always said that they didn't need to see the stars in the sky, because the stars that mattered were there in the city. They were each other's stars.

Guilt waved over her again. She hadn't spoken to Bexley since before she was imprisoned here. As much as she didn't want to worry her friend, she knew she couldn't handle the idea of dying before she got the chance to hear her voice again. She dug her hand into her pocket to find her phone, pulling it out and swiping through it until she found her name and pressed it.

It rang for a long time, then finally, the sound of laughing people, clinking glasses and loud music came through.

"Hello? Bex?"

"Hello?! Hello?! Ugh, hold on, I can't hear you! Let me go outside!"

The sound of people moving, dancing and screaming filtered through the phone until they thinned out and were replaced by cars rushing by and honking their horns.

"Bex?"

"Ana! I'm sorry, it was super loud in there. Are you okay? Are you feeling better? Please tell me you are back in the city."

Bexley sounded drunk but happy. The tone of her voice was light and playful, and she could practically hear the smile in her voice.

"No, not yet. I . . ." Ana paused. She couldn't tell her the truth. Like anything in her life now, she could never tell Bexley everything going through her mind like she was used to. "I was getting better, for a bit, but they think I have taken a bad turn. I–"

"Okay, where are you? I will have my driver take me to you. Just give me the address, please. If you are that sick, you need to let me be there for you."

"No! You can't."

"*What? Why? Ana, I'm not taking no for an answer. Just give me the damn address!*"

Ana sighed and closed her eyes, feeling tears pressing against her lids. She wanted to see Bexley. She wanted to see her so much it felt like her heart was tearing out of her chest just hearing her words. She couldn't risk seeing her, though, not when there was a chance she could go dark at any moment. She couldn't be responsible for hurting her.

"Because I am contagious." It just came out, and the second she said it, she placed her hand on her forehead and squirmed. "If I make you sick, you will miss all of your wedding planning, and you have so much to do, right?"

There was a deep groan from the other side of the phone. It sounded far away, like she had dropped her phone, and Bexley muffled a few words she didn't quite hear. It clicked again, coming back to her ear.

"*Okay. I'll not come, then. But the second you are better, drop me a pin and I will be there to collect you, all right? Everyone is wondering where you are. I had to talk our friends out of making missing posters.*"

Ana hiccupped and opened her eyes. "Was it a good photo of me, at least?"

"*Always. You know I would never let a bad photo of you go on a missing poster. You never know who might see it.*" Bexley sniggered until her voice became sad again. "*But I need my wingwoman back. I need someone to go dress shopping with me, and it has to be you. So, you will get better, you hear me?*"

"I hear you." She sniffled. "Bex? I love you. You know that, don't you? I need to know that you know that."

"*Yeah, of course. I love you too.*" Bexley said, a smile in her voice. "*I need to go. My song is on. Ciao, amore mio.*"

The phone went dead, and Ana took it down from her ear to switch it off with a black finger. She frowned at it, raising her hand in front of her face. The tincture Abby created for her had certainly helped with slowing the blackness down and stopping her nausea, but she knew it was only a matter of time before they came flooding back, overtaking her body and forcing her to become something else.

Something not Ana.

Something *monstrous*.

CHAPTER 22

The cells in the dungeon looked exactly the same as they had when she left. She could still smell the fumes from the cell beside hers that Silas set on fire. She blushed, remembering being completely naked and loving how the flames licked against her skin. It was cruel, what he had done to her down here, but it was a baptism of fire. She had flown from these cells like a phoenix from the ashes, completely in control of herself and excited about the future of her life with magic.

She rested her hand against the bars of the cell door, feeling the cold of the iron under her fingertips. Walking inside, Ana looked at the dirty mattress and the stained blood on the blankets. They were filthy, but it strangely felt comforting to be back in the dark room instead of out in the open where anything could happen. In here, the only thing she had to fear was Silas, and it wasn't like he was going to come down here again with his knife. Not yet, anyway.

Ana pulled a new candle from the drawer and put it in the candelabra, waving her hand and watching it light before she moved to the little bathroom. She knelt on the floor, lifting the discarded tin from the Mabon pie and the note, and brought them back into the room where she slumped onto the mattress and ran her finger over the writing.

"You got my pie, then."

Ana looked up, smiling when she saw Ezra standing by the cell door. He had a soft smile back on his face as he looked around the stone walls.

"I did." She waved him inside.

"You know, this was the same cell I was in when the Council arrested me." He walked inside and sat beside her, his arms resting on his knees as he leaned back against the wall.

"After you *killed* that boy?" She looked at him with a raised eyebrow.

"Yep." Ezra nodded, shrugging and grinning. "What are you doing down here?"

Ana set the note on the table and leaned back against the wall beside him, resting her head on his shoulder and watching the candle flicker. "I don't know. I guess as depressing as it sounds, I find my cell comforting. Like the world outside doesn't exist, like I'm safe. That, and if there is a chance that I can turn dark at any moment, it might be best if I stay down here."

"Nothing is going to happen to you." Ezra reached to take her black hand. "The blackness has slowed down. Abby's tonic must be working."

"She knows her stuff." Ana nodded, biting her lip and sighing. "She is trying to make me a serum just in case the Marions don't pull through."

Ezra noticed the sadness in her voice, and he wrapped his arm around her, pulling her in to his side. "So, what else did Silas do to you down here? I promise I won't get mad." He smirked.

Ana rolled her eyes, tilting her head up to look at him. "Yeah, right." She smirked, then shrugged when he nudged her to continue. "He shouted *a lot* to convince me to let my magic go. He taught me to heal by slicing my arm open and leaving me to work it out myself, like I said. Oh, and he starved me. That was super fun. He is a horrible teacher."

Ezra's body tensed, and he stroked her arm with the back of his fingers. "I promised I wouldn't get mad."

Ana smiled, tilting her head at his furrowed frown. "He took me to the next cell and set it on fire with us inside, to teach me to rapidly heal and learn to manipulate fire. It was kind of thrilling once it stopped burning."

She straightened her back and looked at his hand stroking the blackness of her wrists. "But I have been wondering: If a witch can heal themselves faster than fire can burn them, how did witches get burned at the stake? How did Alexander not escape?"

Ezra considered his words for a long moment before he spoke. "Most of the people who were burned in the European witch trials were not witches. They were patsies for the church to help them explain things they didn't like. But real witches, like my father? The only way you can burn a real witch is to bind their magic with a blood spell. It won't last long, for the witch can break it if given enough time. Another witch would have taken the blood from the person they wanted to burn and performed the blood ritual, rendering the witch's magic useless just long enough to burn them."

"But what kind of witch would do that to their own kind? If there needed to be a witch to do the blood ritual for the magistrate responsible for the burnings, how were they not burned themselves?"

"That is a harder question to answer. Remember how the Marion coven was almost completely wiped out in the burnings at the monument in 1588?" Ezra said, watching her to make sure she understood.

"I am familiar," Ana said sarcastically, pinching him.

"Yes, of course, well, the magistrate was working with a local witch. The Marions were intending to rise up and come into the public eye about their magical practices. Every other coven disagreed, for they wanted to stay hidden. Our coven performed the blood ritual against the Marion coven in return for a free pass from death."

"The witch who was responsible for the Marions' burnings came from *our* coven?"

Ezra gave a small laugh. "Ana, the witch who betrayed them was a *Sullivan*. Which is funny, considering a Sullivan was just killed for trying to do the same thing the Marions wanted to do. Full circles and all that, I guess."

Ana looked up at him in surprise, but she remained silent. She wasn't sure what she *could* say.

"Anyway, all of this depressing stuff aside . . ." Ezra started, taking her black hand again and lacing his fingers with hers and looking over her long Obsidian nails. "When we fix this–"

"Ezra. We need to be realistic." She sighed.

"Please, indulge me," Ezra said with a raised eyebrow and a smile. "*When* we fix this, I have a little proposition for you. I got a new job."

"A job?" Ana blinked, sitting up off his side and smiling at him. "That's amazing! What kind of job?"

"Well, over the summer, I applied to be part of a new dig in the South. It is a newly discovered witch monument that was unearthed on the cliffs last year in a little town called Coral Bay. It is right on the shoreline, and it is *beautiful*. I didn't think I was going to get it, because usually the job goes to the most experienced and I am only working my way up, but I think before my dad died, he must have pulled a few strings." He gulped, his muscles flinching to keep his smile on his face.

"My dad's estate has been halved between my sister and me, so I have the money to move. I found a cottage by the sea. It has the best views over the ocean, a beach right on the doorstep. It's small, but I don't need mansions like the Aldens seem to."

"That's amazing news, Ezra." Ana clenched his hand, but her smile fell. "I am going to miss you."

"That's the thing." Ezra took a small breath, avoiding her eyes. "I thought, maybe, once we have cured you, that you might need a bit of a break. I thought you might like to come with me to Coral Bay."

Ana's breath hitched in her chest, and her eyes watered as she watched the small smile creep over his anxious expression.

"I have already checked and there is an opening in the local paper down there, but it's not as grand as you are used to. They mostly cover bake sales, country fairs and escaped sheep, but it would give you time to relax. You could maybe write a book or something? I don't know. I am rambling." He frowned. "It's just an idea."

Ana blushed deeply, tilting her head at him with a shaky smile and squeezing his hand. "You really want me to go with you?"

Ezra nodded, gulping thickly and looking at her with an unsure shrug. "I just want to be where you are. I want to take you somewhere magic can't hurt us, somewhere we can just relax, and plan for all the tomorrows I *know* you are going to have."

Ana sniffled and let go of his hand so that she could hold his face in her black taloned hands. "I just want to be where you are too," she said honestly.

She leaned in and kissed him before he could speak, and he wrapped his arms around her middle, pulling her onto his lap so that she could straddle him. She fluttered her eyes closed, feeling him place his hands on the small of her back and press his fingers against her skin. They felt warm, and when she kissed him deeper, he tightened his grip on her hips.

"Ana . . ."

"Shh," she mumbled against his lips, snaking her black hands up and into his hair. It felt so good to be close to him again. She wanted to get completely lost in him and forget everything for just a *moment*.

Ezra tilted his head back enough to look at her, his face looking torn and his fingers playing with the hem of her jacket. "Ana, you should be resting. I can't be responsible for making you feel worse."

"I want you, Ezra," she whispered with a smile, leaning in to nuzzle her nose against his. "I feel fine. Please don't make me go into what could be my last days without feeling you touch me again."

She trailed her hands down to his chest, to the buttons of his shirt, popping the first few open and squirming in his lap when she heard him groan deep in his chest. He looked like he was battling with his conscience, but she could tell she was winning when he pushed his hand under her jacket and up her back, pulling her close to him.

"One condition," he said, leaning back against the wall with his now open shirt and watching her as she tugged her leather jacket off and threw it to the side.

"Anything." She placed her hands on the hem of her shirt and pulled it up over her head.

Ezra's hips twitched under her as he watched her discard her clothing. She almost thought he had stopped breathing for a second when he didn't speak, but when she dropped her hands back to his shirt and pushed it off his shoulders, he finally grinned. "Don't kill me."

She laughed, leaning forward to kiss him again. This time, he wrapped his arms around her and fiddled with the clasp of her bra until it came away in his hand and he threw it somewhere behind her. His kisses turned feverish, and his hands worked their way into her blonde hair as he moved his head to her neck, nipping at her skin with his teeth. She gasped, her hips jerking as tingles shot up her back and into her skull, forcing her to close her eyes tightly. She missed this. She missed him so much it *ached*.

Ana's hands traced his taut chest, his abs, his stomach, and found the buckle of his belt. She clawed at it with black taloned nails. It took a few tries to undo, and she almost got frustrated until the leather came apart and she opened his trousers. They were already tight, and the fabric strained under her in a way that made her heart leap into her chest. He moved his hands from holding her and shoved them underneath the hem of his trousers, tugging at them until he shuffled them down enough while she raised on his lap to give him access.

"You need to get up so you can take these off," Ezra murmured, tugging the fabric of her leggings.

Ana didn't have time to stand. Her body was on fire, and she could see her vision darken as her eyes turned black, her magic purring happily in her stomach. "No, just rip them."

Ezra didn't need to be asked twice. He grabbed the fabric at her waist in two fists and ripped it apart, the sound filling the room and making her squirm under his hands. He was gritting his teeth when the fabric came away in his hands as he ripped them all the way down her legs, then turned his attention to her underwear. The pink lace didn't stand a chance when he roughly grabbed the straps, tearing them apart and pushing them aside so that he could slip his hand between her legs. She gasped, having to lean forward and kiss him so her moan wouldn't escape into the air and echo around the cell. When he rolled his thumb, Ana was sent reeling, her body trembling and her tongue seeking his. When he removed his hand, she fluttered her eyes open, looking at him through hooded black eyes.

"Your eyes . . ." He panted, holding onto her hips again.

"I'm fine, don't stop." She gulped, shuffling her legs and her hips until she was comfortably straddling him again. "I need you *now*."

Ezra studied her for a moment, his body tense and his eyebrows furrowed until his conscience lost its moral battle and he grabbed her thighs, placing himself between her legs and forcing her down until their hips flushed.

This time, Ana couldn't stop the sharp moan that escaped her. It echoed off the stone walls and back into her brain, scrambling her thoughts to nothing except how *good* he felt. She looked down at him and placed a black hand on his chest to push him, making him lean against the wall so she could roll her hips. His eyes closed, and his hands moved from her thighs up to her waist, clinging to her there so that he could pull her down on him firmly. He was just as lost as she was, and she enjoyed watching how his face contorted when she raised up on her knees and he instantly pulled her back down on him. The sensation forced her eyes to roll into the back of her head, the lids fluttering closed as her back arched, pushing her chest towards him. Ezra took his chance, driving his hips up into her at the same time he pulled her nipple into his mouth.

Ana lost it. She gasped sharply, her black hand reaching to snake her fingers into his hair and gripping him there, pushing her chest further into his face until she was gliding on him so quickly her body trembled. Before she knew what she was doing, her other hand moved from where it was hugging his shoulder, reaching to wrap her fingers around his throat and push him back from her to look down at his face. Her eyes opened as her hand clenched, and Ezra blinked up at her in surprise. She smiled at him, her hips grinding harder against his while her hand tightened.

"Ana," Ezra said, his voice thin and his hands gripping her hips, trying to slow her movements on him as his muscles tensed.

Ana moaned, leaning down to kiss him. Pressure was building in her hips and stomach, sending shock waves up her spine and into her skull. The better it felt, the tighter her hand clutched his throat until Ezra said her name again sharply and let her hip go, grabbing her wrist and pulling it away from his neck. Her taloned nails scratched over his skin, leaving long cuts on his neck that beaded with blood.

Ana panted, her hips stilling against his and her body tense. The magic in her ears slipped away when she saw she had hurt him, and her eyes slowly returned to normal, looking down into his as he watched her with a furrow of his brow.

"I-I'm sorry." She gasped.

Ezra gulped, looking between her eyes, to her black hands, then over her body. Her heart stilled in her chest, panic coming down on her when he said nothing. Instead of pushing her away or shouting at her, Ezra wrapped his arm around her sides and fused his mouth to hers, kissing her hard and suddenly flipping them. Her world spun, and her head felt dizzy as she found herself on her back with her thighs pinned against his sides and Ezra over her. He was bleeding, but not badly, and the cuts had seemed to set a fire inside him. His body was tense, and his muscles were shaking as he rocked into her, his hips becoming a blur.

Ezra pinned her black hands above her head with one hand,

his other holding her thigh until the pressure in her hips started to overflow. She trembled under him, lips seeking his to silence herself. He was sending her into *heaven*, throwing sensations into her body she didn't know existed.

"Ezra!" She gasped.

With ragged breathing, he buried his face into the crook of her neck. His hips jerked, and he growled loudly into her shoulder, his teeth digging into her skin when his body stiffened. She felt him pulse, and the second she felt his warmth, the pressure burning inside her hips burst, sending her reeling while her legs clenched around his waist, her voice echoing off the cell walls and sending her moaning back to her.

Ezra's hips slowed to a stop, his body slacking and relaxing from its tense state, and he slumped on top of her, breathing heavily into her shoulder. Ana blinked the spots from her eyes, tilting her head sideways to see him. His hand loosened its grip on her wrists above her head, and when he finally let them go, she took them down and grabbed his head, pushing him up so she could smile at him. His brow was beaded with sweat and his hair was sticking up, but he had a tired grin on his face. She leaned up and kissed him softly, then lay back and flicked her eyes towards the scratches on his neck.

"I'm sorry."

"What did I say about the whole *trying to kill me* thing?" he asked with a pant.

Ana chuckled and rolled her hips to free herself from him, making him hiss through his teeth in response. He flopped down beside her, staring at the ceiling tiredly as she curled up into his side and pulled the musty blanket over them to save them from the chill of the cell. Resting her head on his chest, Ana stared at the patterns in the grey brick on the wall, biting her lip happily and enjoying her glow. If she was going to go dark or die, she was happy that, at least for now, she wasn't alone.

"Thank you," she whispered.

Ezra scoffed, grinning dumbly. "No, thank *you*."

Ana swatted his chest with a roll of her eyes. "Not for the *sex*, idiot." She laughed, then tipped her head up to look at him. "For never giving up on me."

Ezra reached to pinch her chin between his thumb and fingers, then leaned down to kiss her softly. "Never."

CHAPTER 23

Ana blinked awake when she heard the chirps of little birds outside the wall. She had grown used to them over the time she spent locked in the cell, and she almost thought she was still locked inside again until she saw the open door and felt Ezra shift beside her. She turned, rolling onto her side to face him, watching his closed eyes and smiling softly at how peaceful he looked. She didn't want to have to get up off this mattress or peel herself out of his arms and face the day that lay ahead. For all she knew, she could be dead soon, or worse, and she would never get to see him sleeping so peacefully again.

"Are you really watching me sleep?" Ezra mumbled, cracking an eye open and catching her staring at him. He smiled and groaned tiredly, pulling her back into his embrace. "Just a few more minutes."

Ana relented and snuggled against him, her head on his chest as she listened to his heart beating steadily. "I want to stay here with you too, but I am starving." She smirked.

Ezra opened his eyes again and nodded, reaching for her hand. He inspected the blackness, which spread up to her elbows, and his eyes widened. He sat up sharply and studied her whole body.

"Shit. We need to get going. Is your magic still moving?" Ezra stood from the mattress and grabbed his clothes, pulling them on as quickly as he could. His hands were fumbling, and his body seemed tense.

"Yeah, always. It's like a clawing demon, but I am getting used to it now." Ana got up as well, looking for her bra and shirt. She pulled them on, and he reached forward to clasp her bra for her before she pulled her shirt over her head.

"That is not something you should be getting used to, Ana. We need to find Abby and get you another tincture. Thaddeus should be back by now, so he can point us in the direction of the diamond." His eyes travelled over her bare thighs, and a smirk crept over his face. "You are still half naked, not that I am complaining, but I'm not sure how Thaddeus will feel if you walk into his office with your ass out." He laughed.

"Or it will make him give us the diamond faster." Ana winked at him as she collected her torn leggings and panties from the floor. They were *destroyed*. "This is your fault! What am I going to do?"

"*My fault*? How is it my fault? You told me to rip them, remember?" Ezra made his voice a pitch higher to mock her. "*Rip them, Ezra, I can't wait any longer!*"

"Stop!" Ana blushed, grinning at him. She pulled her boots on, then threw her leggings and panties at his face and pushed past him, out of the cell. "Or you will never get to rip my panties again."

She walked down the corridor and towards the steps that led

to the upper levels, smiling when she heard Ezra rushing after her.

"Ana! Seriously, Ana, you are *naked*." He hissed, chasing her.

"And?" She grinned, jogging up the steps and spinning around when she reached the door that led to the ballroom, her hands on her hips.

"And as much as I *loved* watching you jog up those steps," Ezra said, reaching her and holding her maroon leather jacket out to her, "that is a view I would like to keep all for myself."

Ana opened her mouth to give him a playful reply, but before she could, daylight illuminated the stairwell, and Ezra's eyes went wide. Her mouth dropped open at his shocked expression as she felt a breeze from the ballroom roll over her bare ass and thighs. "Someone is standing behind me, aren't they?"

"Yes."

Ana was about to turn towards the gruff voice, but Ezra gasped and pushed his hands around her sides, looping the jacket around her waist and tying the sleeves around her middle. It didn't do much to hide her front, but the sleeves covered her enough that she could turn around to see Silas's deep frown.

"Hey . . ." She trailed, a sheepish grin on her face.

"I don't know what is going on here and I don't care, but Thaddeus is back. Thought you should know." He looked over her once, a smirk coming over his face as he turned and walked away. "At least it's not on fire this time!"

Ezra puffed an angry sigh from behind her, and she reached to hold his hand and pull him out into the ballroom. "Okay, stud, don't get mad," she said with a roll of her eyes.

Ana walked close to his side to shield herself until they got to the foyer of House Alden. He stopped at the staircase, looking around to make sure no one else was walking down the steps.

"Go!" he hissed.

Ana smirked, swatting his behind on the way past as she ran up the staircase, across the red carpets and finally into her room, where she slammed the door with a laugh. The room hadn't changed, but the bed had been made and the makeup on the vanity table had been tidied. She hurried to the wardrobe, pulling the door open and discarding her leather jacket and T-shirt before grabbing a new pair of panties and slipping them on. She opted for a new pair of clean black leggings, her clunky boots, and a red wool jumper. It had long sleeves that dropped past her wrists, covering the blackness in her arms.

Sitting down at the vanity, she brought her hands up to her face to study them. The skin was normal, maybe a little dry, but her nails had grown longer overnight. She wouldn't be able to fit her gloves over the sharp obsidian tips anymore. As she looked at her fingers, the beautiful morning haze she had felt when waking up in Ezra's arms dissipated, hollowing her chest and welcoming fear. If her darkness was spreading this rapidly, she wasn't sure how much longer she had left.

She gulped, looking at her face in the mirror. Her face wasn't as pale anymore, but as she leaned forward to inspect her eyes, she noticed the usual bright blues were darkening to a navy. She didn't like how different it made her look. She tilted her head, and the stranger tipped their head back. Frowning, she rolled her head the other way, watching as her reflection mimicked the gesture. Then she smiled, even though Ana's own mouth didn't move.

Ana's heart leapt into her chest. She scrambled from the chair, stumbling into the middle of the room with a pant, watching her reflection. It seemed normal again, and her face stared back at her with the same scared expression. Maybe she imagined it.

She *hoped* she imagined it.

She walked out of the room, lingering in the hallway for a moment while she willed her heart to beat again. The only thing that could help slow down the darkness was Abby's tincture. She looked down the stairs to where Ezra was waiting on her, then moved her eyes down the hallway to her left, in the direction of Abby's room. Willing her feet to move, she made her way to her door, knocking on it with a light fist.

"Abby?"

There was no response. She cleared her throat, then knocked harder. Silence screamed back at her, forcing a frown upon her face. She gulped, reaching for the handle of the door and opening it, and winced when it creaked in protest.

"Abby?"

Peeking her head around Abby's door, Ana noted that the room was smaller than hers but lighter in colour. Soft lilacs and pinks spread across the walls, and her bed was a light natural wood. It surprised her, considering how Abby seemed so "rock 'n' roll" with her leather, boots and weapons. What was more surprising, though, was how much of a mess Abby's room was. It was not only a mess but also *trashed*.

She frowned, opening the door wide and entering with her hands at her sides and her eyes wide. Books littered the floor, her table was overturned, her bed sheets were tousled and her weapons were knocked off the wall. Abby was nowhere to be seen.

Ana turned and ran from the room, rushing across the landing and back down the grand staircase to Ezra, pulling his arm and looking up into his confused face. "Abby isn't in her room, and it's trashed!"

Ezra's eyebrows furrowed, his eyes flicking from her face to the landing of the upper floors. "Silas might know where she is. It wouldn't be the first time she has gotten frustrated and trashed her room. Sullivan trait."

He was smiling, but the smile didn't reach his eyes. She could feel his anxiousness flowing through his skin when she took his hand.

After looking up the staircase one more time, he cleared his throat and led her down the corridor towards Thaddeus's office. Coming to the door, they could hear voices on the other side as Ezra raised his hand and hammered his fist against the wood in three hard knocks. There was shuffling from the other side and then a pause before the door opened widely, Thaddeus standing on the other side. Silas was looming near the window in his usual spot, his arms crossed as he stared out the window.

"Must you be so loud?" Thaddeus sighed, leaving the door open and walking back to his desk.

"I don't have time to be quiet," Ezra said, guiding Ana inside and indicating her hands. "The darkness in her magic is increasing at a rapid rate. It started off small, but it is spreading fast. The Marion coven said it will spread until it reaches her brain and–"

"I know how dark magic works, Ezra," Thaddeus interrupted with a deep, exasperated frown, sitting down in his chair. "Did they give you the spell to cure it as your father suggested?"

"No, but they will . . ." Ezra winced, like he was bracing himself for Thaddeus to throw him out of his office at any second. "If we give them The Blue Draíocht."

"Excuse me?" Thaddeus said, tilting his head like he hadn't quite heard him correctly. His eyes narrowed when Ezra shrugged, and he raised from his seat again, his hands leaning on the desk in front of him. "That is a rare diamond, Ezra. It was gifted to us *hundreds* of years ago. I can't just hand over one of our most precious stones to give to a rival coven."

"A rival coven? How are they a *rival* coven? There are a handful of them left, and they can't even leave the safety of their home. How is that threatening to us, exactly?"

Thaddeus looked sideways at Silas, as if asking for confirmation if what Ezra said was true. Silas nodded once without looking at them, and Thaddeus puffed out a sigh before looking back at Ezra.

"Regardless of how valuable it is, if we don't take it to them, Ana is going dark. Once that happens, our hiding in the shadows as a coven is over, and the world will know the truth about our kind. That is something I *know* you don't want. Isn't that worth more to you than a ridiculous blue diamond?"

Thaddeus watched him for a beat longer, then lifted his hands from where they were resting on the table to stroke his beard. "Ezra, I cannot give you The Blue Draíocht because I do not know where it is."

Ana's heart stilled in her chest, her eyes watering as Ezra's face whitened, a look of defeat descending upon his features. "What?"

"The diamond is not in my possession. I do not know where it is kept. Only the treasurer of the coven knows the location of our most precious possessions. It is the one way we can assure a witch does not become high priest simply to access them."

Silas snorted a laugh, then cleared his throat to stop himself when his father shot him a look. When Ana looked up at Ezra, his shoulders were slacked.

"Well, if I get the treasurer to agree to tell me its location, do I have your permission to take it to the Marions?" His hands were clenched into fists at his sides.

Thaddeus frowned in thought as he stared down at the table. "Yes. Fine."

"Thank you." Ezra sighed as he ran a hand through his floppy hair in stress. "Second, I want the ban on my magic lifted until we smooth all of this out."

"No," Thaddeus said, sitting down at his desk and leaning back tiredly. "Absolutely not. Your ban will always stand."

"Thaddeus, we won't have any time to waste getting her back here for you to do the spell. The second I get the spell, I need to perform it on her so that she doesn't go dark. Silas can't help; he is an idiot when it comes to incantations, you know that. He can barely pronounce the words."

Silas growled in warning from his position beside the window, his arms dropping from crossing across his chest.

"God damn it, Ezra–fine, but the second you arrive back here, your ban will be reinstated. Silas will accompany you to the Marions. They may be small in number, but I still don't trust them."

"Perfect," Ezra said, then looked at Silas. "While we find out where the diamond is located, you need to locate Abby. Her room is trashed, and she is not there."

"She is probably in the alchemy tower. That's where I saw her last. I will track her down."

"Get the tincture from her when you find her. We will meet you in the van."

Ezra grabbed Ana's hand, pulling her quickly out of Thaddeus's office and down the hall, weaving through the labyrinth of corridors so quickly that Ana couldn't keep track of where they were headed.

"Where are we going?"

"To find the treasurer," Ezra said, his face focused but his eyes panicked.

She yelped, jolting when he pulled her down another corridor and finally up a black spiral staircase. "Who is the treasurer?"

He sighed, pausing in the middle of the stairwell and leaning over the railing to look up through the levels. His voice sounded dry when he spoke.

"Anora Alden."

CHAPTER 24

Anora's living area, like the rest of House Alden, was plunged into darkness. The ceilings were high, and the windows were arched, with beautiful crushed red velvet curtains that hung all the way to the floor. Large black bookcases lined the old brick walls, filled with vials of blood and jars containing various specimens Ana couldn't recognise. The gothic fireplace that sat at the back wall was roaring, sending a red glow bouncing around the room and casting shadows on the walls from the various marble statues positioned on the floor.

"Anora?" Ezra called.

Ana clasped Ezra's hand as she looked over her shoulders, in case Anora jumped out at them from some dark corner. Over the sound of the crackling fire, a gentle, eerie hum rose from somewhere beyond the wall at the back near the fireplace.

"Anora?" he said again.

"Come to me."

Anora's voice echoed all the way to her ears, but she was nowhere to be seen. Ezra's hand flinched in hers, but his feet moved anyway, guiding her across the dark wood floor and towards the back wall as if he knew exactly where she would be. That made her frown, jealousy thudding inside her heart when they passed the four-poster gothic bed with the silk sheets. She imagined how many times he had lain there with her. It made the magic in her stomach scratch angrily, and she had to force herself to breathe deeply to stop the darkness from forming at the corners of her eyes.

Tearing her eyes away from the bed, she looked around the wall, her eyes falling upon the enormous bath sitting in front of a large arched window. The glass was stained, depicting a battle with dying men and horses, and it cast a strange colour over the candlelit room. Anora sat among the bubbles, looking up at them from under her eyelashes as she waded her hands along the surface of the water. The candlelight reflected off her eyes as she stared at them.

"Ezra, my love. What can I do for you?" she said, tilting her head.

Ezra's shoulders tensed. In fact, his whole body was standing at attention in a way that made Ana tug his arm when he didn't reply right away.

"Uh. Yes," he said sheepishly. "Thaddeus said we could come and talk to you about something you may have in the treasury's inventory."

"Ah, I see." Anora sighed, reaching to finish the last sip of whatever liquid was in her wineglass.

She stared at them with her feline eyes before rolling them and setting her glass aside. Gripping the sides of the bathtub, she pushed herself to stand, the bubbles spilling over her perfectly toned body and down her legs. She stepped out of the water with barely a splash and stood on the towel that lay on the floor, ringing out her hair while she watched them. Ezra's breath hitched, and Ana frowned, looking up at him and how big his eyes were.

Anora grinned, seeming satisfied. "Why do you need into the treasury?"

Ezra choked and stuttered over his words until he let Ana's hand go and clenched his fist at his side. "We need The Blue Draíocht. Without it, Ana's magic will take over, and she could die."

Anora stood up tall again, her back straight and her tanned skin glowing from her bath oils. She closed the space between them, completely ignoring Ana as she reached to rest her hand on Ezra's chest, playing with the buttons of his shirt and smiling up at him under a sultry gaze.

"And pray tell, my love, why should I care?" She pulled him by his shirt so that his face was inches from hers. She was staring at him so intensely that he had no choice but to gaze right back, his eyes hooded.

Ana's face reddened as she noticed Ezra's hands relax at his sides, his fingers flicking like he wanted to reach out and hold on to her. He was lost somewhere inside his mind, completely forgetting Ana was even standing there as Anora pressed her naked body against him. She narrowed her eyes, then cleared her throat loudly, making Ezra jolt.

Ezra reached out and wrapped his fingers around Anora's wrist that was gripping his shirt, his eyes harder now when he looked at her. "Nice try. Stop fucking with my head, Anora. This is serious."

Anora pouted childishly and tutted at him, then tilted her head to look at Ana with a wicked smile. "But it's so much fun."

"Please, just tell us what we need to know so we can leave," Ana demanded with a frown. She tried not to flick her eyes over Anora's body. She was pushing her chest against Ezra, clearly to elicit some sort of response from her. She refused to give her one.

"No." Anora sighed, turning back to look at Ezra.

"Anora," Ezra warned. He moved the hand gripping her wrist to twist it. "I like you. I am the *only* person who likes you in this coven. Don't make an enemy out of me and don't make me hurt you."

"Ooh, don't threaten *me* with a good time." She chuckled, wriggling her wrist out of his grip and strutting towards her full-length mirror, where she looked at her reflection and ran a gentle finger over the tanned skin of her clavicle. "You know better than anyone, Ezra, that I do not do anything for free."

Ana didn't want to know what that meant. The tone that laced her words sent a jealous shiver through her body, and the hands at her sides turned to fists. Her eyes went instantly dark, and she took a threatening step forward but not before Ezra pulled his face into a scowl and raised an angry fist. The mirror in front of Anora exploded, sending shards flying through the air towards her naked body. She barely had time to turn her head and push her arms up in front of her face, blocking the glass from scratching her body with some unseen barrier.

Anora dropped her arms angrily, turning to face him fully with wide eyes. A few of the shards had cut her forearms. She calmed her breathing, then flicked her wet hair over her shoulder. "Someone got their magic back."

"I always had it," Ezra replied, his hand relaxing. "Now, if you could put some clothes on and stop fucking around, Anora, that would be great."

She rolled her eyes and turned her back to him, walking over the shards of mirror and towards a changing screen, which she disappeared behind. Within seconds, she emerged from the other side, dressed in a glittering emerald green dress. It had her signature plunging bustline, and it fanned out behind her in a fishtail. Her hair was dry, perfectly straight and shining, falling to the middle of her back, and her makeup was fixed with a dark smoky eye and flicked eyeliner.

"Better?" she asked, her hands fanning out beside her.

"Much," Ana said softly.

She wouldn't admit it aloud, but she understood why Ezra was so enthralled when Anora was around. She was alluring and beautiful, and magic or not, she had a presence one couldn't ignore. Her cheeks flushed as she watched her turn in the low light of the room and walk towards the table near another arched window.

"Let's talk terms, then," she said, filling a crystal glass with wine from a golden jug. "If you want access to the treasury, and if you want The Blue Draíocht, I have some demands of my own."

Anora turned, her wine glass hovering at her lips as she flashed them both a wicked grin. "As Ana and I previously discussed, and from your own *personal* experience, Ezra, you know I deal in blood." She took a long sip of her wine and looked into the glass as she continued. "I want a cup of her blood."

Ezra opened his mouth to answer, but Anora flashed him a smile and held up a finger to silence him. "I am not done."

Anora set her wine glass aside and approached him again, her eyes staring him down once more as she rested her hand against the buttons of his shirt. "And from you, a kiss. Call it our last goodbye . . ."

Ana frowned, reaching out to take Ezra's arm before he could answer. She didn't like that they were at Anora's mercy. It pooled anger in her stomach and pushed nausea up against her throat.

"I had a lot of reading time in those cells, Anora. I know that the blood of a witch is a powerful tool. If I give you my blood, how can I trust you will not use it against me?" Her brows furrowed as she studied the woman. Anora could use her blood for anything. Should she so choose, she could curse her without ever needing to touch her.

"You are not as stupid as you look." Anora looked sideways at her and chuckled. "But I do not need your blood for any spell, so you do not need to worry about that. Ezra can vouch for me; I only want to see what your magic *tastes* like. A magic such as yours must have a unique taste. All I need is one cup"–she directed her eyes back to Ezra–"and one kiss, and the diamond is yours. You can take my offer or leave it, but we both know she will go dark if you do not."

Ezra sighed, reaching for Ana's black taloned hand and frowning at her. "Ana, we have no choice and no time. It is just some blood, and I trust her when she says she will not use it for anything other than she means to."

Trust Anora. That was a peculiar concept. The woman couldn't be trusted, *shouldn't* be trusted, but Ezra was right–she didn't have a choice.

"All right. One cup," Ana said, snapping her eyes to Anora. "No spells."

"Cross my heart." She winked, stepping away from them to reach for a silver chalice from one of the bookcases and an athame.

The dagger was long and thin, with a silver snake that curled around the hilt and stared at them with red rubies for eyes. Anora walked to her, holding the athame out for Ana to take while she readied the silver chalice eagerly. Ana took the athame. The last time she was this close to an athame, it was lodged inside her stomach and almost killed her. It felt strange, to be holding another in her hand and willingly drawing more blood with it.

Ana gulped thickly, looking up at Ezra as he gave her a soft, encouraging smile. She smiled back weakly.

"I will not wait all day," Anora warned, holding the chalice upright in the space between them.

Ana frowned and rolled the sleeve of her red wool cardigan up to her elbow, staring down at the charcoal black skin that spanned her entire arm, seeping above the elbow and out of sight under her clothes. Setting her face and forcing her nerves to calm, she placed the blade against the skin of her inner forearm beside the scars Silas had left there. Without thinking about what she was doing or how badly it would feel, she pressed the sharp blade against her arm and sliced hard. The athame cut deep, causing a sharp gasp to escape her throat. It *hurt*, and it bled freely, dripping onto the floor.

Anora's eyes flashed with excitement as she grabbed Ana's wrist in a crushing grip. She pushed the chalice under her arm, catching the blood as it poured from her wound. Anora's hand shook as she clutched her wrist, and she could tell from how still her chest was that she had stopped breathing.

Ana's brows pulled together, and her teeth clenched as she hissed through them to push away the burning sting that radiated up her arm. Her blood was a deep red that looked almost black in the light of the room. Anora leaned her face close to it, a grin spread over her perfect face.

"That is enough, Anora," Ezra said, looking uncomfortable as he came to Ana's side.

Anora held tight, seeming to be lost inside her head as she shook Ana's wrist, sending the blood flowing faster until the cup overflowed. Ana swayed, her face paling at the sight of how much blood was coming from her, making her knees buckle and her head feel light.

"Anora, I said that is enough!" Ezra shouted, taking Ana's

elbow and yanking her away while Anora steadied her cup and brought it to her chest as if she were cradling something precious.

Ezra frowned deeply at her, then turned his back on her as he placed his hand over the wound on Ana's arm, pressing hard to stop the blood from flowing freely. She watched his face, his brows furrowing in concentration. The greens in his eyes sparked to life and grew brighter. It was startling to see how vibrant they were when she wasn't used to seeing magic swirling in his eyes. It was hypnotising, and she found herself lost in them until she felt the stinging pressure in her arm fading away to nothing but gentle tingling.

Looking down at her arm, Ezra pulled his hand away, revealing the healed wound. The scar was difficult to see because of the darkness of her arm, but when she tilted it in the light, she could see how it was raised on her skin beside the others.

"Thank you."

"You are welcome," Ezra said, giving her a soft smile, then turned his attention to Anora. She was placing the chalice of Ana's blood carefully on the table and wiping her hands clean of any blood that had spilled over onto her fingers. "You got what you wanted, Anora. Tell us where the treasury is."

Anora spun around to look at them again, her face returning to its natural coy smile instead of the wide-eyed wonder that graced her features when she was looking at the blood. "I will, when I get my kiss." She flicked her eyes to look at Ana. "You can go now; I will send Ezra out to you in a moment."

Gulping down her nausea, Ana shook her head and pulled the sleeve of her red wool cardigan down over her arm again. If she thought for a second that she was going to leave Ezra within her grasp when she had such a hold over him, Anora had another thing coming. "No."

"It's okay. I will meet you outside," Ezra said, reaching to pinch her chin and giving her another smile to calm her nerves. "I won't be long."

Anora smiled triumphantly, wiggling her fingers in a wave goodbye.

Frowning angrily, Ana turned on her heel and stormed out of the room. Her feet took her around the wall that separated the bath area and the bedroom, but they refused to walk her any further, instead forcing her to stand with her back against the wall. She waited until she heard Anora walking across the stone floor and whispering something softly to Ezra. Curiosity chewed at her insides, making her bite down on her lip hard as she poked her head around the wall to peek at them.

Ezra was standing still, with his hands on his hips, and watching Anora, who was tilting her head at him and drinking him in. She said something to him that Ana couldn't hear, but Ezra cut her off. The only word she could hear clearly was "treasury." Anora rolled her eyes, cupped the side of his face with her hand and leaned into his ear. She stayed there, whispering something to him for a moment too long, then pulled away so she could look back into his eyes.

Ezra nodded once, then grabbed Anora's head in his hands and kissed her fully. It was passionate and obsessive, and Ana gaped at them while her heart pounded against the inside of her chest. It *hurt* to watch them. His hands enveloped Anora's body hugging her close just like he did with her, while she bit his lip and let her hands roam his chest.

At the sound of a moan filtering from Ezra's chest, Ana turned from the wall and rushed silently across the room and out through the door to the spiral staircase. Tears were filling her eyes, and the magic in her stomach pulled angrily. Somehow, watching that kiss hurt worse than the slice of her arm had.

Rushing down the staircase, Ana sped through the many weaving corridors of House Alden until she arrived in the foyer. She sniffled and wiped her cheeks, setting her face when she found Silas standing at the open door.

"What's wrong with you?" he asked, glancing at her from where he was staring outside. "You look like someone just pissed on your breakfast."

"I haven't even *had* breakfast," Ana snapped, coming to his side and trying to calm the anger that had pooled in her stomach. It fed the magic there, and she could see her vision darken in response. "Did you find Abby? I could really use one of those tinctures right about now."

"No." Silas pushed off the door and looked over Ana's shoulder.

Ezra emerged from the corridor, reaching to place his hand on the small of her back to let her know he was there. She stepped forward and away from his hand, staring at Silas instead.

"What do you mean? Where is she?" she asked, crossing her arms over her chest.

"Abby," he elaborated for Ezra, looking between them. "She is not in the alchemy tower or in her room, nor is she anywhere on Alden grounds. We did a tracking spell, but she cannot be located."

"What?" Ezra asked, his face awash with worry. "That makes no sense. She wouldn't just *leave* without telling anyone. We need to find her."

"I have my men on it." He was frowning, which Ana was used to, but there was something else behind it that she hadn't seen in his expression before. Fear.

He turned, walking outside and across the pathway towards Genevieve's brown van, Ezra hot on his heels.

"Silas! We can't leave without knowing where she is. She is my *sister*. She could be in trouble!"

Silas whipped around, his eyes boring a hole into Ezra and making him stop in his tracks. "You think I don't know that? I said, I'm handling it." He growled. "We don't have time to wait for her to return. There was no tincture left for Ana, which means we have less time to find this stupid blue rock and fix her. I have my best men looking for Abby. By the time we come back with Ana cured, she will be here."

He walked again, passion in his step as he pulled the door of the van open roughly and got inside the passenger seat, leaving Ana and Ezra to follow silently. She jumped into the back again, while Ezra took his place in the driver's seat and placed the key into the ignition. He stared at House Alden before finally setting his face and turning the key.

The van sputtered to life, sounding just as angry as everyone inside felt, sending them down the smooth road and out of the gates of House Alden.

"Where are we going?" Ana asked, her voice quiet.

Ezra held the steering wheel with one hand, his other holding his head up as he leaned against the window of the van. "The place where our ancestors lie."

CHAPTER 25

The van pulled to a stop.

Looking out of the window, Ana saw two tall iron gates. They were arched and had arrowhead spikes poking out of the top, with high grey brick walls that lined the property. Through the bars of the gate, she spotted old gravestones sticking out of the ground like loose, broken teeth. Behind them stood an old stone building that looked like a crypt. Gargoyles sat on its roof, and crying statues were positioned on either side of the solid stone doorway, while trees swayed with red and orange leaves in the background, framing it. There was a mist in the air, and it hovered just above the ground and wove its way between the headstones like dissipated ghosts clinging to their last remnants of existence.

"Where are we?" she asked, looking between Silas and Ezra. It was drizzling, and the water stuck to the window in a light spray.

"The treasury, apparently," Ezra said, shutting the engine off and turning to look at her with a soft smile.

Ana didn't return it. She shrugged and turned to Silas, nudging him. "Are you coming?"

Silas wasn't paying attention. He flicked through his phone with heavy fingers. "Hm?"

She reached out a hand and shoved his shoulder, making him lift his head and flash her a warning look. "I said, Are you coming?"

"No," he said through gritted teeth. "Lifting a diamond isn't exactly a three-man job, and I am waiting for updates on Abby."

Ezra didn't argue. He opened his door and jumped out, slamming it closed and walking around to the sliding door. He yanked it open with a loud squeak, offering Ana his hand. She eyed it for a moment, then frowned and got out of the van herself, walking towards the large gates.

He sighed, taking his hand back and closing the door of the van before he jogged to catch up with her. His face was pulled into a confused expression when he looked sideways at her, his hands working the iron lock. It clicked open, and he pulled the chain free, letting it drop to the ground.

"Are you okay?"

"Yep," Ana mumbled, pushing the gate open and slipping through.

She didn't wait on him, instead walking up the cobblestone path that led up the hill between the headstones. It was cold today, and the drizzle that came down upon them was heavier than she expected. It dampened her hair and seeped into her clothes, making frizzy hair stick to her face. Wrapping her arms around herself, she arrived at the door of the crypt, looking up at the stonework. It was carved in beautiful filigree, with symbols and sigils lining the frame.

"Ana . . ." Ezra jogged to catch up. He reached a hand to touch her elbow when he got to her, then frowned deeply when she stepped back from him. "What's wrong? Are you feeling all right?"

"Just open the door."

Ezra raised his eyebrow at her, then blinked and looked to the doorway. He puffed out a sigh, then nodded and stood back to look at the etching that spanned the stone frame. He studied it for a long moment, reading them with muttering lips.

"The incantation is in our own coven alphabet, so that is helpful. We need the blood of the coven to open it, meaning one of us." He reached into his pocket and pulled out a pocketknife, flicking it open and looking at her. "I'll do it, unless you would rather stab me yourself?"

"Tempting, but no," she said, trying not to pout.

She glanced at him and noted his weak smile. His smile always softened her heart, but every time she flicked her eyes to his lips, all she could see was Anora all over him and how much he enjoyed kissing her. Her magic screamed, sending a shock of pain over her body that made her double over and grip the wool cardigan at her stomach. She yelled, shutting her eyes tightly and falling forward against the door to keep herself on her feet until she felt Ezra's arms around her, pulling her close to him.

"Ana! What is going on?!" he said, his hand grabbing her shoulders and helping her stand upright.

She fluttered her eyes open to look at him, trying not to whimper at the pain. It ached, like her bones were shifting and her blood was boiling. She could see the corners of her vision darken.

"It hurts." She groaned, lifting her hand to rest it against the wall of the crypt. "Open the door, please. I don't think I have much time left."

Ezra's face was pale as he studied her eyes. He reached out a hand to her cheek, rubbing his thumb along the black veins that leaked from her eyes into her face. "Just hold on a little longer."

Stepping back from her, he raised his hand and placed the blade into his palm, slicing it quickly. He didn't even flinch, and when he raised his head to look at the door, his eyes were glowing in bright, magical greens. Reaching forward, Ezra placed his bleeding hand onto the sigil in the middle of the door, letting his blood seep into the cracks and reading the incantation aloud. His voice sounded strong, even though she knew he was worried, and it travelled over the mist-covered graveyard like silk.

The blood moved along the cracks and filled the sigils, running along the side of the door, making Ana stumble back from it and stand beside him. The ground rumbled loudly, shaking the cobblestones under her feet and loosening the tiles on the roof. Some came crashing down, making Ana yelp when they smashed by their feet.

The rumbling halted, and Ezra took his hand back from the door, flicking his fingers to swipe the blood from them onto the floor. Somewhere behind it she could hear clicking, then turning, and finally, the door opened a crack, a plume of dust bursting from the gap.

Ana gaped up at it, hardly noticing when Ezra clenched his hand to heal it. It flashed in gold in the corner of her eye, then dissipated when he rubbed the smeared blood on his thigh.

"Let's go." He pushed the door open and peeked inside, then reached out for her hand. Despite still feeling anger in her gut, she took it and followed him inside.

The room inside was small and dark. For a moment, Ana couldn't see anything except the back of Ezra's head as he walked into the darkness. They stopped walking, the door closing behind them and leaving them blind until Ezra mumbled something. The room illuminated with light, torches that lined the walls of the small room bursting into flame and casting shadows along the damp stone. The whole crypt smelled stale, like rotten wood and rain.

Ana glanced at the stone pillars, tombs and chests that littered the back wall. In the middle of the room, a stairway led underground. There was light down there too; she could see the flickering of fire dancing along the floor and up the steps, almost inviting them downward.

"This way, I guess," he said, pulling her down the stairs.

Ana took her hand back now that she was inside, crossing her arms over her chest and avoiding his gaze.

"Are you going to tell me what is eating you?" he asked, his footsteps heavy.

Ana didn't say anything. Instead, she walked around him on the steps and rushed down the rest of them until she came to the bottom. A long, wide corridor met her feet, either side of it filled with person-sized holes that were filled with stone caskets.

"Who are the caskets for?" she asked, trying to change the subject while she walked among them.

"Coffins," Ezra corrected. When she raised her brow, he continued, "Casket lids are held on with a hinge. Coffin lids are completely removable."

"Good to know," Ana said with a sarcastic roll of her eyes. "But that doesn't answer my question."

Ezra looked around at the stonework, walking past them and running his fingers along the stone. "Sullivans, Aldens, the rest of the coven families. The most prominent of our ancestors are kept here, in the main corridor, and the rest are in the wings." He paused at one of the coffins and brushed his finger over the name.

Ana approached his side, looking over his arm to read it.

"Emily Sullivan," Ezra said, then examined the other coffins. "Her father, mother, and her daughter."

"Did they die young?"

"No. They lived long lives, actually. Emily was unmarried when she had her daughter, though. That didn't go down well with the village, but the coven kept her safe. Back then, our coven had an understanding with Thomas Harrow. That is the only reason Emily was not burned for being a witch." He lifted his finger and moved on.

Ana walked with him, looking over her shoulder at the coffin of Emily Sullivan, then up to his face again as they reached a second door. This entrance was much simpler. It was wooden, with a large padlock hanging from the lock.

"I assume *Anora* gave you a key?" she said, unsuccessfully keeping the venom from her tone, which made Ezra stand up straighter and glare at her.

"Okay, that's enough. What is your problem? Are you mad at me?" He put his hands on his hips. When she looked away, he grabbed her by the shoulders and forced her to look at him. "Is this about Anora?"

Ana pouted, shrugging him off and hugging herself. "I saw your kiss."

Ezra's eyes went wide, then a smile crept over his features and he laughed. "What?"

"Don't laugh at me. It's not funny," she said through gritted teeth, shoving him.

"Ana, come on, I had to! She wouldn't have led us here if I didn't. I kissed her for *you*." He raised his hands up defensively.

"For me? You kissed her like *that*, for me?" Ana asked. His features turned confused, then amused. "I know you had to, but you didn't have to enjoy it *that* much."

"Anora is a narcissist. If I hadn't given her exactly what she wanted, she was never going to leave us alone. If I didn't kiss her like that, she would have let you go dark. Would you rather that?"

Rage worked its way through her magic and into her head, fuelling her blood and filling the rest of her eyes with darkness. Her hands shook, and when he reached out to hold her, she thrashed out, grabbing onto his wrists. Something inside her snapped, and before she knew what she was doing, Ezra collapsed to his knees and the room was filled with fog, the ground rumbling under her feet. His nose was bleeding, and he looked faint at her mere touch.

"Ana . . ." He released raspy breaths, trying to wriggle his hands out of her grip.

She held on tighter, then leaned her face into his to watch his scared eyes. The thrill she felt when she burned his father burst open inside her chest, making her shiver. She knew he could fight back, just like Silas had done when she tried to hurt him, but he didn't. He just sat there, looking up at her.

"Ana, this isn't you." He gasped, tugging his hands weakly. "Let me go."

"Fight back!" she shouted.

This time when she spoke, she could hear her voice was not her own. It held a metallic sound, like several voices were screaming in harmony. It startled her, and her hands weakened on his wrists, giving him enough time to break the contact and stand. He reached for her, ignoring her feral growl as he studied her form. Her eyes were leaking black into her cheeks, and the blackness that covered her arms was now spreading to her shoulders and collarbone.

"Ana . . ." He gulped. "This isn't you. This is the dark magic talking. I need you to push it back."

She panted thick, angry breaths as she listened to his words through the loud ringing in her ears. The magic in her stomach was screaming loudly, pulling and chewing her insides with a rage she had never felt before, yet she had no idea why. She didn't know why she was mad at him for kissing Anora, when he did it to keep her alive. She didn't know why she hated him. She didn't know why she wanted so badly to reach out and rip his throat out. Her clawed hand twitched. He was completely still, his eyes begging for her to see reason.

"You are Ana Davenport. You are good, and you are perfect, and you are mine, and you are *okay*." He reached out to cradle her face. "Calm. Down."

Ana flinched at his touch, but she didn't otherwise move. Her body felt hot and sweaty, like she had a fever that just wouldn't break. "I hate you," she seethed, her teeth gritting.

She didn't hate him. She didn't know why she was saying these things to him. She *loved* him. The normal part of her brain wanted to reach out and hold him, but she couldn't move. She was scared that if she did, she wouldn't be able to control herself.

Ezra flashed her a handsome smile. "No, you don't." Then he leaned in and kissed her softly.

Ana squirmed, her hands gripping his wrists tightly with her taloned fingers. He deepened the kiss so much she had no choice but to relax. She could feel the magic in his hands seeping into her body, filling her with warmth and love. It pushed away all the hate, and the rage faded until she finally started to shake and cry.

The fury was gone, and she spluttered against his lips, breaking the kiss to bring in a deep lungful of stale air into herself, clinging to him as she cried more loudly and leaned against his chest.

"W-what is happening to me?" She whimpered. "I'm so

sorry! I-I don't even know why I am so angry. It won't go away!"

Ezra wrapped his arms around her tightly and buried his face into her hair, keeping her there while she tried to calm down. "It's okay. It's the magic, that's all. It isn't you."

He waited until she was breathing evenly again before he pulled out of the hug and held her by the shoulders. His eyes found the places on her shoulders and collarbone that were turning black, making their way upwards towards her neck and head.

"We don't have much time, Ana. Your eyes won't turn back to normal anymore, and the darkness has almost reached your head. We need to go to the Marions now."

"It h-hurts," she stammered, hiccupping a sob.

"I know. I know," he cooed, kissing her forehead.

Letting her go, Ezra turned back to the lock and fished into his pocket, retrieving the key. He slipped it into the lock and turned it with shaky hands. He opened it, pulling the heavy padlock off the door and throwing it onto the floor before yanking the door wide and taking her hand to bring her inside the next room.

The light of torches already filled the room. It flickered along the walls and shone among the many chests and wooden boxes that cluttered the floor. Paintings covered in dirty sheets were stacked together against the wall beside marble statues, gold chalices and glass cabinets with strange artefacts inside.

"This wasn't exactly what I expected," Ana mumbled, hugging her stomach and wincing against the pain.

"And what did you expect? The cave of wonders?" Ezra joked, coming into the middle of the room. "There are no wonders in this place, just cursed objects and valuables that only mean something to the coven."

"Cursed objects. Fantastic." She gazed at the objects and bit her lip hard. "Where should we look?"

"Everywhere."

Ezra approached one of the chests, pulling it open with a creak and digging inside, leaving her to walk around the room and stare into the glass cabinets. Inside were potion bottles sealed with wax, old tin whistles, music boxes and little dolls. Their beaded eyes stared back at her, and when she narrowed her eyes, their wicked smiles seemed to deepen.

Ana sighed and opened the glass door, holding the handle in one taloned hand as the other reached out towards them.

"No!" Ezra was suddenly behind her, pulling her arm back and closing the cabinet door with wide eyes. "Don't touch them. Don't touch *anything*. Just look."

"Why?"

"Because if you touch them, this day will get a whole lot worse, and we really don't have time for a curse on top of everything else. Just . . . stay here. I will find it."

Ana frowned as he moved away from her and opened more chests, rummaging through their contents. His search through the items and how easily he could discern which of those he could touch and which to stay clear of made her feel like a fraud. She had magic, yes, but it wasn't hers. This wasn't her world, nor was it ever going to be. She didn't know the things that were normal to him, and she could never understand what it was like to grow up around cursed objects and daily magical practices. She felt like one of those dolls in the cabinet, full of cursed magic and staring out at a magical room, yet kept behind glass just out of reach of it.

"Ah. I think this is it," Ezra mumbled, pulling a box from a chest and turning to look at her.

He walked to her, then undid the little clasp. Inside, on a bed of white silk, was a light blue diamond. Ana reached out and lifted it with taloned fingers, setting it in the palm of her hand. It fit snuggly there, reflecting the light back at her beautifully. It was stunning, and she realised as she looked at it in the palm of her black hand, that no matter the beauty of it, this diamond was the only thing that stood between her and the darkness.

"We should go, while we still have time," Ezra said, taking it from her and placing it back into the box before he clasped it and took her hand.

She nodded, allowing him to guide her out of the room and lock the door before pulling her past the closed coffins of his family, up the steps and back out into the mist and chill of the graveyard. The second their feet hit the path outside, the door slammed closed, and she heard mechanical locks turning and clicking back into place. Ezra led her down the hill, letting her go to jump into the van while he closed the gates.

"Did you get it?" Silas asked, looking up from his phone.

"Yes, but we don't have much time left. I am starting to lose control." Ana gulped, settling herself into her seat when Ezra opened the driver's side door and got into the van.

When Ezra passed the box to her, Silas studied her all-black eyes and the darkness spreading up her neck. "I can see that."

"Any news of Abby?" Ezra asked, starting the engine and fastening his seatbelt with fumbling fingers.

"No. The Venator has concluded their tracking spells, they have found that she used the mirror in her bedroom as transport somewhere, but they couldn't tell where. Wherever she went was protected. Thaddeus has called a Council meeting; they will be arriving shortly to discuss it further."

Ezra gulped thickly, his anxiety over his sister evident on his face. "Right. Well." He cleared his throat. "If they have it handled, we need to go to the Marions. We can help find her when we have cured Ana."

He reversed the van and whipped around the corner of the wall, pushing the gearstick forward. He slammed his foot down on the accelerator, speeding down the road and away from the graveyard as fast as the little van could take them.

CHAPTER 26

"Are you ready?"

Ana looked up at the mountain when they parked. Her stomach clenched, and her magic cramped, knowing it was home. Gripping the box in her hand, she took a steadying breath. Ezra was looking at her, and she gave him a weak nod.

He smiled softly back and got out of the van. Walking around it and opening the door for her, he offered her his hand, which she took and got out of the van slowly, trying not to wince at how her body responded to the movement. She felt weak, like her body was beginning to shut down and her mind fading.

Ezra pinched her chin with his finger and thumb, like he always did when he was trying to get her to look him in the eye. "Hey." He smiled at her. "We've got this."

"Yeah." Ana tried to stop her lip from trembling.

Hand in hand, Ana and Ezra followed Silas, who was already up ahead on the pathway that led to the Marion caves. The doorway was already open and waiting for them, the hallways inside dark and brooding. Silas paused at the entrance as if he were willing his feet to keep moving but they rooted him to the spot. The mountain had an eeriness that radiated out of the stone and crept through the cracks, leaving her hollow. The Marion coven themselves were creepy, too, and as she stood staring at the open doorway, she felt a pang of panic. She didn't want to have to walk inside those caves, to be at the mercy of a coven they didn't know if they could even trust.

Not that they had a choice.

They walked over the threshold, through the caves and into the carved-out palace. The black obsidian walls were glittering with the reflecting light that came from the many hovering light orbs that fluttered in the air near the ceiling. A smirking Mallory Marion was already seated in her obsidian glass chair, her hands folded delicately on her knee and her white eyes trained on them. Her ivory skin was practically glowing, her white hair billowing down her back and her silver dress fanning out beside her legs perfectly.

The closer Ana got to the woman, the more she felt woozy and the shakier her vision became, the magic in her stomach clawing to get out. Ezra pulled her close to his side and rubbed her arm, steadying her.

"I have been waiting for you," Mallory said with a tilted head when they got close enough.

They all stopped in front of her chair. Silas was looking up at the staircase, where the rest of the coven was standing. They peered down at the trio with their white hair, glowing skin and moonstone eyes. Silas shivered.

The grand foyer was freezing, or maybe it was the magic inside her, but it was making her breath come out of her body in plumes of clouds, like her lungs themselves were freezing.

"Why all the long faces?" Mallory asked with a wide grin as she stood. She sauntered towards them, her white eyes scrutinising every inch of their bodies. "I am actually surprised she is still standing. I thought she would have gone dark and come to me on her own by now." She chuckled.

"Why would I come here if I was going dark?" Ana asked, her head following Mal as she stalked them.

"You have Marion magic inside you, so why wouldn't your dark version return to its home?"

She came to a stop in front of Ezra, smiling widely at him and coming in close to his face so she could gaze into his eyes. "Your eyes are the most spectacular shade of green when they have magic running through them." She outstretched a finger and ran it down his face.

Ezra flinched, stepping back from her and clearing his throat. "Stop playing with us. We don't have time for games, Mallory. We brought The Blue Draíocht. We need the spell now; she doesn't have much time."

Mallory retracted her hand with a pout. "No, she does not." She sighed, walking on to Ana again and standing in front of her, grinning and narrowing her eyes. "Give me my diamond." She extended her hand.

Ana's hand shook as she forfeited it over to her, dropping it into her palm and watching her face. Mallory closed her hand around it the second it touched her skin and turned, gliding back to her chair and sitting down. She set the box on her lap, and with long beautiful fingers, she flipped the lid open, revealing the diamond.

"It is stunning. Absolute perfection." Mallory gasped, a bright smile on her face as she held it up in front of her. She blinked, and the stone in her palm disappeared, leaving her hand bare again. She leaned back in her chair.

"You got what you wanted. Give us the spell, Mallory," Ezra

demanded. He took a step towards her, and Ana followed, wanting to stay as close as she could to him.

Mallory chuckled, watching them in amusement before she laughed, throwing her head back and almost doubling over in hysterics. She tried to catch a breath through them. "I never thought the Sullivans were the stupid ones, but I guess I was wrong."

Ezra's jaw tensed as he gritted his teeth, his hand clenched in a fist on his side. "Mallory, I am not fucking around anymore. Give me the spell!"

"There is no spell." Mallory grinned, tilting her head.

Ana's heart stopped in her chest, and her knees buckled. "W-what? You were playing us?" She glanced between Ezra and Silas. "She was playing with us?"

Ezra's hand flew out in front of him, his magic igniting in a green glow in his palm as the ground shook in warning. "Give me the fucking spell, Mallory, or I will rip your heart from your chest!"

"Stay with Ana. I've got this," Silas said, patting Ezra on the shoulder as he approached Mallory.

Mal raised a finger with a grin. "Before you do, you might want to hear what I have to say."

Silas stopped, looking back at Ana and Ezra, and Ezra nodded for him to stay still.

"You see, when Alexander came here and told me that our Marion magic had been set free, and in the body of a *human*, no less, I was justifiably furious. I made him the deal because I needed the stone. It is very like the one inside the Marion athame, don't you think? That is because *it is*. It is a carrier stone, just like that one. The problem with The Blue Draíocht is that it doesn't work with an enchanted object like the one inside the athame. No, it will only work with a transference spell."

"We don't have time for this, Mallory!" Ezra shouted angrily. Ana's blackness was nearing her ears now, and climbing.

"I am getting to the point, I promise." Mal waved her hand. "I will admit, I lied. There is no spell to take the magic out of her, but there is another way, though you will not like it. The magic Ana has inside her belongs to *me*. It is Marion magic, and it should be equally shared among my coven. I have cast a spell in the next room. The stone is waiting for a soul to inhabit it. A magical soul."

Ezra's face turned pale. He dropped his arm and extinguished the green magic coming from his palm, staring at Mallory as she stood from her obsidian throne.

"The spell has a time limit. I had the timer set when I felt you coming. The sacred circle and the spell in the next room are working quite masterfully, if I do say so myself. When the timer runs out, whoever is standing in the sacred circle will fall. Their soul and, more importantly, their *magic* will be transferred into The Blue Draíocht, just like my ancestors were in the red diamond of the athame. Then I will take the magic out of it and use it for my coven. Ana will walk into the circle willingly, and the magic, including the darkness, will be transferred."

Mallory looked giddy, as if she knew the magic would be all hers. "It is the only way. She has around five minutes to decide what she wishes to do."

"I will not let you kill her. We are leaving and will find another way. Let's go," Ezra said, anger in his eyes as he grabbed Ana's hand, walking towards the exit.

"I am not finished," Mallory said, tilting her head. Ezra stopped, still gripping Ana's hand. "If she does not walk into the circle willingly, she is going to turn dark before the moon rises anyway, terrorising anyone in her path. If she is transferred, she will not be technically dead; her body will be alive, simply vacant. You can still have some piece of her, for whatever use it will be to you, I do not know, but that is none of my concern."

Ezra clenched Ana's hand harder. "Silas, we are leaving."

"Before you decide to leave, just know that if she does not walk into that circle, her friend will take her place!" Mallory called, her features growing wicked.

Ana turned to look back at the witch as she stood triumphantly at the base of the staircase, her coven behind her waiting. "What friend?"

"I won't spoil the surprise. But before you go, just remember, if no one is standing in the circle when the timer runs out, the spell will explode and kill you all. It is you or everyone you love; it shouldn't be that hard of a choice, Ana. The spell is just down that corridor. The rest of you can leave when it is complete. Happy decision-making." Mallory waved.

Ana gasped, cold sweat engulfing her body as she took off in a run down the corridor, Silas and Ezra hot on her heel. She ran down the dimly lit hallway until she got to the last door and pushed it. It was heavy, and it wouldn't budge until Ezra and Silas flanked her sides and shoved their shoulders into the granite, opening it all the way.

As soon as there was enough space, Ana ran inside and skidded to a stop in the middle of the room. The ceiling was tall, and the walls were white, made from carved marble. At the back wall sat a raised area that almost looked like a stage, white columns on either side of it and a sand timer that was nearing its end on a glass table.

Above the stage, a beam of light came from seemingly nowhere, shining down in the shape of a circle. The magic of the circle hummed so loudly it made the atoms in the air shake. Her vision was blurry, but from what she could see, someone was standing in the middle of the beam of light. It was a woman, and she was crying. Her hands reached out in front of her like she wanted to jump out of the circle of light, but she didn't move. Fear was plastered all over her face as she ran her hands through her black and purple hair.

"Ezra? Silas?" Abby hiccupped from inside the circle.

"Abby?" Ezra gasped, his face losing what was left of its colour. "Shit! Abby, don't move! I am coming!"

They all sprinted to the stage, where Ana looked up above Abby's head. The blue diamond floated above her. The light emerging from the sacred circle went upwards and into its tip, waiting for the time to run out so that it could take Abby's magic and her life.

Ana's hands shook at her sides as she looked among Abby, the diamond, and Ezra, who was ripping at his hair.

"Ezra, please don't let me die," Abby cried.

Ezra flinched like he wanted to move towards her, but Ana reached out and took his arm. "I need to swap with her. If we swap, Mallory will stop, and she will let you all go. She isn't going to stop until she gets my magic. I am going to go dark, anyway; it is the only choice we have."

"There is always a choice!" Ezra said, looking at her with tears in his eyes. "You can't walk into that circle, Ana. If you do, you die, and I can't watch you die. Besides, you don't know what Mallory wants that magic for. It is *dark* magic; she is the last person who should have it."

"Whatever we are going to do, we need to do it fast. The timer is almost finished, and I am *not* losing Abby," Silas said as he walked around the stage, staring between the circle and the stone. "The circle is cast well. There is no breaking it."

"Just let me think!" Ezra shouted, breaking from Ana's grip to approach the side of the stage and study the seams for some kind of loophole.

"Ezra, the time is almost gone!" Silas bellowed, walking to the timer and gripping it, presumably to flip it over. It wouldn't budge.

"I just . . ." Ezra panted, his voice breaking. "I-I just need some more time."

"Abby doesn't have time!" Ana said, walking to him. She took Ezra's face in her hands and looked up at him with a weak smile. "It's *okay*, Ezra. I was supposed to die back in the monument. I have been living on borrowed time ever since. I can't let Abby die for me." She sniffled. "Kiss me, before I have to go."

Ezra trembled, his eyes full of tears as his hands gripped her wrists by his face. He stared into her black eyes, and something in his expression changed. Acceptance, perhaps. He spluttered, then leaned in and kissed her fully.

"Ana . . ." he mumbled, pulling back and peering into her eyes. The magic inside them was flowing so brightly, and as she looked into his green eyes, her own eyes hooded, and her heartbeat slowed.

Ana couldn't move. She hadn't felt his influence seeping under her skin and breaking her senses while she was kissing him, but it had a hold of her and it was clinging tightly. "W-what are you doing?"

"I am so sorry. I need you to know that you mean *everything* to me. A-and I need you to promise me you are going to fight this darkness with everything you have, okay? You can do this without me." Ezra sniffled, keeping his gaze on her until he was sure he had her completely under his control.

Realisation flooded her, and she tried to cry and move her body, but she couldn't. The only thing she could move was her mouth. "No. Ezra, *please*."

Ezra leaned in and kissed her forehead, then steadied himself and cleared his throat. "Your body is frozen here. You can't move from this spot, do you understand? Not until it's over."

Ana wanted to scream at him, but her mouth wasn't working anymore as it obeyed his influence. Her whole body felt numb as tears dripped down her face from eyes that couldn't blink.

"You can bring me back. If I am in that stone, I won't be dead, just transported." He then let her go. "Bring me back."

Ezra tore his eyes away from her, not bothering to wipe his cheeks as he ran up the steps of the marble stage and held his hand out to his sister at the edge of the sacred circle. "Abby, take my hand!"

"If I move off the circle, it will kill everyone, Ezra. I'm scared."

"I know. I am scared too. Just give me your hand, Abby, please," Ezra begged.

Abby reached out for him, and Ezra slipped his foot into the circle, putting pressure on it with his foot. "Jump out now!"

"What?" Abby hiccupped.

"God damn it, Abby, move!" Ezra yelled. He grabbed her wrist and pulled her out of the circle, stepping into it once she was clear.

Abby tumbled down the marble steps and onto the floor at Ana's feet, staring at him as he held his hands at his sides and studied the inside of the circle. He looked back at them with wide eyes.

"No! Ezra, it will kill you!" Abby cried, scrambling to her feet, but Silas was already behind her, wrapping his arm around her middle and lifting her off her feet. She thrashed, hitting his large chest with her elbows and crying. "Stop it, let me go!"

Ana fought against Ezra's influence, but as long as his heart was beating, it wouldn't budge. She wanted to tell him not to do this. She wanted to tell him she loved him and to come back to her, but she couldn't even move her mouth. Tears tripped down her face as she stood frozen, watching as the circle started to grow brighter now the time was almost up.

"The timer is nearly done, Ezra! Are you sure about this?" Silas shouted up at him. Abby was wriggling in his grasp and cursing him, but he ignored her.

Ezra nodded firmly and looked at Silas, giving him a small smile. "Take care of them. Keep Ana safe. Whatever you do, don't let her go dark."

When Silas nodded back, Ezra turned to Ana, and his resolve completely broke. She knew he was trying to stay strong, but his hands at his sides trembled. "Be brave, Ana. I love you."

The timer stopped, and the circle exploded, bathing the room in light. She couldn't see him through it, but his violent screaming pierced the metallic ringing sound of the magic in the room. The longer his screams lasted, the more his influence on her slipped away until she could finally move her body.

"Ezra!" Ana screamed, taking sharp breaths as the light dimmed enough so that she could see him.

His feet were floating off the floor, and his chest was bowed up towards the diamond, silver wisps of life leaving his body through his chest, mouth, ears and nose until his body went completely limp. The light of the circle broke in a flash, and Ezra's body dropped onto the hard marble floor with a sickening *thud*. The room fell silent as they watched the diamond above him disappear, the vibration of the room fading away.

Ana spluttered, rushing forward up the steps and to his side and grabbing his shoulder. Rolling him onto his back, she reached to hold his face, watching him through wide eyes. Her black hands were shaking against his face, gripping his head and trying to shake him awake. He didn't move.

"Ezra?" Ana hiccupped, trying to see him through her tears.

She placed a hand flat on his chest, trying to feel it swell with breath, to feel his heartbeat, to feel *anything*. There was nothing. Her heart shattered inside her chest, the shards piercing her body and her mind cracking.

"No. Ezra, wake up, please!" He was bleeding through his nose and his ears, like his life and his magic had to rip its way out of him the easiest way it could. She cried as she brushed his hair back from his face and wiped her cheeks from her falling tears. "W-we have to go to the cottage in Coral Bay, remember? Remember?! Please wake up!"

"Ana, we need to get out of here," Silas said, suddenly at her side and putting a hand on her shoulder. "When the Marions find out it wasn't you who got taken, we are going to have a problem on our hands. Then Ezra would have done all this for nothing."

"Don't touch me!" Ana spat through gritted teeth, shrugging off his hand and cradling Ezra's head tighter.

"We need to go!" Silas barked.

Abby whimpered as she found her way to them, sinking to her knees by their side and holding her brother's hand, a look of guilt washing over her face as her body shook with sobs. "Silas is right. We need to get him out of here and find a way to bring him back."

Something inside Ana's head snapped. Her body became unsteady as she watched Ezra's lifeless body, how his handsome face held no expression and his green eyes wouldn't open again. The grief that had settled in her stomach shifted, forming into a rage that made her breathing turn to panting and her shaking body turn cold. The darkness in her magic screamed in her ears, making her brows furrow. She let him go, standing and holding her arms out. She could feel the charcoal darkness seep further up her neck and over the back of her head. It made her shiver and flex her hands, then flick her eyes at Silas.

"Ana . . ." Silas mumbled, reaching for the curved blade on his hip. "You need to think clearly. Don't let the darkness take you. Don't make me kill you."

"You promised Ezra you wouldn't," Ana sneered, walking to him and narrowing her eyes. With her dark magic, she brought Silas to his knees, tilting his head upwards. "Besides, you can't. I don't think even you could touch me now."

She raised a taloned finger and ran it over his face, down his nose and over his lips. "You are letting your grief make you weak, Ana. If you are weak, the darkness will take you, and you won't be Ana anymore, you know this!"

"Then it can take me!" Ana shouted, her voice metallic and shrill. "If he is gone, then I don't want to *be* Ana anymore."

"Please, come back home with us. We can fix this," Abby said, sobbing as she stood and ran over to them.

Ana watched them both, then released Silas from the hold her magic had on him. He stood, scowling at her, but his expressions elicited no response from her anymore. She didn't feel scared or sad or sorrowful. She felt nothing except *rage*.

"I want you to take his body back to House Alden. No one touches him except me. Do you understand?" Her gaze flashed to both of them. "I will be along soon. Ezra is inside that stone, and the Marions have it. I will bring it back. Give me your blade." She outstretched her hand to Silas.

Silas didn't move. "If you have so much dark magic, why do you need it?"

"Because I fucking asked you for it, Silas. Don't make me kill you!" Ana growled. Silas's nose bled, making him contort his face in pain and grab the blade from his hip, pushing it out to her. "Good boy, run along."

"There is a mirror over there," Abby said, pointing toward

the back wall with a trembling hand. "That is how they brought me here. We can use it to get back to House Alden."

Ana nodded and strutted down the stage and towards the doors they had come through, the blade by her side. A sense of calm blanketed her body, while Silas scooped to lift Ezra's body over his shoulder.

"What about the Marion coven?" Abby asked, a look of fear all over her face.

Ana turned when she reached the door, holding the knob in her hand. She flashed a wicked smile at Abby over her shoulder.

"When I am finished, there will no longer *be* a Marion coven."

CHAPTER 27

The hallways and corridors of the Marion caves were silent, save for the sound of Ana's footsteps and ragged breathing. Now that the darkness had taken away all the pain and grief, her body was only left with bubbling-hot rage. Her black taloned hand gripped the hilt of Silas's blade so tightly she could feel the metal crushing.

"Mallory . . ." Ana sang.

She pushed the hand with the curved dagger out towards the obsidian glass wall, pressing the sharp tip against it and dragging it along the surface, grinning as she heard the empty corridors filling with the shrill sound it created. It echoed down the hallways and filtered into the rooms, her feet following the sound calmly.

"You can't hide forever, Mallory. You can't leave this mountain, and there are only so many rooms you can hide in. I have a game of my own I would like to play with you." A wicked smile spread across her face. "You like games, right?"

Ana had spent so long running from the idea of turning dark, but now that she was in the throes of embracing it, the power she felt sent waves of euphoric aftershocks through her body. She felt strong, unbreakable and utterly undefeatable. The darkness flowed freely inside her skin now that she was allowing it in. It took away the image of Ezra's face when he fell, patched over the pieces of her broken heart and numbed her body of all anguish. With the darkness by her side as a friend, she didn't feel lost, or broken, or pained. With the darkness, she didn't feel *anything*.

Luckily, she didn't have to walk very far. Mallory and her coven were standing together in the main hall by her throne, and when she walked into the open space, Mallory turned to face her. She had the blue diamond in her hand in a crushing, angry grip, and her face was pulled into a furious expression that looked out of place on her hauntingly perfect features.

"Oh, Mallory, what's wrong?" Ana asked as she flicked the tip of the blade off the wall and brought it in front of her, playing with the tip with the top of her taloned index finger. "Did things not go quite how you planned?"

"I did not ask for the magic of a *Sullivan*!" Mal snapped.

"And yet you had a Sullivan in that circle, so you must have known it could go wrong." She shrugged.

"The girl was supposed to be replaced by *you*, not that man."

Mallory looked frustrated. The coven behind her flanked her sides, all of them wearing grimaces and frowns, ready to strike Ana if she got too close. Ana pressed forward with an aloof sway to her step, glancing at each of them.

"Well, you underestimated Ezra's love for his sister." She sighed, stopping in the middle of the room. "And you underestimated his love for me."

"I do not care about his love! He has ruined *everything*! The diamond is useless to me now! I am a Marion, I cannot use

Sullivan magic, so that is why I needed yours!" Mallory shouted as she took a threatening step forward, but she stopped when Ana flashed an amused look at her. "You stole our magic, so it belongs here, with us."

"The diamond may be useless to you but not to me. If it has Ezra inside it, I need to get him back out again, and you will give it to me and tell me how to do that." She opened her hand.

"You can have him, but there is no way of getting him back out of there again. A Sullivan can syphon the magic from it, but for you, he is worthless."

Mallory flipped the diamond out of her hand, a man catching it beside her. Like Mallory, he had white hair, glowing skin and moonstone-coloured eyes. He glanced at Mal, a look of confusion on his face until she nodded to him, and he sighed, walking toward Ana with the diamond in his hand.

The man stopped in front of her, watching her curiously before he set the diamond in her open palm. It felt exactly the same as the last time she touched it. It was no heavier than before, and the colour was the same, except when she peered into its top, she could see swirling energy inside, like it was filled with glittering liquid.

Ezra.

Something inside Ana's chest pulled, and she gulped, looking away from it quickly and up to Mallory's face. If she didn't think about him or look at his essence, it wouldn't hurt. She forced the bubbling human feeling down, returning to the safety of the darkness in her head, and flashed Mallory a smile.

"You are a liar, Mallory. There must be some way to get him back out of this stone and into his body. I have not studied magic very long, but from what I do know, there is always a spell to counteract another, that's how spell crafting works." Ana clenched the blade in her hand tighter. "Give me the incantation, and I might let you live."

Mallory frowned deeply at her. "Is that a threat?"

"No." She chuckled, slipping the diamond into her pocket. "This is."

Ana turned to the Marion man who had given her the diamond, giving him a grin before she grabbed him by the shoulder and plunged Silas's blade into his stomach. He gasped in surprise, then screamed as Ana held him tight by the shoulder and pushed the curved blade upwards, cutting his stomach open all the way up to his ribcage. The bone of his sternum halted the blade from going any further, and when she tugged and pulled it out, the man screamed again, blood spilling onto the black floor all over their feet.

Ana watched his wide pained eyes as he stared back at her in confusion. Then he turned to look at his family before he fell to his knees, his hands flying to his stomach to try to keep his organs inside. They slipped out around his fingers anyway, and he collapsed.

Mallory's face, if possible, was even paler now as she stared at them, her moonstone eyes wide and fear written all over her expression as her family behind her screamed. The coven bolted for the staircase while Mallory stood frozen, watching the man as he bled all over the floor.

"No one is going anywhere until I get what I want!" Ana hollered, throwing her bloody hand in the air and watching as the running Marion family were all pulled down to their hands and knees, unable to move. She smiled, turning her black eyes back to Mallory.

The dark magic in her stomach whispered to her, purring happily at the smell of blood in the air. It felt good between the tips of her fingers, and her body was tingling with a euphoria she now felt addicted to.

"You wanted this, remember? You wanted me to turn dark and stand at your side as a Marion, right?" Ana stepped over the bloody body on the floor. "But you forget, Mallory, I am not a Marion. I am a Davenport, and I don't play by your rules."

"Ana, listen to me," Mallory begged, stepping forward with her hands outstretched in front of her. "We have no more magic. We used the last of what we had to create that transference spell. My family cannot fight you. Do not kill them."

"Don't make me, then."

Ana locked her eyes on Mallory as she pushed her hand out and extended her fingers. One of the Marion females was pulled across the black floor to Ana, and she gripped her hair, the witch's body trembling as she screamed. Ana tugged on the white hair of her head, pulling her up onto her knees so that Mallory could see her.

"Ana! Please stop!" Mal shouted, watching her with pleading eyes, her brows knitting together. "My family is all that is left of us."

"You should have thought about that before you took him from me!" Ana screamed. The metallic tone of her voice shrieked, echoing along the walls as she reached the curved blade to the woman's throat and pressed the sharp edge against her glowing skin, slicing it right through.

"No!" Mal cried, rushing forward to catch the woman when Ana let her go.

The woman gagged, falling on Mallory as her throat opened up and bled freely all over Mal's beautiful silver dress. She placed her hands on her throat, watching her eyes as the woman thrashed and finally stopped moving, falling limp in her arms.

Screams filled the large foyer while Mallory cradled the

woman's bleeding body on the floor, tears flooding down her cheeks.

"Two down, eleven to go, Mallory. Give me the incantation." Ana warned, her voice steady but growing impatient.

"I told you, there is no spell to reverse it!" she yelled at her, hugging her Marion sister to her chest.

"That is not good enough! You took him from me, and you expect me to just walk away? I loved him, Mallory, and you took him away! Bring him back!"

"I cannot." Mallory sniffled, stroking the back of her fingers over her dead sister's cheek.

"Damn you, Mallory!"

Ana turned, facing the rest of her family and thrusting her hand out roughly, clenching her fists and listening to five of their necks snapping in a sickening chorus. They fell over, the remainder of the family continuing to cry.

Mallory gagged, closing her eyes tightly as she clung to her sister and tried not to look at the bodies of her family. "I cannot give you what you ask of me, Ana. The blood you shed is in vain. I cannot give you something I do not possess!"

Ana panted as she scanned the bodies. Anger pulled at her insides, drowning out the human side of her head that was screaming for her to end this. She was too angry to stop and too lost inside the feeling of euphoria that flooded her veins. If Mallory didn't have the incantation, then she couldn't help her get Ezra out of the diamond.

If there was no spell, there would *be* no Ezra.

Ana flashed her an angry stare through her black eyes, sunk onto her haunches and tilted her head at Mallory. She studied her features and how her expression was pulled in sadness and pain.

"Fine. I believe you," Ana said, narrowing her eyes.

Relief washed over Mallory's face, her shoulders sagging and her eyes closing over gently. "Thank you." She sniffled.

"Hmm." Ana pointed the curved blade towards Mal's face and pressed the tip against her cheek.

Mallory snapped her eyes open, her eyebrows pulling together in the middle. A wicked grin played on Ana's lips, and she chuckled as she trailed the tip of the blade over her perfect face to her chin.

"But if you do not have the incantation, then I no longer have any use for you."

CHAPTER 28

It was strange walking through a mirror for the first time. When Ana pushed her hand into the glass, it rippled like water, sending warped reflections of her face back as it rolled to the edges. It was cold, too, and it tingled all over her skin like pins and needles as she pushed her body through the glass. Colours flooded her vision, blinding her and forcing her to shut her eyes tightly.

She heard the room before she saw it. She could hear Silas barking orders, people panicking and chairs shifting over wooden floors. When she fell through the other side, she blinked rapidly, looking around the main hall of House Alden, then back at the mirror she had come through.

Grinning, she reached out a finger to poke the glass, finding it completely solid again while warmth returned to her skin. "Amazing."

"Ana."

She snapped her head back to the middle of the room. Silas was standing in front of the coven, his body tense and his hand giving an uncharacteristic tremble at his side. His wide eyes took in the state of her body. He was studying the blood dripping off her skin and clothes, and when his eyes finally looked down at her hand by her side, he stumbled back from her, a look of horror on his face.

"What the fuck did you do?!" he shouted, his hands out at his sides, warning the coven behind him to stay back.

Ana glanced down to where he was looking, smiling when she saw Mallory's decapitated head swinging from the grip she had on her white hair. "Oh. This? The Marion coven couldn't help us anymore."

She swung her hand, letting go of her hair and letting the head roll into the crowd.

"Ana, this isn't you! You are out of control; you must push the darkness away!" Silas said, taking a threatening step towards her.

"No, I won't." She frowned, flicking her eyes at him. Silas's legs were swept out from under him, sending him onto his hands and knees in front of her. "The darkness is keeping me from crumbling, Silas! If I let it go, if I push it away, I will *feel* again, and I don't want to feel. I *can't* feel."

"You have to. Ezra didn't want this for you! His last wish was for you to push the darkness away. We need to fix you." He was bleeding from his eyes and his nose, and she approached him.

"Stop telling me what he wanted! Stop talking! I can't listen to your whining anymore!"

Ana sighed, then walked past him and stood up straighter, scanning the scared faces of the coven. They were trembling, appearing like scared mice in a trap they did not know how to get out of. She calmed herself, then flashed them a smile and laced her hands in front of herself.

Genevieve was standing beside Thaddeus in the middle. She was crying and hugging herself, looking absolutely broken, as a mother who just lost her son would.

"Don't cry, Genevieve. We are going to bring him back."

"You can't. You know how those stones work, Ana. He is not coming back from this," Silas said over his shoulder. He still couldn't move from his knees, but he could move his head to get a glimpse of her.

"He has to. Before he went into that circle, he told me I could get him out. He wouldn't have done it if there wasn't a way we could get him out, and you . . ." Ana said, turning back to the coven. "You are going to help me free him."

The coven stayed silent. She paced the floor in front of them. Pulling the diamond from her pocket, she stroked it with the tip of her taloned finger.

"He is trapped inside there, alone and cold, when he should be *here*, and alive, with me. Ezra has spent his entire life sacrificing himself for everyone and *everything*, so we cannot let him suffer inside there alone for eternity. I will not let that happen, not when I just found him."

She glanced up at them all, her eyes narrowing and her lip turning into a sneer.

"No one leaves this building until we restore him. No one will eat, and no one will sleep until he is awake and *breathing* by my side again. You will study every magical book in this house, you will scour every potion and remedy you can muster and you will not rest until one of you brings me what I need to wake him up."

Her audience shifted uncomfortably, looking at each other and their feet. When she took a threatening step forward, they flinched, which caused her to laugh.

"If you do not, if you *refuse* me, I will awaken every

shadowy monster inside me and use this dark magic until every single one of you is on your knees *begging* to die. I will pick you off one by one, just like I did with the Marions, and when I have left House Alden razed to the ground, there will no longer be a coven here. It will be a graveyard, filled with the souls of the witches who dared cross me."

She was growling now, her voice a metallic chorus. The evil inside her swelled, engulfing what was left of her human brain.

"I will bring the underneath to the surface, I will obliterate every single happy memory this building holds and I will show you what *hell* looks like."

"Abby, now!"

Ana spun where she was standing. Silas had shouted towards the mirror, and when she flicked her eyes to it, the glass rippled, giving way to Abby's body as she jumped through. She held something in each hand, but Ana couldn't see what it was.

"Abby?"

"I'm sorry, Ana," Abby said, lifting her hand to reveal a potion bottle.

She threw it, and it landed at Ana's feet, smashing and leaking into a puddle that she couldn't step out of no matter how much she tried to shift her feet. Smoke plumed from it and filled her nose and mouth, leaving her spluttering and her eyes tearing. Pain like she had never felt before erupted in her body and she fell to the ground, the diamond rolling out of her hand somewhere beyond her vision in the smoke.

Ana screamed, holding herself on her hands and knees on the floor and writhing in white-hot pain. It felt like her whole body was on fire, like her insides were boiling and her skin was melting from her bones. Howling, she made to stand, but Abby got to her first, kicking her down and back into the smoke again, keeping her contained inside it.

"Ana! This isn't you!"

Abby used the precious seconds she had while Ana was twisting in pain to sneak behind her and wrap her arms around her body. Ana writhed in her grip, searching for the magic in her stomach to help her, but it was silent, unable to break out of the pain from whatever Abby had thrown at her.

"I will kill you." Ana panted.

Abby pressed her face against Ana's shoulder, raising her hand high above her. The smoke was dissipating, and from the corner of her eye, Ana saw a syringe in her grip, the shining, pointed end aimed down at her. A thick blue liquid sloshed inside as Abby struggled to keep hold of her.

"No, you won't." Abby swiped her hand down, plunging the needle of the syringe deep into Ana's neck and emptying the contents into Ana's body. Then she crawled away from Ana and watched her with wide eyes.

Ana growled, her hand flying to her neck and pulling the syringe out with a shaky hand. She looked down at it before glaring at Abby. "What did you put inside me?"

"You'll see," Abby replied, a smile creeping over her features as she sat up on her knees.

"Abby, what did you do?!" she screamed, clenching her hand so tightly the glass syringe smashed, sending pieces of glass and drops of blood to the floor.

Ana gasped, throwing what was left of it away and sitting up on her knees. Her heart was racing in her chest, and her head was becoming dizzy. Her vision blurred, and she swayed, her skin growing hot. She whimpered, pain radiating through her bones. Then she gagged, hunching over on her hands and knees and vomiting thick, black sludge. It clung to the inside of her throat and splashed onto the floor of the room. It sizzled and burned the wood when it landed.

"W-what's h-happening to me?" She gagged through it, retching again and rocking on her hands and knees.

"It's okay, Ana. Let it happen," Abby said softly, scooting across the floor and to her side. She reached out a hand to touch her hair but flinched when Ana pushed her away and vomited thick blackness again.

The weight on Ana's shoulders began to lift. A cooling sensation spread through her veins, rolling through every inch of her body and tingling, like it was purifying her insides. She sat up on her knees and looked down at her hands, watching as the long obsidian talons she had gotten so used to shrank, until her own normal nails appeared in their place.

Confusion pulled at her expression as the darkness that had marred her skin faded from her fingertips. The charcoal of her fingers receded, then disappeared from her wrists, like everything the darkness touched was being erased. She gasped painful breaths, scrambling to pull her bloody wool cardigan up over her head so that she could watch her arms return to normal. Once the skin of her shoulders restored to its natural colour, she could feel it pulling away from her neck, then leaving the back of her head and tugging its influence from her brain.

The last part of her body to restore itself was her eyes. She didn't realise how much the darkness had affected her vision until it was no longer there. She had gotten so used to the dull hue that had blanketed over her world that she hadn't even questioned it. Now, as the bright colours of the ballroom of House Alden returned to her, Ana breathed in fresh air rapidly.

She dropped her hands, looking over the faces of the coven, then to Silas, whose bodily functions had been returned to him. He stood with his arms folded and eyebrows scrunched together. Ana switched her gaze to Abby, who was smiling at her with tears in her eyes, and this time, when Abby reached out to touch her, Ana lunged at her and hugged her tightly, burying her face in the crook of her neck.

Guilt hit her like a train, the images of Mallory and her family that flooded into her brain physically hurt. She shut her eyes tight as Abby hugged her back, trying to force the images of everything she had done to them out of her head, but they flashed again, the expressions on their faces when she killed them now seared into her mind.

"I-I killed them." She gasped, crying hard into her shoulder as they slumped to sit on the ground.

"It's okay! Calm down, Ana. It wasn't you," Abby said, pulling from the hug to take her face in her hands and look into her blue eyes. "It wasn't you."

"I-it was! A-and I couldn't stop myself, Abby! I couldn't stop it. I was so a-angry, and Ezra, he–" Ana paused. The pain she had felt and the relief that now coursed through her veins had been so invasive that she had momentarily forgotten about the diamond.

She inhaled sharply, letting Abby go from her hug and searching for the blue diamond with wild, scared eyes. When she spotted it in the middle of the room, she scrambled over the floor to retrieve it, bringing it close to her chest, then looking down at its insides. It was still swirling inside, with little silver sparkling wisps that pushed against the inside of the stone.

Ezra.

Ana screamed as the pain and grief of remembrance washed over her, shattering what was left of her heart. She felt like her chest might just cave in as she stared down into the diamond, her face leaking with tears that just wouldn't stop. She could barely breathe, spluttering and hiccupping to gasp oxygen into her lungs.

"Ana . . ." Abby sniffled, reaching out to her again and sitting beside her, wrapping her hand around Ana's that held the diamond and pulling her into a hug. "It's going to be okay."

Ana couldn't speak for a long time. She simply sat there, rocking with Abby and crying loudly as the coven was guided away by Genevieve and Thaddeus, leaving her alone in the ballroom with Abby and Silas.

"Is he really gone forever?" Ana asked, looking up at them both. Her eyes were pleading, and her body was shaking violently. "Am I really never going to see him again?"

Abby looked away, gritting her teeth and wiping her own cheeks while Silas closed the space between them. He shrugged, looking down at them.

"I don't know. If there is a spell that can get him out of there, no one has ever heard of it." He frowned.

Ana cried harder at Silas's words, and Abby took her hand again. "But that doesn't mean we can't try. Ezra would never give up if it was one of us inside, so we can't give up on him, either."

She calmed herself, nodding as she studied the skin of her fingers. It was strange, seeing how normal they looked without the darkness infecting them.

"Am I cured?"

"No," Abby replied, her face pulling apologetically. "Before the Marions took me, I finished your blood work. I separated the darkness from your blood, and from that, I made the serum that reverses the side effects of the dark magic. You still have the magic inside you, it will always be there, but so long as you remember to take the serum every day, the dark side effects will be muted while you continue to wield it. I am not sure how long it will work for, though. Eventually, every serum becomes ineffective, so we will need to find a more permanent solution. Until then, this is your answer."

"Thank you, Abby." Ana sighed, wiping her face as she stared at the swirling inside the diamond. "Can I see him?"

"Are you sure that is a good idea?" Silas grunted, his brow furrowed, and his arms folded close against his chest like he was protecting himself.

Ana moved to stand, her legs shaky as she lifted the dirty cardigan from the floor and pulled it back on over her head. "I need to see him. *Please.*"

"I will take her."

She glanced over Silas's shoulder, spotting Genevieve standing near the doorway of the room. Her eyes were ringed red, and her face pulled in a sadness Ana had never seen on a person before. She looked devastated.

"Genevieve . . ." Ana hiccupped. When she opened her arms, Ana took off in a run towards her, enveloping her in a hug and trying not to cry as she held her. "I am so sorry. I tried to stop him."

"I know, love." Her voice was shaky as she ran her hand through Ana's matted hair and rubbed circles over her back. "Come."

Genevieve let her go from the hug, giving her a warm but thin smile that didn't quite reach her eyes. She took Ana's free hand, letting Ana cling to the blue diamond in the other as they walked into the foyer of House Alden and down a long corridor.

"Are you all right? You gave us all quite the fright," Genevieve commented, looking sideways at her.

Ana bit down on her lip. Her body was still wracked with guilt, and her head was still swimming with the faces of the people she hurt. Alexander. Mallory. The Marion family.

Ezra.

She stared at her feet as she walked. They felt numb, like

they were moving on their own. If she could feel them, she wouldn't be able to move.

"No," Ana said honestly. "I . . . I hurt so many people, Genevieve. I *killed* people."

"That wasn't you."

"It was *my* hands, it was *my* face they saw, it was *my* anger. I let it take over when Ezra was gone, and I–"

"Don't torture yourself over something you had no control over, Ana. The Marion coven is gone. They would have done the same to you if given half the chance. It is their fault Ezra is gone; they sealed their own fate when they went down that dark path."

Genevieve stopped outside a large wooden door, releasing Ana's hand and reaching for the handle of the door, pushing it open and leaving it wide enough for Ana to walk through.

Stepping through the threshold, Ana shuffled into the small room. It was bright inside, which was unusual for House Alden. The curtains were open wide, letting sunlight shine through and engulf the room in a hue of gold. In the middle of the room rested a table draped with a red tablecloth, and laying on top of it, completely still, was Ezra.

Ana's breath caught in her chest. The closer her feet carried her to the table, the tighter her chest became, until it felt like the bones of her ribs were caving in and constricting her lungs. Tears welled in her eyes as she reached the side of the table, looking down at his body.

Ezra looked like he was sleeping. His chest was rising and falling, and when she reached a shaky hand out to touch his chest, she found his heartbeat.

Confusion pulled her eyebrows together, and she spun to look at Genevieve in the doorway. She hovered there, like she couldn't face walking too far inside.

"I don't understand. He is breathing, his heart is beating . . ."

"We have spelled him, to keep his body alive. If we don't keep his blood flowing, his body will die. Then he would have no body to return to if we figure out how to get him out of the stone."

What little hope had settled inside Ana's chest fluttered away at her explanation. She nodded in understanding, then turned to look at Ezra's body again, stroking her fingers against his chest. He felt warm, like she could climb up beside him and go to sleep, listening to the beating of his heart like she did when he cuddled her.

The sound of Genevieve closing the door caused Ana to snap her eyes away from him momentarily, and she realised they were alone. She let out a shaky sigh, looking back at Ezra's face and reaching to swipe some of his dark hair out of his face. He looked *perfect*, like he was dreaming of something beautiful that she couldn't reach in and share.

She ran her finger down his nose and over his lips, then pressed her hand back against his chest, enjoying how his heart felt against her palm. She hated that she couldn't see the greens of his eyes staring back at her. Knowing she may never see them again sent her crying again, reaching for his hand and clinging to it.

"Ezra, please wake up."

She cried, lifting the diamond from her other hand and placing it on his chest. She watched as the swirling inside the rock quickened, rolling faster and faster when it was placed against his body. For a second, she thought it was going to pool out the sides and back into his body, but it didn't. It just swirled like liquid, staying inside and glittering.

"Oh, god, Ezra, I'm so sorry." Ana spluttered, looking back to his face and holding his hand against her chest, then lowered her voice into a whisper. "I am going to get you out of there. I promise."

Sitting down on the stool beside the table, she peered into his face, remembering the words he told her before the circle took him.

Be brave, Ana. I love you.

Leaning over the table, Ana leaned down and kissed his lips softly. "I love you, too, Ezra."

She never truly believed in love before she saw his face. She knew that if she believed in the magic of love, then she also needed to believe that love had the power to break a heart.

And hers was utterly broken.

ACKNOWLEDGMENTS

In my wildest dreams I never thought I would ever finish one book, never mind three. This series would never have continued without the support of my readers, my friends and my family.

To Corri, the wonderful human this book is dedicated to: Thank you from the bottom of my heart, for always being there to read my chapters as I write them, and fix my silly plot holes. You are amazing.

To my husband, who gives me ideas and lets me use him as a human sounding board: I love you. Without your patience, I couldn't do this.

My sister, Shalana, and my friend Lainie, who are always there to be my cheerleaders when I am feeling drained.

To my grandparents, Samuel and Lily, I love you both to the moon and back. Thank you for always supporting everything I do.

To Lisa Donnelly who helped me find the right title! Thank you!

And finally, to Kassi Parsons, who reads my work before it is released into the world. Your feedback is always greatly appreciated.

ABOUT THE AUTHOR

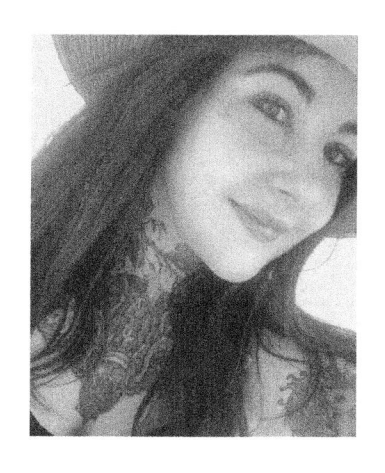

Nikita Rogers lives in a little rustic village in Northern Ireland. She lives with her husband, Lee Rogers, an insanely talented musician, her wonderful step-kids, and their cats, chickens and pygmy goat.

She has been writing for 17 years (as of 2022).

During the day, Nikita spends her time working in her tattoo studio where she has etched designs on her customers since 2008. At night, you will find her curled up on her sofa with a good book, creating sketches and designs, or writing in her pyjamas with a good cup of coffee.

She is currently working on book three of *Whisper of Witches*.

Come say hi on her socials, she promises she doesn't bite.
Instagram: @Nevermoreink
Tiktok: @nikitarogersauthor
Email: nikitarogersauthor@hotmail.com
Find her husband's music also:
Instagram: @leerogersmusic
Facebook: Lee Rogers Music
Twitter: leerogerstweets

ALSO BY NIKITA ROGERS

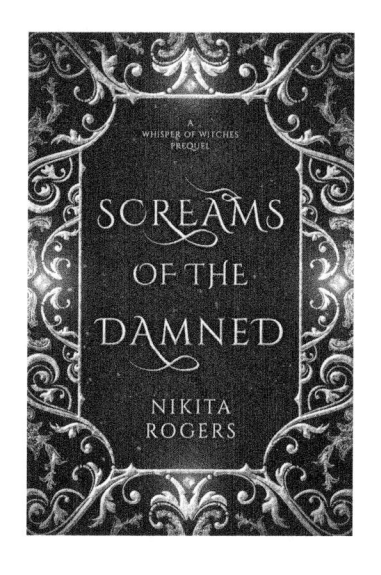

(Prequel to Whisper of Witches)

The year is 1588, and Samuel Marion is in love.

Love *should* be easy. All the melodies and poems told him it would be, but loving Emily Sullivan, the daughter of the High Priest of a rival Witches Coven, has been anything but *easy*. With warnings of repercussions ringing in their ears from both sides of their families, Samuel and Emily have found themselves with no other choice than to keep their love a secret.

A secret that is proving harder and harder to keep.

The return of the notorious witch-hunter Thomas Harrow only seems to heighten the lovers worries, when his arrival marks the start of a new set of witch trials.

Attempting to keep his love a secret, while simultaneously maintaining his promises to his Coven and avoiding the witch-hunters wrath, Samuel embarks on a plan to free himself from the shackles of familial expectations.

Not everything goes to plan, however, and Samuel and Emily find themselves thrown into a world of suspicion, trying to outrun their Covens and the witch-hunter, all for the sake of love.

Printed in Great Britain
by Amazon